# Soul Ties:

## *A Ghetto Love Story*

# Soul Ties:

## *A Ghetto Love Story*

*Wjuanae*

www.urbanbooks.net

Urban Books, LLC
300 Farmingdale Road, NY-Route 109
Farmingdale, NY 11735

ISBN 13: 978-1-64556-613-7

First Mass Market Printing February 2024
First Trade Paperback Printing October 2023
Printed in the United States of America

10 9 8 7 6 5 4 3 2 1

Distributed by Kensington Publishing Corp.
Submit Orders to:
Customer Service
400 Hahn Road
Westminster, MD 21157-4627
Phone: 1-800-733-3000
Fax: 1-800-659-2436

# Soul Ties:

## *A Ghetto Love Story*

*Wjuanae*

# Dedication

I want to dedicate this book to all my dreamers out there. It is never too late to chase your dreams.

To my mother, I dedicate this book to you for introducing me to my love for urban fiction and reading. You're one of my biggest motivations when I write. One of these days, real soon if my intuition is correct, I'm going to make sure you never have to work again. You are my superhero.

To my best friend, Taquashe. Thank you for believing in my dream for so many years and always listening to me rant about my characters. You mean more to me than you know!

To my readers, big ups for y'all! You guys have loved this love story of Nina and Chance's so much that you all literally pushed me to write and keep writing. Look where we are now. I can't thank you all enough for valuing my craft enough to read it and pay for it. Y'all are literally the best, and I can't wait to keep these stories coming for you all.

To that person cheering me on from the sideline, thank you. You don't know how much that random "I'm proud of you" has done for me.

To the haters, I'm still flourishing.

# Acknowledgments

*To the living angel, whom I had the honor of being taught and coached by, Ms. Gara Bell. Your light influenced many and will continue to. We love you. May you rest in peace. #GetYouAGara*

*When it came to the game of Chance's heart, Nina would win every time, no matter the opponent.*

# Chapter One

Chance and Nina rode through the streets of Charlotte in their drop top Lamborghini, blasting their favorite Ja Rule song. The heated summer winds kissed their skin. The two were the definition of a hood Bonnie and Clyde. Chance met Nina at the tender age of 15, when she used to stay with her abusive, alcoholic father. Even though he was three years older than Nina, Chance couldn't help but be infatuated by her innocence and beauty. He was a young hustler at the time, a block boy, but he had bigger dreams: he would run Charlotte one day. And indeed, every one of his dreams came true with Nina by his side.

Nina cherished her relationship with Chance. He rescued her from her father's abuse and had provided for her since that day, showering her with love and his protection. Not once did he have to question her loyalty because she owed him everything, and vice versa. If Chance was sliding on a nigga, Nina would be right by his side, loading his clip. He was her protector, best friend, and lover all wrapped into one. No other man could claim to have ever possessed Nina in the way that Chance could. Many women wished to lock Chance down, but those bragging rights belonged to Nina, and she would physically defend her position if needed.

"We out the game, shorty. We legit. All these years of hustling finally paid off!" Chance reached over with one hand to caress Nina's cheek. He could barely keep his eyes on the road as Nina's natural curls blew in the wind. The sun glistened against her brown skin. He was in love with every part of her, down to the beads of sweat that rolled between her breasts.

Nina smiled and intertwined her fingers with Chance's free hand. She couldn't believe the day had finally arrived when Chance lived up to the promise he had made to her ten years ago. "I told you, baby. Stay down until you come up, and now we all the way up!"

They were headed to Atlanta with five million dollars in their trunk, ready to start a new life. She turned and stretched to reach for her lip gloss out of her purse that sat in the back seat. "Baby, are we being followed?" Nina noticed a black Tahoe truck behind them on I-85. The car had been trailing behind them since they got out of Charlotte, but she thought nothing of it until now. Out of instinct, Nina placed her hand in her purse and clutched her gold nine millimeter.

Chance glanced at his rearview mirror. "Fuck." He was so caught up in being out of the game scot-free that he had let his guard down, breaking his cardinal rule. "I'm about to take this exit. Let's see." Chance clenched his teeth as his trigger finger started itching. The black Tahoe still trailed behind. "Niggas think they can try me since I'm leaving town. They got me fucked up!" Pulling into the closest gas station, Chance pulled his gun from his waist. "You rocking, bae?"

She kissed his lips. "Until the wheels fall off," Nina replied fearlessly.

Seconds passed before the Tahoe turned into the gas station. The tint in the window was so dark that Nina didn't understand how the police didn't pull over the truck. It circled the parking lot until it slowly crept by the gas pump opposite the Lambo. The passenger-side window rolled down, and an AK-47 greeted Chance and Nina.

"What's up, young bull?" a familiar voice asked.

Nina's breath caught in her throat, and her stomach dropped as horrific memories flashed before her eyes.

"Hey, baby girl." Nina's dad, Nino, greeted her with a devilish smile. The scar that ran from his left eye to the side of his mouth made him appear even more menacing than Nina last remembered.

"Chance, I thought you killed him." Nina's voice shook as she stared at the only thing she ever feared in her life.

*BLAT BLAT BLAT.*

Chance didn't have a chance to answer before bullets rained down on the Lambo.

Nina's ears rang from the impact, and her legs became as heavy as a bag of bricks. Her hands shook uncontrollably, and her heart thumped so hard that she thought it would come out of her chest. It was as if Nina were paralyzed. She couldn't bring herself to lift her gun and bust back at her dad, the man who was supposed to want to protect her, not bring harm to her. She never understood why the man who gave her life hated her so much.

Shots rang out like a scene from a war movie. Nino's goon opened fire onto the Lambo, and Chance returned fire with one hand while the other shielded Nina from the bullets coming their way.

"*Nina!*" Chance's voice snapped her out of her daze. "I'm hit, ma."

She heard an agony in his voice that she never heard before. Those words caused her to raise her gun and fire until her clip was empty. She didn't know if she had hit anyone, but the Tahoe recklessly pulled off in the midst of her shots. An uneasy feeling settled in Nina's gut. Something deep down inside of her screamed that this was only the beginning.

"Baby . . . Chance . . . are you good?" Nina panicked when she saw blood pouring profusely from his abdomen and right leg. Tears formed in her eyes as she watched the man she loved weakly slide himself to the passenger seat as she got out of the convertible.

"We have to get the fuck out of here!" She revved the engine, and it purred loudly. "Fuck!" Nina realized she didn't even put the car in drive. Taking a deep breath, she put the car in drive and sped out of the gas station's parking lot, leaving traces of their tire marks behind.

"Get us out of Charlotte." Chance managed to speak through his heavy breathing. "I'm not about to die here, Nina. I worked too hard to die in this bitch." He spat out a mouthful of blood. "You gotta . . . drive."

Never had she seen her man so weak and vulnerable. "Baby, you won't make it if I get on the road. I refuse to let you die. Over my fucking dead body! Nah. We not going out like that. Till death do us part, remember?"

Chance fought against the heavy burning sensation in his chest. He watched the blood slowly seep from the bullet wound in his abdomen, and he placed his hand over it, trying to slow the bleeding. The more blood that left his body, the heavier his eyelids felt. Despite the agonizing pain, Chance was still able to smile at his girl's gangster. "I love your crazy ass."

Smiling weakly, Nina headed for the nearest hospital. "I love you more." She dipped through traffic, bypassing slow cars, and ran a few red lights. "You remember our first date, bae?" She glanced over at Chance. His eyes fluttered as he drifted in and out of consciousness. "Stay with me, Chance!" She clapped her hands together. "Don't fucking die on me! I can't lose you now. Our baby needs you."

Nina had wanted to wait until they were settled in Atlanta to give him the big news. She had found out that morning that she was carrying Chance's child and wanted the delivery of the news to be special, but she never expected their day would end up like this.

Chance could feel his life slowly coming to an end. Memories flashed through his mind like the behind-the-scenes credits at the end of a movie premiere. Even while unconscious, Nina's words rang clearly through his head. *I'm holding on for you baby*, he thought, but Nina could not hear him.

Pulling into the emergency entrance wildly, Nina held the horn down until medics came running out. "Help! He's been shot!" she screamed. Chance barely appeared to be breathing when Nina looked at him.

"Ma'am, can you give us any information on this man?" the paramedic asked as they lifted Chance's body onto a stretcher.

Nina leaned over, placing her hands on her knees, and dry heaved. She fisted her natural curls and bit on her bottom lip until she felt the salty specks of blood on her tongue. She wanted to break down and cry. She wanted to jump on the stretcher with Chance. Shit, she wanted to be lying right beside him on a stretcher herself.

"Excuse me, miss?"

"I—I don't know him. I picked him up like that." Nina backed up slowly and opened the door to the Lamborghini. "Just make sure he makes it." Nina knew she couldn't give them her identity because they would ask too many questions. Situations like this brought cops, and Nina and Chance didn't fuck with the Feds. "I love you, Chance."

"He's flatlining!" the nurse screamed as they rushed his body into the hospital.

Banging on the steering wheel, Nina finally let her tears fall. In a matter of an hour, her entire life had been turned upside down. The man she imagined spending the rest of her life with risked his life to save hers once again. Just when she thought of putting her past behind her, Nino had ripped the carpet from under her feet, leaving Nina alone and confused about her next move.

"I'm going to kill him, if that's the last thing I do. Hang on, Chance baby. I'll be back for you." Nina made up her mind that Nino was dead. There wouldn't be any hits on his head. No drive-by to put him down. Nina would put a bullet through his head herself this time. For Chance.

"Atlanta, here I come."

*But you was my bitch, the one who'd never snitch. Love me when I'm broke or if I'm filthy fucking rich.*

Notorious B.I.G.'s lyrics blared from the system. Nina couldn't stop the tears from falling as she cruised down the highway. Drops of Chance's blood still stained her Prada T-shirt. She thanked herself for talking Chance into purchasing this particular vehicle with the matte leather interior. The blood dried onto the seats rather than staining it.

"God, it's Nina. I know it's been a while, and I'm not even sure if you'll hear me, but I really need you to wrap your arms around Chance. I love that man more than life itself. I don't know if I can go on without him. Please heal him." Nina knew she had reached a low point. Praying and going to church wasn't a part of her lifestyle. To be honest, she couldn't even remember the last time she prayed. Or could she?

**2008**

*"Nina, where the fuck you at?"* Her dad's voice raged from the front door. Nino was in another

one of his moods, and Nina wasn't trying to be around to see it.

Sitting on the sidewalk with Chance, she wanted to be as far away from her dad as possible. "Do you have somewhere we can go? I hate when he gets like this." Nina asked while biting at her nail beds.

Chance had been coming to see Nina every day for a few months straight now. Even though she was younger than him, he saw something different in her.

"Yeah, Nina. Let's go." Chance knew Nino had a drinking problem, but he never pushed Nina to talk about him. Not until she was ready. "Let me call my man Quan and tell him to watch the block for me." He pulled out his cellphone and texted Quan.

"You hungry?" Chance asked as they walked to his 2005 Honda Accord.

Nina shrugged. Her mind seemed to be somewhere else. "I could eat."

"Cool. Let me take you to Red Lobster. I've been wanting that for a good minute." Chance opened the passenger door for Nina and shut it. As he jogged to the driver's side, he noticed the worry in Nina's eyes. "What's wrong, shorty?"

"Look at me. I'm not dressed for Red Lobster, Chance." Nina frowned. "We can get takeout or something."

*"Takeout?" Chance chuckled and shook his head. "A nigga trying to take you on a first date, and you worried about how you look? You look beautiful without even trying."*

*Nina's cheeks warmed, and she blushed. Chance knew all the right things to do to make Nina feel like she mattered. Like she was valued. "Well, let's go then, nigga."*

*Being with Chance was exactly what Nina needed to take her mind off her life at home. Little did Chance know that Nino was so verbally and physically abusive sometimes that she had no self-esteem. She didn't think she was pretty, even though people would tell her she was all the time. In the words of her father, Nina was "an ugly little bitch just like her mother."*

*Nina's mother, Jaslynn, was murdered when Nina was just 12 years old. The Philadelphia Police Department never solved the murder case, but Nina had a feeling Nino knew something about it. Jaslynn was the most beautiful woman ever. Her smooth caramel skin, curly jet-black hair, and slender body with all the right dips and curves left many men heartbroken. Nino had her heart, until his drinking and anger problems pushed her away.*

*Nina remembered her mother bringing around Mike, a new boyfriend, and Nino hated that. His jealousy caused him to beat Mike to death with his bare hands. A few weeks later, Jaslynn was found dead also.*

*"You want to stop by the mall before I take you home?" Chance asked, snapping her out of her daze.*

*"Nah, Chance, you've spent enough money on me today. I'm good. Anyway, I need to get home before it gets too late." As much as she hated to go, she knew Nino would fuck her up if she came in after her curfew.*

*"Bet." Chance had never met a chick like Nina. Most girls he dealt with wanted him to spend money on them just to chill or smash. Not Nina, though. Matter of fact, she never asked him for anything. His company was enough to keep her satisfied. The fact that Nina never asked for anything made Chance want to give her everything.*

*"Look, I want you to take this phone and call me if you need me. My number to my second cellphone is the only number programmed in it. I'm just a call away, a'ight?"*

*Smiling lightly, Nina leaned in to place a soft kiss on Chance's lips. They were so soft and full. "Thank you, Chance. I'll see you later." She blushed as she opened the door to the Honda and ran to her front door. Looking over her shoulder, she saw Chance was still there, waiting for her to enter the house safely, just like she suspected.*

Nina unlocked the door and entered the home. She leaned on the door, closed her eyes, and smiled brightly.

SMACK!

"You think I didn't see that li'l nigga drop you off?" Nino yelled in Nina's face so close she could smell the alcohol on his breath. "I'm not raising you to be a whore like your mother!"

Nina grabbed her face as tears slipped down it. Nino had never hit her face before. "I'm nobody's whore!" she boldly yelled in his face. "And neither was my mama! You're just mad because she left you, you fucking drunk!" Nina spat.

Her words must have struck a nerve because Nino punched Nina in the stomach like she was another nigga off the streets. Doubling over in pain, Nina stumbled and cried out in agony. "You don't know shit, little girl! Keep talking like that, and I'm going to leave you stanking, just like ya moms!" He kicked her one time for good measure and stormed out of the house.

God please don't let him come back, she prayed as she lay on the floor, crying out in pain. She hated Nino.

It took all her strength to pull the phone Chance had given her out of her pocket and dial his number. "Chance, he hit me!" She sobbed into the phone.

*Enraged, Chance sped to Nina's house without a second thought. He didn't have a whole army with him, just his right-hand man, Quan. His heart broke as he saw Nina lying in the same spot she had been in since Nino left.*

*"Shit, I got you." Chance scooped Nina up in his arms and carried her to his car. "You're coming with me. I'm never letting that bitch nigga get close to you again. He's fucking dead, Nina!" He rubbed her black eye gently. "Let me holler at Quan real quick."*

*"What type of father puts his hands on his daughter?" Quan asked, his trigger finger itching. Quan didn't respect a man who put his hands on a woman, especially a man who abused his own child. Although this was none of his business, Quan wanted to help Chance make an example out of Nino. Niggas feared him in the streets too much to try him, and it'd been weeks since he got active. Thoughts of handling Nino excited him.*

*Chance pinched the bridge of his nose as he tried to gather his thoughts. In that moment, he knew he was in love with Nina. He was ready to commit the ultimate sin for her. He knew how to shoot and wouldn't hesitate to defend himself, but Chance had never killed anyone. He made the rules but rarely enforced them on his own. Chance was the brains of the operation, and Quan was the muscle. The lines had never blurred be-*

*tween the two until this day; however, Chance
decided he would catch a body that night.*

*"I'ma dead that nigga!" he vowed.*

*"I know where that pussy be at. We can pull up
on his ass right now, nigga!"*

*"Tonight, nigga. Let me get Nina to my apart-
ment and settled. I'ma hit you up." Chance dapped
Quan up and got into his car and sped off. "I'm
never going to let anyone else hurt you again,
shorty. That's my word." Chance held Nina's left
hand in his right and kissed it softly. He wiped
the tears that ran down her face and wrapped an
arm around her shoulder. From that day forward,
they were inseparable.*

The ringing of Nina's iPhone brought her back
to reality. She remembered that night clearly. It
was the day that she realized how much she loved
Chance. For the first time in her life, she slept without fear that night.

Looking down at her caller ID, she saw Quan's
name flash across the screen.

"Please tell me you have some good news, Quan.
I can't take anything but that."

"Where you at, sis?" Quan asked.

"I'm almost in Atlanta. How is he?" The last few
hours of worrying whether Chance survived had
been agonizing. There wasn't any time to mince
words. Nina needed to hear that Chance had made

it out of the hospital and would be following her to Atlanta shortly. She needed to hear that she was the first person he'd asked for after the surgery. She needed something to hold onto.

The silence on the line was deafening. Nothing could be heard for seconds but Quan's heavy breathing on the other end. "Nina . . . I don't even know how to put this to you."

"Don't say it, Quan. Please. Don't say it."

"He put up a fight," Quan replied quietly. "He tried for you, sis."

Nina dropped the phone and released her hands from the wheel, covering her sobs with her trembling hands. It felt like someone had pulled a carpet from underneath her feet. She'd been confident that Chance would survive his injuries.

Images of Chance flashed in her mind. She never expected today to be the last day she saw the love of her life. Before she knew it, the Lamborghini slammed into the back of a black Toyota, causing her to spin wildly off the road.

"Nina!!" She heard Quan yelling into the phone from a distance before everything went black.


*Beep. Beep. Beep.*

Nina's eyes fluttered open, and she shielded her face with her hands, attempting to block the bright lights in the room. The smell of peroxide and disinfectants invaded her nostrils. The hairs on her forearms rose from the cool air blowing above Nina's head.

"Hmmm," she moaned, trying to sit up. Her hands reached for the IV coming from her right arm. Just as she started to pull the IV from her arm, a sharp pain shot through her entire upper body. *What the fuck?* The recollection of events that had occurred over the last day of her life came flooding back like water from a broken dam. Tears slid down her face as she realized this was not just a bad dream she was waking up from. The man she loved had died. Chance was gone. Her menace of a father mysteriously rose from the dead and attacked them. How had he survived? That night over ten years ago, Chance had come home and assured Nina that he sent Nino to meet his maker. She saw all the blood on his clothes the night he came home, so how did Nino make it out alive?

*Does the nigga have nine lives or something?*

"You're woke." A stranger's voice greeted Nina.

She looked up to find a tall, dark-skinned man sitting by the end of the hospital bed. Confused, Nina placed her hands on her hip out of instinct. "Fuck," she mumbled as she realized her nine wasn't there. "Who the fuck are you?" she barked. She didn't know this nigga from Adam. For all she knew, he could have been someone Nino sent to finish off the job. Nina's eyes darted to the room door, which was slightly ajar. The hallway was bustling with doctors, nurses, and visitors passing by. She sighed in relief.

He sensed Nina's apprehension and remembered that he was a strange face to her. "No need for the hostility, ma. I found you on the side of the highway all fucked up. The ambulance was twenty minutes out, so I brought you here myself," he informed Nina.

Nina twisted her face up and eyed the man suspiciously. She didn't know if she quite trusted the good Samaritan story this guy gave. She felt naked without her gun on her, and the unfamiliar setting made her feel nauseous. Calculating her next response, Nina asked, "Where is my car?" There was still five million dollars in the trunk that she and Chance had stacked over the years. She had so many questions, but her priority was to get out of this hospital.

"I had it towed to my spot. I can take you there once they release you and let you be on your way. What's your name, ma?"

"It's definitely not ma." Nina recognized his northern accent and hoped he didn't think his lingo flattered her. "I'm the one asking the questions right now. What is your name, and why did you help me?"

He laughed at her straightforwardness. He could tell that she wasn't an average chick. "I'm Yasin." He placed his hand on his chest and surveyed Nina. "Honestly, I don't know why I helped you. Would you have rather I left you to die on the side of that highway?"

*That wouldn't have been so bad*, Nina thought sadly. "I appreciate it, but you didn't have to save me. I'm Nina by the way," she mumbled.

Yasin wouldn't admit it out loud, but he was floored by Nina's beauty. Even with minor scratches on her face and her hair in complete disarray, Nina's beauty could not be concealed. The mysterious allure she exuded piqued his interests. Yasin had been in Atlanta for a few months, and no female moved him enough to want to pursue anything serious. He dated to satisfy his needs as a man. But there was something about this girl that he couldn't put his hands on. If his homies were around, they would tell him he was acting like a straight sucker for a chick he didn't even know. Since he'd picked Nina up, Yasin had not checked one message or answered any calls. He never put his business on hold for anything or anyone, but he had to make sure Nina was safe.

"It's nice to officially meet you, Nina."

Before she could respond, the doctor and a nurse entered the room. Nina could not read their faces or expressions. "What's going on?" she asked.

"It's great to see you up and responsive, Miss Doe." The doctor referred to Nina by the alias Jane Doe. "Do you know where you are or recall anything that happened?"

Nina rolled her eyes impatiently. "My name is Nina Singleton. I'm from Charlotte, North Carolina, and I was driving to Atlanta from there. So, I'm assuming that's where I am. I can't move my damn shoulder. Why?"

The doctor took a deep breath before responding. "Well, Ms. Singleton, you dislocated your shoulder in the crash. Also, after running some tests, we became aware that you were four weeks pregnant." The doctor paused to give Nina some time to process information. "I'm sorry, but we couldn't detect a fetal heartbeat. I'm sorry for your loss."

Her lips trembled as the doctor delivered the news. She had thought her day couldn't get any worse after losing Chance. The baby she carried was the last piece of Chance she had. Knowing that she would hold a child they had made in eight months had eased her devastation. She questioned why God would take what she loved most from her. Had she not suffered enough in her life?

"Get out," she whispered. No one made a move. "Get the *fuck* out!" she yelled before bursting into tears.

"Fam, I think Nina hung up on me." Quan said as he sat in the chair next to Chance's bed. When he got a call from his right hand saying that he'd been shot up, he wasted no time getting to the hospital. Per Chance's request, Quan discharged Chance after the surgeons successfully removed all four bullets from Chance's body and stopped the bleeding. Quan called up a private doctor he had on payroll who was treating Chance from his secret spot right outside of Charlotte. The setup of the room looked like a scene out of *Grey's Anatomy*. Quan spared no cost on medical equipment or supplies. He wanted to make sure Chance was as comfortable as possible as he healed.

"She didn't take it well, man."

Chance hated the fact that he couldn't speak to his woman, but it was in her best interest. If she knew he'd survived, she wouldn't hesitate to be by his side. "Nina's strong. She'll be a'ight, man. I need her to be out of the loop and just raise my seed away from all this chaos. I need them safe and out of harm's way. They're all I have left."

Quan nodded in agreement.

"I want the streets to think I'm dead so that bitch nigga Nino can sleep peacefully at night." Chance gritted his teeth. The thought of Nino's violation made his blood boil. Chance risked losing everything he had worked hard for behind Nino, and he couldn't let it slide. "He had to know we were leaving town and took that as an opportunity to catch us off guard. But on my unborn child, it's war. And this time, I'm going to make sure I put him six feet under," Chance vowed.

The silence tortured Yasin as he and Nina headed to his place to retrieve her belongings. Nina hadn't spoken a word since she got the unfortunate news of her loss. He didn't know what say to console her. He wanted to give her space because he knew she was grieving, but he couldn't help but be curious. Where was the father of the child? What was she doing in Atlanta if she was from Charlotte? What type of work did she do to be pushing a Lamborghini? This mysterious beauty had Yasin's mental wheels turning.

"I need to find a spot." Nina finally spoke. She thumbed away a tear and sat up in the seat. "A nice condo maybe. Could you help me with that?"

Instead of asking the questions that were on his mind, Yasin simply responded, "I can link you with my realtor."

"Thanks," Nina mumbled and stared out of the window. She aimlessly watched the buildings pass by. She had no willpower left to say anything. Her intention wasn't to be rude to Yasin, but she couldn't fake the small talk.

No more words were spoken until the two pulled into Yasin's two-car garage attached to his townhouse. "Everything should be exactly where you left it, ma. Once you grab all of that, I'll take you the nearest Marriott."

Nina nodded and hurried to grab her belongings. "Thank you, God!" She whispered when she saw the two duffle bags filled with money still in the car. Grabbing those two bags and the only suitcase of clothes she had packed, Nina loaded the things into the backseat of Yasin's Audi. "I really appreciate all that you've done to help me. I owe you one."

Waving his hands in dismissal, Yasin gave Nina a half smile. "It's nothing, ma. Just know you always have a friend here in Atlanta if you ever need me. If you ever need to talk or anything, I'm here," he responded genuinely.

*I sound like a damn sucker*, Yasin thought.

Nina gave a half smile but said nothing. She didn't understand why Yasin was going out of his way for her, yet she was grateful either way. It eased her anxieties knowing there was someone looking out for her in Atlanta. In a way, he reminded her of Chance, sincere and protective, but it would be a while before she looked at another man intimately again. There was no way she could give her heart to another like she had with Chance. Their love would go down as the greatest love of her life. No one could ever replace that. If she couldn't be with Chance, then Nina didn't see the point of falling in love again. Here she was in

Atlanta, sitting on millions of dollars, but her other half wasn't by her side. It just didn't feel right. Despite it all, she promised to live the life Chance always wanted her to.

Chance's voice echoed through her mind. "You only live once, shorty. Live it up while you're here," he would say often. Tears threatened to escape her eyes as she thought of her man, but she didn't let them fall.

*I have to be strong*, she thought.

"Here we are, ma. Do you need help taking those bags up?" Yasin asked as they pulled into the Marriott hotel's parking lot. Nina shook her head. "Well, look, here's my realtor's card. Her name is Amanda Riley. Tell her Yasin referred you, and she'll get you right." Yasin slipped the card to Nina. As his hand briefly touched hers, he stared into her eyes. "I meant what I said, Nina. I'm here if you ever need anything. My number is on the back of that card, so don't hesitate to call me."

"Thank you, Yasin, but you've helped me enough. Have a nice night." Nina backed away from the car and shuffled through the front doors of the hotel.

# Chapter Two

The whole hood showed up to Chance's funeral to give their love, even though some people just wanted to know if the young rich nigga was really gone. Little did they know it wasn't Chance's body lying in that casket. Quan had put together the funeral upon Chance's request. They set the whole event up to get Nino to send one of his shooters there to make sure Chance was put into the ground. Chance surmised that Nino would let his guard down after the funeral. He would use that moment to catch Nino slacking.

"Yo, you think Nina going to show up?" Quan asked as he sat in the limo with Chance.

Rocking his disguise as an old man, Chance nodded. He held a cane in his left hand, which supported him. The gunshot he had taken to his leg would cause him to walk with a limp until he completed his physical therapy. "She'll be here. I don't know if I can stand watching her break down in here, G. That's my world."

Nina felt so close but so far away at the same time, like the feeling of knowing something on the tip of your tongue, but not being quite able to voice it. That's how he felt about Nina. There wasn't a day that went by within the ten years they'd been together without Chance talking to or checking on Nina. For her safety, freezing her out of his life seemed to be the safest option.

"It's only right." Quan sympathized with Chance. He knew his man worshipped the ground Nina walked on. For years, the three of them were the only family they knew. It took a lot for him not to reach out to Nina and let her know what was up. After all, she was like a sister to him, but in the end, his loyalty lay with Chance. Nina received that loyalty initially as an extension of his love for Chance, until Quan grew to love her also.

"You ready to do this, nigga?"

"Let's go, bruh." Chance checked his appearance one more time in the rearview mirror. No one would ever recognize him.

Walking into the church, Chance wanted to laugh at how packed it was. Yeah, he had love in the city, but half of the people there he didn't fuck with, and they didn't really fuck with him. It was true that people didn't show you love until you were dead and gone. Walking slowly with his cane, Chance observed every face in the building intensely. There was one face in the crowd that made his knees weak. It was Nina, sitting on the front row with huge Tom Ford shades resting on her face. He knew it was to conceal her tears. Nina was too classy to show her ass at this funeral. She knew her love for Chance was real, so there was no need to put on a show at his homegoing.

*Damn, she's so beautiful,* Chance thought. He sat a few rows behind her and waited for the service to start.

"You okay?" Angela, Chance's aunt, asked as she noticed Nina bouncing her leg uncontrollably. Like everyone else in the family, she had been shocked to hear the news. She felt it was only right to make sure Nina was good because she knew her nephew had intended on marrying this girl one day.

"Huh?" Nina closed her eyes and shook her head, turning her attention to Angela. "Oh . . . yes." Physically, she was there, but mentally, she drifted down memory lane. A part of her hadn't even wanted to come to the funeral, but her loyalty to Chance had compelled her to.

Over the past few days in Atlanta, she had managed to purchase a condo and a new Mercedes

Benz. Nina didn't intend on blowing through the money at all. In fact, she planned to invest some of it and flip it. One thing Chance had taught her was how to turn five dollars into a five hundred, and it was a lesson she'd never take in vain. When she had enough money behind her, she would go after Nino.

"Is there anyone who would like to speak of their experience with brother Chance?" Reverend Davis asked.

Nina hadn't even noticed the funeral pass her by. She started to stand and go speak about her love for Chance, but someone beat her to it. Nina noticed a familiar female walking to the front of the altar. She was dressed in all black, with her red weave cascading down her back.

"Who the fuck is she?" Nina mumbled. She had seen that face before, but she couldn't quite put a name to the face.

Tears were rolling down the girl's face before she could even start speaking. "Anyone who knows me knows how much Chance meant to me. I loved that man so much." The girl's voice cracked.

Nina whipped her head to Angela for answers, but she just shrugged. "The fucking audacity!" Nina whispered through clenched teeth. As bad as she wanted to snatch the girl from the stage by her weave, Nina decided to let her finish her speech. She wouldn't disrespect Chance's memory by making a scene. But afterwards, answers would be found.

"Chance was the most selfless person I ever met." The crowd mumbled their agreements and nodded their heads. "No matter how far we drifted apart, we would always find our way back to each other. That's how it tends to go with your first love." She turned toward Nina's direction. "Unfortunately, a bad seed in his life got him to this point. I just wish I could have said goodbye." Wiping her tears, the girl quietly walked back to her seat.

"No the fuck she didn't just blame this on me," Nina mumbled as her back stiffened. Scoffing, she clutched the straps of her purse tightly while biting the inside of her cheek.

When Chance was alive, she never had to deal with the disrespect from any woman on the side. Though Nina wasn't naïve enough to believe that she was the only woman Chance had been with all these years, she believed that only she dwelled in his heart. They went through their breakups and make-ups like any other couple. The difference was that they always found their way back to each other. No one could come between their bond, or so she had thought. Watching this woman speak about Chance with so much passion made Nina's stomach hollow. She second-guessed Chance's devotion.

*He had to be fucking her. Did Chance love this woman?*

Feeling petty, Nina stood up and made her way to the altar. Her natural tresses were silk pressed and cascaded down her back in loose curls. She adjusted the blazer to her all-black pant suit. The clicking of her YSL heels echoed throughout the church. It was so quiet that if a penny dropped, it would be heard at the altar. Rubbing her red lips together, Nina stepped onto the stage and tapped the mic twice. She inhaled deeply before facing the crowd.

"Give me a moment," Nina stated, rubbing her sweaty hands against the sides of her pants. She spun around, clasping her hands together as if she were praying, shaking them back and forth. Tears pooled in her eyes and a lump settled in her throat. Blowing out a shaky breath, she closed her eyes and counted to ten silently.

"Take your time, niece," Angela said, standing and waving her hand in Nina's direction.

"Fuck!" Chance uttered under his breath. He made eye contact with Quan, who was sitting a few pews over, and shook his head, his eyebrows furrowing. He couldn't believe Tiana had the nerve to show up to his funeral and speak like they were so in love. There were a few occasions over the years when he and Nina had broken up. Chance made the mistake of entertaining Tiana during those times. He had explicitly told Tiana that he could never offer her anything serious because Nina had his heart. Tiana envied Nina for that reason. As he watched Nina walk to the altar, he knew she would take it completely wrong, and he had no way to defend himself. This was bad.

"How y'all doing?" Nina spoke quietly into the mic. Rounds of applause erupted throughout the church. The crowd showed Nina love because she had respect in the hood as Chance's girl. "I don't have to speak on me and Chance's relationship because everyone knows what it was and what it will forever be. Anyone else claiming otherwise can kick rocks." Nina removed her designer frames, rolling her neck in the redhead's direction. "My last moments with Chance are moments I will cherish forever. We were finally leaving this place and starting over somewhere else. We wanted to start fresh with our family." Nina looked down and placed her hand on her stomach. "But now, he's gone too soon, and I'll forever miss him. Chance,

I'll always love you, and even in death, I'll continue to hold you down. My love is real. Always has been and always will be. I love you, baby."

*I love you and my seed too,* Chance thought. He took in every inch of Nina. She looked delectable in the pantsuit. There was a diamond *C* brooch attached to the right breast of her blazer. He loved everything about her from the way her hair bounced to the small bruise above her eyebrow. He presumed it had come from them escaping after Nino's attack. In his eyes, that small bruise proved he had failed to keep the promise he made to Nina many years ago. Nino was able to harm her again. Chance wouldn't be able to sleep peacefully at night until Nino was obliterated.

The crowd gathered in the graveyard behind the church. The burial was brief and intimate. Nina accepted the words of condolences from people and picked at the plate of food Angela prepared for her.

Thoughts of confronting the girl preoccupied Nina.

She spotted the redhead talking to one of Chance's workers after the funeral. Nina pulled her hair over her shoulder and approached her. "You wanted my attention? You have it," Nina stated. She crossed her arms in front of her, allowing her quilted Chanel purse to dangle inches above the ground.

A slick smile spread across the girl's face. "So, Nina, we finally meet. I'm Tiana." Tiana held out her hand for Nina to shake.

Nina looked down at her extra-long nails and scoffed. Hell would freeze over before Nina allowed Tiana to feel like she had one up on her. "Don't say my name like you know me. You don't know me, and I don't care to get to know you. What I want to know is why you're showing up to *my* man's funeral being disrespectful?" Nina had never pictured herself arguing with a woman at Chance's funeral. It still hadn't even registered that she buried Chance. If Tiana had pulled this stunt a year or two ago, Nina probably would've physically assaulted her and made Chance bail her out. But Chance was dead, and she'd be damned if she allowed a temporary bitch to claim any parts of Chance's heart.

Tiana sucked her teeth and wiggled her finger at Nina. "Your man? Honey, I can't tell! Did your man tell you we've been fucking around for years? Nah, he can't, can he? Because he got killed behind your bullshit!" Tiana's heels sunk into the dirt as she shifted the weight from her left hip to the right.

Nina knew Tiana had scrambled for anything to say to get under her skin. She thought she had the tea on Nina, but it was piss. No one in the streets knew the truth about Chance's demise. They only could tell rumors that were made up by people who had nothing better to do with their time but gossip. If Tiana's goals were to make Nina despise Chance now that he was gone, her plan was failing.

"Is that so? Well, you might as well line up behind every other slut claiming to be the side bitch."

"I'll be the side bitch, but this side bitch has the receipts." Tiana pulled out her phone and showed Nina screenshots of messages between her and Chance.

Nina's heart dropped to the pit of her stomach as she briefly glanced over the messages. There were no dates showing, but it was indeed Chance's number. However, Nina put on her poker face. Tiana wouldn't see her sweat. "That's cute. But Chance never claimed you. Why you trying to claim a man that never wanted you?" Honestly, Nina wanted to know. There were plenty of women over the years who thought they had a chance of stealing Chance from Nina. Each failed miserably. Nina didn't believe in the idea of a man being able to be stolen from another woman. The man made the decision to leave, and Nina knew Chance would never leave her voluntarily. She never had to worry about bitches popping up to her home or a string of late-night calls. If Chance did step out on her while they were together, he hid it well.

"Because I'm pregnant with his child." Tiana's smile widened as she held up an ultrasound image.

Nina's heart dropped as she looked at the ultrasound. The fact that she had suffered a miscarriage while this sack chaser could potentially be carrying Chance's child was like a slap to the face. Nina felt like she'd been tackled and had the wind knocked out of her. It hurt to know that if what Tiana said was true, Chance couldn't even offer any explanation. How could she hate a dead man?

"Yeah right. That could be anybody's baby," Nina commented.

"We'll see in five months, honey! You remember when you and Chance had that argument five months ago? Yeah, baby, he came to me after that. So, who's the side bitch now?" Tiana smirked and walked away, leaving Nina seething.

Thinking back five months ago, Nina did recall getting into an argument with Chance and sending him away for a few weeks. She didn't believe that he was committed to leaving Charlotte, and they had gotten into a big argument. Nina questioned whether there was any truth to Tiana's words.

She hated that she couldn't ask Chance to give her the truth of the matter. She would forever be tormented with the question of *what if*? All she was sure of was that she had to get out of Charlotte before anything else bad about Chance could come to the light.


Chance discreetly watched the scene between Nina and Tiana unfold from the limo. He couldn't hear the words they exchanged, but the body language told it all. He kicked himself for ever dealing with an envious chick like Tiana.

"Yo, there's no telling what she said to Nina. I need you to get to the bottom of this, man. The last thing I need is Nina leaving here feeling some type of way. I can't lose her, man," Chance said to Quan. "It's going to take some time for me to put my plan together, and there's no telling what could happen between now and then." He bit his lip while the unharmed leg bounced up and down.

"You really fucked with that bitch?" Quan asked in disbelief. He and Chance usually told each other everything, no matter the situation. He knew Chance like he knew himself— he had been too ashamed to admit to seeing Tiana. Quan's response would've been the same as now. If sides had to be chosen, Quan picked Nina's over any other female.

He thought about how Nina must've felt for a second. "This ain't good, bro."

"I fucked up, Q." Chance dropped his head in his hands. "If I could take it back, I would." He watched Nina power walk to her Benz. She was pissed. The haste she walked with gave it away. Nina naturally sauntered when she walked, slowly and sensually. She only walked quickly when someone upset her.

Nina pointed her lock to the car, brows furrowing deeply as the stress lines appeared in her forehead. Chance hoped Nina would find it in her heart to forgive him one day.

"She got my seed, man. She can't stay mad forever."


Nina sped down the highway, listening to "Resentment" by Beyoncé. She finally allowed the tears to fall. There was no one inside the vehicle to judge her. Whatever she couldn't voice to anyone about the situation, she let Bey lay it all out on the track. A part of her didn't want to believe Chance had cheated on her; to believe that after holding him down for ten years, he would make a fool of

her. Her biggest fear had been that Chance would
wake up one day and not feel the same anymore.
For years, she never worried about him stepping
out on her. She was so sure their union meant too
much for him to put it in jeopardy. But the more
money he made in the streets, the bolder the
women became. Did she misplace her trust? Was
she naïve to believe that Chance wouldn't grow
bored of her? Her head throbbed as her mind pro-
cessed her confrontation with Tiana.

There were five missed calls from Quan on her
phone. She had left without saying goodbye, which
was unusual for her. She ignored every one of the
calls. There was no doubt in her mind that Quan
knew about Tiana. She needed time to calm down
before talking to him. Nina had no shoulder to
cry on or no one to vent to. She had just buried
her best friend. Although she had a few female
associates in Charlotte, she didn't trust any of
them enough to reveal anything so personal. All
her family was back in Philadelphia, where her
parents were originally from. Times like this, she
really wished she could get advice from her mother.
Besides Quan, there was no one in Nina's corner.

Yasin's words crossed her mind when she
passed a sign indicating she was fifteen miles
outside of Atlanta. His words seemed so genuine

to her, and in this moment, she needed something to take her mind off the tornado that blew through and destroyed the life she knew. Pulling out her iPhone, she dialed Yasin's number.

Just as Nina was about to hang up, Yasin answered. "Yo," his smooth voice called into the phone.

"I thought you wouldn't answer." Nina bit her lip lightly. "It's Nina."

"I know, ma. I can recognize your voice anywhere." Yasin was surprised to hear from Nina, since their last encounter was a week ago. She didn't seem interested at all from the vibes she gave him. "I didn't expect to hear from you so soon. What changed your mind?"

That was a question Nina didn't have an answer to quite yet. She knew she wanted to vent to someone, but was she calling Yasin out of spite? There was no denying that he was attractive and interested in her, but if none of the drama had unfolded at the funeral, would she even be on the phone right now?

"I wanted to thank you for hooking me up with ya realtor. She found a nice spot for me." Nina laughed.

Yasin chuckled on the other end of the line.

"What's funny?" she asked.

"Let's keep it a hunnit, Nina. I know you didn't call me to thank me." Yasin knew getting to know Nina wouldn't be easy, but he would give her all the time she needed. He was willing to chase her if that's what Nina liked. "How about you meet me in two hours for dinner?"

"Are you asking me on a date?"

"I wouldn't take you to dinner as a first date, ma. That's child's play. Our first day will be way more elaborate," Yasin replied. The spark of a light could be heard on his end of the line. "It seems like you want to talk. So, how about we do that over a friendly dinner and drinks? I just want to get to know you. You're the realest thing that's happened to me since I've been here," he sincerely admitted. Nina possessed the type of personality that made Yasin want to bring her into his world and shield her with his safety.

Nina bit her lip as she contemplated his offer. "Okay, I'll call you in an hour for details."

"No doubt."

Chance paced back and forth across his living room floor, limping slightly. "She didn't answer?" he asked Quan while running his hands over his waves.

"Take it easy, nigga." Quan motioned for Chance to have a seat. At the rate Chance moved around the living room, he would surely rip his stitches if he wasn't careful. Quan had never seen Chance so stressed before. "Nina don't want to talk. That was like my tenth time calling. She thinks I knew about you and shorty. She ain't fucking with me right now."

Quan wanted to slap Chance across the head for cheating on Nina. He really loved her like a sister, and he could tell she was hurting. Seeing Chance with Nina gave Quan hope that he'd someday find the woman meant for him to love. There were enough instances in the world for him to not ever want to fall in love. On the days he figured love wasn't meant for him, Quan looked to Chance and Nina for inspiration. Now, he had no one to look to.

"How about I call Tiana ho ass?" Quan asked.

Chance nodded as he finally took a seat. "I should have never fucked with her." He kicked himself for giving in to temptation.

"Hello?" Tiana answered on the third ring. "Quan, what do I owe the pleasure?" she asked seductively.

"Fuck did you say to Nina at the funeral, Tiana?" Quan didn't even bother asking how she knew it was him. The two had fucked around on a few occasions, too. Tiana was known to get around.

That's why Quan couldn't understand why Chance would step out on a woman like Nina for this ho.

Tiana smacked her lips. "Nina, Nina, Nina. I'm tired of hearing that bitch name! I told her the truth! I fucked the shit out of her man on several occasions. And he left me with his baby." Tiana laughed.

Chance's eyes bulged, and he lunged to snatch the phone from Quan's hands. "Baby!" he exclaimed, forgetting the role he was supposed to be playing.

*What the fuck, nigga!* Quan mouthed to him, pushing Chance away from the phone.

"Who was that?"

"Don't worry about all that." Quan motioned for Chance to sit on the couch. "Watch ya mouth when you're referring to Nina. She ain't no bitch. You, on the other hand, that's a different story," Quan spat. "So, you're saying you pregnant and the baby is Chance's?"

Smacking her lips, Tiana replied "Mm-hmm, and I know there's some money Chance left behind. I'm carrying his child, and I deserve a piece of that."

*Straight gold digger*, Quan thought. "You out yo' rabid-ass mind, Tiana. You acting like you was wifed up or something!" Quan laughed into the phone. Women like Tiana purposely leveraged pregnancies and babies as meal tickets. All it took was spreading their legs for the right man and they could be set for life. Quan didn't respect it. "Any money my nigga left behind is with Nina and the child she's carrying. Have a nice life, ma." He hung up in her ear.

"No wonder Nina left so fast." Chance shook his head and bit his balled fist. If he had doubted that Nina resented him before, he was sure of it now. "I wrapped up every time I fucked her. I didn't even let her give me head." Chance questioned Tiana's intentions. Her affections were for sale, and Chance suspected that there were multiple invested parties when it came to her. He hoped that she was bluffing. "Fuck, man!"

Quan shook his head too. For Chance to be as smart as he was, that was a dumb move. "You know these hoes like to trap a nigga." If Quan had to name the smartest person he knew, it would be Chance. The nigga really possessed the intellect of a Harvard graduate. He didn't understand how a nigga so smart could make the dumbest decisions. "You know I got yo' back like no other, but I ain't finna tiptoe around your feelings. You fucked this up."

"A'ight, nigga, I know I fucked up," Chance expressed. He didn't need anyone else reminding

him of his shortcomings. He realized hurting Nina
was a decision he'd regret for the rest of his life.
Temptation may have cost him the love of his
life. "Damn!" He brought his closed fit down on
the coffee table.


The blues really hit Nina as she got dressed in
her condo. Monica crooned in the background as
Nina touched up the curls from her silk press. She
couldn't believe the series of events that had unfolded in her life throughout the last two weeks.
Battling the grief of losing her baby and Chance
had left her depleted. She had cried more tears
than she knew her body could produce. The betrayal she felt from Chance confused her. She
didn't know how to be upset with him while still
holding onto the beautiful memories they shared
together. She decided that it wasn't fair to allow
anyone to skew her last impression of Chance. For
the sake of her healing, she forgave Chance. Remembering him as the man she deeply loved was
more important than acknowledging his shortcomings.

"What to wear?" Nina asked aloud as she fingered through the suitcase of clothes she had
brought from Charlotte. "I definitely have to go

shopping." She settled with her new black Gucci bodysuit, a red kimono, and her all-black, thigh-high Louboutins.

*I hope I'm not too overdressed.* Nina admired her appearance in the mirror. The bodysuit complemented her slim curves perfectly. Her bare skin glowed to Nina's surprise. She had abandoned her skincare regimen since arriving to Atlanta. She brushed her eyelash extensions and applied a clear coat of lip gloss to her full lips.

"Okay, Nina. You're ready."

Nina's palms moistened when her GPS projected her estimated arrival to be in less than five minutes. Even though Yasin had made it clear that it wasn't a date, Nina felt awkward. She'd never dated anyone besides Chance. She felt so far removed from the dating scene. What if she said the wrong thing or made a wrong move? Romance with Chance came easily. Nina didn't know if she was equipped to find love in today's market.

Yasin was sitting at the bar when Nina arrived. The sleeves of his button-down were rolled up to his elbows. He had the appeal of a mafia boss. Someone who could parlay with the elite and always survive in the trenches; it's what Yasin gave. His dark skin complemented his freshly tapered haircut.

"Hey," Nina said softly, announcing her presence.

Yasin turned and licked his lips when he spotted Nina. His eyes scanned over her, and the sides of his mouth curled into a grin. Nina looked even better dressed up. The bodysuit she wore put her slim-thick frame on display. Her hair was different from the last time he saw her. Her tresses were pressed and curled. He noticed the beauty mark above her lip for the first time. She barely wore makeup and still stunned him.

Yasin stood and embraced her. "I thought you stood me up, ma. You look amazing. How you?" he asked, pulling the seat out for Nina to sit.

"I'm okay," Nina replied as she slid into the seat beside Yasin's. "I thought we were eating."

"You can go ahead and order something. It's been a long day for me, so I'm settling for a drink." Yasin had been ripping and running through the city handling business. The illegal empire he ran occupied most of his free time. There weren't many he trusted to run his operations, so he remained a one-man army.

Nina nodded, understanding the feeling of having an overwhelming day. Shit, it'd been an overwhelming two weeks for her. *A drink or two couldn't hurt.*

"I'll take a margarita," she told the bartender. Nina checked Yasin out. She assumed he had worked all day because he was still dressed in his suit. The jacket hung on the back of the barstool he sat in. She had to admit that she thought Yasin was fine. His smooth, ebony skin shone with no traces of blemishes. He had the aura of a city nigga, and Nina dug it. "I've had a long fucking two weeks," Nina admitted bitterly as she sipped the margarita.

Yasin studied the expression on her face. Her eyes. They were dim and faraway. Her eyes told the story that her mouth never voiced. Sorrow. Grief. Yasin could read those emotions on anyone. Even though she tried to hide it, he recognized the hurt all over Nina's face.

"Well, shit, let's drink to that." Yasin leaned back in his seat, cupping his elbow with one hand and rubbing his goatee with the other. He wanted to know more about the mysterious beauty in front of him, but he didn't want to ask the wrong questions. Nina had a guard up that he hadn't quite figured how to disband. "I'm glad you came out with me tonight, though."

Nina smiled tightly and rolled her eyes up, pausing before she responded. She barely had the mental capacity to be around anyone right now. She desperately yearned to curl up in her bed and sleep, but Nina knew if she succumbed to the grief, she'd never find her way out of it.

"Honestly, I am too. It feels good to be in a new environment, meeting new people. Just the distraction I need," she admitted before tilting her glass back, finishing the rest of the margarita. Nina signaled for the bartender to bring her another round.

"Damn. Distraction?" Yasin clutched his heart as if he were wounded by Nina's words. He nodded to the bartender and handed him a fifty-dollar bill as a tip.

Blushing, Nina rolled her eyes playfully before focusing on Yasin with a smirk on her face. "I didn't mean it like that. It's just been a rough couple of weeks, to say the least. Being occupied keeps my mind off things," she said while swirling the straw around her drink.

"I feel you," Yasin admitted.

"Life can just be so hard sometimes, you know? Nothing in this life is guaranteed. And when you've lost so much, you're constantly waiting for the rug to be pulled from under you, like shit could be turned upside down at any moment. It's not fair," Nina stated quietly, lowering her gaze to her margarita and blinking away tears. "I lost one of the closest people to me in a blink of an eye. Someone who helped me grow into the woman I am today, and I just don't know how to make sense of it."

She looked up to find Yasin glancing at her curiously. Her cheeks flushed, and she took a gulp of her drink to fill the awkward silence. "I'm sorry. I don't mean to pour all of this on you." Being with Chance for so many years made dating feel like a foreign territory to Nina. She had forgotten what people talked about on first dates.

Although they both agreed this wasn't a date, Nina felt a connection with Yasin that she couldn't explain. *First date or not, don't run this nigga off with your baggage*, she thought.

Licking his lips, Yasin curled his finger and placed it under Nina's chin, bringing her gaze to meet his. "Don't apologize for speaking what's on your mind. I know exactly what you mean, but something tells me you're strong enough to make it through it. We gotta make the best of the cards we dealt." He empathized with Nina's plight. He, too, took many losses to be in the position he was in today. "I'm here to listen if you want to talk."

"Thank you." Nina bit her bottom lip and shook her head lightly. The only person she trusted mourning Chance with was Quan. After the funeral's revelations, however, Nina needed space from him too. There was no one she could share this pain with. She had to become numb to it all. "I'm just going to take it day by day."

"Tell me something about yourself," Yasin stated.

Nina shrugged and gently bit her bottom lip. It'd been so long since she shared intimate details about herself with any other man besides Chance. The most basic things like a person's favorite color or food—Nina had forgotten that this was the type of information single people shared when dating.

"I love dogs, but I never actually owned one," she blurted out. It wasn't the most interesting fact about herself, but it was the first thought that came to her mind.

Yasin's lips curled into a smirk as he finished off his second double shot. "Why not?"

"Too much maintenance. The idea of cleaning up dog shit doesn't excite me," Nina responded, chuckling lightly. "What about you?"

"I feel that. Let me see . . . I love music, but I've never been to a concert," Yasin stated, brushing the back of his head.

Nina cocked her head to the side and squinted her eyes in Yasin's direction. "No?"

"Nah, plenty of opportunities, but big crowd's not my vibe. I'm a low-key dude. You'll learn that if you stick around me." He hoped that this wouldn't be the last time he saw Nina. There were multiple reasons he desired her, but her vibe topped the list.

"We'll see," Nina replied.

A few drinks later, Nina was more comfortable with Yasin. He was surprisingly easy to talk to. He allowed Nina to lead the conversation and only contributed when she asked him a question or for his thoughts.

Nina's phone interrupted the conversation. It was a FaceTime call from Quan. In her inebriated state, she didn't think twice about answering Quan's call. She was supposed to still be upset with him.

"Excuse me." Nina said to Yasin as she accepted the call.

"Yo, Nina, what the fuck is up, sis?" Quan spoke into the phone. He'd lost count of the number of times he'd called Nina by this point. He breathed a sigh of relief, knowing Nina was safe, because Chance could get off his back now. He loved his brother to death, but the persistent talk about Nina gave Quan a headache.

"Wassup, bro." Nina smiled into the camera. Looking at Quan reminded her so much of Chance. The two were almost one in the same. That fact alone was bittersweet. Pieces of Chance would always live on through Quan. Yet, the reminder of Chance that Quan presented crippled Nina at the same time. She needed to establish distance between Quan and herself for a while. Her healing couldn't happen as long as she grieved Chance. She hoped Quan would understand.

Chance looked at Nina from a distance. Hearing her voice was a relief to him. His heart ached when he saw the smile on Nina's face. She had her hair down and straightened, one of his favorite styles for her to wear. "Where she at?" he whispered to Quan, waving his hands back and forth, attempting to get Quan's attention. Quan stood a few feet across the room from him.

"What you up to, Nina? I been hitting you up like shit all day. You dipped out of the funeral so quick I couldn't even talk to you." Quan said. He barely allowed Nina time to finish her statement before he bombarded her with his questions.

Nina sighed. She appreciated Quan's concern, but she didn't have the mental capacity to have this discussion at the moment. Quan had questions that she wasn't ready to answer yet. "My mind was fucked up, Quan. I just couldn't stay there." She didn't let Quan in on the information Tiana had given her. To be honest, she didn't want to hear the words come from her own mouth. It was embarrassing to even think about. She wanted to drown it all out tonight. "I'm out having a drink, ya know. Take my mind off some things."

"I feel you. I know you taking losing Chance the hardest." Quan sympathized, laying his act down thick. As much as he hated keeping Nina in the dark, he had to respect his man's wishes. "You out drinking alone?" Quan asked as if he read Chance's mind. Chance pointed his finger at Quan, shaking his head while wagging his finger. That was his indication that Quan asked all the right questions.

Nina paused, and she remembered she was sitting across from Yasin. She smiled at Yasin and stepped away from the bar. "Nah, I've made a friend actually. Shit has been crazy for me, and he's been helpful."

"He?" Quan and Chance repeated at the same time. Before Nina could respond, the video call disconnected.

"Her phone must have died."

"Bro, did she just say she met a nigga that's been helping her?" Chance asked. His nostrils flared at the thought of Nina out having drinks with another man.

Quan ignored the question. He knew Chance heard Nina as clearly as he had. He knew Chance well enough to understand that he didn't want an answer to that question.

"Fuck, man. Nina's a good girl, my nigga. Any nigga would be lucky to have her. So, I know all those niggas out there on her hard. I just hope shorty can wait long enough for me to get my shit together." Chance shook his head and pinched the bridge of his nose. The thought of another man lusting over Nina made his skin crawl. He realized it was typical nigga shit to be upset over Nina getting to know another man although she was technically single, while he had a female showing up to his funeral, professing her love. He could admit that he wouldn't be able to handle the heat if he switched roles with Nina. Still, that revelation didn't ward off his fuming anger. The situation was all fucked up.

"We gotta make a trip to Atlanta and scope some shit out, bro," Chance concluded.

"Nigga!" Quan scoffed while throwing his hands in the air. "Fuck you wanna do? Play dead or check on sis? Why not just bring her in on all this shit?" It was hard to follow Chance's logic. One minute he wanted to ice Nina out, and the next he wanted to keep close tabs on her. Quan usually trusted Chance's plans, but the incident with Nino had him moving erratically. "This shit got you moving crazy, bruh."

Chance clasped his hands together in a fist as his brows furrowed. Inhaling deeply, he gazed directly into Quan's eyes. "I'm doing this my way.

The first thing Nino will suspect is me making contact with Nina. This nigga knows the tricks of playing possum. He got years of practice with this shit. I gotta be two steps ahead of him." He didn't expect Quan to understand his reasoning. Hell, he barely agreed with it himself, but the only way to keep Nina safe was to kill Nino. With Nino believing he was dead, it gave Chance the upper hand to execute his plan. Contact with Nina risked blowing his cover.

"Why go to Atlanta then?" Quan asked.

"I got a feeling. We'll check it out and head back. Just trust me." Chance wasn't going to expose his hand yet, but there was no way he would let another nigga get close to Nina. No way in hell. If he had to lay down bodies for her, then so be it. He'd done it before. He would kill, steal, and lie if that meant Nina's heart remained with him.

"I'm sorry. That was my brother," Nina said to Yasin.

Yasin waved his hand, saying it was no big deal. He didn't mean to eavesdrop on Nina's call, but it was hard not to. Putting two and two together, Yasin figured Nina had lost her boyfriend, and the baby she lost must have been his also. That explained the sadness that her eyes revealed.

"I'm sorry for your loss, ma, for real."

Nina's lips pursed together tightly to keep the tears from falling. She didn't want Yasin to see her waterworks. "It's hard, ya know? But I'm dealing with it." A single tear fell down her cheek. Bottling up her emotions had been her only resort. Soon enough, however, Nina sensed that everything she held in would boil over and explode in her face if she didn't face it head on.

Thumbing the tear away from her cheek lightly, Yasin lifted Nina's chin with his index finger. "I can tell you're strong. I won't lie and say it'll get easier, but it gets better with time." He offered Nina a little consolation. Grief was a feeling he was well acquainted with. If things went well with Nina, Yasin promised to open up to her about his own sad stories too.

Nina nodded, and she turned away from Yasin. The words he spoke were the type of words that broke a grieving person down. While they were meant to sound encouraging, they only sank you deeper into sorrow.

"Can I have two shots of Hennessy?" Nina asked the bartender. Her emotions were coming down hard right now, and she just wanted to drown them out. Hennessy promised her the mental escape she desperately needed. "Just promise you'll get me home safely if I'm too fucked up."

"You don't have to worry, ma. I won't let anything happen to you," Yasin reassured her sincerely. Nina was broken, and he wanted to be the one to help put the pieces back together. Then and there, he made up his mind. Nina was going to be his. He wouldn't rush her. If she ever decided to give him a shot, Yasin would be there for her.

"Whew, I'm feeling nice." Nina flipped her hair over her shoulders as she nodded her head to the music playing in the Black-owned restaurant. The alcohol had her feeling lovely, and she knew she had reached her limit. Being sloppy drunk wasn't usually Nina's thing unless she was in the confinement of her own home.

She and Yasin had been enjoying each other's company for the past two hours. She looked at the digital clock hanging above the bar and gasped. Three hours had passed since they'd entered the bar. "Yeah, I think it's about that time," she said as she stood up, swaying lightly.

Yasin placed his arm around Nina's waist to hold her steady. "I don't think you're in any condition to drive home, ma." He could tell she was a lightweight when it came to alcohol. Furthermore, he respected the fact that she knew when to stop drinking. It let him know that Nina was disciplined. "I told you I would get you home safely. I can't let you drive like this. Give me your keys."

Nina sucked her teeth as she waved Yasin off. "Nah, I'm good. I can make it home. Plus, I don't want you to have to leave your car." Nina reached in her bag for her car keys, fumbling around the many unnecessary items inside. "Fuck!" she exclaimed as the contents of her purse spilled on the floor. Yasin bent down and helped Nina retrieve the contents.

Yasin held the keys out of her reach and smirked. Nina jumped in the air slightly, but her attempts were futile. Her five-foot-six frame didn't stand a chance over Yasin, who stood well over six feet. "Like I said, I can't let you drive." He ignored Nina as she smacked her lips and rolled her eyes. "And don't worry about my car. I own this restaurant," he stated humbly.

Nina was impressed—not by the fact that Yasin had money, because she was used to being spoiled by Chance. But she liked the fact that he had something to show for his money. "It seems like I've been talking about me all night, yet I don't know much about you, Yasin." Her first instinct told her that he was a drug dealer, but she knew not to ask. Nina had always been attracted to Chance because of his hustle, not how much money he brought home. If her dad had taught her anything, he taught her that a man with hustle in him would never be broke. A man who could go into the jungle naked and come out with a fur coat; a man who could make a dollar out of nothing; a man who could lose it all one day and get it back with no complaints. Not every man had it. Yasin seemed to possess that hustler mentality. The only question was, what was his hustle?

"Next time, shorty. Let's get you home." Placing his hand on the small of Nina's back, he guided her out of the restaurant. "There's still a lot I don't know about you, too," Yasin said as he opened the passenger door to Nina's Benz. He noticed she had just totaled her Lamborghini and was able to turn right around and purchase a brand-new Mercedes like it was nothing. The condo she purchased rested on the penthouse floor of one of the hottest complexes in downtown Atlanta. It was nothing to brush shoulders with celebrities in Nina's building. Money talks, and Nina's spoke volumes.

As Yasin slid into the drivers' seat, he looked over to find Nina sleeping lightly. Yasin ended up carrying Nina to her condo, cradling her in his arms. He didn't want to disturb her peaceful slumber.

"Nina, we here, ma." He placed her on her queen-sized bed. "Yo." He shook her arm lightly.

"I'm so tired," Nina moaned and stirred in her sleep, rolling over onto her side.

Yasin took the liberty of removing her heels from her feet, and then slid the kimono off her shoulders. Once he felt she was comfortable, he slowly backed out of the room.

"Yasin," Nina called out lightly. He turned around and nodded. "Can you stay?" she asked softly. "I don't want to be alone."

"Uhh . . . okay." Hesitantly, Yasin kicked off his loafers and climbed into the bed with Nina. As he wrapped his arms around her, tears fell from her eyes. She desperately wished they were Chance's arms around her.

Yasin noticed that Nina was crying, but he didn't say anything. He only held her closer and rubbed her hair. It would be clown behavior for him to try to make a move on Nina in this vulnerable state. Nina had experienced a lot of losses in a short period of time, and right now, she just needed a shoulder to cry on. Little did she know, a bond between her and Yasin was already developing.

# Chapter Three

"This nigga Nino been laying low as a mother-fucker," Quan said to Chance as they sat in a car discreetly outside of Nino's girlfriend's spot. They had been clocking him all day, trying to get familiar with his movements. Chance wanted to find the best opportunity to take a shot at Nino by familiarizing himself with his daily routine.

However, Chance's mind drifted to Nina. It drove him crazy thinking that she was in another man's company. He couldn't focus on the task at hand as long as he worried about Nina. "Man, let's get back to this later. I told you I'm trying to make this quick move to the A." Chance clenched his teeth, checking the time on Quan's phone again. It'd been hours since Nina's call disconnected.

Quan shook his head. Chance couldn't take the heat. He should have known that his master plan of faking his death would come with repercussions. "Nigga, you can't go to Atlanta and blow your cover.

We have to get this shit done before anything else. Nina still grieving, man. She ain't thinking about no nigga."

"Nah, because that's the best time for a nigga to think he can slide in. Quan, I'm not new to this shit. I know how niggas think," Chance stressed. He knew how men preyed on vulnerable women. Niggas would surely shoot their shot at Nina.

Quan ignored him and watched one of Nino's hitters walk out of the house. "It's showtime." He smiled devilishly as his trigger finger began to itch. They planned to pick off all of Nino's workers one by one. The only twist was that they would make it seem like his enemy, Black, had ordered the killings, keeping the suspicion off Quan.

Chance rubbed his hands together, hoping some gunplay would take his mind off Nina. "First thing in the morning, I'm heading to Atlanta. I want you to come with me, yo."

Quan sighed as he loaded up his Glock. "A'ight, bruh. Let's handle this shit right now." Pulling the black ski mask over his face, Quan pulled out behind the boy's Charger.

"Niggas don't know that a quick nut can be the reason they get caught slipping." Chance chuckled as he watched the young bull lay pipe on a girl through his car window. They were sitting in the parking lot of a local apartment complex on the east side of Charlotte. Many murders occurred in the crime-ridden complex, and the police barely stopped through. This was the perfect place to off a nigga. "I'ma let this li'l nigga enjoy it a little bit."

Quan laughed along with his man. He knew Chance meant business when it came to Nino because killing wasn't his thing. Chance engaged in his fair share of gunplay, but he wasn't a shooter. That right was reserved to Quan. To see his friend so bloodthirsty let him know that he wanted Nino's head by any means necessary. "You got this, or you want me to handle it?"

Chance shook his head as he opened the car door. There were barely any working streetlights to illuminate the dark block. Creeping up on the Charger, he heard moaning. The li'l nigga was so preoccupied with shorty that he hadn't even bothered to roll his window back up.

"You fucked up now, nigga," Chance said through clenched teeth as he pressed the cold steel against dude's temple. "Aht aht, shorty, don't even do it." Chance shook his gun, warning the girl as she opened her mouth the scream. "Tell Nino, Black sends his regards." He spoke through the ski mask before sending a shot through the guy's brain. Adrenaline rushed through his veins as he jogged back to the car with Quan. "Hit the highway, bro." Chance said nonchalantly as he wiped off his gun.

Quan laughed. "Nigga gon act like he just didn't murk a nigga. Talmbout some fucking 'hit the highway.'" He noticed Chance's demeanor slowly becoming colder and colder, and he wasn't quite sure if it was a change he liked.

Chance smirked but paid Quan no mind. The only thing on his mind was Nina.


Rolling over in bed, Nina's hand fell on a warm, bare chest. She smiled, but it quickly faded as she realized who was lying next to her. Yasin, not Chance.

*Oh, shit!* she thought as she lifted the covers. *I'm dressed. Thank God.* She didn't remember anything after leaving the restaurant, so she didn't know what went down between her and Yasin. Sliding out of the bed, she grabbed her throbbing head.

"Get it together, Nina. You moving real sloppy out here," she said to herself, going to the bathroom for some Advil. Her reflection in the mirror displayed her mood. Her red eyes were swollen, and her disheveled hair covered her head. She knew she had cried herself to sleep. Grabbing her toothbrush, she began brushing her teeth.

"Good morning, beautiful." Yasin's deep voice greeted her as he stood in the bathroom doorway, admiring Nina. Nina even looked beautiful when she woke up.

"Hi," Nina said, adjusting the shirt on her shoulders. She brushed her hair out of her face shyly. "Did we . . .?" Her voice trailed off.

Yasin shook his head. "I'm not that type of dude, ma. You were vulnerable last night. A clown would have taken advantage of that. I ain't a clown." He inched further into the bathroom and stood beside Nina. His six-feet, four-inch frame towered over hers. She took a deep breath as she took notice of his body for the first time this morning. His abs were chiseled to perfection, and a V-line formed at his waist. Tattoos covered his chest and arms. She imagined her hands running along his chest but blinked away the images.

"You got an extra toothbrush?" he asked.

Nina nodded and pointed to the second drawer. She swallowed around a lump in her throat. Yasin had her at a loss for words. She coolly walked past him and out of the bathroom.

*Damn*, she thought. Nina reached for her phone on the nightstand and connected it to the charger.

"I remember you saying you owned that restaurant last night. How did that happen?" she inquired as she sat on the bed.

"Honestly, I built an empire off of dirty money," Yasin replied, walking back into the bedroom. "I had a couple of niggas from up top that owed me some bread before I left Brooklyn six years ago. I collected my shit and invested my money here. I'm legit now."

Nina smiled because she was right about Yasin. She could spot a hustler a mile away. For some reason, she wasn't attracted to a guy if he didn't have some type of hustler mentality. You could tell Yasin was a hood nigga who was just polished and bossed up. "I figured."

Yasin lifted his right eyebrow and eyed Nina. "Oh, really?" He laughed. "I could ask you the same thing. I see how you're living around here. I see the whip you're pushing. The labels you rock. What's your story?"

Telling Yasin the story about how she came into her money never crossed her mind. He seemed like a good person, but she couldn't trust a stranger with her truth. "Inheritance," she stated simply. "My dad was a businessman back in Charlotte. I never really grew up with him in my life, but he cared enough to put me in his will." The lies rolled off Nina's tongue effortlessly. "And I think invest-ing the money is something you can help me with."

"I'm happy to help, but you have to let me take you on a date to share that knowledge." Yasin flashed a flattering smile to Nina. His pearly white teeth complemented his chocolate skin perfectly.

Before Nina could answer, her phone began ringing. Quan's name appeared across the screen. "Hello," she answered. She had guessed that she would be receiving a call from him as soon as her phone powered on.

"Yo, sis, I was blowing your shit up all last night. It just clicked that you were out drinking, but you're pregnant, yo. What's up with you, Nina?" Quan scolded Nina through the phone. He was concerned about Nina. He understood how grief affected people differently, and he didn't want Nina crashing out behind losing Chance.

"I think you need to worry less about me and handle Chance's other baby mama," Nina snapped. She didn't mean to take her ill feelings out on Quan. "Tiana, right, bro?"

Nina could hear Quan sighing through the phone. "On everything, sis, I did not know about Tiana. You know how I rock with you. We don't even know if that's Chance's baby anyway!"

"That's beyond the point! There shouldn't even be a possibility of it at all!" Nina stressed. The thought of Tiana possibly carrying Chance's baby made her stomach turn. She wished Chance could address the situation, but he was gone.

"Listen, I'm in Atlanta right now. I have to get some shit done, then I want to meet up with you."

"Umm." Nina looked over to Yasin, who was making his way into the kitchen. He opened her refrigerator and pulled out a bottle of water. She didn't want to face Quan and admit that she had lost her baby. She hadn't even fully come to terms with that. But she loved Quan like a brother, and she definitely missed him. "Okay. Just let me know when you're ready."

Little did Nina know Chance and Quan had already located her condo. Quan was a pro at tracking people down, and it only took a few hours to find Nina. They were sitting outside of her place, as Chance had requested.

"Nigga, why we staking outside Nina shit like she the enemy?"

Chance sucked his teeth and waved Quan off. "I just need to see something." For some reason, Chance had a bad feeling in his gut. He couldn't quite put his finger on the source of his unease. "You think he in there?" Chance asked.

"Nina ain't the jump-off type. She wouldn't bring a nigga home after the first night," Quan said matter-of-factly. He'd never seen Nina look too long in another man's direction in his years of knowing her. As soon as the words left his lips, Yasin and Nina emerged outside.

"Fuck outta here!" Chance banged on the dashboard as he watched Nina hug Yasin closely. "I know shorty ain't giving it up like that." A part of him was hurt. Seeing Nina embrace another man had him feeling an uncontrollable jealousy. "Nah." Chance grabbed his gun and reached for the door, but Quan slapped his hands away.

"What the fuck, man! What you gon do? Shoot the nigga in broad daylight *and* blow your cover? Chill out, nigga." Quan ordered sternly. Chance was ready to throw caution out of the window, and it irritated Quan. The nigga didn't know if he wanted to be dead or alive. "Don't jump to conclusions."

Chance clenched his teeth as he tried to get a better look at the guy. Squinting his eyes, something clicked in Chance's mind. "Yo, that nigga look real familiar. I can't put my finger on it."

Quan looked along with Chance. "Too familiar," he added. They had made many enemies along their journey. This man could have been one of them and been using Nina to execute his revenge. They had to get to the bottom of this before leaving Atlanta.

"Thank you for everything," Nina said as she hugged Yasin. His smell was intoxicating. She was attracted to Yasin and felt guilty about it.

"You never answered me about that date."

"I'll call you." Nina smiled graciously. She wasn't quite ready to remove the guards from her heart and get to know someone new. When she was ready, Yasin would be the first one she called. Yasin nodded and kissed Nina's hand, then walked away. Blushing, Nina stood outside until Yasin was out of her eyesight.

"Follow him," Chance instructed. He was sure that this nigga was the explanation behind the funny feeling he had when he'd pulled up to Nina's spot. The guy looked so familiar, but Chance could not make any connections with his face. "This shit killing me. I know that nigga from somewhere." He rubbed his temples, deep in thought.

"I need to ask Nina how she met this nigga. Maybe whatever she knows can help us," Quan suggested. They fell two cars behind the Uber Yasin took to his restaurant. "Let me go in and holler at him real quick."

Chance nodded, hating that he couldn't confront the nigga himself. It seemed like everything began going down the drain in his life since Nino attempted to kill him. This only infuriated him even more. He couldn't wait to run into Nino and put an end to him.

"My man, y'all open?" Quan asked as he approached Yasin.

Yasin stood outside the restaurant, talking on the phone, when Quan approached him. "Nah, son." Yasin replied, not even giving Quan any attention. "Tell that nigga I want my money on time, or I'm paying him a visit next!" Yasin yelled into the phone.

Quan took note of Yasin's curt tone. The way he barked the orders into his phone with authority let Quan know that Yasin was the boss of his operation. Only a man engaged in illegal activities spoke like that. "What time will you be opening?" Quan asked.

Yasin studied Quan from head to toe. He didn't recognize him and figured he was just visiting the city. "We open at ten, my man. You look hungry. When you come back, tell your waitress Yasin sent you and they'll hook you up." Yasin headed towards his Audi.

Quan nodded and disregarded Yasin's sarcasm. He disregarded the fact that he could've put Yasin on his back with his bare hands and swallowed the words he really wanted to say. "Good look, bro."

He jogged back to the car where Chance was anxiously waiting. "His name is Yasin."

"Yasin," Chance repeated as he tried to jog his memory. "He had a New York accent?" he asked.

Quan nodded.

"Ain't this some shit!" Chance punched the dashboard.

"What is it?" Quan asked suspiciously. "Fuck is he?"

Chance shook his head as he thought back to how Nina had hugged Yasin. She didn't even know she had invited the enemy into her home. "That nigga used to supply Nino's crew. They must be connected."

"Oh, shit," Quan said as the picture became clear to him. Yasin hadn't met Nina by accident. He'd been planted there to find her. "How did he find Nina?"

A thousand thoughts ran through Chance's mind. Did Nino send Yasin? Did Yasin even know who Nina was? Was Yasin there to finish what

Nino had started? "I don't know, man. That's what I need you to find out from Nina." Chance didn't want to jump to conclusions or try to kill Yasin just yet. He realized that it wouldn't be easy to get Yasin's head. Every move they made from here on out had to be calculated. "Yo, if he tries to hurt Nina, bruh . . ." Chance didn't even finish his sentence as murderous thoughts invaded his mind.

Nina agreed to meet Quan for brunch in the downtown area of Atlanta. She didn't want him to know where she stayed just yet to avoid any surprise visits. She needed to get accustomed to being alone in the privacy of her own home. Quan's existence was a reminder of Chance, and she couldn't heal if all she thought about was him.

"Sis, what's up!" Quan exclaimed as he embraced Nina.

Nina welcomed Quan's embrace and gave him a kiss on the cheek. She had to admit, it did feel good to be in the presence of someone she was close with. "I missed you, man. You brunching with me today?" She chuckled.

"Yeah, minus the mimosas." If Nina was any other female, Quan would have declined the invitation and asked to just meet at her house, but he would do anything for Nina, and she knew it. Just like Chance, Quan would lay down his life for her. That's how deep his loyalty and love ran.

Nina smiled as she reminisced on how her, Chance, and Quan used to kick it all the time. "Chance could never tell me no either." Her mind drifted down memory lane as they were seated by a hostess on the outside patio of the restaurant. "I miss him so much, Q."

Quan didn't say anything because he knew Chance was not too far away outside the restaurant. He hated that he had to keep shit from Nina, but that's what Chance wanted. The whole fake death situation was something Quan didn't agree with, but he respected Chance's call. In Quan's opinion, it was too risky. There were too many uncontrollable variables.

"How's the baby doing?" he asked.

Nina shook her head as her chest contracted. Tears pooled in her eyes, and she blinked them away. "There is no more baby, bro."

Looking at her confused, Quan noticed the pain in her eyes. He didn't want to believe her words. "What you mean, Nina?"

"I was in an accident on the way here. It was bad. I lost my baby." She sobbed, and Quan handed her a napkin from across the table. He sat in silence and allowed Nina to gather her emotions. "I wanted that baby *so* bad. That was the only piece I had left of Chance. But that bitch Tiana is carrying his seed now."

Quan couldn't believe it. He had no idea what Nina had been going through, and he hated the fact that she had to go through it alone. "Damn, sis, I'm so sorry. And I really don't believe that that's my brother's baby." Quan didn't know what else to say to comfort Nina. She had lost everything that meant the most to her and found out that Chance may have another child on the way. He could only imagine how defeated she felt. "I'm sorry you had to go through that alone."

Nina wiped her tears with the napkin and sniffled. "It's all good. Remember the guy I was telling you about? He was the one who rushed me to the hospital from the scene. He's been really good to me, Quan." Nina didn't realize it, but her eyes beamed when she spoke of Yasin, and Quan took note of it.

He wasn't feeling that shit at all. That nigga was too close to Nina. "How much do you know about this dude, sis? What's his name? What is he about?" Quan questioned.

The waitress left an iPad on the table that allowed them to place their orders from the table.

They both entered their orders before continuing the conversation.

"I mean I don't know much, but he's cool peoples," Nina stated as she sipped the mimosa. "His name is Yasin, and he's from up top. He used to hustle, but now he runs multiple businesses. I was thinking about getting him to help me invest some of this money."

"He knows about the money?" Quan asked.

Nina rolled her eyes. She didn't like how Quan was grilling her, but she knew he was just looking out. "No, I'm not stupid, Quan. I told him that I came into some money through an inheritance. Y'all taught me better than that."

"And he just happened to be there when you got into an accident?" Quan was becoming more suspicious of Yasin by the minute. The nigga was connected to Nino at one point, and now he just popped up into Nina's life right after Chance was murdered. Shit didn't add up. "You think that's a coincidence?"

Nina knew what Quan was implying. "Yasin's not the enemy, bro. He hasn't done anything but help me out since I've been here. If he was on some sheisty shit, he would have robbed me and killed my ass when he was at my house last night." Nina hadn't meant to disclose that part.

Quan looked at Nina in disbelief. He didn't want to believe what he was seeing in Nina's eyes. She had fallen for this nigga, and he didn't want to break the news to Chance. He knew no love could amount to the love she had for Chance, but she believed that nigga was dead. That meant in her mind that it was okay to move on. "You moving real sloppy out here, sis. Don't let your feelings cloud your judgment. You don't know this nigga from a can of paint. For all we know, he could be sent to you to get close to you and fuck you over in the end. I can't sit by and let that happen."

Nina shook her head, regretting the fact she had even agreed to meet up with Quan. Yes, he was just acting as a protective big brother, but she was a big girl, too, and she could take care of herself. "I'm a grown-ass woman, bro. If I choose to move on with someone, that's *my* decision. Chance didn't think twice about fucking around on me. I love that man to death, and I always will, but I have to live my life. I have to make decisions for myself and not live every day looking over my damn shoulder." Nina vented. "And I haven't forgotten about Nino. He will get his, and that's on my mother."

Quan clenched his teeth, realizing that this nigga Yasin had Nina's mind all fucked up. But one thing he couldn't do was worry about her and try to handle shit back in Charlotte with Chance. "I hope you're right, sis. Just know that my bro loved you more than life itself, and his heart was always with you. Always will be." Right now, Quan wished more than ever that he could tell Nina that Chance was alive.

"Just stay on your shit. You got your shorties with you, right?" Quan referred to Nina's gun collection.

"I'm always on my p's and q's. That ain't changed," Nina stated.

"Keep it that way."


Chance watched Nina and Quan's conversation from a distance. He stood on the sidewalk outside the restaurant with a fitted cap concealing his identity. From Nina's body language, he could tell the conversation was becoming tense. He could read Nina like a book, and her facial expressions told it all. She had a slight attitude with Quan.

"Damn, I miss her, yo," he said to himself.

A man passing by accidentally bumped into Chance. "My bad, bruh," dude said.

Chance couldn't believe his eyes. Yasin didn't even realize that it was Chance he had bumped into. "You good, b," Chance said through clenched teeth. It took everything in him to not get at Yasin.

"She's gorgeous, right?" Yasin asked. He noticed Chance staring at Nina.

Becoming more and more angry by the second, Chance swallowed his pride and nodded. "Yeah, man, she's beautiful. That's you?" he asked, slipping his hands into his pockets so Yasin couldn't see his clenched fists. The fact that he had to stand here and allow another man to lust after Nina in front of him made him feel like a pussy.

Yasin rubbed his goatee lightly. "I'm trying, yo. I gotta go holler at shorty right now and see who this nigga is talking to her." Yasin smoothly walked off.

Chance couldn't believe how well he had held his composure. He also couldn't believe Yasin hadn't recognized him. If Nino had sent him after Nina, wouldn't he have realized who Chance was? Or had he?


"You like the food?" Nina asked. She had watched Quan pick over his plate for the last ten minutes. The nigga had the appetite of two grown men, so it was unusual for him not to clean a plate.

Quan nodded, half paying attention because he was texting Chance.

Randomly looking behind Quan, Nina noticed Yasin walking toward her. "You stalking me now?" She laughed as she stood to hug Yasin.

"You know better than that, ma." Yasin smiled. "I may or may not have recommended one of my spots as a brunch spot to you."

Nina laughed and put her hands on her hips. "I should've known."

Quan looked Yasin up and down with a scowl on his face. He wasn't feeling this nigga at all.

"Didn't I see you this morning, yo?" Yasin asked, confused. Quan nodded, sizing Yasin up.

"Yasin, this is my brother Quan. Quan, this is the guy I was telling you about," Nina slowly stated. She could feel the tension rising between the men. "Well, I'm going to use this as an opportunity to go to the ladies' room. You two should talk." Nina took one more bite of her bacon before shuffling inside the restaurant. She already knew how Quan got down, and she didn't want to be around to witness it. If Yasin could meet Quan and not be intimidated, Nina would be impressed.

"You and Nina, y'all gotta dead that shit," Quan said aggressively, getting straight to the point once Nina was out of earshot. "You not the type of nigga she needs to be involving herself with."

Yasin chuckled and let Quan's disrespect fly off the strength of Nina. "I think Nina can make her own decisions." There wasn't any bitch in Yasin, so he wasn't about to let Quan scare him off.

Quan rubbed his nose with his thumb and nodded. He wanted to handle Yasin right there, but they were in a public place. "Listen, homeboy, leave my sister alone if you value your life, 'cause I can dead all that shit."

Yasin tilted his head back and laughed. He took a step closer to Quan. "Nah, you listen. Don't let this Armani suit fool you, little nigga." He looked down at his black, double-breasted suit. "Don't ever fucking threaten me. This is my city, and you won't make it back to Charlotte fucking with me. Tell ya mans Chance over there to stand down, too. Yeah, I know who both of you niggas are." Yasin let Quan know that he knew just as much about them as they knew about him. "I'm not trying to hurt Nina. I want Nino just like y'all do. So, don't ever come at me like that again. Let Chance know that he had his *chance*. Now, a real nigga about to step up and show Nina how to handle shit. If she wants to stop fucking with me, that's her decision."

Quan wanted to pull out his gun and pop Yasin right there, but his words made him think twice. He knew he wasn't playing about him not making it back to Charlotte. Quan wasn't scared of anything or anyone, but he knew that Yasin probably had hitters all over the city. He had one up on him. On top of that, Quan wanted to know what Yasin meant by wanting Nino's head too. This wasn't the time nor the place to pop off. So, he decided to play it smart and walk away.

"You got it, nigga, but know ain't nothing pussy over here." He scowled and pushed his chair back. "Nina don't like secrets, so you better let her know you know who she is before I do. I guarantee you, she not going to fuck with you after that," Quan spat before walking off.

Chance knew by the look on Quan's face that Yasin had pissed him off. He wondered what had been said between them. "What he say?" he asked anxiously when Quan reached him.

"Bruh, that nigga knows everything. He knows who Nina is. He knows who I am. He damn sure knows who you are." Quan gritted in disbelief. He couldn't believe how Yasin had come at him. "Nigga came at me like he was a boss or something. The only thing that kept that nigga breathing was because he claimed he wants Nino too."

Quan and Chance approached their rental car. Chance stopped walking in mid-stride. Now, he was really confused.

"Why would he want Nino?"

Quan shrugged his shoulders in frustration. He was still mad about the fact that Yasin had stepped to him like that. Any other person would have been in a body bag for the disrespect, but they had to play this one smart. "That's what we need to go home and find out, yo."

Everything registered in Chance's head as they got into the car. If Yasin knew who Chance was, then he knew that he wasn't dead. And if that was the case, he could possibly tell Nina. "So, what does Nina know?"

Quan dreaded breaking the news to his boy. Not only did Nina have a miscarriage, but she was also falling for another nigga. He knew that Nina was Chance's motivation for this whole plan, so possibly losing her could send him over the edge. "Sis don't know shit, man. She likes this nigga."

"Fuck you mean she likes him?" Chance asked as they headed toward the interstate.

"She defended him hard when I asked about him. She *feeling* this nigga, bro." Quan sighed.

Chance nodded silently. Those words cut him deep. He never imagined Nina to have feelings for any other man besides him. "She got my baby, though, bro."

Shaking his head, Quan hated that he had to be the one to break the news to Chance. "She lost the baby, bro. She was in an accident," he admitted quietly.

Tears threatened to escape Chance's eyes, but he didn't let any fall. He couldn't imagine the pain Nina had to go through alone. It made sense that she was falling for Yasin because he was there when she needed a shoulder to cry on. "Fuck, man!" Chance yelled in frustration as he kicked the dashboard. It seemed like every reason he'd had for faking his death was slipping away from him. He needed Nina and his seed out of harm's way, but now it seemed like he'd lost Nina along with his unborn child.

Chance questioned God, asking why He would take his child. He wanted someone to blame. Shit, he needed someone to blame. The only person he could think to blame was Nino. He was responsible for this whole mess. Revenge was something Chance wanted before. Now, he wanted Nino to slowly suffer.

"From now on, all our attention is on killing that bitch-ass nigga. He the reason for all of this shit." As much as he wanted to talk to Nina, Chance had to push her to the back of his mind. She would only distract him from getting shit done. The only thing he hoped was that she would wait a little longer before letting Yasin into her heart.


Leaving the bathroom, Nina looked around for Quan. She spotted Yasin sitting in Quan's spot at the table. "Hey, where did my brother go?" she asked.

Yasin looked to be in deep thought. He was trying to figure out how to tell Nina the truth. "He said he had to get back to Charlotte. But look, we need to talk, ma."

Nina cringed at those words. It seemed like nothing good followed those words from experience throughout her life. She slowly took a seat, hoping not to get any bad news. "Wassup?"

"I haven't been completely a hundred with you," Yasin started, looking into Nina's eyes. "I know about you and Chance . . . and your father trying to kill you both."

Her heart dropped as she began to look at Yasin sideways. Quan had been right about him, and she didn't want to believe her ears. "What the hell do you mean? So, you knew who I was this whole time? Are you working with Nino?" she asked, raising her voice and pushing her chair back, away from the table.

Her eyes pierced into his so sharply it felt like a death stare to him. This was the exact reaction Yasin had expected. "Let me explain, ma. I did not know who you were when I first met you."

"Fuck outta here! You expect me to believe that?" Nina was hurt because she was feeling Yasin. "You an opp." She laughed in disbelief and stood to leave.

"Sit down, Nina," Yasin said forcefully, yet gently enough for Nina to abide. "*Listen*. I didn't real-ize who you were until last night when you were on FaceTime with Quan and he said Chance's name. Your father called me when you were back in Charlotte for the funeral. He wanted me to find you because he knew you were in Atlanta. Nino wants the money you're sitting on. When he told me his daughter's name was Nina, I just thought it was a coincidence, until the other night when I put two and two together," Yasin explained.

Nina took in his words, not knowing whether to believe them. She didn't say anything.

Yasin took that as his cue to continue. "Your father and my father used to run together back in Philly and New York. My dad was robbed and murdered when I was younger. I knew Nino was behind it. That's why he up and moved your fam-ily to North Carolina. The nigga thought he was so slick. He doesn't know I know, but I've been wait-ing on the moment to take that nigga out." He punched his fist into his hand.

Nina looked at Yasin and could see the hate in his eyes. Thinking back, she did remember her fa-ther abruptly telling her and her mother to pack their things with no explanation. They moved down south days later. Knowing Nino, he probably did kill Yasin's father. He was grimy like that. She hated the fact that she had his blood running through her veins.

"So, you were going to use me to get to him?" she asked.

"Yes, but it's not how it sounds. I'm really feeling you, ma, and I know that you want to see him dead just as much as I do. I was waiting until the time was right to reveal all of this to you."

"I don't know what to think." Nina shook her head. It was hard to believe anything Yasin was saying. Maybe Quan was right. Maybe she did need to watch her back around Yasin. "I can't trust you," she whispered.

That was something he had expected her to say. Yasin knew it wouldn't be easy gaining Nina's trust, but he was willing to put the work in. "Everything I've said to you is real. I fell for you before I knew who you really were. That ain't changed, Nina. I'm feeling you, and you can't say you don't feel something for me too." Yasin reached for Nina's hand. "And you lied to me too, ma. I didn't believe your little inheritance story anyway." He smiled.

Nina laughed dryly and scratched the back of her neck. He was right. They had both kept things from each other. "I need proof."

"I got you, ma. But for real, you need to talk to ya brother because he ain't keeping it all the way a stack with you either." Yasin was referring to Quan knowing Chance was alive. He wasn't petty enough to throw Chance and Quan all the way under the bus, so he left it up to Nina to find out the truth on her own.

"What do you mean?" Nina asked in confusion. Quan had always kept it real with her. At least that's what she thought.

Yasin kissed Nina's hand. "That's between you and your brother, ma."

# Chapter Four

It had been nearly three months since Chance had heard Nina's voice or even saw her face through FaceTime. The feelings were coming down on him hard now. He kept himself busy with gathering information on Nino and watching his moves. They knew enough now to make a plan to finally get close to Nino, but Chance had to take a break from all of that. His days became consumed with lurking in the shadows, hiding behind tinted windows, and following his enemies around. There was no room for excitement, no one for him to come home to at night, no homecooked meals waiting for him. Life as a dead man was a lonely life, and Chance needed time to himself.

He kicked back on the couch, listening to "Song Cry" by Jay-Z and puffing an L. The song was speaking to him. Just like he rapped, Chance and Nina both started from the bottom and held each other down regardless of the bullshit. Nina never cared about the money or the material things because loving Chance was enough. He knew his girl would ride through whatever.

Fucking around with Tiana was something he regretted every day, but a part of him still believed Nina shouldn't have let his infidelity push her toward another man. She was supposed to stay down for him. Chance wondered if the situation would be different if she knew he was alive. However, Chance loved Nina so much that he wanted to see her happy, even if that meant she would be happy without him. The shit hurt, but it was life.

"Rider" by Future blared through Chance's speakers. He smiled as he listened to the song off one of Future's old mixtapes. This was Nina's favorite song on *Astronaut Status*, and she had dedicated it to Chance.

"I gotta get out my feelings," Chance stated aloud as he took a long hit of the blunt. He sighed as he stood up. Being dead was starting to bore Chance out of his mind. The only thing he could really do in Charlotte was chill at his condo and wait for Quan to report back with some type of news. A lot of his thoughts had been leaning toward making his resurrection public. If he were to go through with this, they would have to move quickly on Nino before he had the opportunity to attack.

Pulling out his phone, Chance dialed Quan's number, letting him know that he was ready to put the plan into action. "Fuck sitting like a fucking duck. I'm ready to make some moves, nigga. This hiding behind closed doors shit ain't me."

"Okay then, nigga. You know what to do next," Quan exclaimed and ended the phone call.

The first part of the plan was what Chance dreaded the most. Quan would bring Tiana over to the condo to see if she was down with helping set Nino up. Chance knew Tiana would be shocked to see him alive and well.

Chanel lounged in her section of Charlotte's most popular nightclub, indulging herself with weed and drinks. This was her first time going out in a few months. She had recently signed a new brand deal and decided to celebrate her success with a night out. The biggest hustlers and get-money niggas filed into the club, and Chanel applauded herself for picking the perfect time to pop out. Her 30-inch weave hung to her ass, and the blue Fendi minidress she wore hugged her curves. A diamond cufflink necklace rested against her light skin. Quan had gifted it to her a few years ago before their breakup. The lavish piece of jewelry reminded her of the love she had shared with him. They had a toxic relationship, but she would always acknowledge him as her first love.

Chanel stepped down from her booth and pushed her way through the crowd. "Fuck," she mumbled. She nearly had to fight her way to the bar. "Bitches act like they can't say excuse me," she spoke aloud when she slid into an open spot at the front of the bar. "Can I get a bottle of Casamigos?" she yelled over the loud music. She held up a hundred-dollar bill.

The female bartender shook her head. "I can give you shots. All the bottles been bought out."

Chanel sucked her teeth. "Give me two shots then. Who bought the bar out?" she inquired.

A loud commotion at the entrance of the club caught her attention, and she turned her body in that direction. People crowded around the front of the club, clamoring like fans at an awards show.

"Pretty sure whoever that is did." The bartender nodded to the entrance of the club and placed two shots in front of Chanel.

Chanel threw the shots back and titled her head toward the crowd. They were doing too much for her liking. "Thanks for the shots." She left the hundred-dollar bill on the bar for the girl. Pushing her way through the people on the dance floor, Chanel kicked herself. She would've stayed home if she had known the club would be packed like this. She wanted a chill night of turning up. She huffed, reaching her section.

A Young Jeezy classic blared throughout the club, and the entire club jumped, singing the lyrics loudly over the music. Chanel stood on top of the couch and bobbed her head. Jeezy rapped about being a trap star. The song reminded her of her younger days of hanging with Nina. They had lived the fast life, blowing money and making memories.

Chanel noticed the crowd circling around someone as they moved closer to the back of the club. She squinted her eyes. It was hard to make anyone out through the darkness. The crowd slowly dispersed when they neared the sections lining the back of the club. Chanel maneuvered her neck, trying to get a glimpse of whoever had the club in a frenzy. People held their cameras up, flashing as they attempted to capture whoever stood in the middle. Her stomach dropped into her ass when the people parted and she realized who stood in the center. Chance stood, alive and well, next to Quan. Chanel rubbed her eyes, clearing her vision with her hands. She had to be seeing shit.

Quan randomly glanced in her direction. He read the surprise on her face with a smirk and nodded his head to salute her.

"Oh, shit," Chanel whispered. She snatched her purse from the couch and fumbled inside for her phone. She wondered if Nina knew of Chance's reappearance. As far as she knew, Nina was grieving Chance's death. There was no way Nina would be miles away if Chance were in Charlotte. She had to call her friend.

With all that had been going on in her crazy life, the past few weeks offered some relief to Nina. It had been so long since she'd let go of every worry and just lived. The feelings she had for Yasin grew stronger the more time she spent with him—and they were together a lot. He reminded her so much of Chance, but in a lot of ways they were so different. Confidence, power, and finesse were qualities that both men possessed. Any stranger could approach Chance or Yasin and know that they were very important men. However, Chance's power was only recognized in the hood. Yasin was respected and even feared by the elite in Atlanta. He introduced Nina to the difference between wealthy and rich. Money never impressed Nina, but Yasin's money was way longer than Chance's.

"Where do you see yourself in five years?" Yasin would ask Nina.

The question caught her off guard. For so long, she had been living day by day with Chance, praying that they could leave the hood eventually. When she was with Chance, they were a team at getting to the money. Nina never had to touch a drug or make any drops for Chance, but she counted his money, handled all his accounts, accompanied him to frequent parties at their supplier's mansion. Her role was to keep up appearances and keep them off the police radar. With Yasin, he stressed the fact that Nina didn't have to lift a finger if she didn't want to. Anything she wanted for, he made sure she had. Nina was Chance's Bonnie, but with Yasin, she was his queen.

None of the comparisons she made between Yasin and Chance took away from her love for Chance, though. There was nothing that could change the fact that Nina was still madly in love with Chance, but she had faced the fact that it was time to move on. Quan hadn't hit her up in about two weeks, and she was grateful. Admitting to the fact that he was right about Yasin was something she didn't look forward to. There were still some doubts she had about Yasin's story of not knowing who she was when they first met, but she gave him the benefit of the doubt.

"You ready, baby?" Yasin's smooth voice greeted Nina from the other end of the phone.

They were going to the Bad Boy reunion concert that night. Yasin had backstage passes, and Nina was so excited to meet Lil Kim. "Yeah, you can head over here now."

She smiled, excited to see what the night would bring. Her titties spilled out of her black lace corset. She paired the top with a pair of black leather pants and black Louboutin booties. Her hair was styled into an updo, resembling a style out of the 90s, with a deep swoop coming across the left side of her face, up into a half-up, half-down ponytail.

"Bet. I'll be there in twenty minutes."

Pouring herself a glass of wine, Nina heard her phone vibrate, indicating she had an incoming FaceTime call. The call was from Chanel, the only female she dealt with in Charlotte. Chanel was her childhood friend and the only person besides Chance and Quan that she trusted with her life. Time had distanced the two women as they built their own lives, but their bond always remained solid. Years could pass without them speaking, and they would remain the same when they finally saw each other.

"Wassup, bitch."

"*Bitchhh!* Guess the fuck what?" Chanel yelled into the phone.

Nina knew whatever she had to tell her would be juicy just from the way her girl greeted her.

"You won't believe who the fuck I'm looking at in the club right now!"

The surprise in Chanel's voice had Nina curious as hell. "Who, bitch?" she asked, figuring Chanel was talking about one of her exes, like Quan.

"See for yourself." Chanel switched the Face-Time view from the front camera to the back.

As Nina squinted her eyes and looked into her phone, the glass of wine fell from her hand as she clutched her chest. She could not believe her eyes. It was as if she'd seen a ghost. Chance stood in the club with Quan, alive and well. He was surrounded by a group of females. "Tell me I'm seeing a damn ghost, 'cause bitch . . .! What's going on, sis? You resurrecting niggas with that pussy now?"

The room spun, and Nina held on to her dresser for support. She couldn't put what she felt into words. *This nigga supposed to be dead!*

"I'll call you back." Abruptly hanging up, Nina ran to the bathroom and vomited. Chance was alive this whole time and she didn't know? Wiping her mouth, Nina leaned over the sink, trying to catch her breath. "Okay, Nina, okay. Calm down." The fact of the matter was, she couldn't keep calm. There were a million things she wanted to do and say.

"I gotta go to Charlotte." Her date with Yasin was the last thing on her mind right now. She was about to do ninety all the way to North Carolina. Fuck the bullshit.

Nina's body operated on autopilot as she gathered her belongings and shuffled out of her home. She was so preoccupied with Chanel's revela-

tion that she didn't bother texting Yasin to cancel.
*Did I hear Chanel wrong?* She questioned herself. Stepping into the driver's seat, Nina replayed
the call in her mind. Even if she had heard Chanel
wrong, Nina had seen Chance with her own eyes.
He stood, in the flesh, beside Quan. Surely her
own eyes weren't deceiving her. Quan seemed to
be in on it and had kept the secret from Nina too.
That decision alone proved that his loyalty lay with
Chance.

"Why keep it away from me?" Nina asked aloud,
sitting at a red light a few miles from the exit to the
interstate. There wasn't an explanation that would
cover the taxing grief Nina had endured by thinking Chance was dead. She hoped the situation was
a cruel joke.

The light changed to green, and Nina's left leg
bounced impatiently. "Go!" Nina yelled, holding
her hand down on the horn. She revved her engine,
switched lanes, and bypassed another car, zoom-
ing toward I-85N.

The club wasn't even Chance's type of scene,
but he knew Nino would eventually show his face.
After all, the party was for him tonight. It would
be Nino's last night of partying, little did he know.
The plan was already in motion as Chance looked

across the club and saw Tiana in her all-black fitted dress. To be four months pregnant, as she claimed, Tiana's shape was still intact: ample breasts, slim waist, fat ass. Any nigga would want to try her.

When Chance had called her earlier to come over, she thought she was being set up.

### Three Hours Earlier . . .

"This is some crazy-ass tv shit, yo!" she exclaimed when she laid eyes on Chance. Tiana could not do anything but stare at him for a few minutes to regroup. "What type of shit you on, Chance?"

This was the reaction he was expecting everyone to have once they saw him, but he had a perfect explanation. "I never died. The nigga y'all buried was some crackhead who OD'd. Why you think I had a closed casket?" Chance asked rhetorically. "Listen, I need your help, though, T."

Placing her hand on her hip, Tiana twirled her red curls around her finger. "Why can't Nina help you?" Jealousy was evident in her voice. Anything Chance asked of her, she would do, but it wouldn't be any fun if she didn't make it hard for him. "I mean, she is the one holding you down, right?" A feeling of superiority surged through Tiana. She figured that because Chance called on her, it meant she still had a shot with him.

"I don't want her in harm's way," he answered simply. Nina was the last thing Chance wanted to think about now. He had to stay focused. Thinking about Nina was a distraction he did not need. When everything was said and done, Chance planned on going to Atlanta and getting his girl back. "Let's cut the bullshit, Tiana. You gon' help a nigga out or what? You know I'm worth it." He pulled out a wad of money and tossed it to Tiana. He cared for her, but not enough to feel bad if things went south with Nino. As long as funds were involved, Tiana would be down to ride.

Thumbing through the hundred-dollar bills, Chance had Tiana's undivided attention.

"What you need, Chance?"

"I need you to pull that nigga Nino tonight. Do whatever it takes to keep him occupied and drunk. There's more in it where that came from." Chance nodded to the ten G's Tiana held.

Licking her lips, Tiana knew that task would be easy. There weren't many guys who could resist her sex appeal and curvy body. She didn't lack in looks either. She could pull a nigga off her face card itself. "You can keep the other half. I'll take you." Her words dripped in seduction.

"You know it ain't that type of party with us no more. If that's really my child you're carrying, I'll be there no doubt, but me and you don't have much more to discuss, shorty." He knew going down that road with Tiana would only lead to more problems.

"You disrespected my lady at the funeral. I peeped that. Just be on point tonight for me, and I might forgive you."

Rolling her eyes, Tiana accepted the challenge. She wanted to take Nina's spot badly. "I'll have that nigga wrapped around my finger."


You would have thought Nina was a NASCAR driver with the time it took her to arrive in Charlotte. She pulled up to the club. After paying her way in, Nina headed straight to the bar. She needed to drown her anxieties with a few shots.

"Three shots of Hennessy, please." She slid a fifty-dollar bill to the bartender.

"Here you go, boo." The girl thanked Nina for her tip and set the shots in front of her.

Throwing each shot back, Nina felt the liquor instantly warm her chest. Peering around the club, Nina took note of all the familiar faces. Some of Nino's workers were in attendance, but Nino was nowhere in sight.

Nina moved throughout the crowd, ignoring several calls from dudes trying to get her attention. None of these niggas in here could afford her or even pique her interest. "Lames," she muttered under her breath. "Where this girl at?" Nina asked herself as she scanned the crowd for Chanel.

"Hey, sexy!" A small hand smacked Nina's ass. She turned around to find Chanel standing there with a devilish smile on her face. She pulled Nina into a hug, rocking back and forth. "You looking for your man, ain't you?"

"Damn right."

Chanel smirked and nodded. "There he goes right over there."

Nina's eyes followed Chanel's hand. Her breath caught in her throat as she spotted Chance sitting at a booth, looking even better than the last time she'd seen him. Her heart dropped. The feelings she had for Chance, which she thought were buried, resurfaced. It was like the first time she ever saw him. All it took was seeing Chance for her to realize how much of a hold he still possessed over her.

"I'ma check you later, girl." Nina took a deep breath and approached Chance. The flock of groupies around him stood with their asses poked out, trying to get Chance's attention. "Y'all bitches can bounce," Nina said loudly enough for each one of the six females to hear. Rolling their eyes and mumbling under their breath, it was obvious they recognized Nina. She stared every single girl in the eyes as they walked away, daring one to pop off.

"Nina." Chance gazed at her with wide eyes. "What are you doing here?"

"I could ask you the same fucking question. You supposed to be six feet under!" She rammed her finger into Chance's chest. Nina was livid. "That's how we rocking now, Chance?"

Chance pulled Nina to the side. The last thing he needed was for her to fuck up the plan. "Can we talk about this later?

"Fuck that! Do you know what I've been through since you've been gone?" Tears welled in Nina's eyes. She wanted to slap the shit out of Chance, but she wasn't here to make a scene. "You better start talking."

Chance stared at her without a word.

"I'm waiting." Nina crossed her arms. There really wasn't any explanation Chance could give that would make her forgive him. As far as Nina could remember, she had held Chance down with any decision he made. They were better than that. Why did he not fill her in on this?

Chance shook his head. He knew that his words wouldn't matter to Nina anyway. When you're with someone for so long, it's easy to read their demeanor. Reading Nina like a book, Chance knew she was trying her hardest to put on her tough act. Yes, she was pissed, but the hurt in her eyes was obvious.

"I done it all to protect you. I've been putting together a plan to handle that shit, ya feel me, baby?" he asked, not wanting to go into the full details of his plan to kill Nino. You never knew who was around listening. "I figured if I was gone, your father wouldn't try you anymore. Nina, I know my words probably don't mean shit to you right now, and I'm sorry for that."

*Smack!*

Nina's hands had a mind of its own. She didn't mean to slap Chance, but it damn sure felt good doing it. "To protect me? Do you think you were protecting me when I was sitting in a cold-ass hospital bed alone, getting the news that I had lost our child?" No longer trying to hold them in, Nina felt hot tears run down her cheeks. "I thought I lost you." Nina finally broke down. She beat her balled fists against Chance's chest as she whimpered. Pretending to be strong was tiring. Yasin was amazing and he treated her like royalty, but he wasn't Chance.

Seeing Nina so broken made Chance feel like shit. Maybe he had been acting selfishly when he decided to fake his death. Taking her in his arms, Chance held Nina close as she cried.

"Where your boy at?" he asked.

"Where is your bitch at?" Nina wiped her tears and put her hands on her hips. "Oh, nah, my bad.

Your baby's mama. Maybe I should be with my boy right now back in Atlanta, enjoying our wonderful night out he put together. But I'm here with you." Was she making the wrong choice? There were still unanswered questions she had about Yasin and where his loyalties lay. As for Chance, the whole time Nina thought he was being loyal, he was stepping out on her. It didn't matter that they were broken up at the time. They always broke up just to make up shortly after.

"Oh, you giving it up like that, Nina? You love him?" Chance asked seriously.

Honestly, Nina didn't know how to answer that question. She did have a lot of love for Yasin, but she was scared to allow herself to completely fall for him. "I have love for him," she answered coolly.

Chance couldn't even be mad. He had allowed another nigga to step into Nina's life and ease his way in. One thing he wasn't worried about was Nina leaving him over Yasin. No matter how she felt about him leaving her in the dark, her loyalty ran deep. "I don't love Tiana, never have. That was a mistake. I never hit her raw, and I'm not saying that to make it seem better. I fucked up, Nina. But if she is carrying my child, I can't abandon it."

"I would never ask you to do that, Chance. I won't ask you to choose."

Just as those words left Nina's lips, Tiana sauntered over to them.

"Well, look who it is." This clearly wasn't the
time for Tiana to step out of line. It would be
the time Nina slid on her ass.

Smirking, Tiana flipped her weave over her
shoulder. She looked Nina up and down, not even
phased by her presence. As far as Tiana was concerned, it wouldn't be long before Nina was out of
the picture.

"Nino is in there," Tiana told Chance, letting him
know she had Nino right where they wanted him.
"There is some out-of-town nigga in the section,
calling shots. Shorty told me to go get a drink while
he chopped it up with him." Tiana shifted her
weight to her left foot and stuck her wide hip out.
"But you know I can't drink, Chance. I'll smoke a L,
but not drink. It's not good for the baby." Rubbing
her nearly flat stomach, Tiana cut her eyes at Nina.

"You trying to be funny, bitch?" Nina asked. The
wound of losing her baby was one that had not
fully healed. Whether Tiana knew Nina was pregnant or not, she wasn't about to let the disrespect
fly.

Chance stood between the girls before either
one could respond. "The last thing I need is for either one of y'all to blow my shit up. Chill out," he
said sternly. "Did the guy say who he was when

you approached him? Anything?" Chance turned to Tiana.

"Jasin, Yasin . . . something like that. I wasn't checking for him like that, but I could tell he's living large," Tiana noted. She wouldn't admit it to Chance, but dude was fine as hell. The way he walked and talked screamed hood rich.

Nina's breath caught in her throat at the mention of Yasin's name. *What the fuck is he doing in Charlotte? And more importantly, what the hell is he doing in Nino's section?*

"When did he get here?" she asked Tiana.

Sighing, Tiana rolled her eyes in irritation. "He literally just got here."

Chance peeled off five hundred-dollar bills from his knot of money and handed it to Tiana. "Go order a bottle of champagne and have it sent to the section with y'all. Make sure the waitress lets them know it's from Chance." Tiana obliged and headed toward the bar.

"What your nigga doing here?" he asked Nina.

Nina was just as lost as he was. She figured Yasin had arrived at her apartment and saw she wasn't there. What she didn't understand was why he coincidentally showed up to Charlotte the same night Chance popped out on the scene. A lot of signs were saying Yasin was shady. His moves didn't show otherwise. "I'on know, but I'm about to find out. I'm about to go to the bathroom and call him. I'll be back."

Chance gave her a slight nod and looked around the club for Quan.


The figure lurking in the shadows of the dark nightclub watched as Nina entered the bathroom. It was expected that Nina would be vigilant. With all that was going on, there was no way she should have been moving around the club unprotected. She made his job easier than it should have been. He hated what he had to do next, but it was all about the money.

Pulling out her phone, Nina dialed Yasin's number as she stood in the bathroom stall. The phone rang until she got his automatic voicemail. "Call me back ASAP!" She left the voicemail and quickly walked out of the bathroom.

"Shit!" Nina exclaimed as she bumped into a stranger on her way out of the bathroom. "Excuse you!" she snapped and began walking away

Swiftly, the guy grabbed Nina from behind and placed a white rag over her mouth and nose. Nina bucked and kicked with all her might, trying to escape the strong hold. Her nine was in her purse all the way in her car. She got caught slipping. The strong chemical she was breathing in caused her vision to blur. Before she knew it, everything went black.

Everything was in place like Chance had planned. Nino sat in the VIP section with Tiana, getting wasted. Yasin was seated beside him, puffing on a Cuban cigar. It wasn't hard to tell that the club wasn't his type of party. Quan and a few of Chance's loyal soldiers were positioned by the rear exit of the club. Now all he had to do was ensure Nina was out of harm's way and get shit started.

Chance called Nina only to immediately meet her voicemail. When he tried again, the same response greeted him: "Hi, you've reached, Nina. Sorry I can't get to the phone right now, but if you . . ."

Chance ended the call. It had only been a few minutes since she ran off to the bathroom to call Yasin. Heading toward the bathroom, Chance tripped and looked down to see Nina's Dior clutch on the floor. "The fuck?" he said aloud. Nina would never lose such an expensive clutch, let alone lose it with money and her wallet in it. Something wasn't right. Chance could feel it in the air.

Nina felt her head hanging as she slowly drifted back into consciousness. She looking around wildly, but blackness filled her vision. There must have been something over her head. Trying to scream, she realized her mouth had been taped. Moving from side to side, Nina could not make any movements. Her hands were tied tightly behind her back, and her feet tied together to what she assumed to be a chair.

"Hmmm! Hmmm!" Nina struggled against her restraints. She had no idea what was going on or where she was. The only thing she hoped was that Chance would find and save her before any harm was brought to her.

Heavy footsteps approached Nina. From what she could hear, there were two people in the room. She tried to use her remaining senses, hearing and smell, to take note of everything around her, because one way or another, she was getting the fuck out of there.

*Today isn't your day to go, Nina! You are not dying*, she thought.

"Why can't we just fuck this bitch and pop her ass?" a male voice asked. He obviously had a Charlotte accent from what Nina could make out.

"We had specific fucking instructions. Follow my lead, nigga," another voice responded.

Whatever was covering Nina's head was removed. Nina's eyes bugged wildly as she was greeted by the face of two strangers, one of whom had snatched her up in the club. There was no inkling in Nina's mind that could suggest why these niggas had kidnapped her out of all people. She was shaking, but not out of fear. It was out of anger.

"You sure are finer than they let on, bitch," the skinnier, light-skinned guy joked. His voice was the first voice she'd heard a few seconds ago. "Too bad we gon' have to fuck that pretty little face up," he said devilishly, sliding his blade up and down Nina's face.

Nina tried to speak, but her words were incoherent. She bucked wildly in the chair. There was no way she could free herself from the right ropes, and tears slid down her face. This was not the way she had imagined her death.

"Here's what's about to happen, ma," the other guy began. He was tall, about six foot three, brown-skinned, and stocky. He had the appearance of a professional football player. "You should already know who sent us. Your pops wants that money, and if you don't give it up, he's really going to put your man six feet under this time."

It all made sense now. While Chance thought he had one up on Nino, Nino had known the whole time—or at least had figured it out in time enough to formulate his own plan. Chance had lured Nina to Charlotte with his back-from-the-dead shit, saving Nino the trouble of doing so.

Fear slowly crept into Nina's heart. There was no way she was giving up the money she and Chance had worked so hard for. If she did that, everything would be in vain. Chance faking his death, Nina losing their baby . . . everything.

"I'm going to take this duct tape from your mouth. I suggest you start talking," the football player-looking dude stated and ripped the duct tape from Nina's mouth. "Where is the money?" he asked roughly.

Nina looked at him as she gathered all the spit in her mouth that she could. She tried to spit on the guy's face, but it landed a few inches from them. "Fuck you."

"Wrong answer!" The light-skinned guy raised his fist and punched Nina in the face with so much might that she was sure her jaw had cracked. "Where's the money?" he demanded.

Tears rolled down Nina's face, but she refused to give them the satisfaction of seeing her in pain. "Kiss my ass!" Blood trickled down her lips.

The guy delivered a fatal two piece to Nina's face and stomach. "You're too pretty for me to beat your ass like this. So how about you just give it the fuck up?"

Nina grunted in pain and contemplated giving them the location of her money. The five million dollars was chump change to Nino. Nina knew this for sure. The money didn't mean shit to him. He wanted to make an example out of Nina and Chance. "Let my sperm donor know if he wants the money, he better come talk to me himself."

Nina was plotting in her head. If Nino came, maybe he'd bring Yasin along with him. Yasin claimed he was secretly plotting against Nino. If he was a man of his word, he would kill Nino before letting him bring any more harm to Nina. She really hoped he wasn't playing games. Her life depended on it.

"The fuck you mean you think someone took her?" Quan shouted to Chance as he paced.

Chance shook his head furiously. He didn't know what to think. Nina was his world, and if she was hurt behind some shit he had started, he would never forgive himself. Whoever took her had to know it would hurt Chance the most.

"Just what the fuck I said! I gotta find her, man. That girl been down for me, yo. If they hurt her . . ." Chance couldn't even bring himself to finish his sentence.

Quan rubbed his face in frustration. He could only imagine the guilt Chance felt. "We gon' get her back, bro, even if we gotta go out in a motherfucking shootout. That's my sister. You know how

I'm riding for her. Ride or die." Quan meant every word. He was always ready to die. You had to be if you lived a life like him. He had made so many enemies and killed so many people. Karma was bound to run up on a nigga like him.

A waitress approached the two men. "Courtesy of the host." The waitress handed Chance a bottle of rosé with a note attached to it.

*If you want to see Tiana or Nina alive, meet at 315 Harper St. in twenty minutes. No guns. Come alone.*

Chance figured Nino was behind this whole ordeal. Not only did he have Nina, but he also had Tiana and the child growing inside of her. Chance wasn't sure if it was even his, but he wasn't about to have any more blood on his hands.

"It's war now." Looking over to the section where Nino, Tiana, and Yasin had been seated, Chance saw that it was empty. "Nino and Yasin about to get it. Somebody not making it out alive, and I don't plan on dying anymore."

"Like I said, you know how I'm riding." Quan didn't need to say any other words. There was no way he was letting his nigga go into this situation blind. They had twenty minutes to come up with a plan. The odds didn't look to be in their favor.

\*\*\*

The silence was killing her. The light-skinned guy, or Big Mouth as Nina called him, made a call on a flip phone. She assumed the call was made to Nino because they no longer interrogated her. She was grateful for that. Nina had fought a lot of fights and taken a few L's in her lifetime, but nothing could amount to the ass whooping these guys were putting down on her tonight. Her biggest fear in this moment wasn't dying, but how her face would look after she got out of this predicament, because one way or another, she vowed to make it out alive.

"What's your name?" Nina asked the buff dude, the one she deemed to be more levelheaded and reasonable. Even with her swollen eye and lips, she knew she still looked good enough to use it to her advantage.

"None of your concern," the guy answered curtly.

Getting into this guy's head was going to be harder than she thought. The wheels in her mind churned as she tried to put together a plan that would turn this unfortunate situation in her favor. Looking over the guy's appearance, she noticed a tattoo on his forearm that indicated he was a part of a local gang. Bleek, the leader of the gang and a rival hustler of Chance's, had tried to spit game to Nina on several occasions.

"Could you go get me some water?" Nina batted her eyelashes at Big Mouth. She needed his hot-headed ass out of earshot. "I might feel like talking, but I'm dying of thirst over here."

Big Mouth looked to the buff dude as if he were asking for his permission.

"Go get the bitch something to drink. The faster she talks, the faster I can go about my business."

Dude nodded and disappeared behind the big steel door.

"You one of Bleek boys?" Nina asked. The guy looked at her but didn't answer. "Ya man is soft as hell on me. If you helped me out here, I can break you off more than what Nino is. I'll even kick it with Bleek and let him know you convinced me to. I'm sure he'll show you his appreciation." Nina lied through her teeth. She would never even waste her time with a nigga like Bleek. He had long pockets and was handsome, but he was a clown. Gang banging was unattractive to her. Why have a whole bunch of niggas behind you to help you do what could be done standing on your own two? Doing that meant you had to break bread when the whole loaf could be yours.

"You talk too fucking much." The guy stood up and walked to Nina. Roughly grabbing her neck, he tapped her mouth closed again. "Nino told me to watch out for you. You the type of bitch to charm a nigga out of his money and his life. I ain't falling for it, shorty."

Nina wanted to tell him that she didn't need to charm a nigga out of shit. She handled hers straight up. Her faith wavered as she ran out of ideas for escaping. Giving up wasn't an option, though. She took note of the shotgun lying a few feet away from her. Ol' dude had a gun tucked in his waist. If she could get to one of those weapons, maybe she'd have a fighting chance.

"We got five minutes before Nino is expecting me. You sure this shit gonna work?" Chance asked Quan seriously. What he carried inside his jacket would put a nigga on his ass for sure. Get down or lay down.

Quan nodded twice. "I'm sure, bro. You just make sure you time that shit right. If not, nobody leaving out," he warned. "I'ma be right out here waiting for you and sis, man. See you soon, my nigga." Quan embraced Chance, giving him a manly hug.

Chance exited the car. This was the moment he had been waiting for well over two months: the opportunity to kill Nino. However, it was more complicated now. Nina's life was at risk, and there was no way Chance was letting her get hurt.

***

Several footsteps approached the steel door before it opened. Nina was shocked to see Tiana and Yasin standing hand in hand next to each other. Nino stood in front of them, a wicked, wide grin plastered on his face.

"Well, well, well, what do we have here?" He laughed.

Nina tried to make eye contact with Yasin, but he looked past her. She didn't know what to think. Why was he standing next to Tiana like she was his bitch? Was Tiana ever on Chance's side like she claimed, or was she working with Nino too? It was hard to believe Yasin had played her the entire time. Every moment they spent together had seemed so genuine and real. His words promised he had her for real, and his actions proved he did. Nina kicked herself for being so gullible. She had allowed Yasin into her heart and even her bed. Spotting a fraud was something she mastered, so how couldn't she see that she was sleeping with the enemy the whole time?

A knock came, followed by the opening of the door. "Ahh." Nino looked down at his presidential Rolex with a diamond-encrusted bezel. "Now we can really get this party started."

Opening the door, Chance marched in. Big Mouth patted Chance down to ensure he had no guns on him. When Nina's eyes met Chance's, she couldn't help but sob. Here stood a man who loved her life more than his own; one that came to her rescue without a second thought, willing to die for her. Guilt ate at her conscience. She had given up on the man who loved her unconditionally for the man who wanted to see both of them dead. In her mind, Yasin had already confirmed his loyalty to Nino.

Chance nodded his head to Nina, trying to tell her that everything was going to be all right. Seeing the bruises on her face infuriated him. He would make every nigga in here slowly suffer for ever laying hands on his woman. At that point, he didn't care what had happened between Nina and Yasin. All he cared about was getting her out alive.

"Tiana, I should have known you were a snake in the grass. You used a baby to try to butter me up." He shook his head in disbelief. He had fallen for the okey-doke. He never should he have trusted a scandalous bitch like Tiana.

Tiana waved her hand in dismissal. "Can I go now, baby?" she asked, kissing Yasin's lips.

Nina turned her head. The sight of the two of them made her sick.

"Yeah, ma. Go ahead."

Watching Tiana waltz out of the door, Nina promised that Tiana would see her. Because she had played a part in Nina losing her baby by being down with Nino, Nina was going to drag her ass. Nina was beyond the point of taking the high road. She would be out for blood.

"Let's make this quick." Nino clapped his hands together. On command, the two guys started punching and stomping Chance.

Nina's muffled screams and the sounds of the guy's shoes stomping Chance out were the only sounds that could be heard. Bucking against her restraints, Nina screamed as the guys beat Chance mercilessly.

Nino enjoyed the show. "Is there something you want to say, baby girl?" he teased, removing the tape from Nina's lips.

"Please stop," she pleaded. "It's me you want, Nino. It always has been. Just kill me and leave Chance out of this."

"I think she has a point," Yasin chimed in. He signaled for the guys to stop beating Chance. "She doesn't even know why you doing this, does she?"

Nino shook his head.

"How could you hate your own daughter so much? Your flesh and blood?" Nina demanded.

Nino twisted his mouth up and looked at Nina in disgust. "I'm not your fucking father! Your mother thought I would never find out that she cheated on me before getting pregnant with you.

That shit was unforgivable. I treated your mother like a queen, and she shitted on me! Had me thinking you were my daughter, even naming you after me. I never loved you. That's why this is so easy for me." Nino pulled out his gun and aimed it at Nina.

It was then and there that Nina saw the insanity in Nino's eyes. He was fucking nuts. There was no compassion in his eyes. Nina knew that he was hell-bent on making her pay for her mother's mistakes. She was sure she was about to die.

"I love you, Chance. I'm sorry." A single tear fell down her face.

As Nino fired his gun, Nina closed her eyes. A burning sensation filled her chest as she heard Chance scream out. Multiple shots rang out after that, but Nina's chair flipped over from the impact of the bullet. She tried to fight the overwhelming heaviness of her eyes as she gasped for air, choking on her own blood. A slight smile came across her face as memories ran throughout her mind. Her life literally flashed before her eyes.

She heard Chance call out to her, "Hold on, Nina!"

Quan's anxiety was at an all-time high. He had been inside the abandoned warehouse for about ten minutes now. The plan they had put together only took about seven minutes to execute. He just hoped Chance could pull it off without getting himself and Nina killed in the process.

Seeing Tiana sneak from the entrance of the building caught Quan's attention. "What the fuck this sneaky bitch up to?" he asked aloud as he exited his car quietly. Approaching Tiana, he pulled out his Glock and aimed it at her back. "Yo, Tiana, wassup?"

Tiana flinched at the sound of Quan's voice. That was the last person she'd expected to see. "Hey, Quan. What are you doing here?"

Mean-mugging, Quan never lowered his gun. His gut was telling him Tiana was on some foul shit. Otherwise, why was she the only one walking out alive right now? "I never trusted ya ho ass." Tiana was about her dollar and would cross anybody while chasing the money. Loyalty wasn't even in her vocabulary. Anyone who praised money over loyalty could never be trusted in Quan's book.

"Where is Chance and Nina?"

"They should have been right behind me." Tiana looked around nervously. "What was I supposed to do? Wait for them to follow me? Fuck that. I had to bounce. Like I said, they should be coming out any minute now. So, I'll go ahead about my business. I've helped y'all enough for the night." She carried on.

*Loose lips*, Quan thought. Tiana's rambling was a dead giveaway. She confirmed Quan's suspicions. "Nah, you're going to stay right here with me until they walk out." He pointed his gun in her face. "And if they don't walk out soon, I'm putting a bullet right between your eyes." Quan's voice was laced with seriousness.

Laughing nervously, Tiana knew she was caught. "Stop playing, Quan."

"Bitch, I'm deadass." One thing Quan did not play about was Chance, his brother from another mother. Their bond was unbreakable. And he damn sure didn't play about Nina.

### Thirteen Years Ago

*Growing up in the hood, life was hard. Drugs were ravishing the community, but ironically, the drug game filtered so much money back into the hood. Many men had to play devil's advocate. Although you didn't want to sell drugs to someone's mother or cousin, you had to put food on your own table. And in order to do that, you needed money. At the age of 13, Quan had seen niggas get killed, crackheads overdosing on the side of the road, females tricking for a come up, you name it. The projects were like a world of*

*their own. Matter of fact, it was more like a jungle.*
*Every man for himself.*

"*Ty'Quan run to the corner store and get me*
*a couple of cigarettes and a forty!*" *Quan's mom*
*yelled to him as he sat on the front porch, watch-*
*ing the people pass by. It was a hot summer day*
*in the middle of July. Everybody was out on the*
*block, kicking it, smoking L's, drinking beer, and*
*listening to music.*

*Exhaling hard, Quan rolled his eyes. "Where*
*the money at?" he asked in an annoyed voice.*

"*I don't have no fucking money! Make some-*
*thing shake, and don't bring your big-headed*
*ass back here until you have my shit!*" *she*
*snapped back. "Every little nigga your age got*
*money in their pocket except you. Get some hus-*
*tle 'bout yourself!*"

*Quan hopped off the porch before his mother*
*could talk anymore shit. He couldn't stand her ass.*
*Ever since his dad left her, she had become content*
*with sitting in the house, getting fat and drunk.*
*Their only source of income was the monthly wel-*
*fare check, since she was too lazy to work. Instead,*
*Quan was expected to bring in money for himself.*

*Walking down the street, Quan ignored the*
*neighborhood boys as they joked on his fit. All his*
*clothes and shoes were either hand-me-downs or*
*bought from Goodwill. A lot of his time was spent*

*fighting to defend his pride. He'd fought so much that everyone knew not to step to him. The dudes could joke all they wanted, but they weren't trying to see Quan's hands.*

*"What up, Quan." Chance greeted Quan as he approached the store.*

*Quan dapped Chance up. Chance was the only friend he had. While everyone else joked on Quan, Chance never tried to clown him. Chance lived with his elderly grandmother and had to hustle to provide money to support himself and her. The two boys bonded over their struggles and developed a mutual respect for each other.*

*"What you up to, nigga?"*

*Chance looked around before pulling Quan close to him. "I'm about to rob this old motherfucker." He looked Quan in the eyes to let him know he was serious.*

*"Let me help," Quan suggested. In his mind, he could get his mom's shit for free and have a little cash in his pocket. Sensing Chance's apprehension, Quan pushed a little more. "I got your back, man."*

*Nodding, Chance entered the store with Quan following closely behind him. "Give me the money!" Chance screamed as he pulled out a small handgun.*

*The old Arabian man at the register put his hands up in fear. He didn't underestimate the*

*young man before him. The criminals were grow-*
*ing younger and younger every day. He wouldn't*
*risk becoming the next victim of the streets. "Okay,*
*be cool, young man." He carefully emptied his*
*register and handed Chance a handful of cash.*

*"You got your shit?" Chance yelled to Quan, who*
*was holding a forty in his hand. "Let's go!"*

*The boys ran out of the store like Olympic*
*gold medalists. They ran four blocks, until they*
*reached a back alley.*

*"Man, we got enough money to flip three times!"*
*Chance exclaimed.*

*Before they knew it, police sirens closed in on*
*them. Panicking, the boys ran, eventually sep-*
*arating from each other. Quan hid behind an*
*abandoned car as two white police officers chased*
*Chance. Out of instinct, Quan yelled, causing the*
*police officers to rush toward him. He didn't know*
*what had made him do that. In the back of his*
*mind, he knew he would be going to jail.*

*Chance was able to get away, but Quan wasn't*
*so lucky. The officers wasted no time locking his*
*young ass up. Quan was sentenced to four years*
*in a juvenile detention center for that, but once he*
*came home, it was all love from his homie. Chance*
*made his way to the top by selling drugs, and he*
*saved a spot beside him for Quan. He even still*
*had his half from the robbery saved up. From that*

*day forward, neither one of the boys had to question each other's loyalty.*

Gunshots were coming from inside the building. Before Quan could run into it, the entire building exploded and went up in flames. The bomb Quan and Chance had picked up from their gun connect detonated.

"Oh my God!" Tiana exclaimed. "Yasin!" she cried out.

Quan glanced at her for a quick second, confused, but quickly dismissed her as he saw a figure emerging from the smoke. It was Chance, carrying Nina's bloody body in his arms.

"We gotta get her to a hospital, man! Now!" Chance yelled to Quan.

Grabbing a crying Tiana by the arm, Quan dragged her to the car. "She's going to make it, bruh!" Quan promised, but things didn't look too good for Nina. She had lost a lot of blood, and her body was limp. "Fuck happened in there?"

"Nino," Chance said simply as he looked at Nina's nearly lifeless body. Placing his forefinger and middle finger on her neck, he felt a faint pulse. Today wasn't the day she would leave him, Chance concluded. They hadn't even experienced the world together. They were supposed to have plenty of children and grow old together. "We wouldn't have made it out if it wasn't for Yasin," Chance stated quietly.

"Hold on, sis!" Quan yelled back to Nina as he drove wildly to the nearest hospital. He could tell Chance was in shock. The explosion had his mans confused. Why else would he give credit to their enemy?

# Chapter Five

"The family of Nina Singleton," a nurse called out in the waiting room.

Chance jumped up at the mention of Nina's name. They had been in the waiting room for over four hours while the doctors operated on Nina. Periodic updates were given to Chance and Quan, but the outcome still wasn't certain. All they could tell Chance was that Nina had lost a lot of blood and needed a blood transfusion. He had been waiting anxiously for hours to hear some good news.

"How is she?"

"We've encountered a complication," the nurse began as she looked over her charts. "What's your relation to Ms. Singleton?"

Chance wanted to tell this broad to get to the point, but he kept it cool. "I'm her fiancé." That was a slight lie. While sitting, waiting, and thinking, Chance had decided that he would propose to Nina as soon as she opened her eyes. "What's wrong?"

"Well, after reviewing some of the bloodwork, it's been determined that Ms. Singleton is about eleven weeks pregnant. It's just standard procedure to consult you with this finding. Your fiancé and unborn child are extremely lucky because if you had gotten here a minute later, we would have lost them both," the nurse explained. "You'll be able to see her once she's transferred from the OR." Giving Chance a warm smile, she walked away.

Chance turned to Quan in disbelief. There was no way that the child Nina was carrying was his. As far as he knew, their child hadn't survived after Nina's car accident. It crushed him to know that Nina had given her body to another man. That was a right that used to be reserved only for him. To make matters worse, Nina now carried Yasin's child.

"That's supposed to be my baby, yo." He shook his head.

Quan didn't know what to say to his homie. He'd never experienced heartbreak. He could only imagine how Chance felt knowing Nina and Yasin had a child on the way. The distraught look on Chance's face spoke for itself. This day would surely go down as one of the craziest days of his life—and he'd seen enough crazy shit for a lifetime.

\*\*\*

*Beep. Beep. Beep.*

As Nina's eyes fluttered open, panic set in. Bright lights greeted her. The beeping of all the machines around her sounded like alarms ringing in her ears. She coughed at the smell of the sterile hospital room. Her throat felt like sandpaper as she lifted her hand to massage it. Her body felt as if it'd been dragged bare on a road for hours.

"Hmm! Hmm!" Tears ran down her face. Looking to her right, Nina saw Chance sleeping. That sight alone calmed her down. She could not remember much about what had happened before she was shot. Thankfully, Chance had made it out alive.

Stirring in his sleep, Chance looked up to see Nina struggling to move. "Yo, she's awake!" Chance shouted from the room. "Hello, beautiful." He gave Nina a warm smile. "You can't talk right now, baby. You're hooked up to a lot of shit, but I'll let the doctors explain that to you."

Chance's words scared her. The way he spoke made her believe she'd endured severe injuries. Nina managed enough strength to lift her finger and point to the whiteboard and marker hanging on the wall. Catching her hint, Chance handed Nina the board.

"Am I paralyzed?" Nina scribbled on the board.

"Nah, Nina." Chance tittered dryly and gripped Nina's hand. "You're blessed to only have the injuries you have now."

As those words left his mouth, Nina's surgeon walked into the room. "Ms. Singleton, I'm delighted to see you have woken up. My name is Dr. Shelby, and I performed your operations." The small Indian woman placed her hand on Nina's forearm gently. "You're connected to a tube that is helping you breathe. You've also been connected to a tube that has been feeding you for this past week. You've been in a coma. The fact that you're already back conscious shows you have a very bright recovery ahead of you."

*Coma? A week?* Nina thought. She knew they said when you're in a coma, you can hear the voices of the people talking to you. Nina didn't recall any of that. Blackness was the only thing she remembered from being in a comatose state. If she had encountered the other side, it didn't appear as any white light to her. It was only never-ending darkness.

"You have a great man, Nina. He's been beside you every second since you got out of surgery." Dr. Shelby turned her doe eyes to Chance and smiled. "I know you would like to speak with him. So, I'm going to remove the tubes from your throat and see how well you breathe on your own."

Once Dr. Shelby removed the tubes, Nina's dry throat still made it hard for her to speak. She swallowed repeatedly, but she barely produced enough saliva to alleviate the scratchiness in her throat. She motioned for the bottle of ice water on the table. Chance handed it to her, and she took a big gulp of it.

"How am I?" she asked in a raspy voice.

"The gunshot wound you sustained should have been fatal, for both you and the fetus," Dr. Shelby began explaining.

Nina coughed in disbelief. "*Fetus*?" Her eyes shot to Chance, and he diverted his attention back to Dr. Shelby. She couldn't read the look on his face, and it worried her.

"I'm sorry. I assumed you were aware." Dr. Shelby peeked at Chance in confusion. "We detected that you are in the late weeks of your first trimester. As I was saying before, the bullet was lodged near your heart. We were fortunate enough to remove it. You have a strong little one growing in there," she said. "I'll give you two some privacy." The doctor left the room and closed the door behind her.

Nina's head spun as the doctor's words echoed in her head. *Late weeks of your first trimester.* When she thought about it, she didn't recall having a period in the few weeks she'd lived in Atlanta. Yasin and Nina only had sex a couple of times. It was unprotected sex, but the pull-out method had never failed Nina before. But like her mom used to tell her, the only way to prevent pregnancy is to keep your legs closed. Looking at Chance, Nina knew he wanted to voice his opinion but bit his tongue out of love and respect for her. However, the look of hurt and betrayal displayed on his face spoke for itself.

*Could our baby possibly have survived? No, the doctor said there was no heartbeat,* Nina thought.

"I'm sorry."

Swallowing his pride, Chance knelt beside Nina's bed. He loved her so much. "You don't have to apologize to me, Nina. I don't care about none of that. Life is too short to worry about the bullshit." Chance kissed Nina's hand. He inconspicuously reached into his pocket and pulled out a small jewelry box. "I want to love every part of you forever. That means I will love this baby. After all we've been through, let's let the past be the past and start our future together. Will you marry me, Nina Aliyah Singleton?"

Looking down at the rock of a diamond sitting pretty on the black box, Nina nodded without a second thought. "Of course I will." Chance was her soulmate. Life tore them apart, only to reunite them. It had to be fate. Thoughts of Yasin didn't even cross her mind. Frankly, Nina didn't care if he was lying six feet under. Little did she know, Yasin was the only reason she and Chance were alive.

\*\*\*

### *One Month Later*

Sitting in the doctor's office, Nina patiently waited to be called to the back. Today marked her sixteenth week of pregnancy, and she would be getting a 4D ultrasound to determine the sex of the baby she was carrying. Nina initially wanted to be surprised by the baby's gender when she delivered, but the suspense made her anxious.

Over the past few weeks, Chance had worked relentlessly to make Nina as comfortable as possible. He accommodated her every need while nursing her back to good health. He never missed a doctor's appointment, other than today.

Chance met with their realtor to seal the deal on a house. Nina's condo in Atlanta was beginning to get cramped. Purchases for the baby were taking up too much space. Chance decided that he would purchase the house of Nina's dreams. They had narrowed the search down to three homes, all equally beautiful. She gave Chance the green light to surprise her with a pick from the options.

It was the first time Nina was truly content in a while. The chaos from the previous weeks subsided, and she breathed easy. Still, she couldn't help but wonder what had happened in those last moments between Chance, Yasin, and Nino. Out of respect for her man, she didn't press for any answers regarding Yasin. Nina longed for a sense of

peace after months of drama and deadly revelations. She craved normalcy in her life. Questions of
the past only threatened to uproot the harmonious
life she'd built over the last month.

"Nina Singleton," a nurse dressed in all pink
scrubs called. She had decorated her uniform with
faux flowers attached, and her hair was pulled into
a bun by two chopsticks.

Nina raised her hand and followed the nurse
into the back.

"I'm Amina. I see you're finding out the sex of
your baby today. Are you excited?"

Nina rubbed her protruding belly. No matter
how this child was conceived, Nina vowed to give
it the best life possible. She was in love with a
child she hadn't even met. Every little kick she felt
reminded her that all her struggles in life had led
up to this moment. She and Chance read to her
growing nugget every night. Nina sang her favorite
songs to the baby even though she could barely
hold a tune. It didn't matter. She loved being a
mother already.

"I'm very excited." Lying back on the table, Nina
lifted her dress over her small baby bump.

Amina clapped her hands and turned on the big
flat screen for Nina's viewing. "Let's take a look,
shall we?" She squeezed the cold ultrasound gel
onto Nina's belly and smeared the ultrasound
probe across it.

Nervously looking at the monitor, Nina hoped that God had blessed her with a baby girl who would possess all her looks and curly hair. Yasin was easy on the eyes, and his chocolate complexion made him nearly irresistible. Nina was sure the two of them would make a beautiful daughter. "Is it a girl?" she asked, crossing her fingers.

Amina tapped her tongue across her teeth, rolling the probe from the left side of her stomach to the right. "Oh, we have a stubborn little nugget here, huh?" She giggled, removing the probe for a second. Amina tapped Nina's bump lightly. "Come on, little one. Open up for Mommy!"

Nina turned anxious eyes to the ultrasound display. "Got those legs closed, huh?"

"Closed tight, too!" Amina placed the probe back onto Nina's bump. "Nugget just wants to play a little. Looka there, moving now," she cooed. "You're having a boy!" Amina landed the probe on the baby just as he uncrossed his legs.

*A boy*, Nina thought. She'd always imagined giving Chance an heir, a little boy to call their own. There were several names she had reserved for their prince.

Chance had loved the idea of being a parent years before Nina accepted the notion. Bringing a child into such a cruel world terrified her. However, experiencing this pregnancy opened her eyes to a kind of love she'd never known. She'd go to the ends of hell to protect her child. If Chance loved her the way she believed he did, he would love the baby as much as she did. *God makes no mistakes*, she thought.

"I love you so much already, my little king," she whispered to her baby bump.

Nina stood in the foyer of her new home, examining the home carefully. She was in awe. The virtual tour had done the home no justice. Chance had gone all out. The house featured six bedrooms with a double set of stairs and white marble floors throughout the entire home. It was undoubtedly a home fit for a queen.

"I love it!" Nina screeched as she hugged Chance. "Thank you, baby."

Smiling, Chance kissed Nina's hand as he led her through every room in the house. "I even made sure you had an extra room for your makeup and all'at." Chance gently held her hand as he guided her up the steps. "Lemme show you where all the magic gon' be happening at."

Nina laughed as she curled her mouth up. "Boy, you so corny."

Chance hadn't touched her intimately since their reunion. He said that he didn't want to put any stress on her recovery, but Nina knew otherwise. Chance would never admit it, but he didn't feel comfortable having sex with Nina while she carried another man's child.

"It's a boy," Nina said quietly.

Looking down at Nina's small pudge, Chance took a few seconds before speaking. It took a lot on his behalf to accept the fact that Nina's firstborn wouldn't be his. But on the other hand, the roles were reversed. Back in Charlotte, Quan played close tabs on Tiana. Her treachery hadn't been forgotten or forgiven. As soon as she gave birth to Chance's seed, he would snatch the baby up, and she would be dealt with accordingly. Tiana's scandalous ways had nearly cost Chance his life, and even Nina's. The baby boy she was carrying kept her breathing in the meantime.

The whole situation was messy in Chance's eyes. He and Nina both had kids on the way, but not together. It wasn't how Chance pictured bringing a life, a part of him, into this world.

"A boy, huh?" He rubbed his goatee lightly and nodded. "I'm going to raise him to be a better man than me." Looking into Nina's eyes, Chance tried to reassure Nina that he accepted this situation, even if a part of him truly hadn't. But it was all for her.

Nina would never admit the fact that she was she was still fragile from all the crazy events that had happened within such a short period of time.

"What's up, baby?" he asked as he pulled Nina into his lap.

Twirling her fingers around each other, Nina shrugged. "What happened to Yasin that night?"

Chance rolled his eyes at the mention of Yasin's name. His nostrils flared. "Why fuck up a good moment, Nina? Don't I keep you stress free and worry free? Don't I make sure that you want for nothing? I make you happy, right?" he demanded, voice rising an octave.

"Yes, baby, but—"

Chance cut Nina off before she could finish her sentence. "But what, Nina? Why do you care what happened to that nigga?"

Nina sprang up and placed her hands on her hips. "Don't fucking raise your voice at me, Chance! I asked a simple question. I've been quiet about it for months out of respect for *you*, but I deserve answers too," she snapped.

Chance rolled his eyes and waved away her statement.

"You know what? Forget I even asked." Nina grabbed her car keys and left Chance sitting in the room by himself.

"Nina!" he yelled after her. Sighing heavily, Chance wiped his face with his hands. Spazzing on Nina wasn't his intention. His jealousy over the Yasin situation burned in his chest. As much as Chance hated to admit it, a part of Nina's heart belonged to another nigga. It was as if what he had done for Nina wasn't enough anymore. And if Nina found out what had actually happened that night, she would be left with a decision to make. That was an ultimatum Chance hoped he never had to propose.

Nina drove aimlessly until her car ended up in the Lennox parking lot. Shopping would clear her mind. In her heart, she knew Chance's intentions weren't to hurt her. Was she asking for too much? Chance did make her happy. He would go to the ends of the earth for her and do whatever in his power to protect and provide for her and her child. Nina understood that that type of love and loyalty was hard to come by these days. They were so much bigger than petty arguments, Nina decided. To be alive was enough of a blessing, especially in her case. This year had taught her that life wasn't promised. Nina didn't want to waste her time with Chance disagreeing over things that didn't matter in the grand scheme of it all.

Nina pulled her iPhone out of her Hermes bag. She dialed Chance's number. "Baby, I don't want to fight with you. I'm going to be home after I pick up a few things from the mall. I love you, Chance." She gushed as she spoke into the phone, leaving a voicemail.

Glancing up, Nina flinched at the sight before her. Her phone crashed to the ground as she released the grip on everything in her hands. "Yasin," she whispered.

In the flesh, Yasin stood before her with a bouquet of roses, wearing his signature suit and designer loafers. He bent over to pick up Nina's phone and bags before handing her the flowers.

"Hello, beautiful," Yasin greeted. His eyes fixated on her small bump curiously. "Is it mine?" he asked, nodding to her belly.

Nina bit her lip and peered around the mall nervously. She exhaled and nodded. "He's yours," Nina admitted. "I thought you were dead." She studied Yasin curiously.

Yasin smirked and shook his head. "I guess your man didn't tell you. If it weren't for me, we'd all be dead," he stated. "I see we have a lot to catch up on, ma." Yasin held out his hand for Nina.

Going against her better judgment, Nina placed her hand inside Yasin's. *What am I doing*? Nina asked herself.


Nina woke up to the sound of her phone ringing. Sitting up groggily, she fumbled for her iPhone. Reality set in as a picture of her and Chance flashed across the screen. They'd taken that picture three years ago on a trip to Jamaica. Their bodies were snuggled together, and they stared into each other's eyes lovingly.

"Fuck." Nina's heart skipped a beat as she looked toward the warm body lying next to her. The body belonged to Yasin, not her longtime lover and friend. "What am I doing?" She shook her head at her reckless actions. There were thirty missed calls from Chance in all. No doubt, Chance was going to spazz on her.

After talking to Yasin at the mall, Nina had agreed to join him for dinner. Yes, she knew it was completely foul and disloyal for her to be in his presence, but what choice did Chance leave her? It was his job to let her know the specific details of that night. He didn't let her know that Yasin had taken out Nino and his two henchmen. He didn't mention that Yasin had risked his life to save not only hers, but Chance's too. He didn't give her the option to choose between him and Yasin. And as of now, Nina didn't know which direction her heart wanted her to follow. Regardless, she acknowledged that she moved foul by being laid up with Yasin.

Slipping out of the bed quietly, Nina went into the bathroom to return Chance's call.

"Yo, Nina, where you at?" Chance's voice blared into the phone.

Nina had known Chance long enough to recognize the emotions in his voice. Anger. Worry.

Doubt.

"I been calling you all damn night and day! Do you understand how worried I've been?"

"I'm sorry, Chance," were the first words to leave her lips. She didn't want to lie to him, but she couldn't tell him the truth either. "I needed some time to think, so I dipped out to Miami for the weekend." Technically, that wasn't a lie. Yasin had asked her to come to Miami with him for the weekend after they had dinner. Her answer should have been no, but Yasin's magnetism always pulled her in his direction. She was, without a doubt, playing with fire.

*I gotta get my shit together before this all blows up in my face*, she vowed.

A deafening silence greeted Nina on the other end of the line. "Say something at least," she muttered in a soft tone.

"Yeah, whatever. You forgot I know you like the back of my hand, right? So, I'ma go ahead and spare myself of this back and forth shit right now, Nina. I love you to death, shorty. No matter what you decide, I'll never love you any less. But I won't share you. Ever. I'm going to stay in my condo until you figure your shit out. The house is yours. Call me if you need me."

With that, Nina met the dial tone. She stared down at the phone in disbelief. Did Chance just break up with her? She hadn't expected that response. She had expected Chance's grace, even though a small part of her knew she didn't deserve grace.

A smirk appeared across Chance's face. He couldn't believe how effortlessly Nina had delivered her lies. Little did she know, Chance had followed her to the mall yesterday. He wasn't trying to be controlling or possessive. He could admit that Nina's discretions with Yasin made him insecure; however, he wasn't moving off insecurity, but off caution. There had been too many times when Nina had come close to death on Chance's watch. He wasn't going to take any more chances. But when he saw her leaving the mall with Yasin, his pride couldn't withstand the blow.

Nina had crossed a line to the point of no return in Chance's book. She was emotional and impulsive now, and pregnancy hormones couldn't excuse her actions. Chance's vision blurred, and he clenched his teeth together. He struggled to understand Nina's reasoning for wanting Yasin. Yes, she was pregnant with the nigga's baby, but in his eyes, she didn't owe Yasin any loyalty. Yes, he saved their lives, but he owed that to Nina. As for Chance, he hoped Yasin didn't want any rewards for saving his life.

"Fuck that nigga," he said aloud. The thought of killing Yasin crossed his mind, but he dismissed it.

The old Nina would have never moved so sloppy.
There was no way Chance could justify Nina's
actions. The only option he had now was to separate himself. Business was one of Chance's main
focuses right now. Nina and her drama distracted
him. Nina put her feelings first and disregarded
his. Chance decided that it was time for him to
separate himself and start doing the same.


"Hey." Nina waved at Yasin as he watched the
news once she came out of the bathroom.

A bare-chested Yasin stood and swaggered over
to Nina. Wrapping his arms around her waist,
Yasin gazed down at Nina.

"I think it's time for me to go back to Atlanta,"
she said.

Yasin nodded as he sat on the edge of the bed.
"You know you got to choose, right, ma?"

Nina nodded with a slight frown on her face.
She had two men who were crazy over her. Chance
was her first love. Yasin, on the other hand, was
the person she was falling for.

"I'll let you choose when you get back to Atlanta.
Right now, I want you to enjoy Miami. I'll give
you your space. A break is exactly what you need,
right?"

"It is," Nina admitted.

"Anything you need, charge it to my account.
There's no expense for you."

"If I choose you, what does that mean for us?" Nina asked Yasin seriously. Games weren't something she was willing to play with anyone anymore. That went for Chance also. "I just don't want to make a mistake."

"Just give me a chance, Nina. Shit been so fucked up lately, I want to make it right for once, feel me?" Yasin kneeled and wrapped his arms around Nina's waist. He rested his forehead against her stomach. "I don't want to waste your time, and I don't want you to waste mine. I know how you feel about Chance. If you not done over there, we can't start anything this way." Yasin made it clear that he wanted to be with Nina, but he wouldn't share her either. So, the ball rested in Nina's court.

Nina knew she had a lot of thinking to do. What she didn't realize was that by being there with Yasin, the decision had been made.

Walking down the beautiful Miami oceanfront, Nina was in deep thought. Yasin walked alongside her. Neither one of them said a word. Yasin enjoyed the serene scenery as he admired Nina's pregnancy glow. All he wanted to do was do right by his son since that chance had been stolen from his own father. There wasn't anything that would get in the way of Yasin being in his son's life.

"It's so amazing how massive and everlasting the ocean is." Nina spoke aloud, more to herself than Yasin. "No matter how much we think we know about the ocean and have seen, there's still so much more to be discovered. That's how I feel about myself." She rubbed her small, round baby bump. "I have to find myself again."

For as long as she could remember, Nina was all about Chance. He was all she had at one point, which was why their breakup hurt her so much. But she owed everything to the little boy growing inside of her. A part of that meant giving Yasin a serious chance. It was worth a try. Death had come knocking at her door one too many times, so it was only right for Nina to live her life to the fullest.

"I'm putting my trust in you, Yasin. I'm not taking any more losses when it comes to my heart. So, if you do me wrong, it might cost you your life." A smile spread across her face, but she was dead-ass. "I'm too grown for the games now. I just want to raise my son and live happily. What I need is stability and attention."

Yasin kissed Nina's hands. "You don't have to want for anything, ma. I got you and my son forever. All you need to do is sit back and raise my son. I'll handle the rest."

The strip club was where Chance found himself later in the night. It was Saturday, and Magic City was lit. Beautiful, voluptuous women and liquor floated everywhere throughout the club. This wasn't his scene, but Chance needed a distraction to take his mind off Nina. He knew he would eventually get over Nina, no matter how hard it would be. He had no other choice.

Migos was hosting the party at the club that night. That meant the baddest chicks Atlanta had to offer were on the scene. There was a girl of every type in the room: tall and short, thick and petite, light skin and dark skin. It was paradise for a nigga, but no one special caught Chance's eye. Nina was a dime for sure, a one-of-a-kind type of beauty. Finding someone on her level would be hard.

"I've never seen you here before," the pretty, dark-skinned bartender commented as Chance took a seat. "You don't even look like the type to trick." She smirked, leaning across the bar slightly, with her titties nearly spilling out of the bralette she wore.

Chance chuckled lightly. "I don't trick, ma," he simply replied. "You gon' serve me or nah?"

"Damn, I got you. What you need, baby?" She licked her lips. The intent behind her words wasn't flirtatious, but she eluded sex appeal without even trying.

Even from behind the bar, Chance noticed her curvy frame. Her sleek, straight hair was pulled into a high ponytail with her baby hairs curling perfectly against her temples. Dimples graced both of her cheeks. What really caught Chance's eye was her radiant chocolate skin. She had potential.

"I'm Naomi, by the way."

"I'm Chance." He smoothly extended his hand for her to shake. "Let me get some D'usse."

Naomi swiftly fixed Chance a drink. The sounds of screams focused the attention of the club on a group of girls surrounding Migos. "These chicks never know how to act when we have celebrities." Naomi rolled her eyes.

Chance recognized the look of disgust on Naomi's face. He couldn't stand a groupie either. "You don't like the young rich niggas?" he joked.

"I like them, but I'm not about to sweat them over some bread. I got my own," Naomi answered confidently. "These bitches break their necks to get close to a baller, only to be played to the left at the end of the night. All those niggas want to do is get their dicks wet." She rolled her tongue against her teeth and waggled her pointer finger. "I'll pass."

Chance laughed. He dug Naomi's demeanor. In a way, she reminded him of Nina. Sipping his drink, Chance enjoyed Naomi's company while she tended to a few customers. By the end of the night, he decided he would take her home. Whatever happened after that, Chance wouldn't regret it.

***

Nina was happy when she arrived back at her home the next day. Miami was cool, but she'd grown accustomed to Atlanta. The only thing she dreaded was facing Chance. Depending on what Chance had to say, Nina would make her decision. She took a deep breath as she unlocked the door to her mansion.

Walking through the door, Nina almost tripped. Looking down, she noticed an unfamiliar pair of high heels in the foyer. "What the fuck?" she asked herself.

"Chance!" Nina called out as she headed up the stairs. The door to their room was slightly ajar, but Nina saw everything she needed to see. Chance's chest was bare as a dark-skinned female slept on it. Her panties, bra, and dress were on the floor in front of the bed. An empty Magnum wrapper was on the nightstand. One of the girl's legs was intertwined with Chance's. Nina gagged at the sight and swallowed hard.

Instead of spazzing out and making a scene, Nina stormed to the closet and grabbed her Gucci luggage. In a rage, she grabbed some of her belongings and stuffed them in the bags. Chance really had her fucked up. No matter what they'd been going through, there was no way Nina would have ever brought another nigga into their bedroom, or home for that matter. Nina admitted that her actions weren't innocent either, but she didn't fuck Yasin. Not while things between her and Chance weren't completely figured out. Chance had obviously made the decision for her. She held back tears as she headed to the bathroom to grab a couple of toiletries.

Chance stirred in the bed and woke up slowly. His eyes bulged wildly when he saw Nina, with her baby bump, moving through the room like a whirlwind. He knew he'd fucked up when he met her sad eyes. He couldn't even say anything as he looked at Naomi lying next to him, still naked and knocked out.

"Nina . . ."

Nina raised her hand up to silence Chance. "Don't say anything." Her voice shook. "No matter the circumstances, I would have never carried things so disrespectful like this. I hope you're happy." Tears fell down her face as she dragged the two duffle bags behind her out of the room. If she didn't plan on leaving Chance before, he had left her with no choice now.

"You left me for Yasin, Nina. What did you expect from me?" Chance yelled at the top of the stairs.

"I expected for you to give me a choice! For *once* in your fucking life! But you've left me with no other choice now." Tears slipped from the corners of Nina's eyes. "Goodbye, Chance." With that, Nina walked out of Chance's life.

***

Sitting in the waitig area of the hospital, Quan scrolled down his Facebook timeline. He wasn't a social media junkie; it was how he stayed connected with his family from up top. Time seemed to be going by slow as hell for him. There was no telling how long it would be before Tiana finished giving birth to her baby boy. Chance had instructed him to stay at the hospital until he arrived.

Today would be the moment of truth. It would be determined whether the baby Tiana caried belonged to Chance. Quan had looked after Tiana since Chance moved to Atlanta. The plan was, if the baby was Chance's, to relocate Tiana and the baby to Atlanta. Tiana might have thought shit was all good, but Chance had big plans for his son, and none included Tiana.

"What's good, my nigga?" Chance greeted his best friend as he entered the waiting area. "How you living?" Chance leaned against the wall wearing a navy blue Tom Ford suit. The suit jacket rested in the crook of his arm. His diamond cufflinks alluded to his newfound wealth. All his energy and frustrations had been put into making money. After the morning Nina left him, Chance was all business. Working seemed to be the only thing that kept his heart from missing his woman. It was fucked up how things had gone down, and Chance wished he could turn back the hands of time, but like his grandma always told him, everything happens for a reason. What's meant to be, will be. He wasn't stressing it.

Quan dapped his mans up. "I'm living."

It was a good feeling to know him and his right hand were eating. While Chance was focusing on going legit in Atlanta, Quan had picked up where the empire left off in Charlotte. Everything was everything.

"Shorty in the room. No family or anything showed up. If I didn't know how Tiana got down, I would be feeling bad." Quan didn't know much about childbirth, but he understood enough to know that it was supposed to be the happiest day of a woman's life. He'd seen enough movies to know that babies were meant to be surrounded by loved ones when they came into the world. Tiana had no one, and Quan figured her grimy ways influenced her loneliness. He shook his head.

"Well, if the kid is mine, he's going to know love." Chance tried not to get his hopes up about being a father because he doubted that Tiana knew the true paternity of her child.

"You talked to Nina lately?" he inquired as he sat down in a chair across from Quan. Nina had completely erased him from her life. After leaving the mansion that day, Nina had blocked Chance and blocked his access to all her social media profiles.

She even went as far as to change the passwords on their shared Netflix and Hulu accounts.

"Maybe like a week ago. You know she's going to drop a kid soon too." Quan didn't want to shit on his boy's parade by telling him Nina sounded happy the last time he had talked to her. That was like his sister, and he had known her long enough to know when she was smiling.

He hated how Nina and Chance carried their situations. Love wasn't supposed to go like that. In his eyes, they were always meant to be, like a modern-day Bonnie and Clyde, even Michelle and Barack, depending on the setting you caught them in. Nina and Chance completed each other. But Quan had never been in love before, so he wasn't in a position to judge.

Chance nodded as his thoughts drifted to Nina. Till this day, he couldn't believe that she had left him. After all they'd been through together and all the shit they had to look forward to, was it that easy for Nina to give up? Was that nigga Yasin making her happy? An uneasy feeling settled in Chance's stomach when he thought of Yasin. Together or not, if the nigga caused any harm to Nina, he would put him six feet under.

"Yeah, she's going to be a great mother," Chance said.

"Excuse me, are you the family of Tiana Cruz?" a petite female nurse asked. Chance and Quan

nodded. "The baby is here. Follow me." The nurse
led the two men down the hall, then into the
maternity ward. She knocked on the door before
slowly pushing it open.

Tiana was sitting up on the bed, cradling a small
baby boy with a head full of slick black hair.

Chance approached Tiana slowly. "How you
doing?" he asked as he looked down at the precious little boy. Instantly, there was no doubt in
Chance's mind that the baby was his. The little boy
was practically a spitting image of him, even down
to his bushy eyebrows and mocha complexion.
The feature that stood out to Chance the most was
the baby's birthmark right behind his right ear.
Chance had the exact same mark.

"What's his name?"

"Chase." Tiana smiled as she saw Chance fall in
love with the baby just as she had. As much as she
wanted to be a great mother to the baby, she knew
she wasn't ready. Being a mother wasn't a job she
was up for right now. The lifestyle she lived didn't
cater to mothers. Tiana stripped to provide for
herself and partied almost every day of the week.
She wasn't ashamed to admit that she would make
a bad mother. "I can't take care of him Chance. I
know he'll be better off with you."

Chance stroked his beard in thought. He had
planned on getting full custody of his son regardless, but Tiana was making it too easy for him.

"That was the plan anyway, T, but I need your help while he's a baby. You'll have those motherly instincts. Until he's old enough, I'm going to set you up in a place in Atlanta. Don't worry about bills or anything. I just need your help for now," Chance explained. He peered into the bassinet and reached out to pick up the sleeping baby. Their bond instantly solidified as the baby wrapped his small fingers around Chance's forefinger. "I got you, Tiana. Just help me out here. You owe me that."

Tiana felt shitty as she listened to Chance practically beg her to be a mother to her child. "I can do that."

"Cool." Chance smiled brightly as he walked the baby over for Quan to see. Quan peeked at Chase, beaming, and tapped Chance's shoulder twice. "My li'l man."

As happy as he was in the moment, Chance couldn't help but wish it was Nina lying in that bed.


Yasin puffed a Cuban cigar as he watched Nina practice her favorite yoga moves on the lawn. Every day, Yasin still marveled at Nina's beauty. He couldn't believe that she was finally his. Everything had been great since she walked away from Chance three months ago. Their relationship and love grew stronger by the day. Their son would be here any day now, and they both were ecstatic. Nina looked up and beamed when she noticed Yasin watching her. She blew him a kiss.

Since the day Yasin laid eyes on Nina, she made him feel whole. He wished that they had met under different circumstances, but even then, he knew it was fate that brought them together. His intentions may not have been genuine when he first met Nina, but his love for her was real. Every move he had made since reuniting with Nina was to rectify his previous mishaps, and no one could take that away. This was the woman he intended to marry. Yet, there were still some things they had to talk about before they could get to that point.

"Baby, can you order us some Mexican food? I want an enchilada," Nina called out to him. She enjoyed being pampered by Yasin. Having money wasn't new to her, but Yasin's bankroll seemed like it was endless. There was no limit to how far he would go to spoil Nina. Whatever she wanted, he provided, and it wasn't just the material things that Yasin showered her with. He gave her his undivided attention whenever he was in her presence. With Chance, there had been some days that went by when Nina didn't even see him.

"Yeah, baby, anything you want. I'll run out and go get it for you now. You need anything else?" he asked. Nina shook her head. "I'll be back in a few, ma." Yasin headed toward his multi-car garage.

It was only right for a man of his stature to have multiple foreign cars at his disposal. He spent money so frivolously because the work he put in to be able to afford these luxuries could've killed him. There were things that he did that he would never tell a soul, not even Nina. His past was something he didn't need coming up, because he wasn't proud of it.

Relaxing in the hot tub Jacuzzi, Nina let the melodies of SZA ease her mind. She was more than ready for her son, Nasim, to enter this world. Being pregnant was a tiring experience, and she told herself that this would be her last pregnancy. She'd always imagined herself having Chance's baby and getting married to him, but things didn't always play out how you expected them to.

Her iPhone vibrated, and Yasin's name flashed across the screen. "Wassup, baby?"

"I know I was supposed to bring your food back, but I got caught up at the dealership for a while. How about you meet me in midtown, and we'll go grab something to eat?" Yasin spoke into the phone.

Nina sighed but replied, "Okay." She lifted her body out of the water and wobbled into the house. "I'm so tired of this." Nina pouted as she headed into the house. A small task such as showering took a lot of effort now that she was carrying an extra thirty pounds on her body.

Walking into the enormous master bedroom that she and Yasin shared, Nina smiled. Scenes of lovemaking from the night before flashed in her mind. Yasin took her to heights in the bedroom that she'd never climbed before. He was gentle and deliberate when they made love. He paid attention to every one of her impulses and acted accordingly. Being a few years older than her, Yasin was a seasoned lover. That was one of the reasons Nina was so crazy about him.

"What to wear?" she asked herself as she stood in the middle of her huge closet the size of the average person's living room. Nina decided on wearing a ruffled, off-the-shoulder Burberry dress and a pair of Moschino sandals. She took a quick shower and got dressed. Brushing her hair into a sleek, curly puffball, Nina applied her Fenty lip gloss before grabbing her keys.

Naomi accompanied Chance for a dinner date. They weren't an exclusive couple, but they'd been seeing each other often since the night they met. Neither one of them wanted a serious relationship. They were just having fun and enjoying each other's company.

"How's the baby doing?" Naomi asked as she savored the delicious Mexican dish in front of her. Chance had informed Naomi that he had newborn son when he linked with her for the second time. Naomi didn't run away from the fact, which made Chance dig her even more.

Chance gave her a slight smile. "He's doing good. Getting bigger every day." Being a father fulfilled Chance in ways that he had never imagined. He had grown up without a father of his own and desired to give Chase every experience he'd missed out on. "I'm going to let you meet him soon."

Naomi gasped and held her hand to her chest dramatically. "I'm honored. Does that mean I get to meet your lucky girl too?" she asked and smirked. Naomi could tell that Chance was being careful with his heart and keeping her at a distance. She knew from experience that there had to be someone who had hurt him before. That was the only explanation. "Are you finally going to tell me about her?"

Chance opened his mouth to speak but closed it instantly when he saw the couple walk through the door. They looked like money, dressed in designer garments, and adorned in diamonds. And indeed, they looked happy together. His palms began sweating as Yasin and Nina stood in the entrance of the restaurant, waiting to be seated. His eyes wandered to Nina, who clung closely to Yasin's

shoulder. She looked even more beautiful than the
last time he'd laid eyes on her. Her pregnancy had
her honey brown complexion glistening like an
Egyptian goddess. That smile that used to make
his heart weak graced her face. His temperature
rose as he noticed the shimmer in her eyes. It was
the same look she used to have when she was with
him.

"Chance?" Naomi waves her hand in front of
Chance's face. Then, her attention focused on
what Chance was looking at. "You know them?"

Chance shook his head as Nina's eyes met his.
Something deep down inside of him begged him to
go hug and kiss her and make things right, but shit
wasn't right. Everything that was right about them
had gone wrong. He knew they were both to blame.
Their time together had passed, and he had to
move on. But seeing her in the flesh let him know
that he was far from over her.

"She's gorgeous," Naomi complimented. She
couldn't even hate on the woman that had Chance's
attention. Her eyes roamed to the dude standing
next to the girl. She coughed on her drink when
she noticed who it was. It was the same nigga
her and her girls hit a lick on once before. She
shuddered as he briefly locked eyes with her. That
was the last person she ever wanted to see in her
life, especially after he killed her friend for robbing
him.

"You good?" Chance asked Naomi.

"Can we go?" she asked as she abruptly rose. "Please."

Chance looked at Naomi strangely. "It looks like you seen a ghost," Chance commented, but he didn't protest. He dropped a hundred-dollar bill on the table, and they headed out of the restaurant.

"That nigga is bad news, Chance. If you love that girl, no matter what y'all went through, you better get her away from him," Naomi said once they were safely inside Chance's Benz. Tears rolled down her face. "I can't tell you why, but just take my word."

Nina's heart skipped a beat as she noticed Chance sitting a few feet away from her in the restaurant. A familiar girl was sitting across from him at the table. *The same bitch he was laid up with that day*, she assumed. He looked a little different from the last time they were in each other's presence, in a good way. Despite their time apart, Nina could still read him just from a look. He was just as surprised to see her. Jealousy crept upon Nina, and she locked her arms with Yasin, pulling him close to her. She flipped her hair over her shoulders and turned her nose up. She silently thanked herself for taking the extra time today to complete her full look. The way she turned heads, pregnant and all, she was sure that Chance enjoyed the view.

"You good?" Yasin asked her, but his attention was on Chance and the girl. "Tell ya mans he better watch that ho. She a leech."

"Oh, you know her?" Nina asked. As the words left her mouth, Chance and the girl were exiting the restaurant.

Yasin nodded as the host escorted them to their table. "There's a lot of shit that I done in the past that I'm not proud of. Shorty fits into that category. Her name is Naomi," he responded vaguely.

Nina leaned across the table, ready to hear more. She refused to believe that the world was this small. First Tiana, and now this chick. "Small world. So y'all used to fuck around?" she asked skeptically. "Because shorty rushed out like she seen a ghost." Nina wanted answers. There weren't enough coincidences in the world to believe that there wasn't a connection between these women who were with Yasin and Chance.

"I promise, when the time is right, I'm going to tell you everything," Yasin vowed. He just hoped Nina would still choose him when she heard the truth.


"You haven't said a word since we left the restaurant, Chance. Are you okay?" Naomi asked nervously.

"I don't know what to think about you, shorty. Anybody connected to that nigga is suspect to me." He rubbed his chin hair lightly, deep in thought. All the wheels in his head were turning. Was Naomi sent to Chance by Yasin? Was he just a mark? He didn't know what the fuck was going on, but he didn't want any dealings.

Naomi chuckled in disbelief. "You don't know what's up with me? I haven't given you no reason not to know, Chance! I been a hundred with you since day one." Naomi's body swiveled in the seat until she faced Chance.

"Bet," Chance responded calmly, resting his hand on his waist near his gun. "So, tell me how you know that nigga." If Naomi said one wrong thing, Chance was going to blow her ass away. He wasn't taking no more chances with anybody. He would shoot first and ask questions later.

"It's a long story," she responded curtly, folding her arms.

Chance placed his .380 on his lap.

"So, you're going to shoot me?" Naomi asked indignantly, flinching at the sight of the gun.

Chance remained silent and kept his eyes on the road as he drove.

"Did you question that bitch like you're questioning me?"

Chance clenched his jaws tightly. "Watch your mouth."

"We been kicking it hard for months now, and you want to trip over this? You don't trust me?" Naomi's voice quivered.

"You can either answer my question or get the fuck out my shit." Chance raised his shoulder indifferently. She wasn't giving the responses that Chance wanted to hear. He pulled the car over to the curb.

Naomi was stuck between a rock and a hard place. Telling Chance that she had set up Yasin to be robbed was out of the question. A man like Chance would never respect any treachery like that. He'd cut ties with her off the principle alone. "I'm just asking you to trust me."

"Trust will get you killed," Chance growled. He unlocked the doors and motioned for Naomi to get out.

She scoffed and nodded in disbelief. She snatched her purse from the backseat and exited the car before slamming the door shut. Naomi kicked herself for catching feelings for Chance. Tonight had ruined any possibility of her having a future with Chance. Her pride wouldn't allow her to tell him the truth.

"That nigga is going to pay. Both of them," Naomi vowed as she watched Chance speed off. No man had ever played her like Chance just had. Embarrassed, she strutted into the nearest convenience store as she called an Uber. "Bitch-ass nigga," she spat as her mind began to plot.


Naomi brought her heavy fist against the door repeatedly. Her right leg tapped the floor impatiently. The sun peeked across the horizon, but Naomi couldn't let the night end without making this final stop. Still pissed about how Chance had threatened and humiliated her, she was ready to set her get-back plan in motion.

"Hold the fuck up!" a female's voice yelled from the other side of the door. "Who is it?"

"It's me! Na! Open up, yo!" Naomi waited until she heard the last lock click before she pushed herself through the door. "That nigga is dirty, man! I can't believe I was really feeling him like that." She stormed into the condo and let out a frustrated squeal.

"You banging on my door about to wake the baby up!" Naomi's friend exclaimed. "What happened?" She softened her voice.

Naomi's best friend sat down and listened as she vented. This was one person she knew who had her back no matter what. They held secrets for each other that they vowed to take to their graves.

"I'm so mad at myself because you warned me about this nigga! I had to be hardheaded and continue to fuck with him." Naomi clapped her hands together before throwing them in the air.

Scoffing lightly, Naomi checked her phone to see if she had received a text or call from Chance. A part of her had really fallen for him, even though she could tell the energy wasn't reciprocated. It was obvious he was stuck on his ex.

"That bitch Nina and Yasin's scheming ass." Her words were laced with malice. "We're out having dinner when those two pop up. Nina is pregnant as fuck, acting like wifey on Yasin's arm. She ain't even really all of that." The green-eyed monster crept up Naomi's back. She knew all about Nina, unbeknownst to Chance. "I tried to warn Chance about Yasin, but he started asking questions I couldn't answer. When I didn't answer, he threatened to shoot me, then put my ass out his car!" Naomi exclaimed.

"I told you not to fuck with him. If anybody should know, it's me." The girl twisted her full mouth into a smirk.

"I know, T." Naomi lowered her head. She thought about the argument they'd gotten into when Naomi informed her friend of the first night she met Chance. Naomi recognized Chance as soon as he walked into the club, but they didn't know each other. Naomi knew of Chance through her best friend, Tiana.

Naomi, Tiana, and their deceased friend, Kiki, grew up together. They were known for being some of the most sought-out strippers from their city. Only the ballers stepped to them. Despite their reputation as sack chasers, the niggas lined up to fuck with them. They'd spent years tricking off niggas and even robbing a few. That's how Naomi came up with the idea of robbing Yasin. The two used to flirt all the time when Yasin came into the club. He was new in town at the time but had established himself amongst Atlanta's circle of bosses. Naomi saw him as the come up she and her girls needed.

Naomi played the role of a loyal girlfriend to Yasin. She waited until he was comfortable enough to let her accompany him on trips to pick up his monthly deposits as the distributor. Her plan was to have her girls meet her at a hotel she and Yasin were staying at and rob them. However, things went left quickly. Kiki ended up shot, while Tiana was able to escape. The mask she wore was the only reason Yasin didn't know of her role in the robbery.

Tiana left Atlanta after that incident and moved to Charlotte, where she eventually met Chance. Naomi fled Atlanta for a while after the incident, only returning when she thought Yasin had forgotten about the situation. Unbeknownst to her, he had figured out that she was the mastermind of the whole robbery.

"You risked our friendship to fuck with that nigga when I told you how stupid he was for that bitch Nina! It's like she put roots on him or some shit," Tiana said, jealous about Chance's unconditional love for Nina. "I got this nigga baby, and that ain't even enough. What made you think he'd choose you?" At the end of the day, Tiana wasn't mad at her friend. They had vowed to never let a nigga come between them years ago. "And if Yasin figures out you set me up with him, Chance is the least of our worries."

Chance headed to Tiana's condo to see his son before heading home. That was one person who could change his mood just by being in his presence. Tiana had kept her word by taking care of Chase until Chance took him in. He couldn't wait to spend every day with Chase and watch him grow.

Chance had to do a double take when he saw Naomi emerging from the exit down the hall from Tiana's condo. Instead of parking, Chance circled the block to ensure Naomi was gone. He wanted to know why Naomi was on this side of town when she lived the opposite way. And why did it look like she was sneaking from Tiana's apartment?

He pulled out his phone to call one person he knew could get answers for him. It took a minute before he clicked on the contact to call it. It had been months since he'd last talked to Nina. He hoped she would hear him out.

\*\*\*

Nina was up and indulging her pregnancy cravings while catching up on an episode of *Queen Sugar*. Chips, fruit, and a plate of onion rings were sprawled across the bed. Yasin was out working early this morning. He had left her a note that read:

> Nina,
> *I'm thankful to wake up to you every morning. You carrying my son means so much to me. I have big plans for us. But first, there are some things we gotta discuss. I don't know if you'll want to be with me once I tell you everything, but I'm hoping you do. I love you more and more every day.*
> *Yasin*

She grimaced, wondering what Yasin wanted to tell her. Her heart fluttered and her chest tightened. One thing she knew for sure, she couldn't take any bad news. She'd had enough of that for a lifetime.

The sound of her phone ringing brought her attention back to reality. Her heart felt like it could beat out of her chest when Chance's name flashed across the screen. She stared down at the phone, debating whether she should answer it. Just as she reached to answer, the call ended. Swiping left on his name, Nina took a deep breath as she called Chance back.

"Hello." His voice was deep and velvety on the other end.

"You called me?" she asked nervously, sounding like a little girl.

"We need to talk. Meet me at the mansion in an hour. Be there, Nina."

Nina met the dial tone. She scoffed at Chance's audacity but made up her mind to hear what he had to say.

Quan and Chance sat outside of the mansion, poolside. A big Dutch was passed between the two, filled with the best Kush Atlanta had to offer. Chance was elated that his right-hand man had decided to move to Atlanta. There wasn't anything left in Charlotte that Quan couldn't get right here with his homie. Ever since Nina left, Chance had to admit that he'd been lonely as hell. He had a few women on the side that he entertained, but he knew it would never be anything more. In fact, he even doubted that he'd ever find something as special as his and Nina's bond. It was once in a lifetime. He wanted her back, but he had too much pride.

"Was it worth it, bruh? All that work we put in, the lives we took, the bids we had to do. Is all of this shit worth it?" Quan motioned to the surroundings of the lavish mansion.

Taking a long pull of the pearled cigar, Chance shrugged. He was living the American Dream, the ghetto American Dream. In a span of ten years, Chance had managed to acquire millions of dollars in drug money. On the way to encompassing those millions of dollars, he'd committed unspeakable acts, things that he vowed to never repeat. From project living and robbing niggas to buying mansions and driving lavish cars, Chance had come a long way. A lot of niggas would have lost their minds or turned state if they were in his shoes. Chance remained solid.

"I have everything I ever dreamed of, bro. At first, I hustled to put food on the table and get out of the hood. I been did that. Everything else I done was for Nina, man. I did it so she wouldn't ever have to worry about shit and so our kids would always be straight. I done this for her, yo!" His voice quaked with a mixture of sadness and anger. "I risked my life for this shit. I could be locked down right now doing a life bid! And you know what, bro?"

"What?" Quan questioned as he clung to Chance's words. He knew he needed to get this off his chest.

"For all the shit I ever did in my life, I'd gladly accept the consequences if that meant Nina could live a happy life, no worries," Chance stated genuinely. "That's my world."

Quan tucked his bottom lip between his teeth and lifted the blunt in acknowledgement. He believed every word Chance said. "On some real shit, bro, I never loved anyone like you love Nina. I got someone I care for, but we ain't at that point yet." He hit the blunt and inhaled. "But if we were, I wouldn't let no petty shit keep us apart. And if that meant knocking a couple niggas off, then so be it. You already know how I'm coming."

The men didn't hear Nina creeping on the grass behind them. She'd overheard the last part of their conversation. A part of her wished that she could right everything that went wrong with Chance. But how could she do that when she was carrying another man's child?

"Y'all niggas really slipping. What if I was your enemy?"

Quan stood up and enveloped Nina in a hug. Her protruding belly poked him, and he chuckled at the sight. "Damn, sis, you pregnant as hell. You look good. though."

"I feel like a whale," Nina whined as she sat down in the patio chair. She glared at Chance, who stared into the yard aimlessly, puffing the blunt.

"Hello to you too, Chance." Nina took it upon herself to speak first. As stubborn as they both could be, she decided to be the bigger person. She was grateful for Quan's presence and knew he would act as a mediator.

Chance passed the blunt to Quan and turned to face Nina. He admired her beauty, but his eyes found their way to Nina's pregnant belly.

"You don't have to stare at my stomach. I don't need you throwing the shit in my face any more than you already have," Nina snapped, getting heated, partly due to her raging pregnancy hormones.

"I didn't tell you to fuck the nigga," Chance shot back nonchalantly. He could tell that comment hurt Nina's feelings, but it had slipped out. "You know you really ain't been moving like the Nina I know? Jumping from one nigga to the next."

Nina waved his statement away. She wouldn't sit here and let Chance reduce her to the level of the hoes he fucked with. "I don't know what you're suggesting, but you should stop while you're ahead," Nina warned. "Maybe I wouldn't have been fucking Yasin if you hadn't come up with that *stupid*-ass plan to fake your death. And you know what? The shit was all for nothing because I could have died, and you still couldn't kill Nino! Yasin had to do it!" Nina yelled. "I thought I lost you! Forever! I was good, Chance! I was coping with everything. Why did you have to show back up in my life after all the suffering, just to let me down again?" Nina dropped her head and wiped her streaming tears. "You should have let me be."

"Because after everything, all the bullshit, I still wanted you! You betrayed me, Nina. Don't you get it?" Chance exclaimed, feeling no sympathy for Nina's tears. He had bottled up his feelings for months in order to protect Nina's. He wanted her to know that he suffered as much as she had. "Not even a month after me faking my death, you on to the next nigga dick. I know I made my mistakes, but I never cheated on you. You ain't have to do me like that."

Quan shook his head, understanding both perspectives, but he didn't get between them. This was some shit they needed to get off their chest.

"What was I supposed to do?"

"You were supposed to wait!" Chance pointed his finger in Nina's face. "You were supposed to hold me down."

"I never wanted shit to play out like this, Chance! I never wanted you to get shot. I never wanted to lose our baby. I never wanted to meet Yasin and fall for him! I swear I didn't! But I did. And I can't take it back." Indecision pulled Nina back and forth like a seesaw. If she could change the hands of time and rearrange the events that played out, she would. "But I miss you so much," Nina admitted.

Chance's eyes burned with emotion. "I'm lost out here without you, ma. I need you, Nina." He wrapped his arms around Nina's waist. "Fuck that nigga. Don't go back. You can stay here with me, a'ight?"

Chance planted soft kisses all over Nina's face, breaking down her resolve. She placed one hand on Chance's cheek and pecked his lips. In that moment, everything else was nonexistent. She was home. That was, until Nina felt a warm liquid trickling down her leg.

Everything happened so fast. Right before his eyes, Nina was doubling over in pain. Chance wished there was something he could do to alleviate her pain, but the only assistance he could offer was to rush her to the hospital. It was just his luck that the baby wanted to come at that moment, a moment when Nina and Chance were finally facing their built-up issues.

"*Quannnn*!" Nina hissed through clenched teeth. Beads of sweat ran down her forehead, and she clenched the back of the headrest tightly. "If you don't speed this fucking car up, I'm going to kick your ass!" Nobody had prepared her for the powerful contractions that invaded her midsection. Although Nina never imagined childbirth to be an easy task, she never fathomed this extent of excruciating pain. Another contraction ripped through body, and she clenched her legs together. "Chance, please," Nina whimpered. "It feels like he's about to come."

"*Shhhh*." Chance stroked Nina's curly hair, attempting to soothe her as best as he could. "I'm right here with you. Don't worry. I got you."

*** 

Yasin cruised through the streets of Atlanta, smoking a blunt and enjoying his own thoughts. He cherished this because he didn't usually get much time for himself. He thought back to the time before all the money, back when he was growing up in the grimy streets of New York, a place that took more than it gave. Yasin, however, was grateful for the lessons he'd learned in those treacherous streets.

Growing up, Yasin never had anything. His father, Yoda, was murdered when Yasin was eight years old. Being of Nigerian descent, Yoda was heavily involved with a crime organization in Nigeria. He dealt anything that the mafia supplied him with—guns, drugs, and sometimes even people. Yoda's come up in New York was inevitable, and niggas hated that fact. Envy was deadlier than any man; Yoda started realizing that after niggas that he had fed started challenging his authority. Yoda didn't know who he could trust, and that ultimately led to his murder.

Marissa, Yasin's mother, was a Trinidadian beauty who was crazy in love with Yoda. When she discovered the only man she ever loved murdered in cold blood, she succumbed to the same lifestyle that took Yoda. Marissa turned to drugs, neglecting her only child's well-being. In return, Yasin had to raise himself and put food on the table for both him and his mom. Despite his mother's crack addiction, Yasin loved his mother with everything in him. He physically defended his mother's name on multiple occasions because even as a crack addict, no one could deny Marissa's beauty.

As he got older, Yasin started to understand what had happened to his father. Hustling wasn't Yasin's occupation, unlike every other young nigga in his hood. At the age of seventeen, Yasin was given a job that would change his life forever. Rodrigo Galliano, a member of the Italian mafia, hired Yasin to murder his known enemy. Rodrigo encountered Yasin on a few occasions when he would treat Marissa to dinner at an upscale restaurant in Manhattan. Just from observation, he liked the way Yasin moved. He moved with stealth and had the stature of a professional football player. Rodrigo hired a couple of his men to follow Yasin around his neighborhood. The rest was history. Rodrigo and Yasin developed a mutual relationship: Yasin eliminated Rodrigo's problems, and Rodrigo made Yasin a rich man.

Yasin hadn't planned on becoming a hitman, but he excelled at the job. He never planned on stopping, until karma caught up with him. After returning from a trip to Italy, Yasin found his mother with her throat slit in her apartment. It broke him. Marissa's death triggered something sinister in Yasin. In his mind, Marissa never would have died if his father was alive. Yasin would have never had to become a hitman for Rodrigo if Yoda had survived. Yasin became fixated on finding his father's murderer, vowing to avenge his father.

Feeling indebted to Yasin, Rodrigo made it his business to find Yoda's killer, and he did just that. It didn't take long, with Rodrigo's connections, to trace Yoda's murder back to Nino. Rodrigo delivered the news and a three-million-dollar check to Yasin for his years of loyalty.

Yasin shook his head as the memories, good and bad, flashed through his head. His heart ached as Marissa's distinct smile appeared in his mind. Loving Nina was the closest thing to the love Yasin had for his mother. Nina possessed the same alluring innocence as Marissa. It was easy to understand why men fell captive to Nina's essence, just like Marissa. Yasin regretted the role he played in all the suffering Nina had endured. She deserved the truth, and Yasin was finally ready to give Nina the full story. He just hoped she wouldn't look at him differently.

The nurse informed Nina that she was already four centimeters dilated. There was nothing more to do but wait for baby Nasim to make his grand entrance. Quan and Chance sat in the room with her, even though Quan claimed he would pass out if he watched her give birth. It was only then that Nina realized Yasin was missing.

"I have to call Yasin."

Chance rolled his eyes at the mention of Yasin, but he knew Nina would be asking for him sooner or later. "I'm not leaving you here by yourself. So, until he gets here, I'll be here." He wanted to see the look on Yasin's face when he walked in and saw him at Nina's side.

Nina nodded as she dialed Yasin's number. "It's time," she said into the phone.

"What?" he exclaimed. "Send your location. I'm on my way right now. What happened? You good?"

Taking a deep breath, Nina prepared herself for his response. "Chance brought me."

"Why the fuck that nigga bring you? Nah, don't even worry about that. Just send your location," Yasin said before disconnecting the call.

Walking calmly through the hospital hallways, Yasin made his way to the maternity ward. He coached himself on maintaining his composure when he arrived. His love for Nina was the only reason Chance remained breathing. He knew that Chance would always hold a spot in Nina's heart, but that didn't intimidate him. His confidence in his and Nina's relationship left him with no worries.

Slowly pushing the door open to room 2612, Yasin saw Nina sitting in the middle of the room, bouncing on a huge ball, breathing in and out rhythmically. The sight amused him. "Ain't you supposed to be in the bed?" He kissed Nina's lips softly. "How you feel?"

"I'm trying to stay strong and not get the epidural." Nina inhaled deeply as her midwife massaged her lower back.

Yasin nodded, and his attention turned to Chance and Quan sitting on the other side of the room. A slight scowl appeared across his handsome face. Taking the high road, Yasin held out his hand for Chance to shake. His hand lingered in the air for a few seconds with no returning gesture from Chance. Yasin pulled his hand back and brushed his nose lightly with his thumb.

"If it's like that, then y'all niggas can bounce. Ya presence ain't needed here any longer," he spat.

Nina's midwife lifted her head with wide eyes. It wasn't the first time she'd seen drama unfold in a delivery room. Amber, the brunette, assumed Chance to be the father, but she could tell she was wrong when Yasin walked in. She understood why a pretty girl like Nina was stuck between two men. They were both fine as hell. *Must be nice,* Amber thought.

Quan stood up and walked over to Nina. "Sis, I love you too much to bring any bad vibes right now.

You already know how I get down." He kissed her forehead before giving Yasin a menacing stare. "So, I'ma bounce. I'll check up on you later." Yasin had tainted the energy as soon as he stepped into the room. Quan recognized the difference, and it made him uneasy.

"Thank you." Nina smiled as she turned her attention to the two men she loved. "Can you excuse us, Amber? If I need you, I'll ring you." Nina never stopped bouncing on the ball. She was determined to deliver her son naturally. After being shot, she knew she could handle childbirth.

"I don't want any problems in here," Nina said through gritted teeth once the door closed behind Amber. "I'm so tired of this shit. I have to choose. I understand that now." Nina's heart churned as she glanced between her two lovers. She was torn.

"Chance." Nina groaned as a contraction hit her. "You're my best friend. I wouldn't be half the woman I am today without you. I love you so much. That's something that will never change."

Chance smiled, knowing that Nina's heart belonged to him. "I feel the same way. We got too much history."

Yasin rolled his eyes and snorted. He adjusted the jacket to his suit and dropped his head.

"But that's exactly what it is, Chance. History." A tear rolled down Nina's face. "I love you, but I'm not in love with you anymore." As the words left Nina's mouth, a part of her heart broke. She felt guilty for being in love with Yasin after all Chance had done for her. He had saved her from her abusive dad when she was just a teenager and protected her with his life. He provided for her and catered to her, but his decisions led to their downfall.

The look on Chance's face said it all. He was hurt. For the last couple of months, he'd been hanging on to the idea that he hadn't completely lost Nina. "She will come around," he would tell Quan. There was no way she would throw away all the years they had together over a couple of hiccups down the line. But he was wrong. Chance's decision to fake his death ultimately led Nina into Yasin's arms. It would be a mistake he would regret for the rest of his life.

"I think you're making a mistake, but it's your life." Chance grabbed his keys off the table next to the bed. "I can't live it for you. I'm always gon' be here for you no matter what. I love you enough to let you go."

Nina dropped her head so Chance couldn't see her face. Those words were almost enough to make her regret her decision. But her mind was already made up. She wanted to be with Yasin. In her mind, the crazy-ass events that she had been through in the last year had happened just to bring her to Yasin. It was as if the universe had led them to each other.

"We can be friends."

"Yo, Nina, fuck all of that respectfully. I can't be your friend." Chance waved his hand in dismissal. "Like I said, I'll never turn my back on you. Call me when this nigga fucks up, because trust me, he will." Chance spoke out of bitterness. His pride was bruised. The only woman he ever loved was in love with another man. "I wish you the best." With that, Chance exited the room.

Yasin placed his index finger under Nina's chin and lifted her head. "I got you, Nina. You, me, and Nasim."

Amber knocked lightly on the door to the room before entering, followed by the head OBGYN. "Okay, Nina, we think it's about that time. I'm going to check you and see how much you've dilated."

Helping Nina to her feet, Yasin lifted her body and placed her on the bed. He stood by her side as Amber placed her hand inside Nina. "That doesn't hurt?" he whispered to her.

"A little uncomfortable, but nothing I can't handle." Nina chuckled softly.

Amber removed the gloves from her hands and beamed. "It's time." She clapped her hands.


"You need to go ahead and take Chase to Chance. We got moves to be made," Naomi snapped as she strapped up her stiletto heels.

Tiana entered the living room, carrying Chase in one arm and his baby bag in the other. "Girl, I'm so damn tired of this crying-ass little boy." She wiped the sleep from her eyes. Dark circles rested under her eyes, and her weave was pulled into a messy ponytail. Dried baby spit-up stained her clothing. "I think you're right. We can't get Chance and Yasin if I'm carrying around a baby all day."

"So, you're sure this woman said she has the information that'll bring Yasin and Chance down? I'm not sure if we can trust this bitch," Tiana asked as she checked the time. Payback was what she wanted, but Tiana didn't trust Naomi's plan. She didn't know if she wanted Chance behind bars. Her son needed a stable home, and she couldn't provide that.

"Bitch, I'm sure. She says she works with the Feds. We ain't got to give her much information. Just enough to get us paid." Naomi's devious mind schemed. She wanted payback on Yasin and Chance, and she wouldn't stop until she got it.


Nina was so in love as she lay with her baby boy on her chest. The feeling she had holding Nasim, with his heart beating against her chest, was the most unexplainable thing ever. She instantly fell in love. She knew she would do anything in her power and beyond to protect his little soul. Nasim had slick black hair like Yasin's and a rich brown complexion like Nina's. However, it wasn't hard to tell that he was his mother's twin. They had created an angel.

Yasin looked at the sight before him in amazement. Never had he imagined being a parent, but this was his chance to finish what his father couldn't.

"Nina, I have to talk to you."

Nina peered at him reluctantly. "Look, Yasin, whatever happened before, I just want to move on. I don't care about any of it." She stopped him before he could say something that made her regret her decision to choose him. Nothing good ever followed those words, and she didn't have the capacity to receive any bad news.

"You deserve to know everything, ma. If I'm the one you really want to be with, you need to know."

Nina sighed as she rubbed her baby boy's head softly, shaping it. "Okay. But not today, all right?" She didn't want to ruin this precious moment.

# Chapter Six

*6 months later . . .*

Chance leaned off the railing of the yacht, smoking a Cuban cigar, the finest Miami had to offer. His dark Tom Ford shades covered his eyes. A white silk Gucci button-down shirt graced his smooth chocolate skin. The sun was shining bright on the clear blue ocean, and Chance was enjoying the scenery. Women in bathing suits pranced around the huge boat, dancing, drinking, and smoking. The women came in all shapes, sizes, and ethnicities. There was a flavor for every desire: the African supermodels, black and Latina video vixens, and high-class executives. Everyone on the boat kicked back, vibing, while Chance was in his own world.

The yacht belonged to Chance's newfound business partner, Nikko. After ending things with Nina, Chance had decided that Atlanta was a place he could never live again. Life didn't feel the same without Nina there. Without her in his life, he felt incomplete. The only solution he could think of for that was to start over somewhere fresh, and as a rich young man, what better place to start over than Miami? He put Atlanta in his rearview mirror along with Nina.

"You want some company?" a curvaceous brown beauty asked sweetly.

Chance gave the girl a once over. Her thick thighs and perky breasts immediately caught his attention. Unlike some of the chicks he'd run into in Miami, who were extremely thick but average in the face, the woman in front of him was naturally attractive. She stood an average height, about five feet five inches if Chance had to guess, and she wore a Burberry bathing suit with a sheer white mini skirt tied around her waist. One dimple appeared in her left cheek. The relations he'd had with women in Miami were strictly sexual. Chance wasn't looking for love or commitment. Feelings were something of his past, and he kind of hated it for the next woman who fell for him. She would ask him for something that he couldn't provide to her—his heart.

"I'll take your company any day, gorgeous." Chance smiled slightly, licking his lips. "What's your name?"

"I'm Yasmine. And you're Chance, right?" She licked her tongue out lightly, rolling it across her teeth, and smiled. This was Yasmine's second time seeing Chance, and she'd made it her business to find out who was the new baller in town. It wasn't hard to tell that Chance had a long bankroll. He wasn't flashy, but Yasmine could always spot a wealthy person. Not to say she was a gold digger, but in Miami, it was best to know how to decipher the posers from the real. Her best friend, Maiya, was Nikko's current girlfriend. In return, Yasmine enjoyed all the lavish festivities Nikko hosted.

"Right. Nice to meet you, Yasmine." Chance removed his shades to get a better look at Yasmine. She obviously wasn't lacking in physical appearance. Yet, Chance bagged enough "bad bitches" in his lifetime. Those things didn't impress him. He needed a woman who could stimulate his mind and grind alongside him. He needed a woman who could motivate him all while staying ten toes down with whatever endeavors she had going on in her own life. He needed a solid woman. He needed a woman like . . . Nina. Chance shook his head as his thoughts drifted to Nina. It seemed as if he wasn't allowing himself to open up to another woman because he kept comparing them all to Nina.

"You good?" Yasmine asked as she noticed a faraway look in Chance's eyes. "Who hurt you?" she asked softly. That was a look she was all too familiar with. A faraway sadness beyond the depth of the eyes. Anyone who'd been a part of the heartbreak club could relate to it.

Chance chuckled at Yasmine's concern. "That's a story for another day, shorty. What's up with you?" He licked his lips, pushing Nina to the back of his mind and giving Yasmine his undivided attention.

"I want to get to know you." Yasmine inched closer to Chance. "I've been watching you. Not on no stalker shit." Yasmine laughed, trying to find the right words. Chance made her nervous for some reason. Maybe it was the intense way his dark eyes stared down at her. "I like how you move. But, if you have someone you're stuck on, I don't want any part of you. Hurt people, hurt people. So, when you think you're ready, ask Nikko to get you in touch with me." Yasmine winked at Chance and walked away. She was sure she would be getting a call from Chance soon.

Shaking his head, Chance threw his Cuban cigar into the ocean and went to find Nikko. His connections to Nikko came through Quan, Nikko's cousin. Nikko was plugged in with the Puerto Rican mafia, run by the infamous Don Carlos. Nikko and his camp earned a million dollars on an easy day. They were at the top of the food chain, and Chance wanted a piece of the pie. Although Chance's pockets were laced, without Nina he decided to leverage his most profitable skill: moving weight.

\*\*\*

Nina sat at the vanity and applied her makeup. Today marked Nina and Yasin's official six-month anniversary. They were celebrating by vacationing at Yasin's second property in Miami. Nasim was back in Atlanta with Yasin's grandmother, Diane. This weekend was all about Yasin showering Nina with his appreciation. The couple had a romantic candlelit dinner earlier. Now, their next stop was at a party being hosted by one of Yasin's associates at King of Diamonds.

This would make the first night Nina had really stepped out after giving birth to her son. She would use this as an opportunity to get sexy and show out for her man. Bringing out a recent purchase of an all-white bodysuit, Nina knew her new thickness would accentuate the outfit. Nasim had blessed Nina with wider hips and thicker thighs, plus her booty got bigger. Her natural curls were sewn under her $400 twenty-two-inch Brazilian curly bundles. Becoming a mother proved to be a full-time job that rarely left her with much free time. Protective styles such as weaves, wigs, and braids became Nina's best friend.

Adding the finishing touches to her makeup, Nina slipped into the snug bodysuit. Nina smiled at her hourglass figure in the mirror, turning around to get a view of her ass from the back. She wasn't as thick as the video vixens, but she had just enough of everything for any man to lust over.

In a world where women laid on doctors' tables, enduring hours of pain to achieve the perfect body, Nina thanked God for her natural curves.

"If you aren't the most beautiful woman I've ever seen, I don't know who is." Yasin's voice called out behind Nina. He stood in the doorway with a bouquet full of red and white roses. "For my lovely lady."

"Thank you, baby." Nina kissed Yasin's lips softly. She pulled back so she could admire her man. His hair was freshly lined up, even down to the mustache above his top lip. "You ready?" Nina locked her arms with Yasin as they headed out of the home.

Bottles and women flowed freely throughout the club. Nikko sat to the left of Chance with his girlfriend, Maiya, and their entourage in the VIP section. They overlooked the entire club from their position. The liquor in Chance's system had him looking at Yasmine with lustful eyes.

"You feeling her, my nigga?" Nikko asked, picking up on the flirtatious vibes between Chance and Yasmine.

"She straight," Chance answered modestly, never taking his eyes off Yasmine.

Nikko nodded as he patted Chance's back. "She's a good look, yo. I wouldn't let any regular female around my chick. They know how to compliment a nigga, ya feel me?" Nikko only invited a certain caliber of woman into his bed. He only fucked with women who had something to lose. Someone with nothing to lose would risk sinking a ship quicker than someone who had a lot to lose. Nikko didn't need any sinking ships around him.

Chance laughed lightly as his attention now shifted to a crowd forming around the entrance of the club. He figured it was probably another rapper coming in. However, he recognized two of the last faces he wanted to run into. Yasin and Nina. Nina looked a little different in appearance. Her once slim figure had filled out in her midsection. Her wide hips were accented by her small waist and set of perky breasts. Chance assumed the extra weight came from childbirth and frankly, it looked good on her. The couple headed to the VIP section, and Chance shook his head at his luck. He still couldn't stand the fact that Nina was happy with Yasin.

"Now, she bad," Nikko commented lightly as Yasin and Nina headed in the opposite direction of the VIP section.

Taking a shot to the head, Chance diverted his attention back to Yasmine. "What you on?"

Nina sat back and sipped her glass of Remy Martin. The music in the club blared as strippers danced on stage, making their money. Of course, Yasin had their own private booth in the VIP section. Nina expected no less out of him. Her man had very lavish taste. After months of shopping on Yasin's dime, she had learned that he enjoyed flashy luxuries. She had no problem with it, though. His money was completely legit, so Nina didn't spend her days looking over her shoulders for cops or enemies. That was a big difference between Yasin and Chance. Although Chance never lacked in providing for Nina, he couldn't protect her like she needed. The one time he thought he was protecting her, he had only pushed her further away. Sometimes she asked herself where she would be now if Chance had never faked his death almost two years ago. Maybe their circumstances would be different.

"You enjoying yourself, beautiful?" Yasin asked as he came and took a seat beside Nina. "I have some people I want you to meet." He nodded for her to follow him. They headed for another VIP booth across the club.

"What's good, fam?" Yasin dapped up a handsome, dark-skinned brother. Like Yasin, he had a commanding presence. His jewelry was minimal, but he rocked an exclusive Presidential Rolex. The garments he wore on his body were of high fashion. There was a gold wedding band on his left hand.

*He's a boss*, Nina noted.

"Fam, this is my lady, Nina. Nina, this is my associate, Cassidy. He's from New York."

"Nice to meet you." She greeted him sweetly as she held out her hand for Cassidy to shake.

"Likewise." He gave Nina a quick smile and kissed her hand. "She's beautiful." The gesture wasn't flirtatious at all. Cassidy appeared to be very serious. All the women flocking around did not catch his attention. She inferred that had something to do with the ring on his hand.

Finally, a gorgeous, light- skinned female pranced over to Cassidy and kissed his lips. She had long, curly tresses and the kind of body that women paid thousands of dollars for, but it was homegrown. Her cheekbones were high, and her mouth was full and pouty. Her most striking feature was her hazel, almond-shaped eyes. Nina was secure enough in her own self-confidence to compliment another woman's beauty. This woman defined a bad bitch.

"This is my wife, Miami. Miami, you remember my cousin Yasin. This is his lady, Nina. Why don't you take Nina to get a drink while Yasin and I chop it up for a while?"

Miami nodded and diverted her attention to Nina. She gave Nina a once over and smiled. "I like your shoes," she commented. "Let's go to the bar."

Nina gave Yasin a kiss before following Miami to the bar. "What's the point of these niggas bringing us out if they're just going to talk business all night?" she asked once they reached the bar.

"Four shots of Hennessy, please," Miami called out to the bartender.

"Girl, I learned long ago not to question them when it came to celebrations like this. It's all a front for major boss moves that they have to make. I'm guessing this is the first time Yasin brought you around some of his business partners. Shit, I've never even met any girl of Yasin's. He's really digging you. But you're beautiful as hell, so I see why."

Nina smiled. "Thanks, girl. So are you. And yeah, this is the first time. I usually prefer to stay out of the business aspect. I had to learn that the hard way."

"Facts, honey. I'd rather hold home down while Cassidy takes care of all the business." Miami toasted her shot glass against Nina's as they threw back their shots.

"Exactly." Nina liked Miami's vibe. She wasn't on any envious behavior like many of the females she'd encountered recently. Her man had money, too, so there was no room for hate. Nina didn't usually befriend strangers, but something told her she and Miami would be good friends.

"How long are y'all in town?" Nina asked.

"For the weekend. Then I'm headed back up top, and Cassidy is going to Puerto Rico. If all goes well after tonight, Yasin will be one of his partners."

"And you trust the men in Puerto Rico they're working with?" Nina asked warily. She had been a victim to the street's atrocities firsthand, and she'd be damned if she let Yasin risk their family's safety by doing business with snakes.

Miami looked at Nina with seriousness in her eyes and shook her head slowly. "I don't trust anyone but my husband and sister. Trust is earned. It's a lot you're going to notice if Yasin really involves himself with this team. Keep your eyes open, honey, because everyone's intentions aren't pure." She looked into Nina's eyes. It was as if she were trying to warn her of something. "I'm Cassidy's third eye in a sense. Whenever he's lacking, I'm right there to make sure everything is copacetic. Us women have to protect our men too."

Nina took heed of Miami's words. "Touché!" By this time, the alcohol had her feeling lovely. This was the first time she had consumed alcohol since she had Nasim. Nina had to remind herself that she was supposed to let down her hair a little this weekend and enjoy herself. A good time was well overdue for Nina. "Let's go party, girl. I'm baby free for the weekend, and I wanna turn up. We'll finish this business talk later." Nina slid Miami two shots and quickly threw back the two in front of her.

Grabbing her by the hand, Nina gently pushed her way through the thick crowd on the dance floor. They finally found an open spot that was in clear view of the VIP section where their men were seated. "Bodak Yellow," Cardi B's record-breaking hit, blared throughout the club. The song instantly turned the whole club up.

"Say, li'l bitch, you can't fuck with me if you wanted to!" Miami and Nina rapped out loud as they swayed their bodies to the beat. This was the type of song that every bad, boss bitch felt on a spiritual level. It unleashed every woman's inner ratchetness in a good way.

Nina dipped her body low and brought it back up seductively. Miami and Nina laughed as they enjoyed themselves. Song after song, they danced until they were out of breath. Niggas tried spit their game to Nina and Miami to no avail. They weren't interested in anything the men had to offer. After all, they had two of the richest men in the club already.

Nina told Miami she needed a little bit of air, so they decided to go back to the bar. Switching the vibe of the club completely, the DJ played "Get Money" by Junior Mafia. Nina bobbed her head to the beat, taking a seat at the bar.

"You want another shot?" Miami asked. Nina nodded. "Yo, let me get two shots of Henny," she demanded in her heavy Brooklyn accent.

They downed the shots as soon as they were placed in front of them. The shot burned as it traveled down her throat. Her skin warmed as the shot seemed to charge her body up. She could hear every crescendo in the beat of the music playing throughout the club. When alcohol made her feel like this, she knew she'd reached her limit. That was one thing her father, Nino, did teach. Too many people got caught slipping by being sloppy drunk. "Always stay on your p's and q's. Don't give them an advantage," he would always say.

Lil Kim's sultry voice permeated throughout the club, and Nina rapped along with her word for word. Miami nodded for her to follow her back to the VIP section. They had to have been on the dance floor for about forty-five minutes.

"Nina, I really don't fuck with females on a regular basis, but I dig your vibe. I can tell you aren't on any envious shit. It's only right that we grow to be friends, with our husbands working together."

"Definitely. I could say the same about you. I'm big on energy, and I get no bad vibes from you. Real recognize real," Nina stated. "And Yasin and I aren't married, by the way."

"What are y'all waiting on?" Miami asked as they climbed the stairs.

That question caught Nina a little off guard. She looked at her for a second as she thought of the best explanation. "The right time," Nina answered simply.

"I feel that."

The ladies finally made it to the booth where
Yasin, Cassidy, and a light brown dude with wild,
curly hair were seated.

Yasin held out his hand for Nina to take as he
gently pulled her next to him in the booth. His
mannerisms had been chivalrous since day one,
and he always treated Nina like a queen, even
down to his small actions. "I see you're having fun,"
he whispered in her ear, kissing her neck softly.
She whispered back sweet talk about what she was
going to do to him once they got back home.

"There's one last person I need to introduce everyone to, then this circle will be complete." The
curly-haired man spoke. "I'm Nikko." He looked at
Nina, and she assumed Miami already knew him.
His eyes danced with a wild look, much like his
untamed hair. She figured he was mixed, because
he had a slight Spanish accent and a thuggish air
about him. "He's going to be running my operation here in Miami. My cousin spoke so highly
of him that I had to meet him. It was history after that." Nikko nodded his head to a burly man
standing beside their booth. He must have been
the bodyguard. Nina was curious to see who the final addition to this power circle was.

Nina squinted her eyes and peered in the
bodyguard's direction. Chance approached the bodyguard, and her heart dropped to her stomach. Nina
gasped under her breath. She turned to Yasin, but

he didn't appear to be surprised at all. *Cassidy must have told him when Miami and I were dancing*, she thought.

"Cassidy. Glad to see you again, bro." Chance shook Cassidy's hand. "Miami." He nodded to her.

"No doubt. I want you to meet my nigga Yasin and his girl Nina. Have a seat," Cassidy urged, sliding over in the booth to make room. Ironically, the only open space in the booth was beside Nina.

Chance snorted lightly, thumbing his nostril while he glared at Nina momentarily. He slid into the booth and extended both arms across the top of the couch. "We know each other."

Everybody's eyes lit up with surprise. Miami's eyes met Nina's, and she just shook her head.

"How?" Nikko asked out of curiosity.

Nina snuggled as close to Yasin as space permitted her to be. She fought against the urge to make eye contact with Chance. He looked even better than the last time she had seen him. He'd put on a few pounds and had new artwork inked onto his forearms. Nina thought she was completely over him, until this moment. Would she ever be rid of her feelings for Chance?

"It's a long story," Yasin answered curtly.

"A story for another time then." Cassidy cut his eyes to Miami. She knew they were all dying to know our connection, but that was a complicated story that would have to wait for tomorrow, or never. "Fact of the matter is, we're all here to get money. I don't give a fuck about what happened in the past. Leave it there. Nothing stops the money flow. I'm sure we can all agree on that part."

By this time, Nina had noticed Cassidy asserted himself as the leader of this group. It wasn't as if he meant to take the lead. She could tell it came naturally to him. Miami gazed at her man in admiration. One day, when the time was right, Nina hoped God allowed her to look at the man she loved like that every day.

"Yasin, Nikko, I need you to come outside with me real quick." Cassidy stood up and exited the booth. "We'll be right back, ladies."

Nina rolled her eyes at the fact of being left in Chance's presence. She slid as far away from him as possible.

"I'm not gon' bite you, Nina, so you can calm all that extra shit down," Chance said. He sat back and allowed his eyes to linger over Nina. Something about her energy was off. "You look good though, shorty. Real happy."

Miami sipped her champagne glass as she looked from Chance to Nina.

"I am happy," Nina snapped.

Chance chuckled lightly. "You sure about that?" His question was interrupted as a thick, video vixen—looking chick walked up to the booth.

"I'm leaving with you, right?" she asked seductively. Chance nodded. "I'll be waiting with Maiya." The girl looked at Nina, rolled her eyes, then kissed Chance's lips. He smirked as she walked away, exaggerating the sway of her hips.

"She's not your type," Nina replied bluntly. "Excuse me, Miami."

Miami laughed. "Well, she doesn't like you very much."

"Nah." Chance shook his head with a smirk. "She loves me.

# Chapter Seven

*Two Years Later*

Nina tapped the tip of her YSL heel against the floor. She glanced at her phone and shook her head in disappointment. The dress she wore began to feel a size too small as her lungs contracted. She had spent a month in the gym to ensure she would fit into the dress for this occasion. Nina even went so far as to hire a babysitter for Nasim for the night. Yasin had planned a date for her and gave her six weeks to prepare for it. The date was meant to make up for time he'd been away from home. His excuse was that business had been hectic lately after he got rid of one of his oldest employees for skimming.

"Where are you at?" Nina yelled into her phone when she got Yasin's voicemail once again. She took a seat on the steps in the foyer and scoffed. Her intuition told her that there was something, or rather someone, occupying his time. Nina thought there was another woman, but she had no proof. She promised herself to never be that woman, one complacent with infidelity. Until her theory was confirmed, Nina would play her part.

Twenty minutes later, Yasin pulled into the driveway of their home. Loud music and the blaring of the car horn announced his presence. Nina kissed her teeth and stood. *Nigga can't even come in to greet me,* she thought as she exited the house and locked the door behind her. Nina halted in her steps when she reached the last step, giving Yasin the opportunity to open the car door for her.

"Let's go, Nina! We already late!" Yasin barked, rolling the window down.

"Asshole," Nina muttered under her breath as she opened the car door and climbed into the passenger seat. "We're late because of you. The least you could do is open the door for me," Nina snapped, buckling her seatbelt.

Yasin ignored Nina and turned up the music. He didn't want to hear any of Nina's complaining. It seemed to be all she did, complaining and fussing. Her behavior annoyed Yasin.

Nina reached for the radio and turned it off. "I know you heard me!" she exclaimed.

"Don't start your shit!" Yasin's voice boomed, and he slammed on the brakes, causing Nina's body to jerk forward. Her forehead hit the dashboard, and she recoiled instantly, gripping her head. Small beads of blood dripped from the small gash above her eyebrow.

"Look what you made me do! I try to do something nice for you, but nah! Can't please your ass," Yasin huffed as he resumed driving. "Clean yourself up. It cost me too much for these tickets to this show. We ain't missing it." He opened the armrest and tossed a few napkins Nina's way.

Sniffling her tears away, Nina snatched the napkins and wiped her forehead. Yasin's true colors were beginning to show, and Nina didn't like the picture it portrayed. She knew she had to find her way out before things got worse between her and Yasin.

A few weeks later, Nina sat on the toilet as Nasim played with his cars in the bath. Nasim, who was approaching three years old, ran his cars across the top of the bath water with not a care in the world. Nina smiled lightly as she thought of how innocent he was in this cruel world. She never wanted him to lose that. Nasim was too young to be aware of the struggles his parents were going through.

Yasin had battled a case on tax evasion and fraud against the federal government. After they failed miserably at charging him with drug trafficking a year ago, the assholes went for the next best thing. They had a hard-on for Yasin. Yasin went to extreme extents to keep the Feds off his trail. Every week, he had their home swept for surveillance devices. Before they were able to pull into their driveway, Yasin circled the block three times.

Nina twirled the engagement ring around her finger as she thought of how distant Yasin had become in the last few months. Nina wanted to blame the distance on the stress from the case, but a part of her felt like there was another woman. Call it a woman's intuition. When she approached Yasin with her accusations, he denied it vehemently. "I got enough on my plate with this case as is. I don't have time to entertain another bitch," were Yasin's exact words. Yet, Nina couldn't shake the feeling. She became more suspicious when Yasin said their wedding would be postponed for another year. His reasoning for that was the Feds would come after Nina too if she were his wife, and that he was getting his ducks in place just in case he had to serve some time.

"Mommy, you sad?" Nasim was looking at Nina curiously. "'Cause Dada gone?"

Nina took a deep breath and put on her best poker face. She never wanted to expose Nasim to any of their problems, but he was very intelligent and attentive. He noticed Yasin was spending less time around the mansion and more time gone. Before the trial, Yasin would spend every free minute he had with Nasim, teaching him things about life like a father should. Nina was sure Nasim noticed his father's absence.

"No, baby, I'm not sad." Nina held back her tears.

"Why I no see Daddy? I wrong?" Nasim continued, letting his mother know he was well aware of the changes within their household.

This time, Nina couldn't stop the tears. She leaned over the tub and brought Nasim's face into her chest. "Of course not, baby. Your daddy loves you very much." She rubbed his wet back slowly.

Nasim nodded. "Does Dada love you?"

Those words broke Nina's heart. Gripping her chest, Nina turned away from him as a small sob escaped her lips. She didn't think Nasim would notice Yasin being gone more than normal lately, but the little boy had a sharp mind. Even at three, Nasim was calculating and observant.

Those qualities reminded Nina so much of Chance. It had been months since Chance crossed Nina's mind, and even longer since she had seen him. She often wondered how life was treating him, if he missed her at all, or if he'd moved on with a new woman. Lately, Nina had been regretting all the decisions she'd made in the past.

Things between her and Yasin had been almost perfect for a long time, but he wasn't acting like the man she knew and loved in these last few months. She worried that the man she knew wasn't the real Yasin, and his true colors were showing.

"Daddy will always love me. It's just that some bad men are trying to take your dad away from us, and he's focusing all his attention on doing whatever he can to stay with us," Nina said unconvincingly. "Once all this blows over, our family will be back to normal. Okay, man?" Nina smiled lightly as she kissed Nasim's forehead. "Come on, let's get you out and ready for bed."

After putting Nasim to sleep, Nina took a shower of her own and waited in bed for Yasin to arrive. His new routine consisted of him coming home late and drunk. Nina prayed the trial would be over soon because she didn't know or like this new Yasin. It was as if she were sleeping beside a stranger every night. They hadn't had sex in almost two weeks, which was unusual for them. Normally, you couldn't pay Yasin to keep his hands of Nina. Now, he barely touched her, let alone conversed with her. The only explanation for his weird behavior was another woman. Nina was going to get to the bottom of it because she refused to have her heart broken again.

When Yasin finally entered their bedroom, it was well after midnight. Nina could smell the alcohol on him from the door. Sitting up on their California king-sized bed, Nina was the first to break the silence. "You know your son asked if you still loved him tonight." Yasin sat on the edge of the bed and removed his Tom Ford loafers. "Then he asked if you loved me." Nina's voice cracked.

"You know I love y'all," Yasin said as he removed his slacks and button-down Ralph Lauren shirt. "I'm handling business." He slid to the top of the bed and placed his head on the pillow.

Nina looked down at him in disgust. "All day long, Yasin? At this time of the night?"

Sitting up, Yasin gave Nina a serious look. "Listen, Nina, I don't feel like arguing with you. I deal with enough shit every day. I'm trying to make sure you and my son are good if I go down." Yasin snatched the covers over his body and flipped onto his side, facing the opposite direction from Nina. "I never hear you nagging when your bougie ass out spending my money on all that Gucci and Prada and those hundred thousand–dollar cars in that driveway. So, can a man get some peace and quiet in his own home? Fuck."

Nina was taken aback by Yasin's words. He had never spoken to her in that manner before. She knew at this moment that he was cheating on her. It was like he was a completely different person. And the fragrance of a woman's perfume lingering on his body did not help his case. Nina decided to let him go to sleep and avoid a fight, but she was going to go through his phone as soon as he was out.

It didn't take long for Yasin to fall into a deep slumber. Nina grabbed his iPhone and eased out of the bed quietly. She went straight to his messages.

An unsaved number caught her attention, and she opened the message thread. Her heart dropped as her suspicions were confirmed.

K: I miss you. I want you inside me.

K: $5,000 Apple Pay Request

K: the door is unlocked. I'm waiting for you.

K: $3,000 Apple Pay Request

K: I love you, Yasin. I want to be with you every day.

Nina let out a forceful breath as she scrolled through the seemingly never-ending message thread. Her worst fears had been confirmed. Dropping the phone, Nina slid down the wall, covering her mouth to conceal her cries. Here she was, engaged to a man who couldn't be faithful to her.

*I could have stayed with Chance for all this shit.* At least with Chance, Nina knew she would be happy and loved like only he knew how to love her.

"I'm not putting up with this shit." All Nina needed was to confirm Yasin's disloyalty to her. She couldn't afford to give second chances to anyone anymore. If Yasin stepped out on her when she held him down, helped run his business, and took care of home while raising their child, then he was capable of anything.

Nina reentered their room quietly and went to retrieve her Gucci luggage from the closet. She didn't care what she grabbed to put into the suitcases. She stuffed clothes into them until they were full. She carefully rolled the luggage out, being sure not to wake Yasin. Entering Nasim's room, Nina grabbed a couple of his belongings and threw a sleeping Nasim over her shoulder. She was leaving Yasin. She didn't know where she would go. Her only friend, Miami, lived all the way in New York. She had no family in Atlanta, or even down south for that matter. But she did have enough money to start her life over wherever she desired. That was one thing Yasin did do right by her. He provided for her so well that she didn't have to touch her own money. She collected her funds while blowing Yasin's money. However, no amount of money could forfeit her self-worth.

Exiting the mansion she had called home for the last three years, Nina looked at the lavish cars parked along the driveway. She knew she could only take one, so she opted for the black-on-black custom G wagon. It was Yasin's favorite, and Nina's pettiness impelled her to take it. Yasin spent hours handwashing and detailing the vehicle himself every other day. He treated the luxury SUV as if it were his most prized possession. The truck probably got more of Yasin's time than Nina.

*For my time wasted*, Nina thought incredulously. She safely secured Nasim in his seat and got in the driver's seat. Her destination was unknown as Nina pulled out of the driveway without looking

back. The tears fell as she drove away, but she
didn't bother to wipe them. This pain she had
kept bottled up for months had to come out. Nina
wanted to put Atlanta far in her rear view. There
was only one friend she could call on, and she
knew it was a selfish decision, but she hoped
she would be welcomed until she figured out her
next move.

A loud banging of the front door woke Chance
out of his sleep. Wiping the sleep from his eyes,
Chance grabbed his Glock as he made his way to
the front of his condo. No one ever showed up
to his place uninvited, so he figured the person on
the other end of the door was an enemy. He looked
through the peephole, but it was covered.

"The fuck." He sighed in irritation as he slowly
unlocked his two locks. His gun was the first thing
to greet the person on the other side of the door.

"Chance, it's me," a regretfully familiar voice
called from the other side.

Chance lowered his weapon and looked at the
sight before him. Nina stood outside with a sleeping Nasim on her chest and a few bags of luggage
at her feet. Her eyes were swollen and red, so he
instantly knew she had been crying. Despite it
all, the woman before him was as beautiful as he
remembered.

"Nina, what are you doing here?" he asked, confused. "Are you okay?"

Nina avoided eye contact with Chance because she knew he would see right through her. No, she was not okay. "Can I come in?" Nina noticed Chance's hesitation, and she didn't blame him. It was selfish of her to show up on his doorstep with her problems, but she didn't know where else to go. Hotels were too risky because that would be the first place Yasin checked.

Despite it all, Nina would always have a safe haven with Chance. Chance stepped aside and let Nina enter. A part of him wanted to turn her away, but there was still love there. He knew she had to be damn near desperate to beseech him for help.

"Baby, who's that at the door?" Yasmine, Chance's girlfriend, appeared in the living room with nothing but a robe on. She looked from Nina and Nasim to Chance then back to Nina. "What's going on?"

Nina recollected a memory from two years ago when she and Yasin took a trip to Miami. They were introduced to a round table of drug dealers that included Chance and Cassidy. The video vixen–looking chick standing before her was the same chick Chance had been with that night. "I didn't mean to interrupt anything. Chance, I can really go if there's a problem." Nina turned toward the door, but Chance reached out for her arm.

"You don't have to go. You look like you need some rest. There's a guest room down the hall to the right. Make yourself at home." Chance nodded for Nina to give him some alone time with Yasmine. "That's Nina."

Yasmine scoffed as she shook her head. Chance had finally opened up to her about Nina a few months ago. She needed to know why he was so defensive with his heart. Even after seeing each other for two years, Chance had always avoided her questions about taking things to the next level. That type of behavior only resulted from heartbreak. "The same Nina who left you for another man after you risked your *life* for *her*? And now she shows up years later and expects you to help her out? No way. You don't owe her shit." Yasmine was livid. The way Chance peered at Nina made her skin crawl. He never looked at her that way, like a delicate treasure he wanted to protect.

Chance understood Yasmine's protests, and she was right in a way. Nina made her choice when she left years ago. But Nina and Chance had history, and before becoming lovers, they had been friends. He could never turn his back on her. "She wouldn't have come here if she didn't have any other options, Yas. There's a lot you don't know. I can't see her out on the streets."

"I can't believe this shit." Yasmine shook her head incredulously. "You know I'm not the one to be in competition over you."

Chance walked up to Yasmine slowly and wrapped his arms around her waist. "I'm not asking you to be. All I'm asking is give me a couple days to figure out what's going on."

"Is that your kid?" Yasmine whispered as her bottom lip quivered. Chance's response did not convince her. As much as she wanted to trust him, Yasmine knew she couldn't compete with a kid.

"My only child is back there sleeping in his room." Chance spoke of his three-year-old son, Chase. "Look, why don't you go home and unwind for a couple of hours? I'm going to let Nina rest up, then get to the bottom of things. We should all have dinner tonight." Chance grabbed Yasmine by the waist. He snuggled his chin against her neck before kissing her lips softly. "Okay?"

Yasmine giggled before nodding her head. She could never resist Chance. "But I want her gone in a couple days. Put her in a hotel, find her a house, I don't care as long as she isn't here." She pointed her finger in Chance's face to let him know she meant business.

"Whatever you say." Chance kissed her one last time before she exited the condo. He sighed deeply as he walked down the hall toward the guest room.

Nina was sitting on the bed, alert.

"You were listening huh?"

Nina cracked a smile for the first time in the last ten hours. "She doesn't like me very much, I see." Nina twirled her fingers nervously. Being around Chance again was a bit weird. Not because of how they acted, because it was as if no time had ever passed, but because the circumstances were complicated. A lot had changed within three years. They led two separate lives with two completely different people.

The twirling of her fingers brought Chance's attention to the princess-cut diamond ring on Nina's left hand. "You're married?" he asked, a bit jealous. Nina shook her head. "Why are you here?" he asked as he sat down on the bed beside her.

"He hurt me, Chance." Tears streamed down Nina's face.

Chance's nostrils flared as his temperature rose. "That nigga put his hands on you?"

Nina felt the urge to smile through her tears. Chance had always been her protector, and it was good to know some things remained the same. "No, but he never loved me like he said he did. He's been fucking around on me for months now. I don't know what I'm going to do, Chance." She looked into his eyes for advice. "He doesn't know I left. And I know it's selfish of me to come here, but I didn't know what else to do or where else to go."

Chance's heart softened as he watched Nina break down before him. He never seen her cry like this before, not even after her mother's death. *I told you so*, Chance thought, but didn't say it aloud. It wasn't what Nina needed to hear right now.

"Damn. I always knew there was something I didn't like about that nigga. But, Nina, you can't run from him forever." Chance shrugged. He couldn't believe the words that he just spoken. He hated Yasin, but a spade was a spade. Chance loved Nina enough to tell her the truth, even when she didn't want to hear it. "I mean, you're his fiancée and the mother of his child. Y'all gon' have to come to some type of terms because I'll hate to body that nigga if he come with some hot shit here."

Nina lowered her head and rubbed her hand across her chest. She cleared her throat. "Nasim isn't Yasin's," she said quietly.

"Come again?" Chance asked in disbelief. Surely, he'd heard Nina incorrectly.

"At first, I thought Yasin was Nasim's father. But as he grew up and came into his own personality, I began to question it. He looks like you, Chance. He acts like you. He reads me just like you do. I don't think Nasim is Yasin's son. I'm so sorry." Nina collapsed in Chance's lap as she sobbed.

Chance rubbed his hands over his face in disbelief. Finally, Chance looked down at Nasim and studied his features. The little boy had a striking resemblance to his son Chase. He just didn't know what to say. Whether to be mad or happy. Whether to hate Nina or love her all over again. He needed time to process the bomb Nina had dropped on him.

*I need A DNA test,* he thought. He didn't want to get his hopes up if Nasim could indeed turn out to be Yasin's child.

Chance gently pushed Nina off him. "Yo, Nina, I need time to think right now. I don't know what to say. I got to go clear my head. Chase is sleep and should still be asleep by the time I get back. I'm just going to take a ride." Chance stood up as he shook his head.

"Chance!" Nina called after him as he was almost out the door. "I never meant to hurt you. I'm sorry."

"I know, Nina," Chance replied softly. "Get some rest, beautiful."


Nina woke up to the sounds of kids playing and dishes being moved around in the kitchen. Checking her phone, the time read 4:30 p.m. She had slept for hours and didn't even notice, but the rest was much needed. She felt way better than she had when she went to sleep. There were no missed calls from Yasin, which didn't surprise her. He had probably left the house that morning without even noticing she was gone. However, she knew she would get that call soon. Yasin wouldn't like the fact that Nina took off with Nasim without letting him know first.

Nina got out of bed and walked into the living room, where she found Nasim and Chase playing on the PS5. The boys favored each other so much that it hurt Nina. Chase was conceived when Nina and Chance were broken up, but he was living proof that Chance had been with other women besides Nina. This little boy's existence had influenced Nina's decision to be with Yasin, but she could not hate Chase for being born. He was a part of Chance, and Nina loved every part of Chance, including Chase.

"Mommy, is Chase and his dad my family?" Nasim asked innocently. The boys already shared a bond that warmed Nina's heart. Chase was a few months older than Nasim, but the boys could almost pass for twins. They both shared Chance's smooth brown complexion, dark eyes, and thick eyebrows.

"Yes, they are, baby." Nina kneeled beside the boys. "Chase, my name is Nina, and I'm a friend of your father's."

"I know who you are." Chase gave Nina a big hug. The little boy had never met Nina in person but learned to love her from hearing his dad speak of her. "Daddy keeps a picture of you and him in his room."

"Aw." Nina cooed as she returned Chase's embrace. She could only imagine how the boy longed for a mother's love. From the looks of things, Tiana had never made an effort to be in her son's life. That was something Nina couldn't even fathom.

Life without Nasim wasn't a life worth living. She couldn't wrap her mind around how a parent, especially a mother, could abandon their own flesh and blood without a second thought. Even though Tiana was a shitty person and an envious bitch, Nina wondered if Chase ever crossed her mind. Every woman had a motherly instinct. It was innate. Did she ever wonder about Chase's well-being?

"Is your dad in his room?" Both boys nodded. "I'll be right back." Nina made her way down the hall and knocked on Chance's door, which was slightly ajar.

"Come in," his deep baritone called out. "How was your rest?" Chance sat on his bed, feet propped up on a bed of pillow, with a MacBook Air on his lap.

Nina entered the dark room and sat on the opposite side of the bed from Chance. "It was good. I really needed that. And thank you for watching Nasim."

"It's nothing. My nanny, Charlene, looked after them while I was out."

Nina turned her nose up and scoffed at the mention of a nanny.

"What?" Chance knew Nina well enough to know she had something to say in response. "Speak your mind, Nina."

"Why do you have a nanny when you have a woman living with you?"

Chance chuckled as he closed his laptop. He placed it on his nightstand and turned on the lamp beside it. "I'm a busy man, Nina. And so is Yasmine. I never asked her to step up and help me take care of Chase."

"You shouldn't have to. She lives with you. I'm sure you're fucking her and spending money on her. So, what's the problem with her having a relationship with your son? It doesn't make sense to me."

That was one thing Chance always loved about Nina. She was big on family and would do anything for the people she loved. She was the type of woman you married and raised your kids with. "You're a mother, Nina. Yasmine isn't. I don't want to ask her to stop living her life to help assist with mine. We have an understanding. Charlene lives here and helps out. It's working." Honestly, Chance didn't put those expectations on Yasmine because he wasn't sure if what they shared would be long term.

"I feel you, Chance, but if a woman can't accept your child and love it like their own, she's not worthy of your love. That's just my opinion. Anyway." Nina waved her hand in the air, dismissing that conversation. She could tell Chance was a little defensive when it came to Yasmine, so she didn't push the situation any further.

Nina's attention was drawn to the 5x7 picture that rested on the nightstand next to Chance's bed. She walked around to the picture and picked it up. "Wow." She covered her mouth with her hand. A silly smile spread across Nina's face as she held the photo frame. In the picture were 18-year-old Chance and Quan and 15-year-old Nina, standing in front of Chance's old Honda. Nina stood in the middle of the boys in the picture. They were always her protectors. The three of them used to be as thick as thieves back in the day.

"I can't believe you still have this." It was taken on the day Chance and Nina moved into their first apartment together. "You know I remember this day like it was yesterday?" Nina sat on the bed beside Chance. "We went to Six Flags later that day and had a ball." She reminisced. "Life was so good back then." A tear slipped from Nina's eye.

Chance thumbed Nina's tears away. "Life is still good, shorty. We just have to make the best hand out of the cards we're dealt." He removed the picture from Nina's hand. The nostalgic photo teleported Nina down memory lane, reminding her of the best of her time with Chance. He hated to say what he had to say next. "I need to get a DNA test for Nasim."

Nina nodded slowly as she wiped her tears away. "I know."

"That's all?" Chance had expected an entirely different reaction from Nina. "I expected a li'l more pushback."

"Chance, it's the least I can do for you. I know I never said this, but I am sorry for all the pain I put you through when I chose Yasin. No matter the circumstance, I was supposed to stay solid for you. I let another man infiltrate my heart and get into places only you should have explored." Nina's voice cracked. "I should have listened to you and Quan. The whole time, I was sleeping with a nigga who meant me no good. I feel so fucking stupid." Nina smacked her forehead with her open hand. She hated that she had ignored Chance's and Quan's warnings about Yasin. Allowing Yasin into her world would be something she regretted for the rest of her life.

Chance took Nina's hands in his. "I'm not going to make you feel any worse than you already do by saying I told you so."

Nina stared longingly into Chance's eyes before leaning in for a kiss, but Chance turned his face before their lips could meet.

"I'm with Yasmine now. I can't go down that road with you anymore."

Nina cheeks turned red from embarrassment. She just knew Chance couldn't resist her, or so she thought. Chance had always been soft on Nina, just like any other man who fell victim to her innocent charm. His love was still there, but it wasn't the same, and it was mostly her fault.

"You don't love me anymore?" Nina asked so softly that it was barely audible.

"That's not it." Chance held Nina's hands gently. "I just want to do right by her. I couldn't do right by you, and I lost you. And I know that one thing as simple as a kiss can lead me right back down that road of loving you. You're like a drug to me, Nina. Us being friends is the only way I can stop myself from relapsing."

"There's just something about her that I don't like, Chance." Nina recalled the way Yasmine looked at Nina, as if she were an infectious disease. Yasmine's presence made Nina uneasy, but not because of intimidation. "I can't put my finger on it." Usually, Nina's instincts were always right, and her gut warned her to watch Yasmine. "How well do you know her?"

Chance snickered. "Green isn't a good color on you, shorty." Chance threw a playful jab to Nina's right shoulder, brushing her suspicions off as jealousy. "Have dinner with us tonight. Charlene will have the boys. It'll give you and Yasmine time to get to know each other a little."

"I'll pass." Nina turned her nose up as she shook her head. There was nothing that interested her in knowing Yasmine. Nina's mind was already made up about the situation. She didn't like the bitch. It wasn't because she was with Chance. All Nina wanted was for Chance to be happy, and if that meant without her, so be it. But Yasmine's vibe was all off. It's like meeting a person and instantly knowing you can't fuck with them. Nina knew she would eventually discover the reason why her spirit didn't seem to resonate with Yasmine's.

Chance sighed. "Look, Nina, you still got whatever type of engagement . . . relationship . . . I don't know what the fuck you and that nigga *Yasin* got going on. You know I'll forever love you. If you ever call on me, I'll be there for you, as a friend. If you're going to be a part of my life, I want y'all to get along." He paused as he looked at Nina, trying to read her expression. "I mean, put yourself in Yasmine's shoes. Your nigga's ex shows up on your doorstep with luggage and a *kid*! Honestly, Nina, you would have wilded out." Chance scoffed and chuckled lightly, remembering how Nina had wilded out in the past over way less. "If Nasim turns out to be mine, we're going to have to carry ourselves like adults. The past is the past."

Those words stung Nina's heart, but she knew she deserved them. "All right, all right. What time should I be ready?"

"Eight p.m. We're having Jamaican. Dress for the occasion, shorty." Chance looked down at his phone as he stood up. "I gotta go handle some business. See you later."

"See ya."

*I gotta hit the mall. Yasmine better not come half-stepping because she never met a bitch like me. I'm coming for my man.*

The games were on. The race was for Chance's heart, and Nina didn't plan on fumbling this time.

Nina pushed the earring into her ear as she walked from the bathroom to the living room. She was attempting to get dressed to go shopping before the night ahead of her, but she found herself pausing every five minutes to check on Nasim and Chase. The boys had toys sprawled across the floor and were continuing to pull out more.

"Chase, don't hit the table with that. Nasim, no slime please," she stated. Nina had volunteered to take the boys to the mall with her while Chance handled business. She regretted that decision as she picked up toys and placed them in the toy bin. "Can we work on playing with one toy at a time? Mommy is tired of cleaning the floor every five minutes," she slightly whimpered. She had underestimated the energy of two toddler boys.

"I can watch them while you run out," Charlene offered when she appeared from her bedroom.

Nina looked from the boys to Charlene. The concept of having a nanny was still growing on her, and Nina didn't want to put more on Charlene's plate. "Uh . . . thank you, but I got them. You deserve time off."

Charlene waved her hand dismissively and kneeled down beside Nina, collecting toys with her. "I don't see this as a job, Nina. Don't get me wrong," Charlene said. "Chance pays me well, but I don't do this for the money. My only son Quentin lives miles away in Europe with his wife."

"Europe?" Nina asked. She didn't know anyone personally who lived in Europe.

"He's a politician," Charlene explained. "He's travelled the world because of his career. We don't see each other much, but I'm proud of him. I always tell him don't let the career run his life, though. I'm fifty, and I learned that the hard way." Charlene shook her head.

"You must miss him," Nina commented. She glanced at Nasim and Chase, realizing the day would come when they would have to find their place in the world. "How do you know Chance?" she asked.

Smiling, Charlene stood and dusted her knees off. "Chance is my godson. I grew up with his family. When Chance called and offered me the job, I was so happy. There was nothing left for me in North Carolina. Chance and Nasim are the closest thing I have to grandchildren. I love them like they're my own. Chance loves you, so my love extends to you."

Nina smiled and glanced at the boys. She trusted that they were in good hands with Charlene. Nina got nothing but pure vibes from her. "How do you feel about Yasmine?"

Charlene scoffed and rolled her eyes. Just speaking Yasmine's name left a bad taste in her mouth, and she refused to say it. "That woman ain't got no respect. She doesn't even look me in the eyes when she speaks to me, the few times she has," Charlene told her.

Nina knew she wasn't the only one getting weird vibes from Yasmine. She just didn't understand why Chance couldn't see that shit. *Her shit can't be that good*, she thought in her head.

"We can agree on that," Nina snorted. "Is the offer to watch the boys still on the table?"

"Of course. Take your time. I'm bored around here without these two," Charlene squealed as she pinched the boys' cheeks.

"Okay. I'll see you guys later," Nina said and grabbed her purse and phone off the end table before leaving out the front door.

A few minutes later, Nina's phone vibrated in her purse as she navigated the G-wagon through the busy Miami streets. She fumbled through her purse until she grabbed her iPhone. Nina answered the call without looking at the caller ID and instantly regretted it.

"Where you at, Nina?" Yasin yelled through the phone. "You know you were supposed to make the fucking bank deposit today!"

Nina rolled her eyes in disbelief. This nigga wasn't concerned about her well-being at all. His true colors were really starting to show. He was the worst type of narcissist. "I'm not in town," she responded simply.

"Fuck you mean, you not in town? Why didn't you let me know you were going out of town?"

Nina could hear the annoyance in his voice, but she didn't give a fuck. He didn't care about her feelings while being laid up with another woman.

She pulled the phone away from her ear and looked down at it with her face twisted up. Yasin really had her fucked up. "I don't need your permission to do shit. You're not my father, and really you not even my man anymore. How about you go hit up that bitch Monica that you been texting and calling and fucking? Maybe she'll take your orders, because Nina don't want any parts of your lies and infidelity," she snapped.

Yasin chuckled on the other end of the line, which only further agitated her. "Yo, Nina, let me tell you something. As long as you got my son and wearing that hundred-thousand-dollar engagement ring on your finger, you're *mine*. You understand me?" He paused on the other end of the line. "As long as I'm coming home to you every night and keeping you iced up and in all the latest designer shit that your bougie ass can't seem to live without, don't question me about any other bitch. I make sure you want for nothing, so that's all it is to it."

Nina couldn't believe this nigga's nerve. As if she didn't have her own money. This nigga must have forgot who the fuck she was and who approached who to begin with. "Nigga, you did that shit for me because you *wanted to*. I never asked. As for this fucking engagement ring, I'll mail the bitch back to you because you won't be seeing me anytime soon."

"Oh, you'll be seeing me real soon," Yasin retorted.

"I think the fuck not." Now it was her turn to laugh. "Oh, yeah, baby, *my son* is good. Don't worry about him. You should be asking for a DNA test, nigga, because the older he gets, the more he starts to act like his *real* dad, a real nigga. Call Maury, motherfucker." Nina laughed hysterically before hanging up the phone.

*That was petty*, she thought. Nina wanted Yasin to feel a portion of the hurt he had caused her over the last few months. She tried to shake off the negativity Yasin just tried to bring into her life. She knew she had fucked his head up with her last comment, but he would know sooner or later. Her baby was a product of her and Chance's love. He was the only thing she had to show for what she had shared with Chance. It was real and a once-in-a-lifetime type of love. Nasim was living proof, and she didn't need a DNA test to prove what she already knew.

The driver is about to pull up. I'll meet you at our destination. - Chance 7:30PM

Nina read Chance's message and rolled her eyes. She didn't know why Chance couldn't pick her up himself. Yet, she went with the flow. She couldn't expect too much special treatment out of Chance because then Yasmine would get jealous. *Fuck her feelings.*

Nevertheless, Nina was still anxious about this dinner. She was styled to perfection. A shopping spree and trip to the spa did her justice. None of the clothes she packed would suffice for tonight. She needed brand new everything: a brand-new outfit, a brand-new hairstyle, all that. Since Jamaican was on the menu, Nina assumed there would be some type of dance floor. At least she hoped. Her outfit fit the description perfectly. Nina donned a soft yellow Margiela dress. When she spotted it in Neiman's, she knew it would be perfect for the occasion. The dress had long sleeves, but the material was very light. The fabric clung to every curve on her body. One side of the dress was asymmetrical, exposing her shapely right leg. On her feet were a pair of gold Giuseppe heels. Her wavy weave had been replaced with a curly Indian install. The hair was full and not too long. The curls accented her beautiful face. Nina didn't need a weave, but it was a great alternate for when she was feeling lazy. Her makeup was done to perfection with a full set of mink lash extensions that accented her slanted brown eyes.

On her neck was a lovely Cartier diamond necklace that Chance gave her on her eighteenth birthday. Nina recalled the memory like it was yesterday. Chance was twenty-one and rising in the drug game in Charlotte. All the long nights and work he put in were finally paying off. Up until that point, Chance had never dabbled in expensive luxuries. He'd rather save and stack.

"You can never come up spending money on stupid shit. If I don't need it, I won't get it until I can afford to buy two or more," Chance used to say. But he wanted to surprise Nina with something she could cherish forever. Hence, he dropped twenty thousand dollars on that diamond necklace. Nina had kept the gift close to her ever since. She hoped Chance would appreciate her sentimental choice of jewelry.

Looking in the mirror, Nina touched the shimmering diamonds in the necklace and smiled at her appearance. She looked bomb as fuck. "The one, not the motherfucking two," she said to herself as she snapped a few pictures.

The driver arrived at 7:45 p.m. in a Lincoln Town Car. "Good evening, ma'am. My name is David, and I'll be your driver for the night. You look exquisite." The older black gentleman complimented Nina's appearance as he opened the door for her.

"Thank you," she replied with a smile as she made herself comfortable in the backseat. For some reason, Nina had butterflies. She didn't know if she was nervous to see Chance or if she was anxious to see if Chance had been thinking about her as much as she'd been thinking about him. Either way, she couldn't wait to lay eyes on him.

The Town Car pulled in front of a restaurant in downtown Miami, and Nina knew this was the destination. Attached to the restaurant was a dance floor with a big roof over it. There was a DJ set up, and the reggae tunes permeated through the air.

*Just like I expected. It wouldn't be Jamaican without a dance floor.* Nina smirked at how dead on she was with her predictions.

David opened the door for Nina and gently helped her out. "All right now, Miss Nina, don't hurt them too bad tonight."

"No promises, David." Nina gave him a wink before walking through the front door of the restaurant. She must have been fashionably late because everyone was already seated. She spotted Chance and Yasmine seated in a booth in the rear part of the restaurant. The aroma of jerk chicken invaded her nostrils, and she realized how hungry she was.

"Can I help de lady?" a tall, dark-skinned man asked Nina as soon as she walked through the door. He was as dark as a winter night. A perfect set of white teeth complemented his midnight complexion. His locs sat in a pineapple style on the top of his head. "I'm Zidane." He extended his hand for Nina to shake.

She blushed and shook his hand. The attractive man practically drooled over Nina. His reaction reassured her that she had surely achieved her goal for the night: to look good or shit on anyone who thought otherwise. "I'm Nina." She smiled graciously. "I'm actually joining those two." Nina nodded to Chance and Yasmine.

By this time, Chance looked up and noticed Nina had arrived. Their eyes locked for a second. Chance's eyes danced around Nina's body for a few seconds. He couldn't hide that look in his eyes—a look of love and lust. Nina knew it all too well, but she would play by Chance's rules for now.

"Ahh, you wit' dat bad man," Zidane said jokingly. His accent was heavy and actually sexy in a way. "Do yu ting. Let me walk you to them, beautiful." He placed his hand on the small of Nina's back as he led her to the back of the restaurant.

Chance stood as they approached. "Zidane, I see you've met Nina."

"To di worl." Zidane's tall frame towered over Nina as he looked down at her.

Nina didn't know what the fuck he had said, but she liked the way it sounded coming off his tongue.

"Nina, gwaan. Order anything ya heart pleases. Enjoy." He bowed slightly, winking at Nina before walking away.

Nina laughed lightly as she slid in the booth, sitting directly across from Chance and Yasmine. Yasmine's eyes met Nina's, and they instantly sized each other up. From what Nina could tell, Yasmine was wearing a white bodysuit with a pair of red thigh-high boots. *Typical*, she thought.

"Well." Nina spoke first, breaking the silence. "You look nice, Yasmine." Nina forced herself to play nice and pay the girl a compliment. It was true. Yasmine was a beautiful woman, and she did look good tonight. However, she couldn't fuck with Nina.

Yasmine gave her a tight smile. "So do you. I love those shoes. What are they? Aldo's?"

*No this bitch didn't.* "Giuseppe's." Nina lifted the corner of her mouth into a smirk and cut her eyes in Chance's direction.

"So, ladies, do you know what y'all are ordering?" Chance asked, trying to ease the obvious tension in the air. He had expected Nina to be the one throwing shots, but Yasmine had her gloves out already. He guessed she felt a little underdressed for the occasion when Nina arrived. Chance couldn't lie. Nina donned the dress as if the designer threaded the dress specifically for Nina. The color complemented her brown skin so well that its specks of gold glistened against her body.

"I want oxtails and curry chicken," Nina commented, observing the extensive menu.

Yasmine shrugged. "I'll have whatever you're having, baby."

Chance nodded. "Okay, I'm about to give Zidane the orders. I gotta run some shit by him. Be right back."

An awkward silence filled the air after Chance left the booth. The tension between the two women was so thick a blind man could see it. Nina didn't know what Yasmine's problem was with her, and quite frankly, she didn't care. It was important to Chance that they had this dinner tonight, therefore Nina promised herself to be on her best behavior.

"Sooo, Yasmine, where are you from?" Nina asked as she sipped the water in front of her.

"D.C.," Yasmine answered.

"Oh, really? That's cool. What brought you down south?"

Yasmine hesitated before she answered. "I came here to pursue my modeling career. There were a lot of opportunities in Miami."

"Hmm." Nina nodded. "And by modeling, do you mean like being in videos and shit and doing photo shoots for Instagram, or do you have an actual modeling contract?" Nina threw a little shade of her own this time.

"I do a little bit of everything. I'm versatile," Yasmine responded and rolled her eyes to Nina. She recognized the subtle shade hidden within Nina's words. "And what about you? Are you a housewife? Chance told me he and your fiancé are business partners. I mean, no offense, but isn't that a little awkward for you?"

Nina laughed out loud and took a sip from the glass of water on the table. Yasmine thought she had the tea on Nina, not knowing it was piss. Yasmine assumed that Nina lived off the means of the men she aligned herself with, but that wasn't Nina's truth. She made herself a millionaire before the age of twenty-one. "Not even, honey. I own several businesses in Atlanta. My most prominent are my three spa locations, Nina's Beautique. It's basically like an all-in-one shop. Ladies can get their hair, nails, makeup, eyelashes, and eyebrows done there or any spa services, like massages or waxes. It's a lucrative business." Nina's revenue from the spas alone allowed her to live comfortably. "And it's not awkward for me at all. Not that it's any of your business."

*If this bitch tries me one more time, all this cordial shit going out the window*, Nina thought.

"Take no offense to my comments, Nina. I'm just curious about you." Yasmine sipped her martini, smirking. Yasmine didn't see what all the hype was about. Nina was beautiful, she could admit that, but beauty came a dime a dozen. The only thing Nina had up on Yasmine, in her opinion, was the years she had spent with Chance. Little did she know, Nina was a rare breed. She was loyal to a fault, a natural born hustler, and fearless. Her personality alone was enough to make you fall in love with her. She was different from a lot of other chicks. Nina didn't care for the spotlight or how much money a nigga had. Only a real man could handle the type of love Nina had to offer.

"No offense taken. Your interest in my life is flattering, but Chance should have told you about me." Nina smiled graciously.

Chance approached the table before either woman could respond. "How's the bonding, ladies?" Chance asked and silence followed his question. Nina shook her head and laughed softly. Yasmine cleared her throat. Chance gave Nina a quick look, as if to say, *what happened?*

Nina spotted Zidane and waved him over. Yasmine's bothered ass polluted her energy space. She could sense Yasmine's disdain and jealousy.

"What's up, gal?"

"Can I have a drink? Jose Cuervo. Straight." Nina was usually a Hennessy type of chick, but she knew how she could get off brown. It was best if she stayed away from it tonight.

"Yuh got it, beautiful." Zidane winked at Nina before shuffling to the bar to grab her drink. "Here yuh go." Zidane was back quickly and placed the drink in front of Nina.

By this time, the waitress brought their food to the table. Nina sipped the tequila and thanked God for haste because she was ready for this night to be over. Yasmine kept being extra, whispering shit in Chance's ear. Her childish behavior annoyed Nina.

The three of them engaged in small talk as they ate their food. It was beyond delicious. Zidane stopped by and checked on the trio periodically. Everyone caught the flirtatious vibes he was throwing at Nina. Who could blame him?

Beenie Man's "Girls Dem Sugar" blared from the speakers, and Nina rocked her body back and forth.

"Dance wit' me, gal." Zidane grabbed Nina's hand and gently pulled her from the booth.

"No, I can't." Nina laughed as she shook her head.

Zidane shook his head as he pulled her closer to the dance floor. Looking back at Chance, she saw him smile and nod as if he approved. *Might as well*, Nina thought. Zidane proved to be a good dancer as he matched Nina's rhythm, following every sway and whine of her hips.

"See, why wouldn't yuh want to dance when ya body moves so naturally to the beat?" Zidane asked Nina hypothetically. "Chu have a man?"

Nina shook her head. "It's complicated," she answered, taking a glance over to the booth where Yasmine and Chance were sitting. She caught Chance's gaze, and he quickly turned his attention back to Yasmine. Nina snorted, licking her lips to conceal her grin.

"Ah. I thought yuh were family. So, what's de story with yuh two?" Zidane whispered in Nina's ear.

"That man sitting over there has my heart. Always has, always will."

As if the DJ were listening in to their conversation, "I'm Still in Love with You" by Sean Paul began playing. Glancing over, Nina noticed Chance and Yasmine on the dance floor. The universe sent the signals; it was up to Chance and Nina to take heed.

Zidane never lost tempo as he and Nina danced. He was a little disappointed by her response, but not surprised. With a woman as beautiful and graceful as Nina, Zidane figured there was a man somewhere in the picture. Chance and Zidane were friends with mutual interests.

"So, why aren't de two of yuh together?"

"Long story." She smiled.

"Could you at least try not to stare at her?" Yasmine smacked her lips as she rocked her hips back and forth. Trying to keep up with Nina had her about to break a sweat. She was trying hard to keep Chance's attention and compete with Nina, but little did she know, Nina wasn't even trying. That was the difference between them. Nina naturally captivated people's attention. It wasn't something she tried to do. Nina had everyone's attention, including Chance's, as she danced and laughed so freely. Zidane and Nina appeared to be enjoying each other's company, and Yasmine hoped the two started a romance for her benefit.

"I'm not staring. Just making sure everything is cool," Chance lied. Till this day, Chance churned at the sight of Nina with another man. It was like wanting something, but not needing it at the immediate moment, but also not wanting anyone else to have it either. Like an aged bottle of wine in a wine cellar, Nina's value only grew the older she became. Deep down, Chance knew that he would eventually find his way back to Nina.

Yasmine rolled her eyes and sighed. Nina was like a thorn in her side. Things between her and

Chance flowed like river water, easy, until Nina showed up on his doorstep with those big brown eyes. "Nina's grown, and I'm sure she can take care of herself. She's stringing you along like a damn puppet master, and you can't even see it. I don't like it either. How can I trust you with her staying with you?" Yasmine pouted.

Chance wrapped his arms around her waist and pulled her in close. He knew the minute Nina showed up things with him and Yasmine were going to get complicated. "Look, tomorrow Nina and I will discuss her options. I'll try to find her a place. Everything with us will be back to normal in a few days. A'ight?"

After reluctantly giving him a head nod, Yasmine kissed Chance's lips.

"May I borrow your beautiful lady?" Zidane asked Chance. Nina stood at his side.

"Go ahead, bro." Chance placed Yasmine's hand in Zidane's and took Nina's. "I guess you'll have to do," he joked. The DJ slowed things down a bit by playing a slower paced reggae song.

Nina chuckled as she placed her hands around his neck. "Oh, really?"

For the first time tonight, Chance noticed the sparkling Cartier diamond on Nina's neck. "Wow, I can't believe you still wear this," he said as he lifted the necklace off her neck a little. The jewel held a lot of sentimental value for both. It reminded

Chance of his purpose for everything he had endured to be in the position he was in now: to make a better life for himself and Nina.

Nina's eyes searched Chance's. "Why wouldn't I? It means so much to me."

Silence filled the two of them. Nina placed her head against Chance's chest and listened to his heartbeat as they swayed back and forth to the music.

Even though Zidane made small talk with her while they danced, Yasmine's focus was on Nina and Chance. Their movements were innocent, but Yasmine's heart stung at the sight. The couple looked as if they had stepped out of a scene of a love story. Each one of their movements were in sync with each other. If circumstances were different, Yasmine wouldn't want to be the one standing in the way of true love. However, Nina was the one in the way. She had no right barging into their lives and interrupting the happiness she and Chance had created. It wasn't fair.

"I'm going to sit down." Yasmine spoke softly to Zidane, and he nodded.

"I'ma go chop it up with Zidane for a few. Can you let Yasmine know that we'll be leaving shortly?" Chance gently clutched Nina's shoulder, pulling her body away from his. He inhaled the scent of her perfume before bringing her closer to him again.

"Sure," Nina said, releasing his body, and turned to walk to the booth. She didn't want to break their embrace. She wanted to stay in his arms forever. There, everything felt so right.

"Hey, Chance said we'll be leaving in a minute."

"Yeah, whatever." Yasmine brushed Nina off.

"What's your problem?" Nina challenged Yasmine. There was only so much she could let slide. Bitches like Yasmine started ice skating when you allowed them to slide even an inch. She had been nice to Yasmine off the strength of Chance, but all she received in return was attitude and disrespect.

Yasmine squinted her eyes and twisted her mouth into a scowl. Was Nina really this clueless? "You're my fucking problem. You showed up announced and fucked up everything Chance and I had going on." She waved her hands around for dramatic emphasis. "And then you have the nerve to come here and gloat."

Nina sat down and blew out a sharp breath. Closing her eyes, she inhaled and held her breath for three seconds, regaining her composure before she slapped the scowl off Yasmine's face. She was about to read this bitch. "Look, *Yasmine*, you have every right not to like me, but Chance and I have some unfinished business. You may think you know what happened between us, but you really know nothing. That man and I have history, and we'll always love each other. You're intimidated by me. I understand that." Nina's tongue clicked against her teeth, and she stepped closer to Yasmine. "But what I won't accept is your disrespect, because I could be doing *a lot* more to fuck up what you and Chance got going on. Trust me."

"That may be true, but I think you're scared Chance doesn't love you the same. That's why you showed up tonight all dressed up, doing the most. Me, on the other hand, I don't have to do all of that for his attention," Yasmine snapped back.

Nina laughed out loud this time. "You really don't know me. This is *nothing*. If you're so secure in your relationship with Chance, why are you so bothered by me? I seen you looking at me tonight. You really hate me, and you don't have to admit it. But what you need to admit to yourself is, you can't compete where you don't compare. That man will *always* love me. He'll *always* choose me. And yes, you may have him right now, but you'll never truly have him. So, enjoy him while you can, because I'm coming for my man, and I don't have to fuck him to keep him interested. Our bond is much deeper than that. It's only a matter of time, baby girl. I have his son and his heart. What do you have?" Nina challenged Yasmine.

She smirked as she watched Yasmine's face
flush with anger. Nina waited a minute for a response, but got none. "That's what I thought."
Nina scoffed and walked away. She would find her
own way back to Chance's place because there was
no way she was riding back with Yasmine. Now
that she had spoken her peace, there was no way
she could play cordial with Yasmine. The girl knew
her intentions and would look at Nina as a target
now. It was game on.

By the time Chance wrapped his conversation
up with Zidane, he noticed Nina was no longer
sitting at the booth with Yasmine. Yasmine sat in
the booth with her arms crossed, obviously upset.

"Where did Nina go?" Chance asked.

"Seriously?" Yasmine scoffed as she shook her
head. "That's really the first thing you say to me?"

Chance held his hand out for Yasmine to take.
He purposely ignored her question because he
didn't want to start an argument. It was late, and
he was ready to be in the confinement of his own
home. David was waiting outside of the restaurant
to escort the two of them home. "Let's talk in the
car."

"No! Let's talk right now." Yasmine raised her
voice. Nina had succeeded in getting under her
skin. She hated the fact that Nina had the last word

in their altercation. "Why did you lie to me about her son? She said he's yours."

Sighing, Chance looked around the restaurant. There weren't as many people present as before, but the few in there were now looking at the argument unfolding. "Don't make a scene." Chance gritted through his teeth sternly. That was one thing Chance hated about Yasmine; she didn't know when to listen.

"Don't keep lying to me then!" Yasmine yelled.

Chance took this opportunity to snatch Yasmine up and remove her from the restaurant. He was rough, but sure not to hurt her. He lightly pushed her toward the Town Car. "Get in the car."

Yasmine sucked her teeth. She obliged with a frown on her face. "Where are we going?"

"You're going home. I'll call you tomorrow." Chance tapped the hood of the town car twice and closed Yasmine's door. He instructed David to take her directly home and slipped him a hundred-dollar bill. Chance was glad he had driven to Zidane's restaurant today after he met up with Nikko. Now, he could ride home in peace and spark up a blunt.

# Chapter Eight

The lights were on in the living room of Chance's spacious condo. Nina was still up, watching TV. She was dressed down in silk pajamas, and a bonnet covered her curly weave. Both Nasim and Chase were asleep on a pallet by Nina's feet.

"What happened to you?" Chance asked as he locked the three deadbolts attached to the door.

"*Shh*," Nina whispered, putting her forefinger against her pouty lips. "Let's put them in their beds first, then we can talk."

They picked up the boys and carried them into Chase's room, where his mahogany bunk bed set sat.

"So, what happened?" Chance asked as they were back in the living room on the couch. Pulling out another Dutch stuffed with three grams of Kush, Chance sparked the blunt.

Nina reached her hand out for the blunt and laughed. Chance was on time with this one. She took a long drag before responding. "I just can't fuck with her." Nina sighed and shrugged her shoulders, exhaling the smoke. A relaxation set over her instantly. It had been months since she'd smoked weed, and honestly, she missed it. "I tried to be nice to the girl, but she kept trying me, throwing shade and shit. And the crazy part about it is she only did it when you weren't around. I can't fuck with no wishy-washy shit like that. So, the last time she tried me, I had to put her in her place."

Chance shook his head as Nina passed the blunt back to him.

"I tried for you, though, Chance. I really did, but it's just something about that girl that turns my vibe off so much. You can continue fucking with her, but I don't want *no* dealings."

Chance puffed the blunt and nodded as he listened to Nina. He knew her well enough to know that she meant what she said. If Nina got a bad vibe off you one time, she would not fuck with you again on any level. He just wondered why she didn't catch that vibe from Yasin. Maybe they wouldn't be in the situation they were in now if she had.

"You mentioned Nasim being mine to her. Now she thinks I lied to her because when she first asked me about it, I said no."

"So what?" Nina rolled her eyes. "It's really none of her business. But don't worry, we'll have the results in two weeks. If my son turns out to be yours, I'm sorry about the problems it's going to cause in your relationship. I never wanted him to be a burden." There was sarcasm laced in Nina's tone. Chance acted like he cared more about Yasmine's feelings than finding out Nasim's true paternity. It had Nina feeling a type of way, and she couldn't hide it. With Nina, everything had to be out on the surface. She valued honesty, no matter how hard it could be to bear. That was part of the reason why she was still hurt over how things had played out with Chance two years ago.

Chance shook his head as he crushed the blunt out in the ashtray. He slid closer to Nina before resting his elbows on both knees. "There's nothing I ever wanted more than for Nasim to be mine, Nina, and you know that. When I found out you were in that accident and lost our baby, I thought it was my karma coming back on me. And then after the shootout, the doctor tells us you were pregnant all along, and I dropped to my knees and thanked God, literally. I knew it had to be a miracle or something for real." He paused and glared at Nina.

Tears pooled in her eyes, and her bottom lip quivered.

"That's why I stuck with you. I wasn't concerned about that nigga Yasin because he took advantage of you at a weak point in your life. I could get over that. But you chose that nigga over me." Chance chuckled as he shook his head.

Nina remained silent and waited for him to fin-ish, obviously it was something he'd been waiting to get off his chest for a while.

"Not only did I warn you about that him, but so did Quan. We were supposed to be family before anything, Nina. It was like you said fuck us after you had Nasim. You disregarded the fact that he could indeed be my son, and you isolated yourself from your family. That shit wack as hell. The nigga was never solid like that, Nina, and you should have peeped game."

Nina wiped her tears as her heart ached. A part of her wanted to refute his words and ask about the times he had hurt her, about the fact that he had a baby on her, but she didn't. Chance had every right to feel indignant. Nina had not only broken Chance's heart, but she wounded his pride. Both would need time to heal.

"I know I fucked up. I'm standing here admitting that. So what? I just want my man back." Nina slid closer to Chance and placed both of her hands in his. "I want us." Her big brown eyes searched deeply into Chance's, hoping to find any hint that he felt the same way she did.

"What if Nasim turns out to not be mine? Then what, ma?" Chance kissed both of Nina's hands. "You're not ready for us, Nina. I know you haven't tied up your shit with Yasin. I may not like the cat, but you still owe him an explanation." Chance moved a strand of hair out of Nina's face. "You're an amazing woman, shorty. Make sure that nigga knows you're leaving his life. Life is too short, on some real shit. At the end of the day, you know my feelings for you will never change. Men will always try to win your affection because it's just something about you and your love. It's up to you to decide who's worth it."

"So, what are you saying?" Nina could tell Chance was a little blowed because he was talking in riddles and shit. His intellect was one of the things Nina fell in love with, but that wasn't what she needed right now. Right now, she needed the truth, raw and uncut.

"I'm saying live your life, Nina. What's meant to be already *is*, so if we are meant to be after everything that's happened, it will happen. We don't have to force nothing. We can see other people and live our lives."

Nina scoffed and shook her head. She didn't need time to date other men or find herself. She had known what she wanted since she was 15 years old. Yes, the road they'd been traveling had been rocky, but Nina didn't want to ride this rollercoaster of life with anybody else. Yet, she had to respect his request. The roles were reversed three years ago. Chance gave Nina the decision to choose between him and Yasin. Now, he requested the same level of grace.

"I respect that. I can't be surprised, right?" Her voice shook as she held back tears. She shifted toward the opposite direction and crossed her arms.

"I'm going to set you up in your own condo in a couple of days. I own one right down the hall, so you don't have to stray that far from Charlene. She's clutch, right?"

Nina nodded. "I like her." She wondered why Chance wanted to keep her so close. Deep down, she knew it wasn't because of Charlene. *Chance isn't ready to let me go*, Nina thought. That alone was enough to give her hope.

The two women sat outside Vice City Bean, a local coffee shop off North Miami Avenue. They were waiting for one more person to arrive before they could get into the details of the reason for their meeting. The redhead sitting on the far-left side bounced her leg and tapped her long nails against the table anxiously. Her signature long, wavy tresses were now styled into a short bob.

"Where is this bitch, man?" she asked irritably.

"Will you stop bouncing your fucking leg like that? You're making me nervous," the dark-skinned beauty hissed under her breath. She looked around to make sure no one else noticed her friend's shifty behavior.

"Na, it's bad enough we agreed to do this shit. I feel dirty as hell." The girl scratched both arms, swiveling her head to survey her surroundings.

Naomi cut her eyes at her friend. She couldn't believe Tiana was scared after they had talked about this a thousand times over. "T, this is the only way we can get revenge. We haven't been successful on our own. It's the only way." Naomi put on her best convincing tone.

Tiana nodded reluctantly, but she had a bad feeling in the pit of her stomach. No good was going to come out of what they were about to do, but she pushed the apprehensive thoughts to the back of her mind.

Their thoughts were interrupted as a beautiful, shapely, brown-skinned woman approached the table they were seated at. "Hello, ladies. Thanks for agreeing to meet me." She was dressed down in a two-piece suit that accented her curvaceous frame. "As I informed you over the phone, my name is Angela Tyson, and I am a detective and federal agent. I work alongside the DEA and sometimes even the CIA. We've been building this case against the syndicate of drug dealers for almost three years now. We've failed in our previous attempts to bring charges against Yasin Amos. I don't know if you're aware or not, but there's a whole drug operation being run out of Puerto Rico by these men." Agent Tyson placed five pictures in front of the women. They shuffled through the photos, only recognizing two out of the five men in front of them.

"That's Yasin, and that's Chance McKnight," Naomi stated matter-of-factly as she pointed the two men out. Tiana rolled her eyes and remained silent. She wasn't feeling this at all.

Agent Tyson smiled and removed the pictures from their hands. "Correct. In the other pictures, we have Nikko Ramirez, Cassidy Arrington, and Ty'Quan Mason. These men are big time. If they were just some petty drug dealers, they wouldn't be such a thorn in my ass." She sighed. "But these men move more weight than a fucking dump truck. Out of every dollar made on the East Coast, they are taking home twenty-five cents of it. This makes them a threat for the federal government. This time, however, they won't get off so easily."

"How are you so sure of that?" Tiana interrupted. She couldn't speak on Cassidy or Nikko, but she knew firsthand how conscientiously Chance and Quan ran their operation. She doubted that this woman had the power to bring them down.

Agent Tyson leaned in so only the two of them could hear her next words. "One of our own has infiltrated their inner circle. We are very confident this time," she whispered before pausing. "And with your help, we can put these bastards behind bars for the rest of their lives. If you are willing to help."

Tiana used this opportunity to speak before Naomi did. "What's in it for us?" she asked, rolling her neck and leaning across the table.

Agent Tyson looked Tiana directly in her eyes and pulled out another photograph. It was of baby Chase being held at the park by Nina. "How do you feel about another woman raising your son? A woman who's living the life that you should be living?"

The sight made Tiana's blood boil. It was true that Tiana hated Nina, but she never would have made a good mother anyway. Agent Tyson sensed that the picture wasn't enough to move Tiana, so she went into her manila folder and pulled out one more photo. It was a picture of their deceased best friend, Kiki.

"I know what Yasin did to her. I want justice for her just as much as you do," Agent Tyson lied. All she cared about was winning this case. To be black and a young woman, a case like this was all she needed to reach her pinnacle. She planned on being the chief of her department, a feat that had never been accomplished by a black woman. Nailing this case would ensure her ascent toward the promotion she dreamed of.

"We're in." Naomi spoke up, slapping her hand on the table.

Tiana cut her eyes at her friend and sucked her teeth but said nothing. They were violating the ultimate rules of the streets: no snitching. As much as she wanted revenge on Yasin, a part of her screamed out that Chance didn't deserve to be collateral damage. But it was already too late. They were in bed with the pigs.

The next few weeks were spent getting Nina settled into her place. The boys spent a lot of time there. Chase expressed his admiration for Nina every day. She cared for him with the same tender love she showed Nasim. Chance also had to do a little kissing up to Yasmine. After Yasmine saw Nina move out and received the Chance experience, everything between the two of them was copacetic.

Lyrics from J. Cole's new album, *KOD*, serenaded the luxury vehicle as Chance made his way to the airport. He was picking up his right hand, Quan. He would be coming to Miami for a combination of business and pleasure. Nikko, who was Quan's second cousin, was having a birthday celebration at his mansion. Invitations were extended to everyone in their circle, including a plus one. It'd been a few months since Chance parlayed with his best friend. A celebration amongst them was long overdue.

"What's good, my nigga?" Chance exclaimed as he exited the car to help Quan with his luggage. He pulled Quan into a brotherly embrace. "I see you shinin' and all that!" Chance admired Quan's Audemar Piguet bezel engraved with VVS stones. He knew the bustdown cost his mans a pretty penny. "I see Charlotte treating you well."

Chance had handed the throne to Quan once he made plans to move to Atlanta with Nina. His empire back in NC ran like a well-oiled engine with no hiccups. The meticulousness of his operation was like no other drug dealer around. Chance ran shit like a Fortune 500 company. Everybody had a part that was well-defined. A shooter never tried to play the part of a dealer, and the dealer never had to shoot unless necessary. There were no blurred lines. You either played your part or got dealt with.

"A nigga can't complain. I learned beside the best." Quan thumbed his nostrils as he looked down at his fit. He was chilling in an Essentials tracksuit and a pair of limited-edition Jordans were on his feet. His blinging wrist was what set him apart from an average hustler. The average nigga couldn't afford half the shit he rocked, let alone what he carried in his luggage.

"No doubt, money. Let's ride."

The men loaded luggage into the Maserati and hopped in. Chance already had a spliff rolled and ready for his mans.

"The best that Miami has to offer." Chance smirked as he handed the blunt to Quan.

Quan laughed as he sparked the blunt. "This what life like in Miami, huh? A nigga gets catered to and shit? I could get used to this."

"I told you, nigga. That's why you need to move here. All the money we make here makes that money in Charlotte look like chump change." Chance had been throwing hints to Quan about moving to Miami for months now. He missed hustling alongside Quan. They were like two pieces of the same puzzle. Together, they were a formidable force. No one could outsmart Chance, and no one could outshoot Quan. Chance wanted to run it up one more time with his best friend.

Quan rubbed his chin hair as he thought about Chance's words. The idea sounded tempting, but he was the king in Charlotte now. That was something money couldn't buy. For years, he had chosen to remain in the shadows of their operation and allowed Chance to amass his own notoriety in the streets. Quan wanted to be known for more than his gun play. He wanted to be remembered as a hood legend.

"I'm good for now, fam." Quan passed the blunt to Chance. "How your li'l shorty doing?" he asked, referring to Yasmine.

Chance hit the blunt and exhaled. "Yasmine, she good man. I had to spend some racks and spend a li'l more time with her 'cause her ass been on edge ever since Nina showed up." Chance shrugged and passed the blunt to Quan.

"Wait, what?" Quan laughed a little before taking a pull of the blunt. "Fuck you mean, since Nina showed up? You can't casually mention that and shit, nigga."

Chance laughed, remembering he hadn't even told Quan about Nina showing up a month ago. His laughs turned into coughing from the Kush smoke. "Yo, my nigga, I thought I told you. Nina and Nasim been in Miami for like a month now. She left that nigga Yasin."

*Damn*, Quan thought. He hadn't seen or heard from Nina in years, since the birth of Nasim, to be exact. "And he let her up and leave with his son? Fuck happened?"

"That's where shit gets interesting. Nasim may be mine. We should have the results back from the DNA test any day now." Chance shook his head. He'd been anxious the last few days, awaiting the test results. Either way it came out, Chance would be a little hurt. If Nasim wasn't his, he'd be hurt because he always wanted a child with Nina. If Nasim was his, he'd be hurt because he had missed the first years of life. Not only that, but Nasim already had a father in his mind. It would only confuse the little boy.

"That's wiiiiild," Quan said as he hit the blunt. He couldn't wait to see Nina so they could chop it up. "It's always some shit with sis," he joked, but it was true. There wasn't much wrong she could do in Quan's eyes, though.

***

Nina sat at the foot of her bed with a letter in her hand. She'd been sitting in the same position for the last thirty minutes. The letter contained the DNA results. Her MacBook Air sat on the bed beside her. On FaceTime was her best friend, Miami, there for moral support. Even though Miami was on a jet headed to the city of Miami, she wouldn't dare let her girl go through this alone. Nina was so thankful that God led Miami into her life because she'd never had a friend like her before. They clicked instantly and had been tight ever since the first day they met.

"I'm so scared, Miami."

"I know mami, but you have to open it." Miami spoke into the camera. Cassidy was next to her, sleeping, so she wasn't worried about him overhearing their conversation. "No matter the results, Nasim knows he's loved, and Chance will still love you, too. Nothing can ever change that." Miami was one of the few people who knew the story of Nina and Chance's love. Nina had confided in her because she knew her secrets would never leave Miami's mouth. Their love story touched Miami so much that she advocated for them getting back together.

Nina inhaled deeply. She looked down at her shaking hands and closed them into tight fists. "You're right. Let me stop being scary." Nina slid her forefinger through the letter, ripping it open. There were a lot of numbers on the front page of the letter that she didn't understand. She looked toward the bottom of the letter for the results:

*The alleged father, Chance McKnight, is not excluded as the biological father of the tested child, Nasim Singleton. Based on testing results obtained from analyses of the DNA loci, the probability of paternity is 99.9998%. This probability of paternity is calculated . . .*

Nina read the words aloud and tears started falling. It had to be a miracle. Even though she had suspected Nasim was Chance's child, she didn't understand how it was scientifically possible, unless she had never truly miscarried like the doctor proclaimed.

"How is this possible, Mi? I had a miscarriage."

Miami gave Nina a warm smile. "Sometimes there are no scientific explanation for things, baby. That's where God steps in. I know it's a relief to finally *really* know." She wiped the tears that brimmed at the corner of her eyes. She loved this for Nina.

Wiping her tears, Nina smiled. "You have no idea . . ." A myriad of emotions brewed within her. A part of her was ecstatic. Another part was relieved. A small part of her felt guilty. How could she explain this to her son? The only father Nasim had known for the last three years was Yasin. Nina prayed that this revelation would be easy to explain to her son.

"Go ahead and handle what you got to, ma. I just wanted to be here with you while you got that important news. I'll see you in a few hours, okay?"

"Yeah, girl, I appreciate it. Can't wait until you land because we are popping out this weekend, bitch." Nina wiped her tears and rolled her neck as she spoke.

Miami lived in New York and Nina lived in Atlanta at the time, so it had been months since they'd linked. They both understood they had lives that included husbands, kids, and businesses to keep up with. Nina missed her Miami, and nothing would fuck up her weekend with her friend.

"Okay!" Miami laughed and blew Nina a kiss before hanging up.

Nina stood up and thought about the upcoming events this weekend. It was a sunny Friday morning. Nikko was turning thirty and had a party planned at Cameo, a local nightclub. Everybody from the team would be in town from across the country. Nina was a little apprehensive about attending knowing Yasin could potentially show up. But, as far as she knew, he wasn't allowed to leave Atlanta.

*You never know*, Nina thought.

"Mommy!" Nina heard tiny footsteps running toward her bedroom door. "Someone knocking at the door."

Chase and Nasim ran into the room. The boys had been playing with their toys until the knock came at the door. Nina always told them to never open the door without her permission.

*I wonder who's at the door. Chance is the only one who knows where I live, and he should still be out handling business*, Nina thought.

"Stay here," Nina instructed the boys. Reaching in her top drawer, Nina swiftly pulled out her nine and carefully concealed it so the boys wouldn't see it. If it was an unwelcome guest on the other side of the door, Nina wouldn't be caught lacking. Being a mother had tamed her, but she'd never hesitate to squeeze her trigger when presented with a threat.

Nina reached the front door and looked through the peephole. The person had the hole covered, which only irritated Nina. "Who is it?"

"It's me," a female voice replied. It was Miami's voice.

Nina laughed in relief as she opened the door and lowered her weapon by her side. She hadn't expected Miami to pop up at her place this early. "Bitch, you almost got blown the fuck away from here!" she joked as she pulled her friend into an embrace.

Miami hugged Nina back as they rocked back
and forth. "I've missed your crazy ass." Miami
stepped into the condo, looking as fabulous as ever.
Like Nina, fashion was a passion of hers, and she
stayed dripped in the latest trends. High-waisted,
distressed jeans hugged Miami's curvy body along
with a white Dior crop top. On her feet were a
pair of white-and-red Balenciaga sneakers. Her
curly hair was in a high ponytail. With a bare face,
Miami was still effortlessly beautiful.

"You're looking good, girl. Glowing and shit."
Nina complimented her friend. She knew a glow
like that could only come from good loving.

She grabbed a bottle of wine from the kitchen
and poured each of them a glass. "How is life?"

Miami took a sip from the flute. "Thank you,
mami. Life is great. Cassidy and I are doing well.
My kids are growing up so fast, and they are so
smart. I'm blessed, but I try to remain humble."

Nina nodded and smiled. "I admire your marriage so much. Like, you can really tell you two are
in love with each other." Miami and Cassidy were
like a power couple in Nina's eyes. She respected
how they held things down. She knew no relationship was perfect, but Miami and Cassidy were
damn sure close to it.

"That's my baby." Miami blushed, holding the
wine glass in her hand. "Speaking of Cassidy . . ."
Miami rolled her neck and tapped Nina's knee.

"He asked whose condo I was coming to that was in the same building as Chance's. I'm like, nigga, Nina's! Damn!" She laughed. "To be honest, he never really knew you and Chance were like *that*. I knew from the first moment I saw the two of you. I guess he'll find out now." As a friend, Miami figured Nina didn't want everyone in her business. She respected that, and didn't even mention any of it to her husband. There were no secrets between Cassidy and Miami, but this was something she figured Chance would eventually tell Cassidy on his own.

Nina's thoughts lingered back to the DNA test results. She wondered if Chance knew the news yet. "Chance is back?"

Shrugging, Miami pulled a blunt out of her Prada handbag. "I think he is, or he's pulling up, because Cassidy been chopping it up with him since we landed." She lit the blunt and took a pull. "Bad habit of mine right here." She laughed and looked over to Nina, who appeared to be deep in thought. "What's wrong, bae?"

"I can't get the damn DNA test off my mind." Nina sighed heavily and reached for the blunt from Miami. Smoking was something she'd been trying to give up since Nasim was born, but it was a hard habit to shake. The relaxation she felt when the Kush smoke entered her lungs was almost incomparable to anything else she ever felt. The only other thing that could get her high like that was Chance's love.

"What if Chance still decides that he doesn't want to be with me? Miami, what if I'm trying to force something that's not meant to be anymore?" Nina exhaled a cloud of smoke.

Grabbing both of Nina's hands, Miami looked her in the eyes. "Fuck that. Y'all are made for each other. Ya energy around each other is on another level. I can even feel it, so I know you do. And I've only been around the two of you together *once*." Miami held up one finger for emphasis. "Don't give up, Nina." Miami squeezed her hands. "And if we got to fuck Yasmine up, then I'm down with that, too! Bitch in the way."

Nina's cheeks warmed as she blushed. Miami's words reassured her that her love for Chance was worth fighting for. "I just might have to make the bitch disappear," Nina jokingly replied.

"Deadass. I got a man for the job," Miami noted coolly. She took a hit of the blunt and winked at Nina. "However you want to carry it."

Nina laughed out loud, geeked. The Kush was finally hitting her. "Bitch, you're crazy! Nah, I'm going to win him fair and square."

"I'm with that, too. Now, where are these handsome little boys of yours?" Miami put the blunt in the ashtray. The women went into the master bedroom, where the boys sat watching cartoons. They both waved to Nina and Miami.

"Oh, they are definitely brothers." Miami instantly recognized the resemblance between the two boys. They both had Chance's smooth brown skin and dark eyes. Nasim had a lot of Nina's features, but he surely looked more like his father. "Bitch, how you ain't know this from jump street?"

Nina shrugged. "He looked so much like me when he was younger. As he grew, he started looking more like Chance and even acting like him. I guess a part of me was so hurt by Chance and confused. I thought I had a miscarriage." Nina's brows furrowed, thinking back to the sorrow she endured when she mourned losing her child. "And Chase's mom was pregnant at the same time as me. She's a sorry excuse for a mother because she hasn't even attempted to check on her son since he was born. Shit is crazy."

Miami shook her head in disgust. Her mother, too, used to go months without checking on her and her twin sister, Paris. There was bad blood between the women for years, until Cassidy urged the two to reconcile. "Girl, I've had my experiences with my mother like that. She was supposed to raise my sister and me after my dad got killed. She was there, but she really wasn't there. We've come a long way. Nothing's worse than a deadbeat mom."

Nina tapped the blunt against the ashtray and nodded her head. "My mom was killed when I was younger, too. I always had my dad, but that nigga hated me." She chuckled, thinking of how much

she had in common with Miami. They were from
two completely different places but bonded over
their shared experiences and struggles. There was
still a lot the two women didn't know about each
other, but they were forming a solid friendship, a
sisterhood. They were from different places and
had different stories, yet they had the same struggles. "But look at us now. Prospering and shit."
She changed the topic quickly. She didn't want to
pollute the weekend with bad vibes or memories.

"I'll drink to that." Miami smiled and tipped
her glass of wine in the air. Nina reminded her a
lot of herself. If you had asked Miami two years
ago if she wanted another female best friend, she
would have said no. The only females she dealt
with were her twin and her bestie, Gina. However,
Nina clicked with her so well that their friendship
felt inevitable. Gina had even thrown a little shade
when Miami talked about going to spend the weekend with Nina. She wasn't used to sharing Miami.

The ladies got the boys situated for bed. They
planned on kicking back and getting tipsy. It was
Thursday, and the weekend's festivities wouldn't
start until the next night. Yet, they weren't even
aware of the drama that would unfold.


"What's good, bro?" Chance asked Cassidy as
he stood outside of his door. Chance and Quan
were just arriving back from the airport. He was

surprised to see Cassidy so early. "I'm surprised to see you already, my nigga."

Cassidy laughed as he dapped up Quan and Chance. He followed behind the men as they entered the condo. "Man, Miami wouldn't even let us go to our hotel first. She was saying something about seeing Nina?" Cassidy questioned as he rubbed his goatee lightly.

Chance nodded while unlocking his door.

"Shit, I didn't even know Nina was in town."

"Yeah, that's a long story, bro." Chance sat on his sofa. "You can put your stuff in the guest room, bruh," he said to Quan. "So, Miami over at Nina's place?"

Cassidy nodded as he pulled out a Cuban cigar and lit it. "I think it's time I heard this story." He took a pull of the cigar and exhaled the smoke. "No disrespect, fam, but I thought she was with Yasin. I just don't want anything to fuck up our money flow, nah'mean? Especially with that nigga fighting a fed case already." Honestly, he was interested to hear this story. He remembered meeting Nina for the first time and noticing the tension between her and Chance. The only time he had asked Miami about it, she acted like she was dumbfounded, but he knew his wife better than that. He figured she was just protecting her friend, so Cassidy never sweated it.

"Nah, it's cool, bro. Nina and I used to be to-gether. She always was mine, since she was fifteen years old. She was there when I ain't have shit, feel me?" Memories danced through Chance's mind as he spoke. He missed the times when life was much simpler for them all. The more money he made, the more problems he encountered. "We got rich together, but shit went left when her father tried to kill me. I faked my death, and she moved to Atlanta. That's where she met Yasin. He really took advan-tage of her because she was still vulnerable. Nina thought I was dead, but she was pregnant with my child. She got into an accident, and we thought she lost the baby. Crazy part about it, there's a possi-bility Nasim is my son." Chance tried to simplify the story as much as possible. He knew there was not enough time in the world to ever explain the love they had for each other. Their love was vast, deeper than the ocean. "Yasin was cheating on her, so she left him and ended up here."

"Damn." Cassidy shook his head, taking in the information. "So, y'all back together now?"

"Nah."

"Why not?"

"Shit complicated, fam."

Passing the cigar to Chance, Cassidy nodded. "Well, I can't tell you what to do because you're your own man. Life short, though, my nigga. What I can tell you is I don't know where I'd be without my woman. That's my backbone, yo. Nothing makes me happier in this life than seeing her raise our kids. Fuck the material shit. Just do what you think is right. You don't want to look back thirty years from now and have regrets." Cassidy let his words sink in for a minute. "And I've seen Nina, so I know she got options. She won't be waiting forever."

"Chance, where the alcohol at, nigga?" Quan asked as he fumbled around in the kitchen cabinets. Finally, he located a cabinet full of liquor and grabbed the pint of Hennessy. In Charlotte, he had no time to turn up. His position required him to be on his p's and q's because niggas were always plotting to take his spot. If he wasn't handling business, he was with his shorty. The streets wouldn't catch him lacking. However, here in Miami, Quan could let his guard down a bit, and he planned to take full advantage of this getaway. "Where my sister at? Let me call her and tell her come drink with me. I mean, y'all don't mind if I invite the ladies over, right?"

Chance and Cassidy shook their heads. It felt like home being in the company of like-minded people. Chance needed to see Nina anyway to see if she'd gotten back any news on the DNA testing. Cassidy's words were still fresh in his mind, and he was starting to think he was right. Maybe it was time to stop fighting what seemed to be destiny.

*** 

The night left all parties intoxicated. Nina was the last to remain in Chance's condo.

"Can we talk about the DNA results?" Chance asked as he folded his arms.

Having this conversation drunk was not how Nina had pictured this moment, but maybe it was for the best. "I did, but I really don't want to talk about it right now. I just want to lay down."

"What makes you think you can control when I find out or not?" His patience ran thin with Nina regarding the matter. He had already missed three years of Nasim's life because of Nina's choices. He couldn't help but be agitated by her antics.

"Because that's *my* son! At the end of the day, I'm the person he will always be able to count on. I don't want my son coming second to anyone. I have to protect him." Nina felt the tears coming before they even fell. That brown liquor had her feeling a storm of emotions. "We don't fit into your new life." Nina dropped her head.

Chance checked himself before replying. It had been so easy to forget how sensitive Nina became when she was drunk. He had to remember he was still dealing with a fragile heart. "You know me better than anyone in this world, Nina. Don't try to carry me like that. So wassup, why the ill feelings?"

Nina covered her face with her hands, so Chance couldn't see the embarrassment that was written all over it. "Nasim is yours. I was just scared to tell you because I was scared that you still wouldn't choose me." Her eyes burned, and she blinked, opening her floodgate of tears.

*Damn*, Chance thought as he ran his right hand over his beard. The sight of Nina crying was slowly breaking down the walls he had built to guard his heart. "Come here." Chance pulled Nina into his arms and held her tightly. "Don't cry. We're a family, Nina. I will never abandon you or Nasim."

"But you don't love me anymore." Nina sobbed. She felt weak as hell for breaking down like this. No other man would ever have her crying like this, but this was Chance. He wasn't just any other man. He was *her* man. Yasmine didn't deserve being with him in her mind.

"I'll always love you," Chance said just above a whisper. He lifted Nina's chin up and looked deeply into her eyes. "You got me, ma. I can't shake this shit. Maybe we need to stop fighting it."

Those were just the words Nina needed to hear. She stood on her tiptoes and leaned in for a kiss. Chance hesitated, but he eventually began kissing her back with so much passion. Wrapping her arms around his neck, Nina pressed her body against Chance's. She knew he wanted her just as much as she wanted him as she felt him harden against her stomach. They explored each other's mouths with their tongues. So caught up in the moment, neither noticed the table behind them as they kissed. Nina tripped on the table's leg and fell backwards. She laughed loudly as Chance helped her up.

"I got you." Chance scooped Nina up into his arms and cradled her like a baby all the way to his bedroom before placing her onto her feet.

Nina pushed Chance down on the bed and closed the door behind her. She pulled her shirt over her head and crawled on the bed slowly. Nina kissed Chance's neck softly. It had been so long since she'd felt a man's touch intimately that she was already dripping in anticipation.

Their lips locked sensually as Chance left trails of hickeys from Nina's neck to her shoulder. Chance turned on some slow jams to drown out the lovemaking that was about to take place. "Fire and Desire" by Rick James and Teena Marie was the first to come on the playlist. The song captured the moment perfectly. Chance and Nina brought out the fire and desire within each other.

Both stripped completely naked and stared at each other. The sexual tension between them was strong enough to ignite a flame. No one knew Nina's body better than Chance, and vice versa, yet they were still amazed by the sight of each other naked.

Chance made the first move as he instructed Nina to lay on the bed flat on her back. He wanted to make sure he kissed every inch of her immaculate body before he entered her. Each kiss he planted on her body was so deliberate and slow that it caused Nina to shudder. Chance took each of Nina's breasts into his mouth, slowly circling her nipples with his tongue. She moaned in ecstasy. Next, Chance travelled further south and planted kisses on the inside of Nina's thighs. His face met her freshly waxed vagina and smiled at the sight. She didn't smell of anything really—like water, just like he remembered. He kissed both lips before flicking his tongue over her clitoris repeatedly. Nina arched her back from the mind-blowing sensation. When it came to the art of giving head, Chance was a pussy connoisseur.

"Ahh, my God." Nina moaned loudly. Luckily, her moans were drowned out by the loud music. She grinded her midsection into Chance's face, which he happily accepted by digging his tongue deeper inside of her.

Chance inserted one finger into Nina while still licking her clit with expertise. It only took two minutes before Nina was on the verge of an orgasm. "Shittt," She hissed when her body finally stopped shaking.

Sitting up with a smile, she positioned her ass over Chance's face and brought his long, thick dick into her mouth. She knew exactly how Chance liked his head, especially since he was the one who taught her how to suck it like a pro. Hearing him moan from the pleasure she brought him from her mouth only turned her on more.

Chance tapped her ass, signaling he was ready for her. Nina laid on her back and bit her lip anxiously as she watched him stroke himself before putting the tip of his dick at her opening. Entering her slowly, Chance threw his head back from the incredible and incomparable sensation of Nina's muscles contracting around him. Nina was tight and wet, just like he remembered. He stroked slowly at first, making sure she was taking all of him.

"Fuck." He groaned.

Nina's moans grew louder as Chance picked up his pace. She no longer cared if anyone heard them because she couldn't contain herself any longer. She had deprived herself of Chance for far too long. Her body hadn't been worked like this in months, and she wanted to savor every second of pleasure.

"I wanna ride it."

Chance obliged her request as he lay on his back. Nina got on top and lowered herself, then began riding Chance like a champ. He gripped her breasts as she bounced up and down, back and forth.

"Ooooooh, I love you, Chance!" Nina screamed as she had another orgasm.

For hours into the morning, Chance and Nina fell into each other, changing positions and making love. They brought each other to multiple orgasms, never getting the desire to stop. They were like animals mating, aggressive yet passionate.

Little did they know there was a camera set up in the bedroom, and they had a one-person audience watching them.


Yasmine seethed at the sight before her. It was the wee hours of the night. Yasmine sat on her bed, nothing illuminating her bedroom except the screen light of her MacBook Pro. She had officially reached crazy bitch status. The little devil on her right shoulder had given her the idea to plant cameras in Chance's condo. The entire night, she'd been tuned in. There wasn't much interesting information that had come out from her watching the night's interactions. However, she learned that Nasim was indeed Chance's son, and Chance had been playing her the whole time.

Looking at the way Chance made love to Nina, she knew he had to still be in love with Nina. He never treated Yasmine's body like he was doing Nina's in the live stream. So deliberately and delicately. His kisses, his touch, hell even his stroke was different. Finally, Yasmine closed the laptop. Seeing Nina moan in pleasure made her sick to her stomach.

Yet, Yasmine had to admit she was a little turned on. She reached into the drawer of her nightstand and pulled out her vibrator. She turned it on high speed and placed it on her clitoris until she came.

Yasmine regained her composure and walked into the bathroom. She turned the shower on and stepped in. While bathing, Yasmine thought of how stupid she was for falling for a man she knew it could never work out with from jump street. For one, Chance had made it clear he wasn't over his ex when they first met. Secondly, she always told herself to never get involved with any of Nikko's associates. Yet, Yasmine still fell in love with him. His charisma captured her before he even laid a finger on her body. He had a way of making Yasmine feel like the only girl in the world. The superb dick he gave her only sealed the package. Chance was like that.

It would have been better for Chance if he never fucked with Yasmine at all. See now, everything was personal. In Yasmine's mind, all Chance had to do was keep it real about Nina. Yet, he strung her along like a puppet master. What he didn't know was that Yasmine was the bitch really pulling all the strings. His freedom rested in her hands.

By the time her shower ended, Yasmine had devised a plan. She would play coy and shy until the time was right. If and when Chance brought the situation to Yasmine, she would brush it off.

She hadn't gathered enough evidence on Chance yet. Besides, she wasn't done fucking him.

*When it's all said and done, Chance and Nina will regret ever crossing a bitch like me,* Yasmine thought.

# Chapter Nine

Morning came quickly for Chance. Nina was still sleeping. The sunshine reflected on her brown skin. He didn't bother to wake her as he slid off the California king bed.

Grabbing his iPhone and an authentic Cuban cigar out of a full box on the dresser, Chance stepped out onto his balcony overlooking the city. Miami was beautiful. Every aspect of life was lovely here for Chance. It wasn't where he wanted to settle and raise a family, but he had a plan. Now that Nina and his son Nasim were back in his life, he had to grind even harder to execute it. He lit the cigar and pulled deeply. His phone vibrated, indicating a new message.

If it's space you want, you got it. That's all you had to say. I'll hit you up later.

Yas 8:30 AM

Chance shook his head as he scrolled and saw all the missed phone calls and text messages from Yasmine. She was bugging with the all the notifications. *At least she's out of my hair now*, he thought. All his efforts would be focused on getting things right with Nina. Chance hoped Yasmine would take the hint.

"Good morning." Nina greeted him from behind, wrapping her arms around his exposed abdomen. "That's ya girlfriend texting you?" she asked jokingly.

Chance turned around and kissed Nina's forehead. She had his white silk robe covering her body, but the material did little to hide the curves. "You mean more like my distraction." Chance grinned at Nina as he cupped her ass. "You dead-ass been my only girlfriend in my life. I've been with plenty of women, but none of them ever made me feel the way that you do."

Nina blushed at the statement. She hadn't been up but for five minutes and was still as beautiful as ever. That was something Chance loved about Nina. Her beauty was effortless. She could rock her gold hoop earrings with lip-gloss and kill any scene she was on. Period.

Nina pecked his lips softly. "You better let her know her place, because I don't do second place." She gave him a smirk as she traced the outlines of his lips with her forefinger. "If I can't have all of you, I don't want none of you at all." Nina looked into his eyes to make sure he understood her seriousness.

Chance nodded his head. "I got you, Nina." After all the years of history they shared, Chance knew Nina like a book. She was extremely loyal and lived by a code: family first. If you crossed her, she would reveal another side of herself. Nina could be as lethal as any killer or gangster. There was no telling what Nina would do to Yasmine if she came at her wrong. Chance knew the only way to keep the peace was by cutting Yasmine off.

"Good. I'ma go shower and make breakfast." Nina turned around and opened the balcony door. She knew Chance was watching, so she put an extra sway in her walk.

The table was filled with pancakes, scrambled eggs with cheese, bacon and sausage, grits, and toast. Nasim and Chase were seated at the table, ready to dig in. Charlene fixed everyone's plates. Nina was dressed for her nail date with Miami later. The only person they were waiting on was Chance.

"Boys, you can go ahead and eat." She smiled at the two handsome boys. They both looked so much like each other and their father. You really couldn't tell they had different mothers and a few months in age difference.

"Nasim, you know that Chase is your brother, right?" The little boy shrugged his shoulders as he ate a spoonful of eggs. Nina continued, "Well, you are brothers. And Chance is your dad."

"No, he's not!" Nasim interjected. The only dad he knew was Yasin. It hurt Nina knowing she had to confuse her son's young mind, but he was smart and would eventually get used to the idea of Chance being his real father.

"I am your father, Nasim." Chance's deep baritone announced his presence.

"You're my father, too!" Chase shouted cheerfully.

Chance kissed Charlene's cheek, greeting her good morning. "That's right, son. You are brothers. Do you know what that means?" he asked as he took a seat next to Nina. The boys looked at each other and chuckled. "It means you protect each other. Always have each other's backs. You are your brother's keeper. Never forget that." Chance fed his sons wisdom. He was an only child growing up, so Quan was the closest thing he had to a brother. The bond they shared meant so much to him that he wouldn't trade it for anything in the world. There weren't any parents in his household to raise him. His mother died when he was only three years old. As far as he knew, his father died along with his mother. Rose, Chance's grandmother, raised him in her house until he graduated and decided it was time to become his own man. It was important that his kids were raised to value the strength of family because he never properly experienced it.

Nina smiled and nodded her head. "That's right. Family is everything."

"So, Mommy, are you Chase's mom too?" Nasim asked.

"If he wants me to be." Nina looked to Chase. "Can I be your mom, Chase?" she asked. Chase nodded shyly and smiled. Chance rubbed Nina's thigh softly under the table.

Charlene finished the last bite of her food and stood up. "I think you all make a beautiful family." She grabbed her plate and placed it in the sink. "Thanks for the breakfast, Nina. I'll take care of all the dishes." Charlene headed for her room.

"No problem," Nina replied. She was used to doing everything around her house. Having Charlene there was a luxury most parents couldn't afford. "I'm going out for a few. The boys good with you for a few hours?" she asked Chance as she stood up and rubbed his shoulders.

He nodded and smiled at the two boys as they talked. "That's cool. As long as you're back by five. I have a few moves to make before the party tonight. Me and the boys will find something to get into."

Nina placed her empty plate in the sink and kissed each of her son's cheeks. "Thank you." She kissed Chance's lips softly before exiting the condo.

***

"Hey, bitch." Miami greeted Nina as she got into the passenger side of the Tesla. She sported a cream-colored Fendi crop top, an olive pair of biker shorts, and a pair of real fox fur Chanel slides.

"Wassup, girl. You look cute." Nina complimented Miami.

Miami flipped her big, curly tresses over her shoulder. "I mean, it's slight work, you know. You looking good too." Most females who encountered Miami thought she was stuck up because of her demeanor. Nina never got that vibe from her, though. Maybe because girls thought she was bougie, too, but that was the furthest thing from the truth.

Nina was chilling in a pair of distressed American Eagle jean shorts with a red tube top and the Jordan 10s. A pair of oversized Tom Ford shades adorned her face. "Chill shit, you feel me?"

Miami and Nina laughed.

"I was lit up last night," Miami exclaimed. She barely remembered her car ride home with Cassidy last night. All she remembered was sexing Cassidy before she went to sleep.

"It was the Hennessy," Nina commented as she navigated the foreign car through the Miami streets.

"You were turnt yourself, too. You get some dick?" Miami asked. She didn't even need an answer once she saw Nina's mouth curl into a smile.

Her brown skin was glowing. "I told you Chance wouldn't be able to resist for long."

Flashbacks of last night's lovemaking sessions ran across Nina's mind. The thought of it alone had her wanting more. "It's like the universe is pushing us into each other's arms. I feel like he needs me. I don't trust that bitch Yasmine." She rolled her eyes. Yasmine moved like she had ulterior motives, in Nina's opinion.

"What's the deal on shorty? Tell me you done your homework on her." Miami cut her eyes at Nina.

"Nah, I don't even be around her for that." Nina dismissed the thought. She knew she would end up slapping fire from Yasmine if she stayed around her too long.

Sighing, Miami pulled out her phone. "You can't be doing that." She shook her head as her fingers typed a message.

Nina's eyes peered over to Miami, then focused back on the road. "I mean, I know her name is Yasmine Alvarez. She's from D.C. Nikko's chick, Maya, is her friend."

Miami nodded as she finished up her text message. "I just got a friend of mine to check into her. He's a private investigator," she explained. "I'm always extra careful about these broads ever since Cassidy got caught up in that shit."

*Miami's right*, Nina thought. She should have put her lurking skills to use after her first encounter with Yasmine. She couldn't pinpoint where along the line she had lost faith in her intuitive nudges, but she intended on heeding its warnings again. "Everything better check out, or else I'll end up fucking her up, on my son."

Standing in the doorway of her walk-in closet, Nina contemplated the night's fit. She wouldn't go all out; she would wait until tomorrow to shit on bitches. Her nails, feet, hair, and makeup were already done to perfection. The long, wavy weave she sported had been replaced by a blunt bob. The hair was colored to a burgundy, reddish hue. It complemented her brown skin nicely.

Her ringing phone interrupted her search for an outfit. "Hello?" she answered, placing the iPhone on speaker.

"Bitch!" Miami yelled into the phone. "You're not going to believe what I have to tell you!"

Nina looked at the phone curiously. "What?" A part of her knew the news had something to do with Yasmine.

"The private investigator just called me a few minutes ago with an update on shorty. Now, Cole is fucking great at what he does. If there is any dirt to be found on a person, that nigga will go lengths

to dig all that shit up. I know that from experience."
Miami paused on the other end of the phone.

"And?" Nina asked, ready to hear the rest of the
story.

"*And* the crazy thing is, he said he couldn't find
anything on a Yasmine Alvarez. No birth certificate,
hospital records, tax information. *Nada*," Miami
explained. "So, me being thorough, I'm like, *Cole,
what about a national search*? I sent him a picture
of her that I got from her Instagram. Still nothing.
He found other women with that name, but none
fitting her description."

The news made Nina take a seat on the bed.
Who was Yasmine for real? What were her motives? Was she really feeling Chance, or was it just
a front? How did she meet Maya? Could she be
an enemy? These were all the questions running
through Nina's mind right now. "What the fuck?"
she finally said. "We have to find out who this bitch
is and what she wants."

"Most definitely. I got Cole doing some more
digging. He said he'll hit me as soon as something
comes up."

"That's a bet." Nina nodded her head as her mind
thought of possible scenarios to explain Yasmine's
unknown identity. One scenario included Yasmine
up and changing her name and identity. However,
the only people she knew who had done that were
either trying to run from something or someone,

or a person who was down with the Feds. "Keep this between us until we have more information."

"I got you, sis. I'll see you in a few." Miami ended the call.

Nina had been off her square for a minute now. She hated to admit it, but becoming a mother had softened her up. Not that it was a bad thing; however, it made her realize how much of a secure lifestyle Yasin had offered her. Being with him, she had never needed her guard up. Now that he was out of her life, it was essential that she got back to the old Nina—the vigilant and on point Nina. She had always been a shooter, but with a family of her own now, she had to move smart. She should have sniffed Yasmine and her secrets out from the jump.

"You're slipping, Nina," she said aloud as she stared into the mirror. Taking a deep breath, Nina headed back into her closet to find an outfit for the night. She settled for a black bodysuit by Balenciaga with the brand's name printed in white letters. Nina fingered through various pairs of jeans on hangers until she located her favorite pair of black Fashion Nova pants. It was like the pants were painted on every time she wore them. None of her designer jeans hugged her curves like the Fashion Nova did. Like Cardi B said, she could afford designer shit, but the Fashion Nova *fits*. Her outfit would be completed with a pair of thigh-high Balenciaga boots.

Everyone from their camp was expected to come out and show love this weekend. Nina prayed that everyone was on their best behavior as she got dressed. Anyone was liable to make an appearance, friend or foe.

Zidane had texted her earlier, expressing his hopes of seeing her tonight. His interest flattered her, but Nina would never be able to be more than a friend to him. Chance and Zidane were business associates, so that made him off limits. In another world, he was her caliber of a man and would definitely have a chance with her.

A FaceTime call from Chance interrupted Nina's thoughts. She knew it was him because he had a personalized ringtone.

"What's up, love?" he asked after Nina answered.

"Trying to finish getting ready. What you doing?" Nina saw that he was driving. They hadn't gotten a chance to talk much since breakfast.

"I'm making a few money moves before the party starts. I just wanted to see your beautiful face." He gave Nina a smile. "I like the hair, too. It looks good on you." Chance always paid close attention to Nina, so it was easy to notice a change in her appearance. She usually wore her natural hair, and he loved that the most. It was nothing like seeing Nina in her organic essence, but he dug the weaves too. He loved whatever made her feel beautiful.

Blushing, Nina smiled into the camera. "Thank you. I wanted to try something new." She paused as she slipped the jeans over her thighs. "Ol' girl coming tonight?" Nina asked, referring to Yasmine. She tried not to arouse too much suspicion from Chance with her question.

"I haven't talked to her, so I couldn't tell you," Chance replied nonchalantly.

"I guess we'll see." Nina slipped the long boots over her feet. "I have to finish getting ready. I'll see you later." Nina blew Chance a kiss before hanging up.


Chance, Cassidy, and Nikko all pulled into the back of Zidane's restaurant at the same time. All three men looked more like business executives instead of drug traffickers in their designer suits. The naked eye would never guess how much dope these men were about to flood the streets with. They had a big shipment coming in that needed to be discussed with Zidane, who was their number one distributor in Miami. He got first dibs on the weight.

"Zidane, my man." Chance greeted Zidane with a firm handshake after he exited his cocaine white S-class Mercedes Benz.

"Wa'gwaan." Zidane replied in his thick Jamaican accent. He nodded his head to greet Cassidy and

Nikko. "Come inside." He held the doors open to his restaurant. "Feel free to grab a drink or bite to eat while we parlay."

"We won't be long," Cassidy interjected with his hands crossed in front of him forming an X. "We're here to discuss the expectations for the upcoming shipment. It's been brought to our attention that you may not be quite clear on what we expect from you." He pointed his finger at Zidane.

Nikko took a step closer to where Zidane was standing. "Your niggas on the east end came up short last month," Nikko began. His usual wild and curly hair was neatly braided down. It gave him a less menacing appearance. "Now, Chance vouches for *you*. For that, I let your boys slide on that one." Nikko adjusted his diamond cufflinks before making eye contact with Zidane. "But there won't be a next time. You feel me?" He delivered a blanketed threat. Zidane had hitters on almost every perimeter of the restaurant, but Nikko wasn't concerned with that. His only concern was to ensure Zidane understood his words.

Zidane looked to Chance, who had a straight face. He knew Nikko meant no harm, but he didn't like how he went about it. Nikko was obviously asserting his power. Chance was the only nigga he dealt with when it came to his supply. He had heard about Nikko's arrogance on the streets. Today, he had the pleasure of seeing it firsthand.

"I feel you" Zidane replied coolly. He could have easily ended Nikko right then and there, but that wasn't in the best interest of any of them. "We all just trying to eat out here."

"That's right. I'm the nigga that's allowing you to be fed. Never forget that," Nikko said before turning to exit the restaurant with Cassidy by his side.

Chance smirked as he rubbed his goatee lightly. Nikko was the hothead of their team. He was materialistic and flashy, but he ran his operation with no hiccups. His motto was that fear can rule the masses far longer than love can. That was his only flaw in Chance's eyes. He would never become the big man with that thinking. A wise man once told Chance that the key to a king's successful reign was neither fear nor love, but respect. And he lived by that.

"We'll have those joints ready for you tomorrow night after the ball." Chance looked into Zidane's eyes to search for any sign of malice. "I know the type of cat you are. Don't let them little niggas fuck up this money flow. Get them in line." He attempted to ease some of the tension in the air.

"You coming through tonight, right?" Chance asked as he turned and started to walk away.

"I wouldn't miss it, especially if it means I get to see the lovely Nina again."

Those words compelled Chance to stop dead in his tracks. "I really like how we're getting this money, my nigga. Don't fuck it up for yourself," he warned Zidane without even turning around.

Adjusting the jacket to his suit, Chance opened the door to the restaurant and exited. As he got into his coupe, he noticed a black Suburban speeding off from the curb in front of the restaurant. He didn't give the speeding truck much thought as he reversed out of the parking lot.

"This shit is lit!" Nina exclaimed as David pulled the Wraith up to the valet parking area of the club. The entire block was filled with people trying to enter the club. Nikko had brought almost all of Miami to celebrate with him tonight.

"Oh, we're going to have a good time." Miami smiled devilishly as she looked out to the crowd. She was dressed down in a liquid Fendi printed bodysuit that literally looked like it was painted on her. Her slim waist and fat ass were on full display. Miami's curly tresses were pressed bone straight.

David opened the door and helped the two women out of the luxury vehicle. Cameras instantly flashed as Nina stepped foot on the gold carpet, which led to the entrance of the club. She and Miami posed for a second then proceeded to enter the club. It paid to have VIP treatment when there were long lines like tonight.

Cameo was known to host some of the best parties Miami Beach had to offer. Nikko had teamed up with one of the biggest promoters in the industry. Nina had to admit the outcome of all the planning had turned out well.

Miami locked arms with Nina as they entered the club and saw the thick crowd of people already on the dance floor. Future's newest hit, "Racks Blue," vibrated through the entire club. Both women bobbed their heads to the beat as they navigated through the crowd. They stopped by the first bar in their sight.

"Two shots of Hennessy for me and my girl," Miami shouted to the bartender as she placed a blue face hundred-dollar bill on the bar.

Nina placed a blue face of her own on the bar after the male bartender slid her the two shots. "Keep the change." She knew employees of the club didn't mind working tonight. It was plenty of money floating around. Nina and Miami had plenty of it, so they didn't mind sharing. Like Future said, *What you supposed to do when the racks is blue*?

"You want to go to VIP now, or chill this way for a while?" Miami whispered loudly into Nina's ear.

"Yeah," Nina answered as she surveyed her surroundings. There were security guards at every entrance and exit. The exclusive crowd was moving into the club faster, leaving the regular folks outside, hoping to get in.

A familiar face entered the club.

"Let's go to VIP." Nina quickly turned her head, hoping to not be seen. She locked arms with Miami and held tightly.

"You good?" Miami asked as she looked at Nina for a second.

Nodding, Nina eased her arm's grip a little. She kicked herself for leaving her gun at home. Unwanted guests could come in and ruin the party at any moment.

*Please let everyone be on their best behavior*, Nina prayed silently.

"Miami, is that you?" A dark-skinned woman grabbed Miami by the wrists. She had high cheekbones and dark, alluring eyes.

"Remy?" Miami asked as she took a good look at the woman. "You look good, bitch!" she exclaimed as she pulled the woman into an embrace.

"So the fuck do you!" The woman had a strong New York accent, so Nina figured she was an old friend.

"How's Houston treating you?" Miami asked.

Remy spun around, rubbing her hands down her petite body. "Great, as you can see," she said. "My country nigga treating me even better." She showed off a diamond ring on her left hand.

"Fuck outta here!" Miami exclaimed as she brought her hand to her heart. "Bitch, we gotta catch up." She turned her attention to Nina. "You don't mind if I chop it up with my homegirl? I'll meet you in VIP."

"A'ight, call me if you need me." Nina continued to push through the crowd to get to VIP. She felt a hand on the small of her back and rolled her eyes because she already knew who it was.

"Long time no see." A smiling Yasin greeted Nina.

"Boy, fuck you." Nina sucked her teeth as she attempted to walk pass Yasin. However, he blocked her path. The crowd was so thick she couldn't move at the moment. "What are you doing here?" Nina finally asked after realizing Yasin wouldn't leave her alone.

Yasin smirked as he moved a flying piece of hair out of Nina's face. She flinched at his touch, but he ignored it. "I came to enjoy my weekend just like everyone else."

Nina rolled her eyes again and looked around for a familiar face to save her. It had to be apparent that she was uncomfortable.

"You don't have to fuck with me, shorty. I just want to see my son."

Nina laughed as if someone had told her a joke. She didn't trust Yasin at all. This calm, cool, and collected front he put on was almost believable. However, Nina knew better. She had spent almost three years with Yasin only to find out she never knew the real him. Nina blamed herself for it all, though.

"That's not happening."

"Why not?" he asked before taking a step closer to Nina.

"Nasim isn't your son. When the fuck you gon' get that through your head? I had a DNA test done. My son is a McKnight," Nina replied bluntly.

Yasin's nostrils flared as the words left Nina's mouth. The music in the club was loud, but Yasin heard every word Nina said. "Oh, and let me guess. You back with that flaw-ass nigga Chance?" Yasin asked aggressively, grabbing Nina by the elbow.

Nina gritted her teeth and snatched away from Yasin. "First off, keep your motherfucking hands off of me. Secondly, ain't no flaw in my nigga. Watch ya mouth." Nina dusted her arm off. "Lastly, it's none of your fucking business. I'm not with you. I'm not your baby moms. I have no ties with you. I'm good."

Quan had been watching the encounter from across the club. He opted to stay out of it until he saw Yasin put his hands on Nina. Now, he was headed to confront this nigga Yasin.

"Yo, sis, you good?" Quan got to Nina and Yasin within thirty seconds. He stood toe to toe with Yasin and looked him straight in the eyes. He had never liked the nigga. He prayed for the day he got to end his shit. In the past, he'd killed niggas for less, so he wouldn't mind sending Yasin to meet his maker for fucking with Nina.

Yasin looked Quan up and down. "We good, *bro*. This a grown woman right here. She can handle herself. Right, Nina?"

Nina hesitated to answer. She didn't know if a threat lurked behind Yasin's words or not. All she could think about was the deranged look in his eyes when she said she wanted no ties.

"I could give a fuck about what you saying. She don't want no dealing with you, nigga. I suggest you leave her alone." Quan nodded down to his stomach as he lifted the jacket to his suit enough for Yasin to see the .45 tucked safely against his waist.

Yasin chuckled. "Damn, my nigga, was I fucking her or you?" Yasin always expected Quan to have feelings for Nina, and this confirmed it. "No offense," he said sarcastically.

Nina placed her hand on Quan's shoulders. "We good, bro." She tried not to make a big deal out of Yasin's words because she knew there was some truth to what he was hinting at. A woman knows when a man has feelings for her. Nina suspected Quan loved her more than he let on years ago. She was grateful he never acted on his feelings because she could only see him as a brother.

By this time, Miami had found her way back to Nina. She noticed the tension between the three people and figured her girl needed saving. "Nina, I have someone I want you to meet." Miami was quick on her feet with an excuse to rescue Nina from the awkward encounter.

Nina nodded and grabbed Miami's hand. The women disappeared into the crowd.

Yasin looked at Quan with a smirk on his face. "What would ya mans say if he knew you were in love with his ol' lady?" Yasin stood there for a second after asking his question. "At least I got a piece of that. You'll never even taste the pussy. Sucks to be you, my nigga." Yasin patted Quan on the back before disappearing into the crowd.

*What a way to start the night*, Nina thought. But her night was about to get more interesting, as she spotted Yasmine at the bar with a familiar-looking dark-skinned chick. Nina could have sworn the girl looked exactly like the chick she had caught Chance in the bed with. *Nah, the world can't be that fucking small. Or can it?* She made sure to keep the woman in her eyesight as she took a seat in VIP.


Chance, Cassidy, and Nikko arrived at Cameo two hours later. Fashionably late was the perfect term for the three men as they walked through the main entrance of the club. Each man looked different in appearance, but they were equally dashing in their designer suits.

Yasmine spotted Chance's handsome face easily from the bar. If she wasn't so set on bringing Chance down, she really would have fallen in love with him.

"There he is." Yasmine nodded her head in the direction of the men. "Here's the plan: don't let Chance see us together. I want you to try and get close to his right-hand man, Quan. He's too loyal to Nina. We need to sever that bond," Yasmine explained. As long as Quan was close to Chance and Nina, it would be nearly impossible for Yasmine to execute her plan.

"Isn't this risky for you? Like, aren't you scared what could happen if they found out? You don't know what these men are capable of," Naomi said nervously.

"I cover my tracks very well. I've been close to Chance for about two years now. I've gotten way too far for any slip-ups, and I won't let anyone ruin this for me. So, please tell me you aren't getting second thoughts, because if you blow my cover or fuck this up in *any* way for me, that'll be your ass," Yasmine stated calmly. "Now, go get Quan, and don't come back until you have something I can work with."

Naomi rolled her eyes as she walked away from the bar. She devised a plan in her head to get close to Quan. She didn't know much about Quan except for what Tiana had told her about him: *"He's loyal as fuck and overprotective of Nina. Pussy don't excite him. Money and violence do."* Naomi recalled the conversation she'd had with Tiana earlier that night. *"Be careful, Na,"* were her final words.

The men made their way to VIP after greeting a few important guests. Chance noticed Nina sitting by herself, looking around. "A beautiful woman like you should never be alone in a club," Chance whispered in her ear from behind.

A wide smile spread across Nina's face at the sound of her lover's voice. "Where have you been?" she asked as she turned around and kissed his lips softly.

"Handling business, but I'm here now. Everything good?" Chance asked.

Nina shook her head. "I spoke to Yasin." She drank the remaining champagne that sat in front of her. It wouldn't be long before she was throwed, so Nina decided that was her last drink. "He didn't take the news well."

"Fuck him. We'll deal with him later." Chance took both of Nina's hands in his and stood her up.

"Tonight ain't for any of the bullshit. Yasin better tread lightly," Chance responded before pulling Nina into a hug. "I wanna marry you," Chance whispered into Nina's ear.

"You must be in a good mood." Nina laughed as she shook her head. She didn't think Chance was serious since they'd just gotten back on track. Nina waved him off.

Chance nodded and smirked. He was going to let Nina think he was playing for now. He would let his actions speak for themselves. "I'm in a great mood." Thoughts of the money they were about to come into lingered in Chance's mind. "Let's mingle, baby. You sitting by yourself and shit. I'm surprised you ain't with Miami."

Chance's brows furrowed. He didn't like the fact that Yasin's presence had control over Nina. "I'm here now. Let's see if Yasin got that same energy." Still holding Nina's hand, Chance walked over to where the rest of the crew was.

"Wassup, Nina," Cassidy said with a blunt in his right hand and a stack of hundred-dollar bills in his left. Miami was right by his side with a bottle of Hennessy in her hands.

"Wassup, Cash." Nina greeted him as she hugged Maiya, who was seated beside her man. Nina had never had a problem with Maiya. Even though she was Yasmine's friend, she had always shown Nina love. Nina figured Yasmine was using the poor girl anyway. She made a mental note to search Chance's condo for any evidence on the bitch.

"Hey, Nikko." Nina greeted the last of the men's trio.

"You good, mami?" Miami asked as Nina took a seat beside her.

Nina nodded her head. "I just needed a few minutes to myself. I'm 'bout tipsy now, though." She laughed. The music was literally vibrating through her. It was a feeling she always got when she was drinking around loud music.

Chance placed his hands on Nina's thigh and gave it a light squeeze. The liquor had Chance looking edible in Nina's eyes. She could eat him up right there in front of everyone.

"Where Quan at?" Chance asked, noticing his brother wasn't anywhere in the VIP section.

"I haven't seen him since earlier," Nina said, thinking back to her encounter with Yasin and Quan. "He in here somewhere."

Nodding, Chance took a pull from the backwood Cassidy rolled. He figured Yasin would show his face sooner or later.

Miami slid the bottle of Hennessy to Nina. "I take a shot. You take a shot. Then we go to the dance floor," she proposed with a smirk on her face.

"Dancing sounds good." Nina shrugged her shoulders before taking the bottle to the head.

"Whew." She scrunched her face up as the liquor hit the back of her throat. Hennessy was nasty in her opinion, but it always got her drunk with no hangovers the next day.

She passed the bottle back to Miami, who took a shot without hesitation. Miami and Cassidy were about that life when it came to drinking Hennessy.

"I'll be back, baby," Nina told Chance before being pulled to the dance floor by Miami.

Naomi spotted Quan sitting by himself at a booth on the second floor of the club. She thought of a quick way to access him without arousing any suspicions. This was her best opportunity to get close to Quan, so it was now or never. Thinking on her feet, Naomi purchased a bottle of Ace of Spades from the bar. Security at the entrance of VIP didn't give Naomi a hard time because she posed as a bottle girl.

"It's do or die," she said to herself quietly and took a deep breath.

Adding an extra sway in her steps, Naomi sauntered over to Quan. "You mind if I join you?" Naomi asked, announcing her presence. Her perky C-cup breasts were sitting pretty in her Tom Ford mini dress.

Quan checked Naomi out and was impressed by what he saw. Shorty was thick and pretty in the face. "Sit down." Quan nodded to the open seat across from him. "That for me?" he asked as he nodded to the bottle in her hands.

The dark-skinned beauty laughed as she slid the bottle across the table. Naomi licked her lips as she leaned across the table. "That and whatever you see that you like," she said seductively. "Courtesy of Nikko." She added a small lie to kill any of Quan's suspicions.

Naomi had to admit that the pictures she'd seen of Quan didn't do him any justice. He looked even better in person. He was just as handsome as Chance, but his vibe was different. He had a dangerous yet alluring aura about him that made Naomi want to test his fire.

Leaning back and crossing her arms, Naomi studied Quan from across the table. "So, what's up with you?"

"What's your name, beautiful?" Quan asked as he popped the top to the bottle of Ace. He poured a glass for Naomi and himself. Big Bank by YG blasted throughout the club. From their position in the club, you could look down and see everyone on the dance floor. It was a *lituation* tonight.

"I'm Na." She held her hand out for him to shake. "Quan, right?"

Quan nodded, but his eyes were focused on the dance floor. He spotted Nina dancing with Miami. He couldn't help but notice how effortlessly Nina's body movements matched the beat of the music. Guilt crept into his mind as he thought of Yasin's words.

"Can I ask you something?" Quan asked. He needed to get this off his chest. What better person to vent to than a beautiful stranger? "What do you do when you love a person that you can never have?"

Naomi sighed as she rolled her eyes. It was a topic she knew all too well. "Love someone else," Naomi suggested. The question had caught her off guard. As good as she looked, she didn't understand why Quan didn't ask her to go home with him. "Distractions help," she added, speaking from experience. She knew this because she had fallen for Chance when it was clear she would never have his heart. "I could be your distraction. I don't mind. I, uh, actually need one of those myself."

Quan's eyes surveyed the dance floor as he laughed. "I already have one of those," he said, referring to his girlfriend back in Charlotte. It was harsh for Quan to think of Jada as a distraction, but it was the truth. Jada wanted something that Quan just couldn't provide to her: his undivided love. In another lifetime, Quan hoped he would have his shot at love with Nina. He fought a constant battle with his feelings for her. He indeed loved Nina like a sister, but he couldn't ignore his deeper feelings that brewed beneath the surface.

Fighting the feelings was his only option. What did being in love with his best friend's woman say about him?

"Who's the special girl?" Naomi asked curiously. She looked in the direction of the dance floor that Quan was focused on. Coincidentally, Naomi recognized Nina on the dance floor instantly.

*Oooo, I know Nina isn't the woman he's talking about. What that bitch got that make niggas go crazy over her?* Naomi thought.

Eyeing Naomi suspiciously, Quan wondered why she was so interested in his business. "What's up with all of the questions?"

Naomi figured Quan was referring to Nina. "I mean, you asked for my opinion," she explained with a slight attitude. "But I'm sorry if I offended you. Enjoy the drink." Naomi abruptly stood up and walked away from Quan. She smirked as she thought about how easy Quan had made her task. He gave her all the leverage she needed to save her ass. She pulled out her phone and shot Yasmine a quick text.

Quan is in love with Nina and Chance doesn't know.

A smile spread across Yasmine's face as she read the text from Naomi. The new information made it ten times easier for Yasmine to break Chance's bond with Quan. Much of her night had been spent lurking in the shadows of the club. Now it was showtime.

***

The night was approaching an end as the DJ played the last couple of songs. Chance stood outside of the club, finishing up a call from Charlene. He didn't notice Yasmine sneak up behind him. "We'll be home soon," Chance said before ending the call.

"I was wondering if I would get a chance to talk to you tonight," Yasmine said before Chance turned around.

Sighing, Chance slipped his iPhone into his pocket. "Wassup?" he asked with a hint of impatience in his voice.

"You back with Nina now? I seen you flexing with her on your arm all night." Yasmine's jealousy was evident. She hated that she had caught real feelings for Chance.

He nodded.

"And you didn't think I deserved to know that?"

"Why?" Chance shrugged his shoulders. "I thought you would catch the drift."

"*Catch the drift?*" Yasmine scoffed as she mocked Chance. The arrogance that had once attracted Yasmine to Chance was now turning her off in a major way. "I was fucking with you for two years. We spent almost every day together. I thought I at least meant enough to you to deserve a heads up." Yasmine chuckled in disbelief. "It's all good, though."

"So, what's up, Yasmine? 'Cause I know you got more to say." Chance had to admit he'd had some good times with Yasmine, but she couldn't hold a candle to Nina. When it came to the game of Chance's heart, Nina would win every time, no matter the opponent.

Yasmine's mouth formed a pout as she rubbed Chance's chest. "I miss you."

Chance sighed as he removed Yasmine's hands. "It ain't that type of party no more. I got a family now."

Chance's rejection stung. Ulterior motives aside, Yasmine felt cheated out of two years of her life. Chance had made her fall in love with him only to leave her high and dry. "Speaking of family, you ought to check the ones in your circle." Yasmine used this as an opportunity to throw shade.

"Oh, yeah?" Chance gave Yasmine an unconvinced look.

Yasmine placed her hand on her right hip and nodded her head. "Yeah," she said matter-of-factly. "Why don't you ask your homeboy Quan how long he's been in love with your girl Nina?" she spat.

Chance roughly grabbed Yasmine by both of her shoulders. "The fuck you just say?" he demanded.

"You heard me. Ask your girl. I'm sure she knows. We females know shit like that." Yasmine couldn't help but laugh. The look on Chance's face was priceless. "I'm waiting for you whenever you're ready, baby." Yasmine mocked Chance's apparent anger.

"Go the fuck home," Chance warned Yasmine before re-entering the club. Her words had his mind spinning. He had to confront his right-hand and make sure Yasmine had things twisted.

He found Quan sitting in VIP with Nikko and Cassidy, smoking a blunt. Chance approached the table without saying a word. He placed both hands in front of him as he waited for Quan to look up.

"What's good, bro?" Quan asked with an inviting smile on his face.

"Let me talk to you for a second," Chance stated emotionlessly. He stepped over to the side so their conversation wouldn't be overheard. "I got a question for you."

Quan caught Chance's vibe. He had known Chance long enough to know when he was upset. A lump formed in his throat because he knew what his best friend was about to ask him. "Wassup?" Quan replied.

"How long have you had feelings for Nina?" Chance's jaw clenched as he waited for a response.

Quan lowered his head before answering. He knew he owed his friend the truth, so lying didn't even cross his mind. He would accept the conse-quences like a man. "Years," he admitted. "But—"

Chance's fist met Quan's left jaw before he could get the rest of his words out. It seemed as if the entire club froze, and all eyes were on them after that. Quan grabbed his jaw in disbelief. He couldn't believe Chance had hit him. Out of all their years of friendship, they had never gotten into one fight. Out of pure instinct, Quan responded with a right hook of his own. All hell broke loose after that. Nikko and Cassidy struggled to pull the two men off each other.

The commotion coming from VIP compelled Miami and Nina to see what was going on. When Nina realized it was Quan and Chance, she ran to pull Chance off Quan. The way the men were fighting, you would think they were strangers off the street.

"Chance! *Stop!*" Nina shrieked as she grabbed him by the jacket.

"Aye! Chill, nigga!" Cassidy was finally able to separate Chance from Quan. "What the fuck going on?" Cassidy demanded.

"You know this nigga in love with you?" Chance yelled after regaining his composure. Beyond the anger, the look of hurt was evident in his eyes.

Chance put Nina on the spot with that question. All eyes were on her. She looked at Quan, who was wiping blood from his lip, in desperation. She didn't want to admit to the fact, nor did she want to throw Quan further under the bus. "I suspected it, but I didn't really know for sure." Nina threw her hands up in frustration. "It's not that deep,

Chance. Quan never acted on his feelings!" she insisted. All she wanted to do was defuse the situation.

"Not that deep?" Chance yelled. "I trusted that nigga with *everything*. Fuck you mean?"

"I never wanted it to come to this, yo." Quan tried to explain himself.

Chance shook his head. "I'm good!" he said to Cassidy. "Go back to Charlotte, nigga. I'on want no dealings with you. Consider our business null and void." Chance bumped Quan as he walked past him.

Tears fell from Nina's eyes. She was distraught. Two men who meant the most to her in life were at odds. She couldn't recall anything being serious enough to separate the two men. Being at the center of their dispute put Nina in an uncomfortable position. She never wanted to see Chance and Quan fall out, especially over her.

"Quan, I'm sorry." Nina cried into his chest.

Quan brushed his nose with his thumbs. He didn't care that he had just gotten into a fight in a club full of people. "It's not your fault, Nina. Take care of yourself." He kissed Nina's forehead before exiting the club.

"What the fuck y'all looking at?" Nina yelled to the spectators. One smirking face in the crowd caught Nina's attention. "Bitch," Nina mumbled as she looked in Yasmine's face.

"I'ma fuck you up," Nina mouthed to her before turning to exit the club.

Naomi waited outside of the club for Quan. She knew it was risky, but she was lonely and didn't want to be alone tonight. She figured Quan would be rushing out of the club any moment now. A part of her felt bad for setting Quan up, but she was looking out for herself.

People started filing out of the club. It had to be her luck because Chance walked straight into Naomi as he stormed out of the club.

"Well, excuse you," Naomi said as she smoothed out her dress. "Long time, no see. I can't get any love?"

Chance clenched his teeth together. He wasn't in the mood for Naomi's games. "You can't get shit from this way." He brushed past Naomi without a second thought.

She laughed and flipped her wavy weave over her shoulders. A small part of her hoped Chance would at least acknowledge her. "It's cool. I fuck with Quan more anyway!" Naomi yelled after him. She knew why Chance was leaving the club so angrily. A poke at Chance's pride amused Naomi. Really, it was just another way for her not to feel played by Chance, yet again.

Chance paused mid-stride and looked in Naomi's direction. "Well, we always passed them around back in the day. I see ain't much changed." He smirked, not giving Naomi the reaction she wanted. "You look real suspect even showing up here."

Before Naomi could reply, Nina approached them. She put her hand on her hip and looked Naomi up and down. She had watched their interaction from the door. "Bitch, can we help you?" By this point, Nina was already mad about the fight between Chance and Quan. She was sure Yasmine's sheisty ass was behind it all. On top of that, she was still feeling her liquor. Nina was down with however Naomi wanted to carry it. "'Cause you all up on my nigga for what?"

Naomi contemplated either giving Nina a show or maintaining her composure, so she wouldn't blow her cover. "I'm just talking to an old friend." Naomi plastered a fake smile on her face.

Nina handed her Chanel clutch to Chance. He smiled as he waited for Nina to give Naomi what she had coming.

"Don't think for a second I don't know who you are. I seen you with Yasmine earlier. You're a snake. I can tell. So, I may as well whoop your ass before I find out what you bitches is up to." Nina removed her 24 karat gold hoops from her ears.

"I don't even know a Yasmine! Fuck are you talking about?" Naomi was honestly confused. The only person she had been with was Jessica. She couldn't believe Nina really wanted to square up right now. Fighting was something Tiana did, not Naomi, so she was a little shook. "Girl, I am not about to fight you. It's not even that serious!" Naomi exclaimed, placing her hands up in surrender.

"This is my *life,* bitch! It is that serious. I know you and that bitch Yasmine set my brother up. You cross a line when you fuck with my family."

"The only female I've been with tonight is my homegirl, Jessica. As far as your brother, I don't even know what you're talking about. I see you want to fight, but I'm not on none of that. I respect Chance, so I'm not even trying to go there with you."

Nina smirked. *Bitches always wanna cop pleas when shit get real. Could Yasmine's real name be Jessica?* Nina thought.

"That's like I thought. But this ain't the last you'll see of me. Let's go, baby." Nina shook her head at Naomi's scary ass. She locked arms with Chance and headed to their whip.

Embarrassed, Naomi walked in the opposite direction of the couple. She walked right into the person she wanted to see: Quan.

"Jeez, you okay?" Naomi asked, looking at Quan's bloody and bruised lip. "I'm not even going to ask what happened." She pulled a Kleenex from her purse and handed it to Quan. Naomi's acting skills could win her an Emmy. She already knew what had happened, but it was important for her to play dumb.

"You should go home, shorty." Quan brushed past Naomi, but she was hot on his heels.

"I'm trying to go home with you," Naomi insisted.

Quan shook his head as he waited for his Uber to pull up. "I'm on the next flight out of here. I got to get back to Charlotte tonight."

"Stay until the morning. Please."

"Why?"

"Because I think you need to end the night better than it's been going. I just need a distraction myself. It's a win for both of us," she said.

The Uber pulled alongside the curb where Quan and Naomi stood.

"One night only," he said as he opened the back door and motioned for Naomi to climb in.

# Chapter Ten

"Smile," Nina commented softly as she tied Chance's tie. He hadn't said much the entire day they'd spent together. Nina knew to give him his space last night once they got home, but today was a new day. It didn't make any sense, in Nina's mind, for Chance to hold a grudge. He had already done the worst by banishing Quan back to Charlotte. Yet, Nina held her tongue because she knew Chance wasn't trying to hear any of that. The Sagittarius in him influenced his stubborn ways. Besides the mean mug, Chance looked dapper in his all-black Gucci suit.

He gave Nina half of a smile and kissed her forehead. After a long night of thinking and contemplating, Chance decided he couldn't be mad at Nina. He knew she didn't put out her suspicions of Quan's feelings because she didn't want to come between the two men. Chance regretted how he had carried the situation last night, but he wasn't sorry for it. His pride wouldn't allow him to call his brother and apologize. The damage was already done.

"I feel lost right now," Chance admitted.

Nina tenderly held his hand. "Friends fall out all the time, baby." She lightly gripped the collar of his shirt, looking into his eyes.

He shook his head, took a seat on the king-sized bed, and kissed Nina's hands. "Nah, it's deeper than that." Chance reached for the blunt on his nightstand and lit it. "We told each other everything, yo. This a secret he kept from me for years. What else could that nigga have been hiding?" Chance pulled the blunt hard.

"Quan has always been loyal to us. He would die for both of us." Nina pointed back and forth between the two of them. "The shit that came out can never change that. Quan's solid. Never once did he make me feel uncomfortable or like he wanted more from me. We're all human, and our emotions can be hard to control. He loves me, but guess what? He loves you way more. Loyalty means more to Quan than his feelings," Nina replied honestly. There had been many opportunities for Quan to make his move on Nina in all the years they'd known each other; however, he never did, and she knew he never would. Nina respected him for that. "He's family."

"Family will cross you, too." Chance kissed Nina's lips and handed her the perfectly rolled big Dutch. "I'll see you at the ball. I have to get there early to chop it up with Nikko and Cassidy. I love you."

Nina shook her head at Chance's stubbornness. It would be a while before he forgave Quan, but she trusted in their bond. She trusted that their love would eventually reunite the two. "I love you, too."

Chance cruised through the beautiful streets of Miami, anticipating the money they were about to make. It was his third year throwing what he called the Player's Ball. The average person who was familiar with the ball knew of it as a fundraising event for black elites such as celebrities, athletes, business owners, etc., to gather and party. Those privileged enough to do business with Chance knew that it was a perfect front. Chance had masterminded the idea so drug dealers, the top dawgs, could come and bid on weight to move. He ensured all the paperwork and legal aspects were squeaky clean. His lawyer handled all of the affairs, just in case the police wanted to sniff around.

The past two years hosting the ball had gone successfully for Chance. This year was going to be even better with all of the hours of preparation they had put in. It would be hosted at the Zen Retreat in Miami. The mansion featured a beautiful white marble floor and a huge living room. It had all of the furniture cleared out upon Chance's request. The event was strictly invite-only. Security would be heavily enforced, with zero tolerance for bullshit.

Everything was pretty much in place when Chance arrived at the estate. They had decided on a masquerade theme for the night with a strict dress code. If you weren't in formal attire, access to the party would be denied.

The hired valet stood at the entrance, ready to park Chance's Tesla. "Thanks, my guy." Chance shook the young man's hand as he stepped out of the car. The kid squeezed Chance's hand firmly and made direct eye contact with him. He didn't look a day over eighteen. Chance respected the hustle the kid had.

"Come find me later if you're looking for another job." Chance recognized the hunger in the young man's eyes. He handed the boy, whose name tag read Kenyan, a hundred-dollar bill as a tip.

"Thanks, man. I'ma find you later. Don't forget about me," he said eagerly.

"No doubt. Do that," Chance replied before entering the mansion's foyer. The stage was set up and the DJ already had the music going. Chance spotted Cassidy and Nikko at the custom bar they paid to have set up.

"What's good, Mayweather?" Cassidy greeted Chance, swinging in the air as if he were boxing, before dapping him up. Cassidy didn't know what had happened between Quan and Chance. He didn't ask questions either. Chance would talk about it when he was ready, Cassidy figured.

Chance shook his head as he thought of last night's drama. He had lost his cool and put his hands on one of the people closest to him. Thinking of Quan lusting over Nina sent his calm demeanor out the window. "Chilling, my nigga. How this shit looking?" He dapped Nikko up and pulled him into a brotherly hug.

"We set to go," Nikko stated as he rubbed both of his hands together.

Those were all the words Chance needed to hear. Now that all the ducks were in place, he would kick back until the party started.

Nina sat down on the couch in the living room as she watched Chase and Nasim play with their toy cars. Charlene was in the kitchen, preparing dinner for the boys. Nina should have been getting ready for the ball, but she wasn't feeling it. The way things had gone down last night didn't sit well with her. Quan crossed her mind multiple times. There was a nagging feeling in her gut that wouldn't settle until she checked on him. *Call him*, the voice in the back of her mind urged. Nina picked up her new iPhone and dialed Quan's number.

On nearly the last ring, Quan answered the call. "Wassup, Nina?" he answered coolly on the other end of the phone.

"I hope you didn't think I won't gon' call and check up on you," Nina said and gave a little laugh to lighten the mood.

"Nah, I know you better than that, sis. I'm surprised I'm just now hearing from you." He returned the laugh. "I'm back home, though. Making slight moves."

"Oh, okay," Nina replied.

An awkward silence filled the air. Nina had called because she wanted to make sure Quan got home safe. Now, she didn't know what to say. A part of her wanted to ask Quan how long he had harbored these feelings for her, but she didn't want to make him feel uncomfortable.

"Bro, I gotta ask," she finally said. "How long have you loved me? Like, really *loved* me?"

Quan sighed heavily on the other end of the phone. The question didn't surprise him. He actually knew it was coming. "Nina, you know we go way back. Shit, I'm the one who introduced you to Chance. I always had love for you. It's easy falling for you after being around you for so long. You're a good-ass woman, yo. Solid as they come, straight up."

Nina listened silently on the other end as he began explaining.

"I watched you grow into a woman. You always held Chance down, even when he didn't deserve your loyalty. I would always tell bro when I was

ready for a girl, I wanted her to be just like you."
He chuckled before continuing. "I had plenty of
times to try you, but I'm not even built like that.
You and Chance always been right for each other.
I respected that. Y'all are my only family, besides
Jada. I chose my family over my feelings."

Nina sat quietly for a second as she thought
back to the times Chance had hurt her in the
past. Quan always came to Chance's defense. He
never threw Chance under the bus. On so many
occasions, he acted as the glue that brought Nina
and Chance back to each other during the trials
their relationship faced. Quan's loyalty ran deep.
He lived by a code that a lot of niggas preached but
never practiced: family over everything. There was
nothing in the world that could make him turn on
his family. He would die before he allowed that.

"Chance will come around soon."

"No disrespect, sis, but I don't think shit will ever
be the same between me and Chance," Quan replied bluntly. Both men were stubborn. They had
never come to blows before or exchanged hateful
words with each other. They prided themselves
on being bigger than that. If Chance couldn't see
that Quan always moved from a place of love and
loyalty, Quan wouldn't waste time convincing him.

Nina hated to hear those words, but she knew
it was true. "How is Jada? I never got to meet her."
She changed the subject.

"She's good. I told her so much about y'all. She's a li'l' sad that she didn't get a chance to meet everyone so we could share the news."

"Don't tell me I'm going to be an auntie!" The thought of having a little nephew or niece around instantly excited Nina. "I am so happy for you, bro. This is a blessing. Congratulations!"

"Thanks, Nina. Look, I don't want to rush you off the phone, but I got some business to handle."

"Oh, no, it's cool bro. You just been on my mind heavy. You know I love you forever. I'll never turn my back on you. Be safe out there."

"I love you too, sis. You already know how we rocking. Kiss my nephews for me."

"I got you," Nina said before hanging up the phone. A weight felt like it had been lifted off of her shoulders. She worried about Quan's well-being, but now that she knew he was fine, her mind was at ease.

A knock came on the front door right as Nina started to head for the bedroom. She raised an eyebrow, wondering who could be on the other side of the door.

Nina couldn't believe her eyes once she looked through the peephole. "Boys, go to your room." Nina softly ordered. The boys grabbed their toy cars and ran to the back of the condo.

"You got a lot of fucking nerve." Nina's voice dripped in animosity as she snatched the door open. Nina crossed her arms as she stood toe to toe with Tiana.

"I wasn't expecting to see you either," Tiana replied sarcastically. She had hoped to catch Chance before he went to the ball. She decided that being on Chance's team was safer than working for Agent Tyson. Days spent thinking about getting caught by Chance or someone in his organization haunted her. The baby mama title wouldn't save her if they found out she was snitching. Snitching equaled a death sentence in their hood.

"I told myself I would fuck you up the next time I saw you. Now, why shouldn't I?" Nina asked seriously. This was the same bitch who had fucked with both of her niggas.

Tiana pulled out her phone and held it in Nina's face. "Because I think you want to fuck her up more. Save your energy. You'll need it after the story I have to tell you." On Tiana's phone was a photo of Yasmine.

Nina wasn't convinced. "And why would I trust anything that comes out of your mouth?"

"I owe you and Chance. You stepped up when I failed as a parent. Just hear me out," she pleaded. Her eyes watered in desperation. She was ready to get on her knees and plead if it went that far.

Reluctantly, Nina stepped aside, allowing Tiana to enter the condo. "No further. Sit." Nina ordered Tiana to sit on the couch closest to the door. "Talk."

Nina discreetly opened the voice recorder app on her iPhone and started recording.

"First off, woman to woman, I want to apologize for any hurt I caused you. It was petty and childish on my behalf."

Nina chuckled as she shook her head. "You're sorry for fucking my man and getting pregnant?" She gave Tiana a confused look. "Or are you sorry you got pregnant when you never wanted a kid in the first place?" Nina read her like a book. "I don't want your apologies because it ain't coming from a place of sincerity. I don't believe a person as scandalous as you can change. You don't have to apologize because you're in my presence. What's next?" She waved her hand and crossed her legs.

Tiana sighed and shifted uncomfortably. She hadn't expected Nina to accept her apology, but she gave it anyway. With all the chaos she had caused in Nina's life, apologizing was the least she could do. "I have to admit whenever Chance and I fucked around, he always used protection. The only reason I got pregnant is because I froze his sperm and injected it in myself," she admitted shamelessly.

"Bitch, what?" Nina exclaimed. "You done *all* of that just to leave your son? I can't." Nina waved her hand no. "Just get to why you came here." Nina couldn't stand to hear anymore of Tiana's trifling stories. "What do you know about Yasmine?"

"I know for one her real name isn't Yasmine." Tiana crossed her legs and leaned forward, ready to spill all the tea. Nina motioned for her to continue. "Her name is Jessica Tyson. Or shall I say *federal agent* Jessica Tyson?"

Tiana had Nina's undivided attention now.


Chance looked down at his watch as he surveyed the crowd for Nina. She should have made it to the ball over an hour ago. He would have started to worry if Nina hadn't sent him a text saying she was on the way a half hour ago. The ball was approaching the final bidding and donation section before it ended. Thus far, over a million dollars had been raised for this year's scholarship winners.

"Well, hello, handsome," a female voice said behind him.

Chance turned to find Yasmine. "Who invited you?" he asked curiously. Chance thought he had made sure Yasmine's name wasn't on the guest list.

Yasmine removed the burgundy masquerade mask from her face. "I see last night still has you uptight." She grinned devilishly. "Tell me what I can do to help you," she purred sensually.

"How did you even know about that?" Chance wondered how Yasmine knew about Quan when the two barely spoke to each other.

Yasmine shrugged her shoulders. "I have my ways."

Cassidy interrupted their conversation. "We have a problem." Cassidy nodded for Chance to follow him outside. "The Feds are all over our shit at the docks!" he whispered harshly.

"The fuck you mean? They got our shit?" Chance questioned angrily. This was the last day he needed the Feds sniffing around.

"I don't know. I mean, I'm guessing so. All Nikko said was they had the whole ship surrounded," Cassidy explained.

"Fuck!" Chance shouted. A few people hanging outside turned their attention to the two men. "How the fuck did this happen?" Chance asked hypothetically as he paced back and forth. They'd never attracted the attention of the Feds before. How did they even know where the shipment was coming to? A thousand questions raced through Chance's mind. Either they were moving extremely sloppy, or someone was snitching, he concluded.

*Where the fuck is Nina*? Chance thought. Times like this, he could count on Nina or Quan to advise him on the next move to make.

He pulled out his phone and dialed Quan's number. Like he expected, Chance got his voicemail. "Aye, bro, we need to talk. I know what happened last night can't be forgotten, but I need you, bro. I love you. Hit me back."

Chance hung up the phone and nodded to Cassidy. "Come on. Let's figure out how to tell these niggas their weight on back order."

Cassidy shook his head. He was thinking the same thing as Chance. "We got a rat, b."

The news Nina received from Tiana had her floored. Nina knew something was off with Yasmine, but she never expected her to be a Fed. Everything Chance and Nina had built—their family, their business, *everything*, was at risk now. There was no telling what evidence Yasmine had on Chance, let alone Cassidy and Nikko. She'd been playing the part of the loyal girlfriend so well that she deserved a damn Oscar.

*Two years she's been undercover*, Nina thought as she sped to get to the ball. She hadn't even bothered getting dressed. Nina had instructed Charlene to look over every inch of the condo for wires, cameras, anything that could incriminate Chance.

A bad feeling settled in Nina's gut as she got closer to her destination. Luxury vehicles lined the block of the affluent neighborhood as Nina sped down its streets.

"Oh my God." Nina's heart dropped as she saw flashing blue lights in the distance. She parked her car quickly and hopped out. Nina thanked God she had worn her Yeezys instead of heels because as soon as her feet touched the ground, she ran toward the mansion. When she passed through the gates of mansion, she saw the one sight she had hoped to never see: Chance in handcuffs. Not only was Chance in cuffs, but so were Cassidy, Nikko, and Yasin.

"What the fuck do y'all think you're doing?" Nina spazzed on the cop who was roughly handling Chance. "You *pig*! Don't touch him like that!" She pushed the fat white cop.

"Ma'am, back up or you'll be in cuffs next," another cop warned her.

By this time, guests had formed a crowd outside of the mansion. Many had phones in their hands, recording just in case the cops wanted to try some crazy shit.

"Fuck y'all!" Nina yelled, fueled by anger. Nina spotted Yasmine in the crowd and locked eyes with her. She wanted to fuck this bitch up so bad it hurt, but Nina knew she had to play it smart if she wanted to get her man out of this jam.

*We play chess, not checkers.* Chance's words rang out in Nina's head.

"Nina!" Chance yelled. "Call my lawyer. Go home with the boys and wait on my call. I love you!" he shouted before being shoved into the back of the police car.

"Girl, where have you been?" Miami asked Nina as she hugged her tightly. "Them motherfuckers stormed in there like they were trying to get Osama Bin Laden or some shit!" Miami spoke quickly.

The vibrating of Nina's phone interrupted their conversation. Nina gave a sigh of relief when she saw Quan's face flash across her screen. "Bro, you won't believe what just happened!"

Instead of Quan's voice replying on the other end, a distraught woman's cry answered. "Nina, he's gone!" the voice cried out. "They killed him! Oh my God!"

"Jada?" Nina asked in confusion. "Slow down. Tell me what happened." If Nina had heard her correctly, she'd said someone killed someone. She knew Jada couldn't be talking about Quan because Nina had just talked to him.

"Quan, Nina. They killed Quan. They shot him!" Jada sobbed into the phone. "He's gone, Nina. He's gone. They robbed and shot him. Oh my God, why?"

Nina dropped her phone and covered her mouth with her hands. Her phone instantly shattered as it hit the concrete. "*Noooo!*" she yelled before letting out a gut-wrenching cry. It was like her world had come crashing down. Things couldn't possibly get any worse. That was news Nina never wanted to hear in a million years. Her brother, her protector, was gone. How did something happen that quick? Nina had just talked to him on the phone. He couldn't be gone that fast; Nina so desperately wanted to believe. But she knew the price that came with the streets. You could be here one minute and gone the next. Nina had seen it too many times. Never did she think she would be mourning one of her best friends. The grief she felt was immeasurable.

"Mami, what is it?" Miami held Nina's arms, keeping her steady as her knees tried to give out. "Talk to me. What happened?" Miami held Nina's face in her hands.

"It's Quan. They killed him," Nina said weakly as she wept into Miami's shoulders.

"Oh my God, baby. I am so sorry. Let's get you home." Miami's heart ached for Nina. She knew the feeling all too well. Quan was a good nigga from what she saw. It was so fucked up that some-one took his life. Miami sighed as she walked Nina to her car. She was a mess. After tonight's events, all Miami wanted to do was crawl in bed and cry with her friend.

"How am I . . . gonna tell Chance?" Nina asked as she cried. She knew this would completely crush Chance. He already had enough on his plate; this would surely push him to the edge.

Nina silently prayed. *God, I know I don't talk to you much, but please hear me out. Look over my brother's soul. He may have done some bad things in his life, but his heart has always been pure. Protect and guide his soul into your eternal heaven. And please help me get Chance out of this bind. I need you, Lord. Amen.*

*Numb.* That was the perfect word to describe how Nina was feeling. She hadn't gotten a minute of sleep since she'd been home. She sat in one spot on the bed with her phone in her hand. Its cracked screen mirrored the sentiments of her shattered heart. Red eyes stared back at her. The thought of Quan being dead just wasn't registering in her mind. It had to be a cruel joke. She hoped for a phone call from him saying he had faked his death just like Chance had, but after hours of waiting, no call came. Reality was beginning to set in. Quan died, and she would never be able to hug him again.

Miami never left her side. She held Nina as she cried all night long. The pain she was feeling no one could understand—except Chance, and he was sitting in a jail cell at the moment. It was the weekend, so Nina knew they would be held there until Monday. It was well into the morning, and Nina prayed she would be receiving a call from Chance sooner than later. How could she tell him this horrible news? Nina had never been so afraid to tell Chance anything in her life. She knew this would break him. The last encounter between Chance and Quan was physical. Words were exchanged that could never be unsaid. That would be what would hurt Chance the most.

"How am I gonna tell Chance?" Nina asked, voice raspy and eyes swollen and red from crying.

Miami yawned as she wiped the sleep from her eyes. She'd been dozing in and out of sleep all night. Tired wasn't the word to describe how exhausted she was, but she tried her best to stay up throughout the night with Nina.

"Honestly, I wouldn't tell him while he's locked up. He has enough to worry about in there."

More tears fell from Nina's eyes. She was in a tough position right now. Not only did she have to deal with Quan's death, but she also had to figure out how she was going to get Chance and Cassidy out of this predicament.

"I have something to tell you. But you have to promise me you won't tell Cassidy."

Miami sat up completely in bed. "What is it?"

"That bitch Yasmine," Nina said venomously. She had so much hatred for Yasmine in her heart that she had to take a deep breath. "She's behind all of this shit. She's a fucking Fed. All of the shit that went wrong tonight leads directly back to her."

"Hold up. How do you know this?" Miami sat up quickly.

"She recruited Chance's baby mama Tiana to do her dirty work. But Tiana ain't built like that.

She knows a lot, but one thing for sure, she knows Chance wouldn't hesitate to off her ass for going against the grain," Nina explained. "We have one up on her. I went to confront her last night, but then I saw all the cops there. I had to play it smart as much as I wanted to kill that bitch. I think I have a plan."

"So, am I gonna beat her ass first, or are you? My husband is sitting in a cell because of that bitch! Ya body will be found floating in the Hudson for shit like this in New York. She has to be dealt with. Period." Miami shook her head as she thought of the severity of this situation. She seethed with anger. "There's no telling what information she had on them. Or us for that matter! I know how this shit goes, Nina. First, they'll charge our men, then they'll be coming after us next. I'm especially fucked because I'm married to Cassidy. And I'll send a motherfucker to meet his maker before I leave my kids or my man." Miami stared Nina in her eyes so she could see how serious she was.

"I know, Miami. I live by that same code. But Yasmine is better off alive right now. Trust me." Nina held Miami's hands.

"You're my bitch, so I trust you. At the end of the day, though, you know our little problem is eventually going to have to be eliminated." Miami spoke in code. "A loose end." Miami shrugged her shoulders. She'd much rather have Yasmine killed immediately, but maybe Nina was right. Yasmine could possibly be their only key to getting their men off these charges.

Their conversation was interrupted by Nina's ringing cell phone. Nina looked at the unknown number and knew it was her man.

"You have a collect call from . . . *Chance pick up,*" at the Miami Federal Correctional Institution. To accept these charges, please press one."

Nina pressed one and held her breath. She didn't like keeping the fact that Quan had died from Chance, but it was the last thing he needed to hear right now.

"What's up, baby," he said in his deep baritone from the other end of the phone.

"Hey, baby. I'm so glad you called." Nina spoke softly, taking a deep breath. "What they saying?"

Miami motioned for Nina to put him on speakerphone, and she did.

"It's the weekend. They gotta hold us until Monday until we can go before a judge. Them motherfuckers trying to pin that shit the Feds found on the boat on us. I don't want to say too much over the phone about it. You contacted my lawyer yet?" Irritation in Chance's voice was evident.

"No, a lot of shit has been going on, but—"

Chance sighed heavily into the phone. "Damn, Nina, that should have been the first thing you done!"

Nina rolled her eyes, trying to hold back tears. She knew Chance wasn't trying to upset her considering his circumstances, but he didn't even know the type of night she'd had herself, the type of crippling grief she battled. "I know, Chance. It's hard to explain."

"Nah, explain it to me, Nina. Tell me what could be more important than getting me my freedom. First, you get to the ball late as hell. Now this. Who or what got your attention?"

Miami looked at Nina and shook her head no, already knowing what she was about to say.

"I have some bad news, and I can't tell you this over the phone, baby. Please don't make me say it."

Chance was silent for a moment. Amid all the bullshit going on, he didn't want to hear any more bad news. "A'ight, I hear you." He sighed. "Contact my lawyer for me. Have him ready first thing Monday morning. I'm trying to be out this bitch asap."

"We got you, Chance. Where's my husband? He good?" Miami yelled in the speaker phone.

"He's good, sis. He should be calling you soon. Nina, I love you. I'll see you soon, baby."

Nina expressed her love for Chance before ending the call. She desperately wished she could break into the jail herself and free her man, but that was not how the American justice system worked. As broken as it was, there were rules and regulations in place that had to be followed. Innocent until proven guilty; Nina was thankful for that decree, even though the media was running with the story and making Chance out to be a cartel leader. She would do whatever in her power to kill that narrative and ensure Chance's freedom.

By Monday morning, Nina and Miami were up bright and early to meet with their lawyers. Chance and Cassidy would be going before a judge in less than one hour. They prayed the judge would grant bail. Both women carefully climbed the steps to the entrance of Harper and Stevens Law Firm. It housed two of Miami's most cutthroat defense attorneys. Jay Harper and Austin Stevens were the only men with the balls to take this case. Chance had spoken highly of Jay Harper on numerous occasions, but Nina had never met him.

"Hello, ladies. How can I help you?" The blonde receptionist greeted them with a smile.

"Nina Singleton. Miami Santana. Mr. Harper is expecting us," Nina answered while looking at the time on her iPhone.

"Of course. Right this way." The thin beauty led Nina and Miami down a hallway until they reached Harper's office. "He's been expecting you." The girl motioned for them to enter the immaculate office space. They found a middle-aged black man sitting at the desk. His goatee displayed hints of salt and pepper, and his head was bald. He was easy on the eyes for sure.

"Good morning, ladies. You must be Nina." Mr. Harper stood up and shook Nina's hand. "I've heard a lot about you."

"Likewise." Nina took a seat as she observed the award plaques hanging from the wall. "This is my girlfriend, Miami. Her husband is one of the men that was picked up with Chance. I know you and Chance are familiar from your past business transactions."

"Chance worked with Stevens. He handles contractual business. I'm defense." Harper sat down behind his desk and crossed his legs. "Nevertheless, you also know this will not be cheap?"

Nina nodded her head as she crossed her legs. "I'm well aware. Whatever it takes. We need someone like you, Mr. Harper."

"Call me Jay," he insisted with a gracious smile. "I'm confident we can bring your men home today and beat these charges. The only evidence the Feds have right now is a shitload of cocaine and a Colombian immigrant who illegally delivered it. He's not talking, and the Colombian government requested he be tried in his own country. So, they're back at square one," Jay explained.

"Thank God!" Miami exclaimed as she squeezed Nina's hand.

"Don't rejoice just yet, love. The Feds will not give up after this. It's an embarrassment. They will be coming after your men, your businesses, and your finances. The money you post for bail, make sure it is squeaky clean. They will be after anything that could link them to anything illegal. Is that clear?"

Both women nodded.

"All right. Let's go get your men."

Nina couldn't wait until the moment Chance was released. She had put on her best poker face the last few days, but all she could think about was Quan lying dead on a cold table. This unfathomable reality ate at Nina's heart every second of the day. She'd experienced death before. Her beautiful mother, Jaslynn, was murdered when Nina was just a young girl. There were people she grew up with that had passed. Shit, her own father had tried to kill her and ended up dying at the hands of Yasin. Nina had been close enough to death to kiss it plenty of times. Death seemed to be a distant friend of hers. Yet, losing Quan was different. The pain seemed like it would never stop. Maybe it was because Nina was grieving for Chance, too. He would undoubtedly take the news the worst.

"You good, mami?" Miami asked as she noticed Nina staring out of the car window as they headed to the courthouse. She could sense the sadness pouring out of Nina. Miami knew she was trying to remain strong for the sake of their situation. It was all she knew, what all women who looked like them or related to their struggle knew: strength when life brings you to your lowest point. "We're bringing them home."

Nina nodded as she bit her bottom lip, trying to hold back tears. "My brother is never coming back. I have to live with that." Her voice was barely audible as her bottom lip quivered. "I have to make this right." All of the chaos in her life was a direct product of Yasmine's treachery. Nina would make her suffer for her deeds, but first, she would bail her man out and bury her brother.

# Chapter Eleven

Chance gritted his teeth as he struggled to walk with the tight, heavy shackles on his feet. Being chained up for the last two days had made him come to a realization. This would be his first and last time in chains. The American prison system claimed to rehabilitate criminals, but its sole intention, in Chance's opinion, was to enslave the black man. It was a system that Chance had lost many homies and family members to. He refused to fall victim to this punishment again. Court would be held in the streets before Chance surrendered to prison.

"This way." The guard pushed the four men chained together. He held a big wooden door open that led to the courtroom. The stocky white guard unchained Chance and Cassidy and led them to the table where Harper and Stevens sat. Nina and Miami sat in the row of seats directly behind their lawyers.

Cassidy turned around and planted a big kiss on his wife's lips. "Looking good, baby."

"No touching," the guard warned harshly.

Nina gave Chance a hopeful smile and blew him a kiss. Just the presence of her man lifted her mood. All she wanted to do was collapse into his strong and soothing grasp. She *needed* him. She needed to hear him say that everything would be fine, even if it wasn't.

"All rise," the bailiff stated loudly. "The Honorable Judge Lopez."

Chance gave a sigh of relief when he saw the judge walking up. Maria Lopez was Nikko's distant cousin. She was well compensated for the confidential information she provided to Nikko and Chance on a monthly basis. He locked eyes with Nikko, who was seated across the room. Nikko nodded and gave him a smirk.

"You may be seated," Judge Lopez declared as she sat down comfortably. "Chance McKnight, Cassidy Arrington, Nikko Ramirez, and Yasin Amos. Well, this is my first time seeing these names in my courtroom." Judge Lopez flipped through the files as she tapped her finger impatiently against the stand. "Hmm, drug trafficking."

Nina and Miami looked at each other with puzzled looks on their faces. This woman seemed so uninterested, not like she wanted to lock up four criminals.

"They better have her on payroll," Miami murmured to Nina.

"Attorney Harper, Attorney Stevens, I will not be wasting anymore of your time today. The DEA has dropped all charges against the defendants. It seems there is no direct evidence linking these men to the shipment of cocaine found. On behalf of Dade County, I apologize to you four men. Next case." Lopez banged her gravel and handed their files to the secretary sitting next to her.

Nina looked at Miami in surprise. It couldn't have been that easy, right? *This is only the beginning*, she thought as Harper and Stevens shook her hand.

"At least we didn't have to drop that million," Miami whispered in Nina's ear before walking over to hug Cassidy.

The minute Chance emerged from the entrance of the courthouse, Nina ran into his arms. She couldn't contain the storm of emotions that had been brewing inside of her. With Chance, she could let everything out. Nina was content with the fact that he'd never judge her. Tears poured from her as Chance embraced her tightly, intertwining his fingers in her hair as he massaged her scalp carefully.

"Shh, it's okay, baby. I'm never leaving you again," he whispered in her ear.

"It's not okay. Everything has changed." Nina cried as Chance nearly held her up as they walked to the Town Car. She slid in after he opened the door for her. "I wish I had good news for you, baby, but it's all bad." Nina shook her head, dreading being the bearer of bad news.

"Whatever it is, you can tell me, shorty. I beat this case. That's all that matters." Chance stroked her soft hand as they headed to their home. All he wanted to do right now was see his sons' faces and lay up with his lady.

*If you only knew*, Nina thought with a lump forming in her throat. She cleared her throat and mustered the courage to speak the dreadful news. "I don't even know how to say this—"

The ringing of Chance's phone interrupted Nina's words. Yasmine's name appeared across the screen.

"Answer it," she demanded. "Put her on speaker phone."

Chance looked at Nina as if he were trying to figure out her angle. But from the tone of Nina's voice, he knew she was serious. He slid his finger across the button just in time to catch the call before it forwarded Yasmine to voicemail.

"Yo."

"Oh my God, it's so great to hear your voice. I miss you, Chance. After seeing you get arrested this weekend, you've been on my mind nonstop." Yasmine's voice filled the car.

"Word?" Chance replied, playing it cool.

"Of course, baby. I just think it's funny how shit starts going left for all of us when Nina arrives in town."

Nina scoffed silently as she listened to Yasmine slander her name. The conniving bitch was trying to plant seeds in Chance's mind that could possibly lead to him looking at Nina as if she were the cause of everything. She looked at Chance and raised an eyebrow.

The thought of Nina crossing him was ludicrous. "What you trying to get at, Yasmine? Because you can't insinuate shit like that without Nina being here to defend herself." Yasmine had become a slight annoyance to him since he and Nina got back together. He had tried shunning her politely, but his efforts didn't stop Yasmine from pursuing him. It seemed as if Chance's rejection only added fuel to Yasmine's desire for him.

"I'm just saying. I know you're real lowkey and shit when it comes to your business. Cops never been a problem for your operation. You run that shit like a monopoly. So, why is it a problem all of a sudden?"

"I don't know what you're talking about, Yasmine." Chance frowned. She was getting loose at the lips, and it was time to cancel her ass for good. "Have a good day, shorty." He hung up before Yasmine could get another word out.

"What's that about?" Chance turned to face Nina.

"That's a discussion for later." An unreadable expression came over her face. "Quan died." She spit it out quickly. If she hadn't said it now, she never would. Nina decided ripping the Band-Aid was the best route to go.

Chance laughed lightly as he cocked his head to the side like the words Nina spoke weren't registering in his mind. "You said what?" It was as if time stopped for a second. He read Nina's lips as she said what she said, but he couldn't have possibly heard her correctly. "What did you say?" There was no way niggas got one up on Quan.

Nina looked into Chance's eyes and recognized a dark look. It was the look of the devil that lived inside of Chance, a devil that only came out when his loved ones were harmed. "I said Quan died, baby. Jada called me . . . and told me." Nina's voice quivered as she slowly replied.

Chance pulled out his phone and dialed Quan's number. It was the same reaction Nina had when she received the news. He angrily ended the call when the phone went straight to voicemail. Sweeping his hands over his face, Chance pinched the bridge of his nose, trying to maintain his composure. He was glad he was already sitting down because his knees gave out when he realized Nina was serious.

"I didn't even get to tell him I was sorry." Chance finally broke down when he remembered his last encounter with Quan. He had fought his brother and condemned him back to Charlotte. In his mind, he'd sentenced his brother to death by sending him back home. Chance knew how niggas were in Charlotte. When they saw the next man coming up in a major way, they would take his life to try to take what he built. He would never be able to forgive himself for this.

"My brother, man." Chance placed his face in Nina's lap as he cried like a baby. The last time he cried like this was when his Nana died, the only woman he knew truly loved him besides Nina.

Nina's heart broke seeing Chance like this. She knew the magnitude of her pain couldn't compare to the turmoil Chance was experiencing. He'd lost his best friend, his right hand, his brother. Nina rubbed his back as she sobbed along with him. They were the only people in this world who understood how world-shattering this news was.

"I can't believe it either, baby. We have to go to Charlotte. I don't think Jada will be able to handle funeral arrangements on her own."

Chance sat up and wiped his face. The tears stopped, but the pain would be eternal. He would forever be tormented by his last encounter with Quan. "She doesn't have to worry about anything.

She's carrying my little niece or nephew. She good forever." The thought of having a part of Quan living on through his seed eased the pain a little.

"I never kept anything from you, Chance, and I don't want to start now. I hate even having to tell you this with all the shit that's going on, but you deserve to know," Nina said as the Town Car pulled alongside the curb at the skyscraper where their condo rested. "Yasmine is a fucking Fed. That bitch is the cause of all this shit," Nina whispered into his ear.

"A Fed?" Chance repeated. "I'on know, Nina. We need proof." He knew he wasn't slipping to the point he couldn't point out an undercover agent or not.

"Look at me. We'll figure it out." Nina grabbed Chance's face with her hands. "When we have proof, we're going to make that bitch pay. But we got to play smart first. This is chess, baby. By the time we're done with her, she'll wish she never fucked with our family, and that's on my brother," Nina promised. She never made a promise she couldn't keep. She kissed Chance before releasing his face.

"Your sons have been waiting for you. It's been a long couple of days. Let me take care of you before we go to Charlotte," she said as she dropped to her knees.

***

Nina and Chance had been in Charlotte for two days now. The majority of Nina's time was spent planning a funeral. Chance wasn't much help. Nina knew he was battling the guilt of fighting Quan on top of grieving his death. Like any good woman, Nina picked up the pieces when her man couldn't.

It was the day of the wake. Nina dropped the boys off to Chance's aunt, who lived right outside of Charlotte. She headed to meet Jada for the first time. Nina was going to make it her business to ensure Jada's comfort before going back to Miami.

The GPS indicated Nina had arrived at her destination. She chuckled to herself when she pulled up to a modest brick home. Quan always stated he never wanted to live in a mansion. A nice three-bedroom, two-bathroom home was enough for him. *I know he got that joint decked out inside*, Nina thought. There was a BMW parked in the driveway and Nina assumed it was Jada's.

Her YSL heels sank into the grass as she crossed the yard. Knocking lightly on the door, Nina observed the surroundings of the suburban neighborhood. A person had to be making at least six figures to reside on this side of Charlotte.

"Hi, Nina." Jada and her baby bump greeted Nina. Jada's cinnamon-colored skin was smooth and glowing flawlessly. She wore her hair in a short curly fro that was dyed an orange hue. The hoop nose ring resting in her small nose accentuated her beautiful face. Nina could tell Jada was a petite woman without the bump.

"Come on in." Jada stepped aside and allowed Nina to enter the home.

"Hey, it's nice to finally meet you." Nina felt the urge to hug Jada. She held her tight and close because she knew she needed it. Three years ago, Nina had been in Jada's shoes. The only difference was Chance didn't really die. He faked his death, and Quan's was all too real.

"How are you feeling?" Nina asked as she sat on the gray plush loveseat. Nina noted Jada's resemblance to herself. She wondered if Quan had pursued her because she reminded him of Nina.

Jada exhaled as she took a seat on the couch across from Nina. "I'm trying to stay strong." Jada smiled, but the shaking of her voice let Nina know she was hurting. "I feel like my time with him, my baby's time, was stolen. It's not fair." Jada shook her head as she looked down at her bump.

Nina's heart broke for the beautiful woman before her. That pain Jada was feeling would be felt every time she looked into her child's face. "I can't say I know how you feel, honey, but I almost do. It's going to be hard. I'll always be here for you and that baby. No matter what. We lost a real one." Nina shook her head. She wanted to question God, but there would be no answer, except that everything happens for a reason.

"So, there was nothing out of the ordinary that day?" Nina asked. She hoped Jada could give her some type of insight into this dreadful situation.

Jada nodded her head as she reached into her purse and pulled out a manila envelope. She slid the envelope across the glass table to Nina. "When Ty'Quan got back home, he told me about everything that went down in Miami. He never liked keeping things from me. He told me he spent the night with some bitch named Naomi. They had sex." Jada dropped her head. "I'm like, why would you do this to me and why are you telling me this?" she cried.

Nina was all ears now. "And what did he say to you?"

"He said he had to do it for you and Chance. Apparently, the girl had some information he needed, but he wouldn't tell me what. He said the less I knew, the better." Jada shrugged her shoulders and took a deep breath. "The night he died, he was going to meet up with these new buyers. I told him not to go because I didn't have a good feeling about it. Like always, he told me he had everything under control. Then he handed me two envelopes. One for you, one for Chance. He said if anything ever happened to him, to make sure I gave it to you both. He kissed me, left, and that was the last time I saw him," Jada said as a pool of tears streamed down her face.

Nina picked up the envelope and held it tightly in her hands. Did Quan know Yasmine was the Feds and came to Miami to get more information? What happened with him and Naomi? Who did he meet with that night? There were a million questions Nina wished she could ask her brother.

"I'm sorry, Jada. I promise you we're going to find out who killed Quan," Nina vowed as she slipped the envelope into her Chanel purse.

"Since he died, all of these females are trying to claim him. I can't fight because I'm pregnant, and I can't ask Ty'Quan because he's dead. I just don't know what to do," Jada cried.

Nina moved across the living room to sit beside Jada. "You were the only woman to capture my brother's heart. He *never* brought up a girl to me until he met you. Quan loved you, and he loved that blessing growing inside of you more than you'll ever know. Those bitches can say what they want, but they never had him like you. Never did." Nina put her finger under Jada's chin and lifted her head up. "You can cry all you want, but don't ever let anyone see you with your head down. When you're ready, we'll leave for the wake."

Jada nodded, teary-eyed. "Thank you, Nina. I know he loved you very much, too. You lost him just like me."

Nina blinked away tears as she smiled weakly. "I did." She rubbed Jada's back as she cried.

\*\*\*

Black Ray Ban shades covered Chance's face as he sat outside of the church where Quan's wake took place. Nina was inside with Jada and the rest of the guests. He didn't know how Nina was able to remain strong for everyone. Chance couldn't even bring himself to see his brother's lifeless body lying in the ten thousand—dollar casket he'd purchased. Instead, he was sitting in his rental car, facing blunts of Kush. A semi-automatic pistol rested in his lap. All he wanted to do was make the entire city rain with bullets until he found the niggas responsible for his brother's death. A life for a life. But Chance knew none of that would bring his brother back, so he put it on pause. The streets would talk eventually.

"Tha Crossroads" by Bone Thugs-N-Harmony blared loudly from the speakers of the car. He choked on his blunt as he took a trip down memory lane. There was not a milestone in Chance's life that he hadn't conquered without Quan by his side. How could he go on with such an important figure in his life gone?

### Summer 2011

*The summer heat in Charlotte was blistering. It was one of the hottest days the city had seen* in July. Drake's latest hit blared from someone's car as everyone from the apartment complex gathered at the pool party. All the hustlers, scammers, strippers, and groupies were in attendance. Chance brought everyone out to celebrate Nina's nineteenth birthday.

A year ago, Nina had inherited her mother's half-million-dollar life insurance settlement. She used the money to boss her life up, with Chance's help, of course. At 18 years old, she opened her first Beautique. Plenty of women in the city despised Nina just for the fact that she was young, beautiful, and successful, but they really hated that she had Chance's heart. No one ever tried her, though. They knew the consequences could be dire.

The celebration was also to welcome Quan home from doing a one-year bid for getting caught with a dirty gun. Chance missed his right hand, but he ran it up 365 days straight for his nigga. Now, he had finally touched his first million dollars. Today was reserved for turning up. No business would interfere with Chance showing Nina and Quan a good time.

Nina was poolside with her homegirl, Chanel, when Chance arrived with Quan. "Bro!" Nina exclaimed as she jumped up to hug Quan. "I missed you so much! Check you out." Nina took a good look at Quan. He had put on some muscle weight, but he wore it well. "Feel good to be home, huh?"

"Damn right. I ain't never going back to jail."
Quan nodded down to acknowledge Chanel. She
always tried to flirt with him, but Quan never
made a move. He had a certain type of woman
he liked, and Chanel didn't fit the description. She
was beautiful, but just not his cup of tea. However,
Quan didn't know if it was because he hadn't
gotten pussy in a year, but Chanel was looking
better than ever. He decided that he would finally
give her a chance tonight.

"Oh, I almost forgot." Quan handed Nina a
small, blue Tiffany's box. A beautiful diamond
tennis bracelet sat inside. "Happy birthday, sis. I
couldn't make your eighteenth, so I had to make it
up to you."

"Aww, you didn't have to." Nina kissed Quan's
cheeks lightly. "Thank you. Go ahead and enjoy
yourself, bro. Chanel ain't going anywhere." Nina
playfully nudged Chanel, letting Quan know she
had peeped him checking Chanel out. "Chance
been missing the fuck out of you. Maybe he won't
work so much now that you're home." Nina
winked at him before turning her attention back
to Chanel.

The next few hours, Quan and Chance kicked
back and got drunk. For the first time in 365
days, Chance was able to let go and enjoy himself.
He wasn't worried about a nigga pulling up on
hot shit because niggas knew better than trying
Chance with Quan around, or vice versa.

"Yo, Chance, you my brother forever, nigga. I love you, man." Quan spoke sincerely. The liquor was starting to get to him because he was getting emotional. "I got your back through whatever, with whoever. Family over everything."

Chance laughed because he knew the Hennessy had Quan gone. "No doubt. You know it's nothing but love for you. I never met a realer nigga." Chance dapped Quan up and slyly placed a set of car keys in the palm of his hand. "Welcome home, my nigga."

Quan looked down at the Mercedes Benz key fob in his hands. "Oh, this how we welcome niggas home now?" He smiled.

Chance nodded with a wide grin on his face. He felt like a proud dad at this moment. "That's right. We stayed down until we came up. Now we all the way up, and we ain't never going back to the bottom," Chance modestly bragged.

He led Quan and Nina to the parking lot where Quan's new cocaine white Benz sat. "That's all you, bro. She's paid for. Nina helped me pick it out, so I hope you like it."

"Yeah, bro. I got my first foreign on my birthday last year. We had to get you right," Nina noted.

Quan wiped his hands over his face in excitement. It had been a long time since he'd been behind the wheel of anybody's car. He couldn't wait to spin the block on this baby. "I appreciate it, bro. I'ma pay you back for this for sure."

*"Don't insult me like that. This empire is just as much yours as mine. I wouldn't be where I am today without you, bro. There's nothing that I can give you to repay you for your loyalty. All I can do is continue to give you my loyalty, too. Family over everything, right?"*

*"Family over everything,"* Quan repeated, solidifying their ten-plus-year bond. There was nothing that could come between them.

*Nina couldn't contain her happiness as she brought both men into an embrace. "Group hug,"* she exclaimed playfully. *"I don't know where I would be without you two." Emotion threatened to overcome her, but she didn't want to ruin the moment. "Family forever," she stated proudly.*

*"Family forever,"* both men repeated.

A single tear slid down Chance's face as he thumbed the *Family Forever* tattoo on the inside of his right forearm. It was a matching tattoo that he, Quan, and Nina had gotten years ago. It symbolized their unyielding loyalty to each other, always and forever. A light knock on his window brought Chance back to reality. Nina stood on the other side of the window. Chance turned the music down as he unlocked the door for his beautiful woman. She sighed as her body sank down into the plush leather of the car seats. Nina hadn't slept in nearly two days. Exhaustion was written all over her face. The responsibility of planning a funeral weighed on her, yet her beauty still shone through.

"I need you in there with me."

"I can't see him like that." Chance shook his head as he thought of Quan's lifeless body lying in a casket. "That was the strongest nigga I know. How can I look at him like that, lifeless?" Chance was fighting an internal battle. A part of him wanted to be there for Nina, and even Jada, to be that crutch of support that they needed. Then, a part of him still hadn't accepted the fact that Quan was gone. Seeing his body would confirm one of Chance's biggest fears.

Nina sighed heavily and took a deep breath. "Do you know how tiring it is being the one everyone is looking to for strength? I never asked for this, but I'll proudly accept it because I loved the shit out of Quan. I think you're afraid to face him because of the last encounter you had with him. It's something you can never take back, and now it's too late to apologize. You have to deal with it because I can't do this alone anymore. Get your shit together, Chance!" Nina shook her head at him before slamming the car door and heading back into the wake.

*Nina's right*, Chance thought as he looked down at the tattoo again. Chance groaned as he lifted his body out of the seat of his car and exited. His feet felt heavy as he took steps closer to the church. Heart racing, Chance swung the heavy church doors open. There were about thirty people gathered inside. Chance recognized most of the faces, but there were some he didn't recognize. When his eyes met Nina's, he saw a look of relief come over her face. She was drowning out there trying to keep everyone occupied.

"Ma, how are you?" Chance asked as he hugged Quan's mother.

"Oh my God, Chance." The lady cried into Chance's chest. Lidia wasn't the best mother to her son while he was younger, but Quan had forgiven her a long time ago. He loved his mother more than life, even when she neglected him as a child. "I'm glad you're here. I haven't seen you and Nina in years."

"I'm sorry we had to see each other under these circumstances," Chance stated genuinely. "I know Quan loved you more than the world."

"I could say the same for you, baby. At least he did leave me a grandbaby." Lidia nodded to a very pregnant Jada, who was wobbling in their direction.

"Chance," she said as she held her hand out to him. "I'm Jada."

Instead of shaking her hand, Chance bent down until his was face level with her six-month belly. "Hey, little one, it's ya uncle. You'll never have to worry about anything. Your mommy, your grandma, Auntie Nina, and I will make sure of that." He planted a kiss on Jada's stomach before standing up. He pulled her into a hug, sensing that it was something she needed. "You're family, Jada. We never shake hands," Chance said once he released the embrace.

Jada smiled as she realized how much of a family Quan had with Nina and Chance. He was lucky to have them in their child's life. "He talked so much about you." Jada's voice cracked. "There's something that he left me with that he wanted you and Nina to have."

"What is it?" Nina inquired.

Jada pulled a thick manila envelope out of her Birkin bag. "He gave it to me the same night he died. He told me if anything ever happened to him, to make sure this made it into your hands. I'm not sure what's inside it."

"Thank you, Jada." Chance took the envelope and tucked it on the inside of his suit.

The sun peeked through the curtains of their hotel suite. Chance and Nina rested in the middle of the bed. "You opened your envelope yet?" Chance inquired as he massaged Nina's feet. It was tempting not to open his envelope and see what was in the contents. He thought maybe Nina could enlighten him on the contents of her own envelope. Chance wondered what his slain brother had up his sleeve.

Nina shook her head. She honestly didn't want to open the envelope. Knowing Quan, someone would have to die shortly after revealing the information in the envelope. "I'm anxious to find out what's inside, but I have to be mentally prepared. I'm opening mine after the funeral. What about you?"

"I'll open it once I get back to Miami." Chance traced his finger along Nina's ankle. Thoughts were heavy on his mind tonight. The pain of losing Quan had opened the gates he put over his heart many years ago. There was not much that left Chance wondering what move to make next. He never let his emotions get too invested in situations. Nina was the only person who could penetrate his guarded heart. It was amazing how the ills of the world didn't matter when he was next to her. After all these years of being together, he found a new way to fall in love with Nina every day. She was his sanctuary.

"I can't believe he's gone, yo." Chance couldn't believe he had to bury his brother the next morning.

Nina shook her head as her eyes lowered in sadness. "Me either," she whispered softly as she rubbed Chance's shoulders. "Looking at his

body today, I—I wanted to break down. He was
so strong. He was thorough. Seeing him like that
fucked me up," Nina admitted, laying her head on
his chest.

Chance nodded. He knew exactly what Nina
meant. In the wake, he couldn't muster up the
strength to look at Quan's body. Just as he had
inched closer to the casket earlier, his palms began
sweating and his breathing became erratic. Lying
in a casket was the last place Chance imagined
seeing Quan. The situation was surreal.

"I couldn't look," he replied.

Chance didn't notice that his hands were
shaking. Nina took his hands in hers and firmly
caressed them. "I can feel him. He's still looking after us like he always has." She gently massaged his
hands. His nails were clean and cut down. It was
something Nina had done for him since the beginning of their relationship. She chuckled at the
memory of telling him she hated to see a man with
dirty nails.

Bringing his hands to her face, she kissed them
softly. "We'll get through this together."

Chance brought Nina into an embrace and
kissed her forehead lightly. He followed the
gesture up with a light kiss on the neck. That
alone was enough to send electrifying shivers all
throughout her body. He knew all the places that
turned Nina on, even down to the smallest ones

she thought he hadn't picked up on. His strong hands danced along her waistline, making her womanhood drip in anticipation.

"You always got my back," Chance whispered as he kissed her inner thigh. His hands gripped each of her thighs firmly, making Nina squirm in anticipation.

She licked her tongue out as she watched Chance's manhood rise to attention. The illuminating light from the nightstand was reflecting just right on Nina and the gold satin robe she wore. He knew she was naked underneath the expensive garment, just how he liked it.

"I'ma always have your front." Chance cupped Nina's C-cups in his hands. Having a child had filled her breasts out perfectly. He exalted in the beauty of the grown woman before him. There were scars on her body that revealed trauma that she'd experienced in the past. He kissed every one of them gently. Nina was self-conscious about them, even though she never admitted it to Chance, but he knew. What Nina didn't know was that Chance thought her body was a masterpiece that deserved his worship. Each one of her imperfections symbolized Nina's strength in Chance's eyes. She was a goddess, and she didn't even realize it. A true queen. Without her, Chance wouldn't have amassed half of the things he possessed in life. Most men think it's a woman's place to follow her man's lead, when truly, it's so much more powerful when your woman can lead right by your side.

"Without a doubt," Nina responded as she leaned in for a kiss, taking the lead like a lioness in the wilderness. She playfully pushed Chance back on the bed as she straddled him. Looking him in the eyes, Nina positioned herself on top of his thickness and lowered herself down slowly. Up. Down. Up. Down. Throwing her head back in ecstasy, Nina found her rhythm instantly.

Chance bit his bottom lip and placed his hands on Nina's hip. She grinned devilishly as she removed his hands and picked up her speed.

"Uh-uh, baby." Teasing him turned her on. She knew it would only be so long before Chance flipped her over and took control the way that sent her climbing up walls.

"Damn." Chance grunted as he admired the view. Seeing Nina bouncing up and down on him, titties jiggling, he was almost at his peak, but he never came without making sure Nina got hers first. That was law. In one swift motion, Chance wrapped his hand around Nina's back and flipped her on her back. As he dug deeper inside, Nina scratched his back and grunted in pleasure. Just as he felt Nina's pussy muscles contract around him, Chance bit down on Nina's ear softly. "I'ma marry you," he whispered, his hot breath against her ear.

***

Shaky hands gripped the thick envelope. Nina had been sitting in the same place for ten minutes outside the church. The little voice in her head urged her to discover the contents inside the envelope. It was the last thing Quan had left her. After a long night of sexing, Nina had found herself tossing and turning restlessly. As crazy as it sounded, she believed Quan was trying to send her a message.

Chance walked up to her and placed a finger under her chin. He hated seeing her with her head down, but circumstances were different now. They'd lost a brother. "I want to tell you take all of the time you need, but the service is about to start in a few minutes."

If Nina weren't rocking the dark pair of Ferragamo shades, Chance would have been able to see the tears pooling in her eyes. "I just need ten minutes, baby. I'll be right in, okay?"

Chance gave her a reluctant nod and backpedaled back into the church.

*All right, Nina, just open it,* she thought.

Taking a deep breath, Nina opened the envelope. As she pulled the contents out, a small key fell on the ground. Picking it up and looking at it, she assumed it was a safety deposit box key. There was an envelope inside that contained printed pictures. Nina thumbed through them and saw several pictures of Yasmine meeting up with Tiana and that dark-skinned chick she knew looked familiar. There were also pictures of Yasmine entering the district attorney's office. These photos also corroborated Tiana's story of Yasmine being a Fed. It looked like Quan had discovered Yasmine's real identity and tracked down her immediate family. Quan had printouts of Yasmine when she was younger, information on her from college, and more. This was just the type of collateral information Nina needed to get Yasmine. Nina also noticed that there was a flash drive in the envelope also. She would have to connect that to her laptop on the flight back to Miami.

Nina picked up a handwritten letter that Quan handwrote to her. Tears fell as she looked at his neat handwriting.

*Nina,*
*Phenomenal. That'll be the word I would use to describe you if anyone ever asked. That's exactly what you are. At this point, if you're reading this, that means I have crossed over. I don't want you to cry for me or grieve over me, sis. I knew exactly the type of lifestyle I was living and the consequences that came with it. You live by the gun, you die by it. I hope you find peace*

*in knowing I will be good no matter where life takes me, even in the afterlife. I take a little peace myself in knowing that I always kept it a hundred and told the people I loved that I love them while I'm here. That shit is so important.*

*You've probably met Jada by this point. That's my everything. She always tells me I taught her so much, but the truth is, she taught me more than I could have ever taught her. She taught me love, and that's the lesson of life. I been reading a lot, sis, believe it or not. I read that this journey here on Earth is only temporary. We have to make the best of what we got while we here. I lived my best life, but meeting Jada, I wish I would have met her years ago. Maybe shit would have turned out differently for me.*

*Back to you, sis. I want you to do a couple of things for me that I trust you'll handle. I've included a key to a safety deposit box with some of my belongings. I want Jada to get everything. She's pregnant with my seed. Without a doubt, I know you gon' have her back for me. She's special, Nina, but she ain't built like us. I want you to protect her. I never want harm to come to her. I know it's a lot to ask, but I know you got me.*

*Look out for my brother, man. Money can change a lot of people, and all that money he's making will bring problems with it, too. You know how the shit go, sis. It's better to get out while you can. The only thing Chance loves more than money is you and my nephs. You can get through to him.*

*Take care of yourself, Nina. I may not be there with you physically, but I'm always watching over you. Never stopped. That bitch Yasmine is sheisty. I trust that you learned enough from me to know how to get rid of the bitch. You got the leverage you need on her. Don't let her tear down everything we built. Like we always say, this shit is just a game of chess. Protect your king, even when muhfuckas thinking you ain't. Stay ten toes down. Remember, we may bend, but we never fold. We the last of a dying breed, sis. Hold that shit down like I know you can. Don't cry for me; put one in the air for me. I love you forever.*

*Family over Everything.*

*Quan*

Nina smiled as she wiped the tear falling down her cheek. She knew she felt Quan's spirit. Whenever she was in his presence, she always felt protected and secure. Damn near invincible. And today, like the past few days, she'd felt that same way.

Nina brought her hand to her mouth, kissed it, and extended it toward the sky. Nina lit the bottom of the letter with her lighter. It instantly spread, until the entire page was ash, blowing with the wind. As much as Nina wanted to keep the letter to hold on to one last piece of Quan, she knew it was too risky.

Nina opened the doors to the church just as the service began. She made her way to the front row and sat between Chance and Jada.

"You good?" Chance whispered to her, searching her face for any indication of something wrong.

Nina grabbed Chance's hand and squeezed it tightly as she shook her head no. "Everything's fine, bae. I opened my envelope," she whispered back and then turned to focus her attention on the pastor at the altar.

The service went by fast for Nina. She couldn't stop thinking about what she would do when she finally got her hands on Yasmine. Quan could have possibly risked his life getting Nina this information, so she wasn't going to waste this opportunity he had provided her with.

People were lining up for the final viewing of Quan's body. Many walked by and voiced their condolences to Nina, Chance, and Jada. There were a few female faces in the crowd that Nina recognized from Quan's past. She hoped they wouldn't bring any bad energy or try to be funny with Jada, because neither would fly in her presence. Today would be the day she snapped, and that was the last thing she wanted here.

Jada's feet felt heavy as bricks as she watched the row of people sitting behind her lined up in front of the gold casket. It meant that they were next up. "I can't do this," she whispered to Nina.

Nina noticed Jada's chest start to rise unevenly, and she was sweating. "You can," she replied calmly. "Can't you feel him? Your heart is linked with his, literally, beating through your baby. It's going to hurt, but we'll get through this. Just breathe." Tears of joy and sorrow filled Nina's eyes as she touched Jada's baby bump. "We're family now. I got your back." Nina verbally affirmed that she would honor Quan's dying wish by looking out for Jada. She would love her like her own sister.

Exhaling slowly, Jada nodded her head. Nina didn't know that she had never really had a family before, so those words made her feel safe—how her man made her feel. That fact had intrigued Quan about Jada because he always wondered how a woman who was never shown how to love could give pure and unconditional love.

*Damn, I'm going to miss that man*, Jada thought solemnly. No one ever left the type of imprint on her heart like Quan. No one ever would again.

Nina stood and placed her hand in Chance's. He gave her hand a slight squeeze, letting her know in their language of love that he admired her for comforting Jada. One thing he loved about her from the jump was that she never stood for tearing women down, only uplifting them. But she could be lethal when crossed.

"I love you."

She kissed his lips. He placed his forehead against hers for a few seconds. No other soul in the building mattered in this intimate moment Nina and Chance shared. They were both about to say goodbye to someone they thought they would never live without. It was almost impossible to process the thought, but Nina knew they had to let go for Quan to peacefully make his transition.

"I got you, baby." One foot in front of the other, they slowly made their way to the casket.

Jada was the first in line to view the body. Luckily, Nina was right behind Jada because her knees buckled at the sight of her man lying in a casket. Her baby girl kicked wildly as if she felt her mother's distress. "

Oh my God." Jada sobbed as she placed a hand on Quan's cold face. She had to admit the mortician did his thing because Quan looked normal. He didn't sustain a fatal gun wound to the head, so it made his preparation for viewing easier.

Jada placed her hand over his heart, right where the bullet had pierced him. He had died on impact. "I'm so sorry, baby." She kissed his lips. She didn't give a fuck that hundreds of eyes were on her. This was her final moment with the love of her life, so nothing else mattered in the moment. "I needed you. Why did they have to take you from me?" The pain was unbearable, and now the reality sank in. She'd never be able to wake up to breakfast in bed again. Quan was an amazing cook, unbeknownst to most people. To the outside world, he may have been a gangster, drug dealer, killer, whatever. With Jada, he was loving, affectionate, and patient. He was home.

The sight of Jada breaking down was enough to cause Nina to be filled with so many emotions and memories. She had been in the exact same position years ago, but fate had brought Chance back to her. Jada would never be able to hug Quan again, kiss his lips. Their child would never experience the unconditional love that her father had to offer. It was a tragic love story.

"It's okay." Nina rubbed Jada's back as she looked down at Quan. A small cry escaped her lips unintentionally. All the mental preparation she had coached herself on before the funeral seemed to fly out the window. Nothing could have ever prepared her to see her brother lying in a casket, lifeless. She turned and buried her face in Chance's chest and cried like a baby. She didn't even try holding it in. This had to be the worst day of her life.

Chance gritted his teeth as he held Nina closely, rubbing her back. He had to force himself to look at Quan's body. The sight would fuck him up for the rest of his life. He'd been to plenty of funerals, seen plenty of dead bodies, but none had an effect like this. Even down to the first person he ever killed, the feeling wasn't the same. This was his best friend, his brother that blood couldn't make any closer, lying dead. It was enough to make the strongest man cry. One solemn tear fell down his cheek.

"Family over everything forever, my brother," Chance said as he placed Quan's favorite gold link chain and a fat backwood in his casket with him. "Thug holiday for real, too, bro. You brought the whole city out. Rest up, my nigga." Chance spoke to Quan as if he could hear him. Maybe he could, somewhere out there. He placed each one of his arms out for Jada and Nina to hold onto. Together, they exited the church.

"My condolences, bro." Cassidy and Miami walked up to the couple, looking classy in their all-black attire. He dapped up Chance and brought him into a brotherly embrace. Miami pouted at Nina, reading the sorrow on her face. She pulled her into a tight hug, rocking back and forth. When it came to Nina and Miami, they understood each other. Their lives were so similar yet unique in their own right. It's what made them such good friends. For Nina, Miami was like the sister she never had.

"Appreciate y'all for showing up," Chance stated.

"We family. Real recognize real, and Quan was as real as they come. Me and Miami had to pay our respects," Cassidy replied humbly.

"Sorry to interrupt, but they ready for the pall-bearers," Lidia informed Chance.

"Okay, Ma, I'm right behind you."

Lidia kissed Chance's cheek before going back into the church.

"You good?" Chance held both of Nina's hands, searching her eyes for any signs of Nina slipping into a dark place. Nina had spoken the words he needed to hear yesterday to escape that same dark place—a place filled with regret and grief that felt never ending. He was afraid that the pressure of everything going on would be too overwhelming for Nina.

"I'm okay, bae. Y'all go ahead. We'll be waiting out here." Nina nodded to Miami and Jada and gave Chance a reassuring smile. She wouldn't dare worry Chance with what she knew about Yasmine. Seeing Quan in that casket didn't make her cry only tears of sorrow. Nina was crying because she was angry at the fact that Yasmine played a role in Quan's death. She didn't know the facts yet, but her intuition screamed foul play. She was angry at herself for ignoring her intuition telling her that Yasmine was a snake when she first met her; angry at the world for putting her black men in these positions where they had to sell drugs to feed their families. Quan was brilliant and could have been anything he wanted in life, but from the moment they locked him behind bars at such a young age, he decided his fate was either death or incarceration. That would have to be a conversation for another day, Nina decided.

Chance smiled lightly and pecked Nina's lips before heading into the church with Cassidy.

"Jada, I want you to meet my friend, Miami. Miami, this is Jada, Quan's woman." Nina introduced the two women.

"Hi, Miami. It's nice to finally meet you." Jada forced herself to put a smile on her face through all the pain she was feeling. Quan had spoken nothing but good things of Miami and Cassidy.

"Likewise, mami. You are glowing, honey." Miami admired Jada's beauty and pregnancy glow. "Keep that smile on your face. It's going to be hard, but you got this." Miami pulled Jada into a tight hug.

Nina smiled at the interaction between the two ladies. Then, her attention turned to a group of three women exiting the doors of the church. From

the way they were dressed, you'd think they were
attending a club party instead of a funeral. She
turned her nose up in disgust, figuring they were
typical sack chasers trying to get the attention of a
baller. Quan's name rang bells from the East Coast
all the way to the West Coast, so it was nothing but
getting-money niggas from all over the country
there, paying their respects to a real one.

The three girls must have felt Nina's stare, not
that she gave a fuck, because they were now looking in their direction. "You know them?" Nina
asked, nodding to the three girls. By their stares
and whispers, Nina felt the tension and figured it
may have been bad blood with Jada and the girls.

Jada narrowed her eyes at the girls and scoffed.
"These bitches got some nerve." She laughed to herself and rolled her eyes. "The bitch in the red dress
used to fuck with my ex. I ain't even gon' speak
his name because once I met Quan, he became a
non-factor. The type of woman I am, I never see
bitches like her. I wouldn't even give her my energy whenever she was going around Charlotte,
slandering my name," Jada explained, not caring
if the group overheard her. "I guess that upset her,
so she tried Quan, and that's where she had me
fucked up. I wanted to fight her, but Quan just said,
'Bae, chill. It's my job to put these hoes in their
place, not yours.' And he did just that." Her eyes
glistened with happiness. "Since then, she been

super pressed. She only showed up to try and get under my skin."

"*Tsk*." Nina scoffed at the nerve of some bitches, and she meant bitches because they didn't deserve the title of being a woman. A real woman uplifted other women, even if it was from afar. "Jealousy is a disease, and real bitches come a dime a dozen. She envies you and the way Quan loved you."

Miami nodded her head in agreement. "And it takes a real man to be able to tell these bitches to back the fuck up because he got a wife or a lady at home. And if they try to be funny with you, don't even say shit 'cause me and Nina will handle the light work. You're pregnant. I wish they would try you."

As if the girls really wanted smoke, they approached Jada, Nina, and Miami. "Wassup, Jada. I think it's fucked up how you sitting at Quan's funeral when you won't admit to the fact that the baby ain't even his," the light-skinned girl in the red minidress said.

"Right," one of her sidekicks added.

"Camiko, I really don't have time for your shit today. I know who the father—" Jada couldn't finish her words because Nina cut her off.

"Uh-uh, Jada. You don't have to explain shit to these bitches. We know what was up with you and *my brother*," Nina spat. These petty hoes were really starting to piss her off. They were acting like highschoolers instead of grown-ass women.

"Who you calling a bitch?" the third girl asked, sounding like she wanted to pop off.

"Nah, ma," Miami interjected. "The question is why the fuck you broke-ass *bitches* feel like y'all can disrespect my sister and the mother of *Quan's* child at his funeral?"

"And if you really wanted to know, I'm *Nina*, Quan's crazy-ass sister, and I won't hesitate to fuck you up 'bout Jada or any of my family. Don't disrespect my dead brother like that again. Matter of fact, don't even speak on him at all, or you'll have problems with me. I promise you don't want that," Nina threatened.

"Word to mother," Miami added, daring one of them to jump. "So, what's good?"

The light-skinned girl, Camiko, laughed and flipped her long weave over her shoulder. She was a pretty girl, but from what Nina could tell, her soul was hideous. Beating her ass would do no good because she was the type to get dragged in a fight and still pick at the same bitch who beat her ass. She would be the destruction of her own self.

"We'll see if you still defend her when that baby gets here. That bitch ain't worth saving." Camiko rolled her neck as she spoke. "And you *will* be seeing me, Jada."

The crew of girls walked toward the parking lot. Nina wondered what Camiko had meant by those words. She made a mental note to investigate

Camiko and Jada's history. She could never be too careful these days. For now, Quan had loved and trusted Jada, so Nina would give her the benefit of the doubt.

The doors of the church opened, and six men, including Chance, Cassidy, and Nikko, appeared, carrying the golden casket. It was made from pure gold, the only way to send off a boss like Quan. Each man wore dark designer frames over their eyes. Nina watched along with tears in her eyes as they lifted the casket into the carry-along golden hearse. Two radiant, all white stallions pulled his hearse. The idea was Nina's, to give Quan the homegoing fit for a king. It was a bittersweet sight.

"Aye, Nina, check her out." Miami nodded to a woman dressed in all black across the block, observing. The woman wore a black veil over her face, but Nina could recognize her from a mile away.

Nina's chest rose unevenly as her palms began to sweat. She clenched her fists together and started shaking as she thought about how this woman had conspired with Yasmine, or Jessica, or whatever the bitch's real name was, to bring her family down. The way she was feeling now just from spotting Naomi, Nina could only imagine what she would do to Yasmine.

"Bitches trying me today," Nina mumbled as a dark look came into her eyes.

"Who's that?" Jada asked.

Nina gave no answer as she headed across the street hastily. Ongoing traffic had to stop and honk their horns, but Nina didn't care. They could wait.

*POP! POP!*

Nina hauled off and slapped the dog shit out of Naomi. The echo from the hit was so loud that everyone stopped what they were doing, even down to the horses, and looked in the direction of Nina and Naomi.

"You sheisty little dirty bitch. I'm on to you."

Naomi grabbed her stinging cheek in surprise. She couldn't believe Nina had the nerve to make a scene at a funeral. From what Yasmine had said, Nina was all bark and no bite, too pretty to get her hands dirty. But the look in the eyes of the woman before her was the look of a woman scorned, a deadly combination.

"I don't know what you're talking about. I'm here to pay my respects like everyone else." Naomi feigned ignorance.

Nina shook her head at the fuckery. Never in her life had she been the type of chick to throw rocks and duck when someone threw them back. She had no problem voicing her opinion, and she could stand on everything she said. "I'm sure you are. You were one of the last people to see Quan before he died. I find that *very* fucking ironic."

"Nina, what's going on?" Chance came and stood between the two women.

Shaking her head, Nina smiled at God's grace on this day because Chance saved Naomi. "Ain't nothing, baby, because she ain't gon' shake none," Nina spat. "This bitch is dirty. Yasin warned me about her. I been ignoring shit too much lately. No more, though."

Chance looked down at Naomi in disgust. She obviously had a motive for showing up here, but figuring that out would have to wait. "I feel you, but that shit can wait, Nina. Just chill. All this drama can wait until later," he said sternly.

Nina bit down on her bottom lip as she mentally fought to hold her tongue. *Another fight for another day*, she thought.

"I'm not going to beat your ass, *Naomi*. You already a dead woman walking." Nina chuckled before giving her one final death stare. If looks could kill, Naomi's body would have been chalked out by now. "Now, you better leave. Let us grieve in peace."

Naomi turned on her heels quickly and headed in the opposite direction. She didn't dare try Nina because she knew a crazy-ass bitch when she saw one, and the look in Nina's eyes screamed, *I'm crazy, so try me if you want to*.

For the first time in the past few months, Naomi questioned her decision of dealing with Jessica. Fear set in her heart. To make matters worse, she hadn't seen or spoken with Tiana in about two weeks. She had brushed her paranoia off and figured Tiana was lying low. Little did she know, Tiana had thrown Naomi and Yasmine under the bus to save her own ass. Naomi didn't realize Yasmine was using her, and she wouldn't realize until it was too late.

When she had heard about Quan getting killed, she found it all too much to be deemed a coincidence. She found a bug Jessica had planted in her purse the next morning after staying with Quan. Honestly, she never would have agreed to seduce Quan under the extreme circumstances Jessica put her in without her knowledge. Her stomach dropped as she realized the role she may have played in Quan's death. Jessica was playing dirty, letting her emotions get involved with business. It was fucked up because Naomi had legitimately dug Quan and his demeanor. She never expected Quan to take her seriously because she'd fucked with Chance in the past, and she was cool with that. They vibed the whole night; he didn't pressure her for sex, but she insisted. Even then, he turned her down. He told her he had a lady at home and that Naomi deserved a man who could offer her more than just a night of sex. She'd never had a man treat her the way he did. Quan had conversed with her and held her the entire night.

Now, that phenomenal man was gone, and the blood was on her hands. She kicked herself for ever making a deal with a cold-hearted bitch like Jessica. Naomi had to live with that, if she even lived after the accusations Nina had made. The truth would soon come to light, and Naomi was not ready to face the consequences of her actions.

# Chapter Twelve

It was a relief to land back in Florida. Being in Charlotte even for a few days was a constant reminder of Quan being dead. Nina had been acting extra irritable since her encounter with Naomi. When Chance asked what was bothering her, she said she couldn't talk about it until he opened his envelope. He knew she was hurting more than she would ever admit.

On their first day home, Chance put off all of his business meetings until the next day. Even though Nina didn't voice it, she needed Chance to be there. He held her close in their silk sheets, stroking her hair softly. Life would not have been worth living without Nina by his side. He'd been giving a lot of thought to marriage lately. Though they'd been together over ten years, Chance wanted to have everything set in stone. They weren't getting any younger, and they had a family to raise.

"Baby," Nina called out to him.

"Yeah?" he asked, still stroking her tresses.

"I think Quan was set up and murdered, and I know Yasmine is behind it all."

Chance stopped stroking Nina's hair and sat up straight. "Are you sure? You know what that means."

"I'm positive," Nina stated matter-of-factly. "After I tell you this, you need to open your envelope." Nina looked deep into Chance's eyes to ensure he understood the severity of the situation. Yasmine had proven herself to be a deadly threat, and Nina would not underestimate her again. Yasmine had one up on Nina, but Nina was about to show the bitch she too could play dirty. Nina could be conniving and stealthy; after all, she had learned from Nino. An eye for an eye. That was the motto her deceased father had instilled in her at a young age.

"My suspicions were first confirmed when Miami and I hired a private investigator to look into Yasmine. Nothing came up for her. Then, Tiana came to me and revealed that Yasmine recruited her and another girl to get information out of you. That same woman, Naomi, was the last person with Quan, according to Jada. The same bitch who conveniently showed up in our home in Atlanta. Yasmine instigated the fight between you and Quan because she knew how you'd react. Yasmine's been pulling the strings around you like a fucking puppet master. I don't understand how you missed all this right in front of your eyes," Nina said once she finished with her story.

Chance gripped the bridge of his nose between his index finger and thumb. How had he not seen Yasmine for the snake she was? She had manipulated Chance into fighting with Quan and sending him back to Charlotte. He played directly into her hand. He sent his brother into the lion's den.

"Why would she want Quan dead? What would she gain?" Chance asked as he tried to pinpoint Yasmine's motives.

"I don't know for sure. Maybe he found out her real identity, and she found out. Once you open that envelope, we can piece all this shit together. Either way, we have to get rid of this bitch."

"Who else knows?" Chance quipped.

"Miami. I trust her."

Chance nodded. "I'm going to need Cassidy's help with this one," he said. Usually, Quan would help him eliminate problems like these. The fact that he'd never be able to call on his homie again really fucked him up. Quan was the only person besides Nina to see Chance at his best and worst. He was the person Chance depended on to have his back, right or wrong, and ride accordingly. Chance knew for a fact that Quan would step about him, and vice versa. He was angry at himself for not protecting Quan and allowing Yasmine to infiltrate his heart. She used the love he had for her, as little as he had for her, as his weakness. Yasmine got too secure in her plan, though, and assumed Chance wouldn't care too much about losing Quan. That's where she had fucked up. Chance was lethal when crossed. Just the thought of Yasmine's treachery alone had Chance ready to go on a murderous rampage.

"I'm sure they want our little problem solved just as much as we do." Nina kissed Chance's neck. "I'm about to take the boys out, give you some time alone to open your envelope," Nina said, noting that she still had to figure out what was on that flash drive.

Snaking his tongue in Nina's mouth, Chance held Nina close as he kissed her deeply. "Take Charlene with you. She'll look after you," he instructed once he let Nina go.

Nina raised an eyebrow and gave Chance an inquisitive look. "Trust me," he said before Nina could protest, like he knew exactly what she was thinking.

"All right," Nina said skeptically. *What Charlene old ass got that'll protect me?*

"I'll call you, baby. I love you." Nina grabbed for the doorknob.

"I love you more," Chance replied. Pulling out the nightstand drawer, Chance reached for his stash of the finest Kush Miami had to offer. He would definitely need to get high to ease his anxieties before opening the envelope. He'd deliberately put off opening it because he wasn't sure what he would find. With Quan, he was liable to have put anything in the envelope.

Chance clapped his hands twice and activated his built-in home surround sound system. "Alexa, play Tupac's 'Thugz Mansion,'" he stated aloud. Alexa instantly recognized the command and had the track playing in seconds.

Chance bobbed his head to the beat as he listened to Tupac's mellow lyrics. Ripping open the thick envelope, the first thing Chance pulled out was a Ziploc bag containing three photos. Each photo had the word *SNITCH* written across it in red writing. One of the people in the pictures was Zidane. Chance shook his head in disbelief. He couldn't believe Zidane, who came from a long line of Jamaican gangsters, would do something as stupid as cooperating with the Feds.

Zidane's older brother, Khepri, was Chance's only reason for working with him. Chance had done business with Khepri on several occasions, but the 35-year-old business tycoon retired from the game early and returned home to Jamaica. Out of respect for Khepri, Chance decided he would consult him with the news before taking matters into his own hands. As for the other rats, they were already as good as dead. He would handle them by sundown.

"My nigga, even in death, you still resourceful." Chance chuckled as he spoke aloud to Quan, hoping he could hear him. Chance lit the freshly rolled blunt and inhaled slowly. Shaking his head, Chance couldn't help but reminisce on the good ol' days. *Damn, my nigga really gone,* Chance thought solemnly. Tupac spoke of a place where niggas could go to smoke and chill without worrying about the ills and reality of the world around them. Life on Earth was hard enough as is for the black man. Chance hoped Quan was at peace wherever he was, lighting one at the Thugz Mansion.

*Save a spot for me, bro,* he thought.

The next item he retrieved out of the envelope was a small, black jewelry box. The box contained a beautiful emerald cut diamond ring. Chance admired its simple radiance, figuring it was a gift for Jada. A handwritten letter slipped out of the envelope. Inhaling more smoke, Chance reached down for the letter and smiled when he recognized Quan's neat penmanship. He always teased Quan, saying he wrote like a woman. Chance was the only person he allowed to joke on him. No other person received that pleasure. He smiled slightly as he began reading the letter.

*First off, nigga, fuck you. I know you thinking look at this nigga and his femi-*

*nine-ass handwriting. LOL. But on a heavier note, if you're reading this, it means my journey on Earth has come to an end, and my new journey beyond life has begun. I know neither one of us imagined our departure so soon, but we know the consequences this lifestyle comes with. Don't live in regret or guilt. You were my truest friend and the first person to show me what family and brotherhood meant. You put me on my feet once I touched down from juvie, and we been running it up ever since. You my nigga for life. Blood in, blood out. I forgive you for everything.*

*Who would have known two little niggas from the hood would have conquered all the shit we did? Not many. That's why I don't feel sadness writing this. I've lived my best life. But something I've come to learn is the most important thing in life is family. Money comes and goes, material shit comes and goes, even street cred, all that shit is disposable. Family is everything. Cherish that shit while you can. If you're reading this, it means I'll never be able to watch my daughter be born, never see her take her first steps, never be able to buy her first car or send her to prom, or even walk her down the aisle on her wedding day. That's my biggest regret. Wherever God takes me in the afterlife, I will still mourn that fact.*

*I say this to say, don't make the same mistakes I did. You got two li'l men that's gonna need you in this wicked-ass world we live in. Nina's strong, but she can't do this shit without you. You up right now, brother. Get out that shit while you can. That bitch Yasmine already trying to put you behind bars. We can't take no more losses, bro. You got to break the wheel. Get out before it's too late.*

*I left you the ring you first spotted years ago. You said you'd buy Nina one just like that and marry her. My sister deserves that shit, man. She deserves the life I couldn't give Jada and my unborn child. It don't make you pussy or lame; it makes you a man. Marry Nina, settle the fuck down, and y'all have all the fucking kids you want.*

*I've equipped you with everything you need to solve your little problem. I trust that you will. I don't even have to say look out for Jada and the baby; I know you'll hold shit down.*

*While you looking out for everybody else, I've asked Charlene to look after you. We both know she's more than capable.*

*You forever in my heart. You, Nina, and the entire family. Can't wait to kick it with ya again, my dawg. Hold it down until we meet again. Family. Forever. Always.*
*Quan*

Chance shook his head after reading the letter. From the way Quan spoke, he knew he was going to die. He was basically begging Chance to get out of the game.

"Damn," Chance said with a heavy heart.

"Live in the Sky" by T.I played in the background of the room. In life, Quan had never led him in the wrong direction. His urges felt like a bad omen to Chance. Holding the diamond ring in his hand, he smiled at how Quan remembered the ring after all these years.

"Nigga had the memory of an elephant." Chance laughed to himself.

The blunt was nearly gone, and Chance was stuck in his thoughts. He always meant to make an honest woman out of Nina, but he still had a few reservations. The last time he had proposed to Nina, she left him for another man. He'd never been played like that in his life. It was a wound his pride was still recovering from. He'd spent the last three years of his life *not* committing to a woman, not even Yasmine. While he thought she was upset over their breakup, she was really angry that her access had been revoked.

Thinking back to their first encounter, he realized he had mistaken her ambitions for attraction. Chance would have to tread lightly with this situation. Yasmine had disobeyed the oath she took and ignored warnings from her superiors when she got sexually and emotionally involved with Chance. She very well may have set Quan up to be killed. She sent Tiana and Naomi to do her dirty work. It was clear Yasmine had an unhealthy desire to bring Chance down. Yasmine was willing to risk it all, even if it meant taking down herself along with Chance.

"Fucking psycho," he muttered, marking Yasmine as a top priority.

Another piece of paper was inside the envelope, and Chance slowly pulled it out. It read: *The Will and Estate of Ty'Quan Messiah Galloway*. The ringing of his phone interrupted him before he opened the envelope. Yasmine's name flashed across the screen.

Chance's nostrils flared as he looked down at his phone. He answered, nearly on the last ring.

"Yo," he said coolly, trying to disguise the malice he felt for her.

"Hey, stranger," Yasmine cooed into the phone. "I miss you. I know you got whatever you got with Nina, but I need to see you. At least one last time," Yasmine pleaded.

Chance scoffed at the front she put on. He decided to play her game, but this time, he would defeat her at her own game. He would show her she wasn't the only one with acting skills. "Word? You know I just lost my best friend, right?" he quizzed.

Yasmine gasped on the other end of the line. "Quan died? Stop lying!" she exclaimed, dumbfounded.

If Chance was a dummy, Yasmine would have deceived him with the performance she gave. "How'd you figure it was Quan?" he retorted.

There was a pause on the line. "C'mon now. At least have enough respect to acknowledge the fact that I *was* with you for almost *two years*. Like I don't know who your best friend is. Damn, I'm hurt," Yasmine responded.

Chance was smart enough to catch the message in her words. She was warning him that she possessed knowledge of him that he wasn't even aware of. Yasmine was starting to display signs of sociopath with her behavior.

"You right. I'm sorry." Chance softened his tone. "I miss you too, though, real shit. I been wanting to call you, but Nina's always around with everything going on," Chance lied. The only time Yasmine crossed his mind was when he plotted on how to kill her.

Chance could feel Yasmine smiling through the phone. "Yeah? I'm sorry for your loss, too. I know Quan was like a big brother and guardian angel to you."

Dropping his head, Chance swallowed hard, as if he were swallowing all of the obscenities he wanted to scream at her. Not only was Yasmine acknowledging the fact she was cognizant of how much Quan meant to Chance, but she showed no remorse by rubbing it in his face.

"Yeah," he responded quietly. "I just want to get my mind off it. It's like everything reminds me of him, even Nina. And she doesn't understand how I'm feeling." The lies effortlessly rolled off his tongue.

"That's because she doesn't understand you like I do. I should be the one by your side, but you made your pick. I can't change that." Yasmine sighed. "That doesn't change the fact of what I feel for you. I love you even when I want to hate you," she admitted honestly.

"I'm sorry," Chance added.

"For what?" she asked.

"For hurting you," he replied. "Let me make it up to you. I need to see you tonight."

"Where?" Yasmine asked without hesitation.

"I want to surprise you," he stated.

Yasmine didn't immediately respond. He had to convince her without arousing any suspicion from her.

"Nina took the boys out of town for the night. We can have some alone time. I'll have my driver pick you up. Eight p.m. sharp. Be ready," he demanded, knowing Yasmine was the type that liked to be dominated.

"Okay," she obliged.

"Oh, yeah," Chance added, "don't wear shit. Straight trench coat and heels. Nothing else," Chance said before hanging up.

Grinning devilishly, Chance resumed his chess game as he devised a master plan. He pulled out his phone to contact Kenyan, the young man he had met at the ball. He'd been in contact with Kenyan since he was released from jail. He promised the young man a job once he returned from Charlotte. The time for Kenyan to prove his worth had arrived.

"Wassup, young bull. I got a job for you." Chance spoke into the phone once Kenyan answered. "Real simple. Just a pickup and drop-off. Your money will be waiting for you once the job is complete." Chance purposely left out the details of the job to see how Kenyan would respond.

"Word. You know I'm with whatever. Told you I'm ready to prove myself. Consider it done," Kenyan replied on the other end. He really didn't give a fuck what Chance needed done. His family was barely able to keep food on the table. He needed to get down with Chance and his team.

"That's a bet. Look out for the details," Chance stated before ending the call and powering his phone off. He was wary of giving out too much information over the phone; anybody could be listening. Precautions were necessary if he wished to beat his enemies at their own game. One wrong move from this point on could possibly land Chance in prison for the rest of his life. He had to move smart with this one. Killing a nigga on the streets was one thing. Killing a federal agent was treasonous. Chance would not move wrong.

"How's Lidia doing?" Charlene asked as she loaded the shopping bags into the trunk of the G-wagon.

They'd spent the last couple of hours taking the boys to Fun Center, an amusement center for kids, and shopping at a few boutiques along the way. It was the getaway Nina needed from the current chaos in her life. Her sons provided the perfect distraction. Their purity and innocence always reminded Nina that her purpose in this world was much bigger than her life or Chance's; their purpose was to mold Chase and Nasim into emotionally stable and strong young men. Growing up, Nina nor Chance had a mother or father to show them how to properly love or reciprocate love. Her sons would not grow up that way, and she refused to let anyone take her or Chance away from their kids. It would be over her dead body.

"She's strong," Nina replied as she lifted Chase's sleeping body into his car seat. "You know she didn't have the best relationship with Quan. I think that's the hardest part for her." Nina watched as Charlene placed a sleeping Nasim in his car seat.

"You know I grew up with Lidia and Chance's mother, Faith. Faith stayed down the block from me and Lidia across the street. Lidia loved Ty'Quan very much. The way we grew up, though, no one ever taught us the right way. We nearly raised ourselves. Faith, God rest her soul, always asked me to look after Chance. He's like a son to me," she explained as they sat in the car. "I don't want to bury him. Or you. I need y'all to be careful," Charlene stated seriously.

Nina nodded. Chance never spoke of his mother or father. All Nina knew was his mother died when he was ten from an overdose, and his father was never in the picture as far as she knew. Being motherless left a tremendous void in Nina's heart, so she only imagined how Chance felt growing up without a mother or father. Nino may not have been father of the year; however, he was the only father Nina knew. There were many vital life lessons he instilled in Nina's mind, things that only a father could teach his daughter. Nino taught Nina about survival and the proper way a man should love a woman. He taught her the art of hustling. If Nina wanted, she could have easily become a queen pin with the game she soaked up from Nino for years. As much as she hated him, she had to admit her life would have been drastically different without Nino's influence on her life. She thanked him for that.

"That Chance is a strong one. Rose, his grand-mother, tried to raise him the best she could. God rest her soul. Chance worshipped her." Charlene chuckled as she reminisced. "Faith was so beauti-ful. I wish you could have met her. She was like a magnet. Everybody gravitated to her. Faith didn't take no shit, though."

Nina smiled as she tried to envision Chance's mother. She had only ever seen one picture of the woman who birthed the best man she'd ever known. "He doesn't talk about her. You're probably the closest thing to a relative that Chance has left."

"It's hard growing up without your parents. Sometimes the past can be too painful to talk about. Both of you lost your mothers at a young age. How often do you talk about your mother?" Charlene asked, driving,

Nina sighed heavily as she thought of an answer to that question. "Honestly, I haven't talked with anyone my mother in years. I think about her all the time." Nina swallowed hard as her eyes moistened. "The worst part is not knowing. My mother's murder was never solved. Like her life didn't matter at all. Nino was an awful father, but he was the only parent I had. All for me to find out I really wasn't his child to begin with. It's just crazy." Nina dabbed the creases of her eyes with her fingers and laughed lightly. "You probably think I'm a mess."

Charlene gave Nina a sympathetic look and shook her head no. "I think you're a strong black woman, and your life is important. So was your mother's life. It's tiring carrying those bags around, ain't it?" she asked hypothetically. "You deserve the truth and closure. It may set you free. Maybe finding your real father is what your soul needs."

Nina rested her head on the headrest. "Maybe you're right," she admitted. Closing her eyes, Nina pictured her mother's face in her mind. She distinctly remembered her mother's beautiful smile and single dimple in her right cheek. Growing up, Nina liked to think she looked more like her mom because she was almost opposite of Nino and his light skin. She possessed a deep, honey brown complexion, just like her mom. "I miss her so much."

Charlene was about to respond before a Ford F-150 tapped the back of the G-wagon, causing them to jerk forward slightly.

Nina shot up quickly, alarmed, looking into her rearview mirror. "What the fuck," she mumbled harshly, looking into the backseat where her boys were still sleeping soundly in their seats. A minute later, the truck returned and recklessly rammed into their SUV.

Nasim stirred in his car seat and fisted the sleep away from his eyes. The commotion disturbed his nap, and he looked around curiously. "Mommy?" His innocent voice shook with fear.

Nina swiveled in her seat to find Nasim awake beside a sleeping Chase. "Shh, go back to sleep, baby. Everything is okay." Nina's heart thumped against her rib cage. Seeing her son frightened caused her adrenaline to rush. Her priority was to get her boys home safely.

"Are they following us?" She exclaimed, turning to Charlene. Flashes of traumatic memories of Nino attacking them ran through her mind. Nina automatically went into defense mode.

"I don't know. Let's see," Charlene said calmly as she tightly gripped the steering wheel. She pressed her foot down harder on the gas.

"Shit, they not letting up," Nina said as she watched the truck close in on their tail. She dialed Chance's number only to get voicemail. The dark night sky made it nearly impossible for Nina to see who was behind the wheel. Panic set in once the truck hit the back of the G-wagon again. It wasn't her life she feared for; it was the innocent lives of her sons.

"I want my dada!" Chase shouted this time with hot tears streaming down his face. His little hands tightened around his seatbelt, and his eyes darted from Nina to Charlene.

"It's going to be okay, boys," Nina said, attempting to sound convincing. Both boys were fully awake and crying in the back seat.

Nina glanced into the rearview mirror and gritted her teeth when she saw the pickup truck still on their tail. "What the fuck do they want?" she yelled in frustration. "You got to lose them!" she urged Charlene while tapping the dashboard for emphasis. In this moment, she had underestimated Yasmine's ruthlessness. There was nobody else with balls enough to try to bring harm to Chance's family.

"Oh, I'm going to kill that bitch. On everything I love, I'm going to kill her!" Nina yelled as she punched the dashboard. Her right leg bounced up and down quickly and she gulped down all the obscenities she wanted to shout. Inhaling deeply, Nina rolled her eyes to the back of her head as she tried to gather her thoughts. *How the hell are we going to make it out of this?*

"Nina, listen to me," Charlene said in a soothing voice. "The only chance we have at making it out of this alive is if you do exactly as I say."

"What?" Nina asked hysterically, looking at Charlene as if she were crazy.

"Nina, listen to me! Open the glove compartment. There are two handguns in there. Hand them to me, and you grab the wheel. *Now*!" she commanded sternly.

As many questions as she wanted to ask, Nina kept them to herself because time was of the essence. If these maniacs were sent by Yasmine, they were surely there to kill them. Opening the glove compartment, Nina pulled out a .357 magnum and a nine millimeter with an extended clip. Both guns already had silencers on them. Nina's eyes widened as she handed the weapons to Charlene. She wasn't even aware that the guns were in the vehicle.

"You know how to use them? Nina asked.

Charlene smirked before hanging out of the driver's side window. She didn't hesitate to let the rounds go. The first bullets pierced the driver's shoulder, causing him to swerve a little. The second and third hit the truck's front tires. The last bullet Charlene fired pierced the driver's brain, directly between the eyes, killing him on impact. The car spun out of control before flipping off the road.

Charlene quickly leaned back in the truck and regained control of the wheel.

For the first time, Nina noticed the *DBD* on the right side of Charlene's neck. Charlene had fired those guns with such precision that Nina was intrigued. Four shots, and each hit its intended target.

"What does that mean on your neck?" Nina asked, still a bit shaken.

"Death before dishonor," Charlene replied.

"Who are you?" Nina asked. "You went all 'my nanny is an assassin' on me and shit. What the hell?" She laughed in disbelief.

"I'm Charlene, baby. I was raised to protect my family just like you," Charlene replied vaguely.

Looking into the back seat, she reached out to rub both boys' knees. They were holding each other's hands. Nina silently thanked God for protecting her boys. *Thankful* could not fully describe how Nina felt for Charlene. Chance was right. Nina and her kids were safe under Charlene's protection.

Chance sat patiently in his living room, awaiting Nina's arrival. He had a feeling Yasmine would come after Nina, but he never imagined her putting his two innocent sons in danger. Yasmine wanted to tango, and Chance was about to lace up his dancing shoes and give her the show of her life. When he turned his phone back on and saw the missed calls and text messages from Charlene and Nina, he instantly became infuriated. Had he not followed his intuition and sent Charlene along, he would probably be burying Nina and his children.

Yasmine must have thought that since she'd never seen Chance's vengeful side that he didn't have one. Maybe she thought he had some type of feelings for her that would spare her life. Or maybe she thought he was a dummy all around. An end was about to come to all of that, though. Chance had just gotten confirmation from Kenyan that he'd made the pickup.

The lock on the front door turned, and Charlene and Nina entered, carrying Nasim and Chase. Chance stood to kiss each boy's forehead before tucking them into their beds.

Nina fell into his arms once he emerged from the boys' bedroom. "We have to kill that bitch. I know she was behind this. That bitch put my babies in harm's way." Her nerves were all over the place. Yet again, Nina had come close enough with death to kiss it. The thought would have been easier to bear if her sons hadn't been in that backseat. "This isn't just some Fed shit she's on. It's personal. We have to handle her now," she whispered into Chance's ear as he caressed her back.

"I know. I promise it's going to get handled. *Tonight*." Chance kissed Nina's forehead. "I have a plan."

Nina's eyes got wide. "Tell me. You can't go in with just one plan. You need a plan B, C, and D fucking with this bitch."

Chance ran his hands down Nina's arms and kissed her forehead. He didn't want her worrying about him. "I'm going to invite Yasmine on a date on Cassidy's yacht. When we're far enough out, dinner will be served. Her food will contain something that'll knock her out for a few hours. Then, we'll move her to an old warehouse location until I can question her before she's killed."

"Let me help you," Nina urged.

"I got this, baby. Cassidy got my back with this. I already got Miami on the way here to you. I'll call you when I'll be needing you."

Nina nodded, trusting her man. "Please be careful. I love you." Nina kissed Chance's lips.

"I love you more." He held Nina's chin between his thumb and index finger. "*Mrs*. McKnight." He slipped the ring Quan had gifted him on Nina's ring finger. After carefully contemplating, Chance had decided his life was incomplete without Nina by his side. She was like the glue that kept his life intact. Without her, he would fall apart. She'd proven time and time again that she was willing to fight for their love. Chance had had his pick of beautiful women throughout his life. None he encountered could hold a candle to Nina in any aspect. He didn't get that *feeling* Nina gave him with any other woman. The universe had perfectly crafted her soul for his. She was meant to be his wife.

"You are my queen. The light on my darkest days. Shit, you fight for a nigga even when I can't fight for myself." Chance chuckled lightly, never breaking eye contact with Nina. "You not only gave me a son, but you accepted my son as your own, too. And the way you love them makes me want to learn how to love you better. My mother died, and something was missing in my heart until I met you. Your love makes me whole, and I'm *never* letting go of you again. There's no one else I'd want to spend the rest of my life with. Once this all blows over, I'm marrying you. No ifs, ands, or buts about it."

Nina blushed as she admired the beauty in the simplicity of the ring. Chance had always been a man of his words. Time had matured him from the boy she'd fallen in love with years ago into a man who was ready to love her like she rightfully deserved with no reservations. Her mother always told her if the love is true, it'll always come back. Nina realized that all the trials she and Chance had gone through were only a test of their love. They weren't ready three years ago.

*Time works in mysterious ways*, Nina thought.

"I'll be waiting for that, Mr. McKnight." Nina knew committing wasn't as easy as the first time he proposed.

Chance gave Nina a passionate kiss before grabbing a black duffle bag. "Once everything is in motion, I'll call you. Stay here until then. Two of my men will be outside of this door until I come back."

Nina nodded. "We'll be fine." She knew they had enough weapons in their home to send a hundred niggas to meet their maker. She wasn't sure if Yasmine knew that her little henchmen were unsuccessful with their job. Either way, Nina wanted the bitch's head on a stake, by any means necessary.

"Be careful," Nina said seriously, grabbing Chance by the jacket of his Armani suit.

Resting his forehead on hers, Chance hugged Nina tightly. "I will be. Promise. I love you."

"I love you, too," Nina said, savoring the last few seconds of their embrace. They were about to enter an unforeseen territory. Once they removed Yasmine from the equation, there would be no turning back. Their next move would have to be their best move. Everything depended on it.

Chance kissed Nina's forehead. "Wait on my call," he instructed before exiting the penthouse. "You two stay on point. If anything happens to my family, I'm holding you personally responsible. Understood?" Chance warned the two guards positioned outside of his home. They nodded.

David was outside, waiting with the Town Car exactly as Chance had instructed. David opened the back door and closed it once Chance was securely inside. Sitting inside the car was Khepri, the Jamaican crime boss and Zidane's older brother.

"Thank you for meeting me on such short notice," Chance stated once David had the vehicle in motion. The tint was so dark on the car that no one would ever be able to see two of Miami's most notorious drug traffickers tucked inside.

"Don't mention it," Khepri replied modestly. Unlike his younger brother, Khepri's English was more refined and polished, which came from years of doing business in countries all over the world. "I'm sure whatever you've beseeched me here for is of cardinal regard."

Chance nodded his head slowly. "Of course. I know the risk you've exposed yourself to by being here in the States. I wouldn't call you on no bullshit." He placed the manila envelope on Khepri's lap. *The evidence will speak for itself,* Chance thought as he remained silent while Khepri shuffled through the photos Quan had left behind.

Khepri scoffed as a look of disappointment filled his face. "Where'd you get this?"

"It doesn't matter where or how I got it. What matters is the facts. Your brother is a liability," Chance concluded. Even though he was sitting in the presence of a man who was known to kill for sport, he displayed no signs of fear. His freedom was at stake, so he didn't care if he offended Khepri. The truth remained the truth.

"So, what are you saying?" Khepri asked, looking Chance in the eyes. He had to admit the man had balls.

"You already know what it is, Khepri. I came to you out of respect for *you* first before I take matters into my own hands." Chance returned Khepri's eye contact.

"This is tricky, Chance, my man."

Chance clenched his teeth. He had hoped for a different response. "Your brother had a hand in me getting arrested and a shipment seized. I lost a lot of money behind that. There's nothing tricky about it," Chance retorted.

Khepri laughed lightly. "If my eyes are not deceiving me, this woman my brother is talking to in this picture is the same woman you brought to my birthday celebration last year, no?" Khepri asked as he held up the picture for Chance to see clearly. "Yasmine, right? I never forget a face." He nodded, answering his own question. "It looks to me like you are the one to blame for your own problems, my friend. *You* invited this Judas amongst you. In no way am I saying my brother is not also at fault. I will have him immediately removed to Jamaica, and he will answer to me and only me." Khepri hated a snitch just as much as anyone else from the hood, but he could not condone his brother dying at the hands of another man. His mother would kill him first.

Chance wanted to protest, but he knew Khepri had a point. He had invited Yasmine into his home and life. As much as he despised Zidane for cooperating, he could not afford to go to war with the Jamaicans. Not with the Feds on his ass. "I'll agree to that only if I am recompensated for the five million–dollar loss I took and Zidane's territory."

"I can arrange for the money to be wired to you momentarily. As for the territory, I will be in touch." Khepri nodded as he reached out to shake Chance's hand. "Keep your grass cut, my friend."

As if on cue, David pulled the car over, and Khepri exited without speaking another word.

"*Tsk*." Chance wanted to knock Zidane off badly. Getting his money back and possibly new territory would suffice for now.

# Chapter Thirteen

When the Town Car arrived at the Port of Miami, it was 9:00 p.m. Cassidy had allowed Chance to use his yacht for this occasion. He had a very *special* candlelit dinner prepared for Yasmine.

"Thank you, David. Be back here in about an hour. Grab yourself something to eat," Chance said, slipping him a hundred-dollar bill.

David received a hefty six-figure salary as Chance's chauffer. He was loyal to Chance because he had hired him when David was at his lowest. After David had worked for the city for forty years as a bus driver, his wife, Valerie, fell extremely ill. He'd run through his pension, but they were still drowning in debt from medical bills. Chance hired him when it seemed like no one else would. He also covered all of Valerie's medical expenses in full. Three years later, he'd grown to love his job and Chance. Now, David was making enough to afford the best care for Val. He was grateful and repaid Chance with his unyielding loyalty.

"Sure thing, son." David nodded his head and patted Chance on his back. "Ring me if you need me," he said before pulling off.

Chance boarded the yacht and pulled the jacket of his suit on. The duffle bag was in tow in his right hand. Tonight, he wouldn't be playing the role of the loving father and fiancé. He was a man who wore many faces and assumed many roles when need be. Yasmine had provoked him and forced him to reveal the most barbaric side of himself, the monster inside that he worked hard to contain.

"Wassup, boss." Kenyan greeted Chance with a firm handshake. "Your guest is over there having a drink." He nodded to where Yasmine was seated at a table for two.

"'Preciate it. Hold onto this for me." Chance handed him the duffle bag. "Let's go ahead and get this shit moving. I don't plan on being on the water long."

Kenyan nodded and walked away. He headed to find the captain. It was the first time he'd ever been on anything as lavish as a million-dollar yacht. The yacht's name was *Ayana*, after Cassidy's daughter. He was still in awe. *I want to have one of these one day*, Kenyan thought.

"Aye, my boss man said you can go ahead and get her moving."

The older white man tipped his hat and followed the instructions, puffing a Cuban cigar.

\*\*\*

"Why, hello, handsome." Yasmine sat at the table in her trench coat, just as Chance had commanded. A wine glass was already in her hand. "You done all of this for me?" she asked, motioning to the beautiful scenery.

Chance smirked and pecked Yasmine's cheek. "Good evening. You look beautiful." He fought the urge to strangle Yasmine with his bare hands. Instead, he took a seat across from her. "Why would you expect anything less? Like you said, we have one last night together. I thought I should make it memorable."

*It's going to be a memorable night, a'ight.* Chance taunted Yasmine in his mind.

Yasmine lifted her glass in the air before bringing it to her lips. "I'll drink to that," she replied with a smile. "How are you holding up?" she asked, trying to see where his mind was at.

Chance slightly clenched his teeth. It was taking everything in him not to knock Yasmine out cold and tie her up from there. However, he had to stick to the plan and outsmart Yasmine at her own game. "I'm fucked up, but I'll be straight. It's not the first loss I've took," he said as he stared out to the Miami sea.

Yasmine reached across the table and grabbed Chance's hand. "I'm really sorry. I wish it was something I could do to help."

To the naked eye, Yasmine appeared to be sym-
pathizing with Chance, but he saw her for who she
truly was: a vindictive, insecure woman with a fatal attraction for him. "You being here is enough
help." He gave Yasmine a charming smile. *Because
I got you right where I want you*, Chance thought
mockingly.

"Sorry to interrupt, but tonight's entrée is ready
to be served." The blonde waitress pushed forward
a cart containing silver trays of food. "We were
informed prime steaks were a favorite of the guest
of honor. Cooked medium." She placed a tray in
front of Yasmine and lifted the lid, revealing a
scrumptious filet mignon with a side of asparagus
and sautéed shrimp. "Same for Mr. McKnight."
She refilled Yasmine's wine and placed a glass of
water in front of Chance.

"Thank you," Chance said, giving the waitress a
wink.

"I'll be back out when dessert is ready."

"I must say, I'm impressed, Mr. McKnight."
Yasmine blushed at the thought Chance had put
into planning this romantic night. She was oblivi-
ous to the fact that Chance saw through her façade.
In her twisted mind, she figured she finally had
Chance where she wanted him.

*I can't wait to come out of this trench coat.
When he sees what's underneath, he won't be able
to resist*, Yasmine thought as she took a bite into
the steak.

"This is good," she mumbled in between bites.

"Only the best for you. I realized that I did neglect you when we were dating. I never intended on getting too serious with you. Truth was, I was scared to let anyone close to me again." Chance made conversation, telling Yasmine exactly what she wanted to hear.

"I feel that. What I never understood is why you took Nina back after she hurt you the way she did." Yasmine sipped her wine. Speaking Nina's name left a bitter taste in her mouth.

"I love her, Yas. Always have," he admitted honestly.

"There was a time when you loved me, too," she quietly replied. "You're not ready for that conversation, though."

"I got love for you," he lied.

"But you don't love me in the way you love Nina," she stated flatly.

Chance sighed. "Why are we talking about Nina? I thought tonight was about us."

Yasmine nodded as she pushed her plate in front of her and stood up. She slowly dropped the trench coat, revealing her naked body. Chance's eyes grew wide as his eyes focused on the fresh tattoo above her waist that read his name.

"You like it, baby?" she asked. "I got it about a week ago. It was an impulsive decision, but I don't regret it. Our love story goes way back, even before you and Nina's. I've loved you since I was five." She walked around to Chance and massaged his shoulders. "You don't remember?" Yasmine whispered into his ear.

*This bitch is looney.* "What are you talking about?" Chance asked, his patience running thin. "We've only known each other for two and a half years."

"Wrong," Yasmine said as she slid her hand down Chance's midsection until she gripped his thick tool. "Our parents were neighbors. Our fathers were partners. Our mothers were friends, until . . ." Yasmine's voice trailed off.

"You're tripping. I don't know my father," Chance scoffed and removed Yasmine's hands. He didn't like the mind games she played.

"Wrong again. When someone experiences trauma, the mind sometimes suppresses memories as a coping mechanism. You may not remember now, but you will soon." Yasmine licked her tongue into Chance's ear.

He swatted her hands away and stood up, grabbing Yasmine by the wrists. "You're a lying, conniving bitch. That's what you are. I see you. You couldn't have me, so you went for the people I love. I know who you are, *agent Jessica Tyson.* And there ain't no Jessica in my recollection," Chance spat, fed up with everything. The ketamine Chance had paid the waitress to put into Yasmine's wine should be kicking in soon.

Yasmine's eyes grew wide with fear. "No, no, let me explain. Please," she begged, realizing that her cover was blown. They were in the middle of the ocean, so she was sure her cell phone had no reception.

"I don't feel good," she said weakly as her vision became blurry. "What did you do to me?" Yasmine slurred, reaching out to grab Chance's face before everything went black.


Yasmine woke up to nothing but blackness. She was chained to a chair and still naked. The cold air caused the hairs on her arms to rise. Water dripped from above her head, forming a puddle beside her feet. She wasn't aware of how long she'd been there, but when she woke for the first time a few hours ago, she assumed it was morning from the sounds of the birds chirping. The last thing she remembered was being on the yacht with Chance.

*Chance*, she thought.

"Somebody help me!" she yelled until her throat was dry.

Yasmine cried silently, realizing that no one was coming to her rescue. She was forced to release herself in that chair. Never in her life had she felt so low. She prayed Chance or someone would at least bring her water and food soon.

"Help me! Chance! *Please*. I'm sorry." She sobbed.

A steel door creaked as it opened, filling the dark space with light. A figure emerged from the stairs, and Yasmine figured her prayers had been answered. All she had to do was convince Chance she never intended to harm him and that she wasn't lying about the history they shared.

"Well, well, well. Look what we have here," a female voice called out in the darkness.

Switching the light switch on, Nina came face to face with the woman she despised. "Ain't no fun when the rabbit got the gun, huh?" Nina laughed. She was dressed in an all-black Nike sweat suit with the black Air Max 97s to match. Her natural hair was out and in a bun. She wore no makeup or earrings.

"Good to see you alive." Yasmine laughed.

Nina pulled the nine from her waist and slapped Yasmine across the face with it. "Bitch, don't play with me," she spat. "You think it's cute that you put *my* son's lives in danger?"

Yasmine smirked with a bloody nose. "Collateral damage."

Nina brought the gun across Yasmine's face with more force. She was sure she had broken her nose with the blow. "I can go all day!" Nina screamed, pointing the gun at Yasmine. "Be honest with yourself. *You* hate me because Chance loves *me*. You're a delusional bitch. For the last five years, you've worked as an undercover detective, Jessica. Or would you prefer Yasmine?" Nina chuckled.

"Fuck you." Yasmine spoke despite the throbbing headache she experienced and spat out a mouthful of blood. She would not give Nina the satisfaction of seeing her weak.

"I should kill you, bitch," Nina said through clenched teeth, pointing the gun between Yasmine's eyes. Her finger itched against the trigger. "You killed my brother." Her voice cracked.


Chance sat in the back of the black Escalade with Cassidy heading to where Yasmine was. He'd kept Yasmine locked in the basement beneath an abandoned warehouse for the last twenty-four hours. He wanted to make her suffer before putting her out of her miserable existence. Since Yasmine made the absurd revelation of knowing Chance since childhood, he had hired one of Cassidy's private investigators to find any truth to the claims.

"I just got word that Nina arrived at the warehouse and has been in the basement over twenty minutes," Cassidy informed Chance.

"She probably in there beating the fuck out of that girl." Chance laughed. He knew it was only a matter of time before Nina showed up to the warehouse after Chance disclosed the location.

"We'll be back there in time before Nina kills her."

Cassidy chuckled lightly and shook his head. "I wouldn't blame her if she did."

"Yeah, I'on want her getting involved that way. We both know ain't no turning back once you go down that road." Chance wanted Nina to live a happy life minus the burdens that came with taking a life. The mental repercussions that came with killing someone could break down the strongest person. Chance didn't want Nina to live with that type of regret.

"Speaking of killing, Nikko handled our rat infestation, too. Zidane won't be a problem anymore."

"Whoa, whoa, please tell me y'all niggas didn't." Chance prayed he had heard Cassidy incorrectly.

Cassidy shrugged. "Nikko called me a few hours ago and said he handled it. He thought he was doing you a favor."

Chance brushed his hands over his face and sighed. "Fam, I made a deal with Khepri three nights ago. He wired the five million that we lost and agreed to give me the territory Zidane ran on the condition that Zidane safely returned to Jamaica," he explained. "We got a war on our hands."

Cassidy's iPhone dinged, indicating an unread text message. "Shit is about to get even more complicated, bro. Cole just texted and said your father is alive and has been serving a thirty-year bid for the last twenty years."

"That's impossible," Chance scoffed. It couldn't be true. His father was dead. Period. "Only one person can give me answers until Cole finds more information."

"You sure you can trust that broad, bro?" Cassidy asked reluctantly.

Chance shook his head. "Nah, but she knows her fate. There's no need to lie now." The fact that Yasmine was possibly telling the truth blew his mind. He had to get to her as soon as possible.

"Why did you do it?" Nina asked a bloody and bruised Yasmine. Nina had brought the gun across her face so many times that it was unrecognizable. "What did Quan ever do to you?" Tears filled Nina's eyes. Beating Yasmine's ass wasn't making her feel any better. It definitely wasn't going to bring Quan back to life. She needed closure.

Yasmine laughed like a madman. "He was in my way. I'll gladly do the same to anyone who stands between Chance and me. We're meant to be."

"Bitch, you'll never have Chance. You're sick. You need help," Nina spat, fed up with Yasmine's antics. "I'm his fiancée! I'm the mother of his children, the love of his life. I'm getting really tired of your bullshit." She aimed the gun at Yasmine's chest. "You took so much from me."

Yasmine had accepted the fact that she was going to die. However, she refused to die letting Nina think she won. She had something that would bring her down a notch or two. "If I'm sick, so are you, bitch. Call me what you want. At least I've never fucked my brother."

Nina gave Yasmine's head a crushing blow. "Bitch! I never fucked Quan!"

Yasmine laughed hysterically, like she was at a comedy show. "Not Quan. How does it feel to know that you were in a relationship with your own brother for years? You almost got pregnant by your brother, you sick bitch. Yasin is your brother!" Yasmine exclaimed.

"You're lying." Nina's hands shook as she gripped the gun. Yasmine had to be playing mind games with her.

"It's true, Nina. I'm a federal agent. I have access to files and information that the public doesn't. Nino wasn't your biological father. Your mother was quite the slut back then it seems." She laughed. "Your real father's name is Yoda Amos. He and your mother had a secret love affair for years. You can investigate that yourself. I'm telling the truth. Ms. Perfect here was fucking her own brother." Yasmine's mad laugh came back.

Nina closed her eyes as vomit threatened to escape her throat. "Shut the fuck up!" she yelled. She didn't even feel her finger pressing against the trigger until the bullet escaped the chamber and pierced Yasmine's heart. "Oh my God. What have I done?" Nina asked before leaning over and released the vomit building up.

The steel door cracked open, and two sets of footsteps came running down the stairs. "Nina, what did you do, ma?" Chance asked as he looked at the gruesome scene before him. Yasmine's bloodied body was slumped over, limp. Nina was standing in a pool of her own throw up.

She looked over to Chance with concerned eyes.

"I'll get this cleaned up, bro. Get her out of here," Cassidy stated.

Chance wrapped his arms around Nina's shoulders and looked into her eyes. There was an absent look there that scared him. "Hey, look at me. It's okay. We'll get this fixed. There's nothing you have to worry about," Chance said gently. In the back of his mind, he regretted leaving Nina alone with Yasmine. Now, he would never be able to get the answers from her he needed about his father. "Let's go home. We'll talk about everything there."

Nina nodded repeatedly, still feeling sick to her stomach. She was too embarrassed to tell Chance about her discoveries. She wouldn't tell anybody until she could confirm it. Sighing a breath of relief, she was glad Yasmine was out of the picture for good.

Little did she know, their troubles were just beginning . . .

# *To be continued . . .*